PRIVATEERS IN EXILE

JAMIE MCFARLANE

FICKLE DRAGON PUBLISHING LLC

❀ Created with Vellum

PREFACE

FREE DOWNLOAD

Sign up for Jamie's New Releases mailing list and get free copies of the novellas; *Pete, Popeye and Olive* and *Life of a Miner*.

To get started, please visit:

http://www.fickledragon.com/keep-in-touch

Chapter 1

HOTSPUR

"Mr. Hoffen, Kelly Jangles from *Daily Voice*, Mars' premier news purveyor. Can you confirm the rumors that you've come back to Mars to run for the High Council?" The doe-eyed, blonde reporter asking the question somehow managed to convey trustworthy sincerity in her delivery.

Public interest in our story had reached a fever pitch after we'd returned, the conquering heroes. We'd played an active role in repelling the Kroerak invaders that had very nearly enslaved humanity and then tracked them to their homes. In the end we'd put a permanent end to the threat in spectacular fashion.

Thomas Anino, the inestimably wealthy business tycoon who also happened to be a friend and occasional business partner, had suggested that our lives would be made easier if we fielded some questions today. He'd pitched the press conference as a human-interest, local-boy-and-friends-save-the-world, get-to-know-the-people-behind-the-scenes type of an affair.

For the first twenty minutes that's exactly how things had gone. Kelly Jangles' question, however, caught me completely flat-footed. I'd heard some jokes about my taking political office, but the fact was, we had a life in the Dwingeloo galaxy where I was already in charge of a growing, albeit small, tribe called House of the Bold.

I smiled back at Jangles, which was the wrong thing to do. She turned up the voltage with her own perfect smile and it left me a bit starstruck. "Um," I started, stammering as my brain raced to find an answer.

A comforting hand rested on my shoulder. "What my partner is trying to say ..." Nick James, my best friend, business partner and almost always the smartest person in the room. He knew I wasn't prepared for the question and was about to take a bullet for me. "... is that we are just visiting Mars and will be headed back to Dwingeloo galaxy in a few days."

"Reports obtained by *Daily Voice* show that you and your team did what neither Mars Protectorate nor the entire Earth Alliance fleet could manage. Polling shows you're a lock for a High Council seat this fall, Mr. Hoffen," Kelly Jangles pushed. Her smile had turned from girl next door to salivating predator in seconds.

"That's ridiculous," I said. "We're all lucky to be alive. A lot of brave men and women died defending our home worlds. I'm just grateful we found a solution at all."

"Are you saying that without you and Tabitha Masters acquiring that Piscivoru weapon, the combined fleets would have been triumphant?" Jangles asked.

"I think it's clear that without the Iskstar, things would have turned out differently," I said and immediately regretted it as a surge of reporters pushed forward, all shouting their questions. I caught Jangles' eye. She had a satisfied grin on her face as she spoke into a recording device that hovered in front of her.

Marty Jacks, a publicist who was helping manage the press conference, jumped to his feet and animatedly waved his arms. My AI indicated that Jacks had severed our comm feeds. "That's all we have for today," he announced. Originally, I'd wondered why Anino had felt Jacks' services were necessary. Now, as the room full of reporters began to boil over into a frenzy, I saw the wisdom. Unlike myself, Jacks' team didn't hesitate at the sudden shift in intensity. A group of security personnel poured into the room, creating a physical barrier between where my team had been seated and the gallery. Jacks wasted no time in escorting us off the stage.

"That was intense," Tabby said, smiling and pushing shoulder-length auburn hair out of her face. Tabby was, of course, my soul mate. She was also not one for public speaking. "I think Kelly Jangles has the hots for you."

My grin reflected the irony I found in her new attitude. During the war against the Kroerak, Tabby had almost died by volunteering to serve as a host for the Iskstar mother crystal. To save her life, she'd undergone an extensive round of surgeries to replace much of her damaged musculature and skeletal system. According to Thomas Anino's mother, Dorian, Tabby had something called a hero gene. People with this rare condition had an unusual symbiosis with synthetically grown replacement tissues, resulting in a substantial increase in strength, stamina, and reflexes.

While Tabby had received the same surgeries once before, the doctors failed to notice the existence of her hero gene. Without proper monitoring and intervention, she'd grown more and more aggressive as her body strengthened to an extreme level. The old Tabby wouldn't have found Kelly Jangles amusing. She would have seen her as a threat and likely have already taken steps to deal with it. Hence, the irony.

"Oh, Kelly would show you quite the time," Marty Jacks said, picking up on the conversation. "And you'd bare your soul to her. Guaranteed, she'd manufacture a believable story, just close enough to the truth that most people would believe it."

"I thought you handled those reporters just fine," Marny Bertrand offered. In addition to being one of my closest advisors, she and Nick were married with an adorable six-month-old son, Pete. Marny was unforgettable. Earthers were already big compared to spacers like me, but she was exceptional, heavily muscled and well above the average Earther's height. I wouldn't lie or suggest that having two women in my life who could pound me into dust wasn't somewhat humbling.

"Are you kidding?" This came from the fifth member of our crew, Ada Chen. Unlike Marny and Tabby, Ada had no remarkable strength. She was small with a willowy build, but what she lacked in physical power, she made up for in her capacity to pilot ships of all sizes. "The public already believes the government let them down by allowing the invasion of Earth. Jangles is going to hold you out as a savior."

A door was thrown open, slamming loudly against the wall. The small but enigmatic Thomas Anino entered the room, just catching Ada's last words. "Dammit Jacks, how could you let him answer that frakking question? Who allowed Jangles into the conference?" he spluttered, his adolescent voice cracking awkwardly.

Like so many of the people I knew, outward appearances didn't accurately represent the person within. At first glance, Thomas Anino appeared to be a gawky, unassuming early-teen spacer. Nothing could have been further from the truth. He regularly utilized highly illegal rejuvenation surgeries and was in fact centuries old; a fact known to very few.

"I'm sorry, sir." Marty Jacks bowed and backed up, obviously afraid of Anino's temper.

"Well, frakking go fix it!" Anino pushed. "It's obvious even to Chen that Jangles is going to run with that story. Shite!"

"Is it really that bad?" I asked, stealing a glance at Ada. Her dark-brown cheeks showed a hint of red flush, which was saying something. She knew Anino well enough to understand he hadn't intentionally insulted her, but his flippancy was annoying nonetheless.

Anino shook his head as Jacks disappeared through the door to the press room. A roar erupted as the reporters, hungry for a story, recognized new fodder and pounced. The noise abated when the door finally closed.

"Depends on whether or not you want a target on your back," Anino snapped, holding my gaze for a moment. "Do you have any idea what politicians and their political parties are willing to do to keep themselves in power? You think the Kroerak were vicious? They were nothing. Your life expectancy just dropped in half with that little stunt."

"Hey, it wasn't a stunt. He was just speaking the truth," Tabby said. I grabbed her hand, impressed at how calmly she'd delivered the rebuke. Old Tabby would have been in Anino's face, threatening physical violence.

Anino took in a deep breath and sighed. "It's my fault. I knew there was a chance the question of your political aspirations would be raised. She's right, you know. You wouldn't need much starting capital to run for that open High Council seat." He shrugged his shoulders as an idea floated through his consciousness. "If you want it, we could make it happen."

"This press conference was supposed to reduce the pressure on us," I said. "Before today, we couldn't walk through Puskar Stellar market without being mobbed. There's no way that's getting better now."

Anino shook his head. "Ten standard years," he said.

"For what?" I asked.

"No one will know who you are in ten years. After two years, you'll still get a few people coming up to you. Five years, you'll get funny looks and the occasional *do I know you* questions. By ten years, you'll be forgotten completely."

"We don't have that kind of time," I said. "We need to get back to Mhina. We left Mom in charge of an entire solar system."

"What about our deal?" Anino asked.

"Deal?" I looked from him to Nick. Nick's abashed face suggested he had some knowledge of the *deal* Anino referred to.

"Let's get out of here and we can talk," Anino said. "Are you hungry?"

I'd always been surprised at how easily that old man changed subjects in a conversation.

"Let's make sure to grab Jonathan," I said.

Jonathan was the only crew remaining from those that had originally accompanied us back from the Dwingeloo galaxy. To call the collective of fourteen hundred plus sentients that inhabited a very life-like android body crew wasn't strictly accurate. I suppose consultant was a more apt description.

"He's already in the shuttle," Anino pushed.

We'd originally met Jonathan at the same time we'd met Anino. They had a special bond I still didn't understand but Jonathan had more than earned my trust on multiple occasions. I couldn't say the same for Anino. He was up to something.

"What's going on, Anino?" I asked.

"We need to talk somewhere private," he said. Something in his bearing got my attention. Something was bothering him, and it wasn't the press conference.

"I'm out," Marny said. "Peter is with a temporary babysitter. Meet back at the hotel?"

To call the place we were staying a hotel was something of an understatement. It was more like a private compound for the rich and famous. Each guest or party was given their own mansion with beach-front views of Concord Lake. Interestingly, the resort was only a few kilometers south of the Mars Naval Academy where Tabby had trained in what felt like a lifetime ago.

Poor Nick looked back and forth between me and his wife, then reached out to her. "I'll come with you."

"You should be part of whatever's going on," Marny said to him. “You can link me in on comms when you get to the meat of the conversation."

"I'm afraid I'm out too," Ada said. "Dad's making dinner." Ada's mother had been killed in a pirate attack years ago, and though she could never imagine being planet-bound, she missed her father. Since we'd been back, the two spent as much time as possible together.

I nodded in understanding. "We'll catch you up."

Tabby, Nick, and I followed Anino to an underground lot where we loaded into a small, nondescript passenger craft. From the outside, it looked like any other midsize taxi, but Anino was a master of hiding in plain sight. The vessel was anything but ordinary.

Once we were in the air, I couldn’t wait any longer. "What's on your mind? And what about Jonathan?"

"Jonathan are otherwise engaged," Anino said. It was both weird and correct that he referred to Jonathan in the plural. I tended to think of Jonathan as a single entity even though he, or they, were multitude.

"I assume *our deal* refers to House of the Bold's agreement to chase down the Belirand mission crystals?" Nick got right to the issue and as soon as he said it, I realized what I’d been missing.

"The reason I've been withholding technology and capital from you is because I was afraid you'd get in exactly the position you're in now," Anino replied.

"What position is that?" I asked. "The position where we saved the known universe?"

"Doesn't get old saying it, does it?" The smile Anino gave was genuine, which by itself was unusual. He always seemed to be plotting and planning.

"Probably gets old for everyone else," I said. "But it's kind of cool knowing that no matter what happens, we saved a lot of people. Most won't know the sacrifices that were made, either." I rested my hand on Tabby's knee and gave it a squeeze.

Anino placed a briefcase on a short table and opened it. Sure enough, rows of gleaming quantum communication crystals sat neatly embedded in the cushioned lining.

"The *position* I'm referring to is your confusion of priorities," he said. "Don't get me wrong, it's entirely natural to be wooed by power. How great is it to be able to build your own city, run your own planet, and rule your own solar system? In a few short years, you transformed from asteroid mining space-trash to Abasi royalty."

"Hey, watch it," I said, bristling at the space-trash reference. The people I'd grown up with worked hard as asteroid miners and calling us trash was below the belt.

The squealing sound of bending metal broke the stare-down between me and Anino. Tabby had twisted the metal of her chair. The arm pointed down at a forty-five-degree angle and showed indentations where her fingers had rested. Tabby's face was placid, but her eyes had a slightly crazed look to them.

"Masters?" Anino asked with a gulp. His expression indicated he wondered how deep he'd stepped in it.

Tabby shook her head and smiled. "Sorry. I'm working on positive responses. I guess I squeezed too hard."

I smiled at her and waggled my eyebrows. The kinder, gentler Tabby was nice when sparring in the ring, but I'd always loved when she became the fiery defender of the innocent. I was used to her quick temper and wasn't sure I was ready to give up those honest responses just yet.

Anino breathed a sigh of relief. "Yeah. Good. Keep doing that," he said. "I didn't mean *space-trash* exactly ... but, you know what I mean? You weren't exactly on schedule to take over the world."

She maintained her placid demeanor, but there was a hint of seething just beneath. "He's too successful? That's your issue?"

Anino nodded. "Exactly. I told you early on that the trappings of success would divert you from the core mission."

"In fairness, a lot has changed," Nick said.

"Not from where I sit," Anino said. "There are still over eighty Belirand missions unaccounted for."

"Most of those people are probably dead," I said, making an argument I didn't love.

"Like York settlement or Yishuv or Cradle?" he pushed back, causing me to immediately regret my statement.

"What would you have us do? We have an entire solar system that needs us."

"You can do both," Anino replied.

Tabby looked out the window. "Where are we going?" Instead of sailing out of the city, we'd continued to climb, the cityscape disappearing below us.

"I have a surprise for you," he said.

"Running House of the Bold is going to take a lot of attention," Nick said, uninterested in Anino's surprise. "With Abasi forces reduced, we're going to see increased pirate activity in the region. We need more capital than ever before."

"Good. We're finally negotiating." Anino sounded relieved.

"What?" I asked, skeptically.

"Nick says you need capital and help fighting pirates. I can do you one better than that. I happen to know an elite team that's good at all that fighting stuff. You remember Natalia Lizst?"

"Tali? No way," I said. "Last I knew, she was hanging up her boots."

"Nope. She's hooked up with a team that works with my mother, Dorian. I can get them to look into your pirate problem," he said. "Trust me when I say they're more than effective at their job."

Nick frowned. "I'm not sure a single team can fix these problems. We need ships and patrols and sensor equipment. The list is huge. One of the reasons we're here is to cut some deals and bring industry to York."

"I'll build a shipyard in orbit over York and send four frigates," Anino said. "I'll pay standard Abasi taxes and supply the personnel."

"You don't give things away," Tabby said. "There's more to this than having us chase down these old Belirand missions. What gives?"

"There's really nothing more to it," Anino said. "Granted, I might not be telling you everything I know about the failed missions, but that is truly at the center of it all."

"Timeline to deliver shipyard?" Nick asked.

"Nine months, give or take," Anino said. "I have a facility in mothballs over Tipperary. Wouldn't take much to get it back online."

"Are you talking about the one we blew up?" I asked.

"That's the one," he said. "I've had a crew putting it back together."

"How many employees?" Nick asked.

"Fully operational, the station requires twenty-three hundred," Anino said. "We'd start with eight hundred and try to hire four hundred locals. That'd give us enough to get going. I can ship more if needed. You'd be surprised how many people love the idea of exotic locales."

I chuckled mirthlessly. We were being railroaded and I hated the feeling. "We should walk away," I said, lifting my eyebrows at Nick.

Nick just shook his head. "He's got us. The entire Abasi nation needs ships. Can you imagine the value a shipyard would bring? Why, just the ore demand for steel production alone would jump-start York's economy."

"Four frigates would allow us to run patrols," Tabby said.

"We need to work out a number of details," Anino said, "but it's manageable."

I felt sick. The challenge of running House of the Bold felt daunting, but at the same time, it was exciting to think of reshaping the once-ravaged colony into something brand new. We could handle those challenges and now Anino was taking that all away.

"Holy shite! What is that?" Tabby stood up, pointed out the vessel's window, while at the same time grabbing for me.

I joined her in front of the armored-glass screen. The near space of Mars was cluttered with a myriad of ships, so it took me a minute to notice we were heading toward one in particular, a gleaming, silvery ship.

My heart raced as I recognized the outline. The armor was all wrong, but the lines of the ship had been etched into my heart. She was a little longer and a lot sleeker, but it was definitely our old sloop *Hotspur*.

"Where did you find her?" I asked, my heart thumping in my throat as I spoke.

Chapter 2

GILDED CAGE

Tabby laid a long arm over my shoulder, leaned in, and whispered in my ear. "He knows your weakness for ships. Don't let him take advantage of you."

Anino's transport made a slow arc around the new *Hotspur*. Gone were the pockmarks of previous battle and the stealth armor which had given her the character of old stories and good times. In its place was a gleaming new skin, unbroken by port or turret or even armor-glass. When we reached the bow, a wide strip of armor began to change and fade. In its place was now a glass screen allowing us a peek into the bridge.

"Is that even *Hotspur*?" I asked. "It's her, but it's not."

"It's her," Anino said.

"Where'd you find her?" I asked. Last I heard, *Hotspur* had crash-landed somewhere in North America, having been knocked down by Kroerak.

"Shh." Tabby placed a finger on my lips as we continued around and headed aft.

"It's a whole story," Anino said. "A small group of crazy people put her back together shortly after the invasion. You'd probably like them, but I found them annoying. Interesting fact. The primary engineer was the same guy who prototyped the rail-gun used to drive off the Kroerak invasion."

"Dr. Murray?" I asked, vaguely remembering the scientist to whom we'd delivered the selich root.

"Murray was the guy who put the global dispersal system together for the Kroerak poison," Anino said. "Dr. Jeremy Tinker is the rail-gun guy. Came out of Colorado School of Mines."

"You're missing all the best parts!" Tabby was joking but pulled on my ear to make sure I was still looking at *Hotspur*.

"A bit theatrical, if you ask me," Nick said, annoyed.

"You, Mr. James, negotiate with numbers," Anino answered as we pulled around aft. *Hotspur's* cargo ramp lowered and a dim blue pressure barrier extended, covering the opening. "Mr. Hoffen, however, negotiates with his heart. I can't take him away from his shiny new solar system by negotiating solely based on what I think is best for everyone."

"You think *Hotspur* will change my mind?" I asked. No doubt she was an amazing ship, but I already had *Hornblower,* a frakking battle cruiser, not to mention our recently refitted frigate, *Intrepid.*

Anino set the nose of the transport vessel onto the ramp and through an extended pressure barrier. "Tell me you don't want to take her out for a spin."

The cargo bay was half the size it had been when we'd sailed the ship. While Anino's transport could fit inside the hold if angled correctly, it wouldn't leave much room. The great thing about the pressure barrier was, as long as the shuttle door was past it, we could safely transfer between ships even without vac-suits.

"What gives with the shiny skin?" Tabby asked. "Doesn't that make her easier to see?"

Rather than join us as we exited, Anino stood in the transport's hatch. "The skin is similar to those fighters you flew for the Navy. Lots more armor, though. You can configure their overall reflectiveness and pretty much any color configuration you come up with. The armor is also smart enough that you can patch it so it's good as new."

"You're not getting off?" I asked.

"I am responsible for many things," Anino said. "Your comments stirred up a hornet's nest in the Mars Protectorate hierarchy. I meant what I said. You're not safe on Mars right now. There are currently three contracts out on Liam's life."

"Three?" I squeaked.

"Buck up, buttercup," he said. "I have over a hundred out on me. You get used to it."

"Transfer ownership of *Hotspur* to House of the Bold," Anino ordered his AI.

"Seems like if you knew we'd get into trouble, you might have warned us," Nick said. "Convenient that suddenly Mars is inhospitable."

A youthful grin flashed across Anino's face. "I didn't mention the best part about the ship. She has an experimental FTL drive."

"FTL?" My AI caught the question and flashed *faster-than-lightspeed* onto my HUD. "What? No fold-space or wormhole engines?"

"Wormhole drives, yes. Fold-space engines, no. I've destroyed the remaining stores of Aninonium," Anino said nonchalantly, as if he wasn't telling us he'd disrupted one of the few modes of traveling in the immensity of space. "If people want to travel between systems, they'll have to find a wormhole or construct a TransLoc gate."

Nick wasn't buying it. "Don't TransLoc gates use Aninonium?"

"Not anymore they don't." Anino folded his arms across his chest, a look of ruthless pride on his face. "My company supplies the fold-space generators and performs maintenance. No Anino Enterprise, no fold-space."

"So, we're stuck here?" Tabby asked.

"No," Nick answered. "We have enough Aninonium back in Dwingeloo to have someone come fetch us."

This change made no sense to me. " Why an FTL drive? Isn't that the same as traveling through fold-space?"

The old man in a child's body just rolled his eyes at me. "Completely different principal."

I shrugged, largely uninterested in the details. Anino's genius was second to none, but I wasn't trying to pick his brains about the science of FTL. "My question isn't about how FTL works. Doesn't the spread of FTL technology cause the same problems we had with fold-space? An alien species gets hold of it and bammo, we're right back to fighting off bugs on planet Earth."

"The drive can't be replicated and this ship is one-of-a-kind," Anino said. "Look, there's a group of eight mission locations, all in a cluster, about two-hundred forty thousand light years out in the Small Magellanic Cloud. We've had activity on six of the eight crystals."

"How'd you get the crystals back from the Confederation of Planets?" I asked. We'd lost control of most of the crystals when we entered the Dwingeloo galaxy. We'd managed to recover some, but not all.

"Know your opponent," Anino said. "All I'm asking is that you take a run out there. Trip will take less than a month. You want to cancel our deal after that, just head back to Dwingeloo and we'll be done. I'll recall the frigates and the shipyard, then send someone for *Hotspur.* Play your cards right, though, and maybe I'll drop a pair of TransLoc gates between Tipperary and Mhina."

"You're an asshole," Tabby said.

Anino grinned and stepped back into his transport, allowing the hatch to start closing. "Won't be the worst thing I'm called today. Make sure to check the closet, Masters. I left you a present."

"Can you believe that guy?" she asked, spinning on me.

My HUD filled with details about *Hotspur*. For a moment, I had difficulty processing it all. Fortunately, Nick broke my mental stalemate by palming a security panel next to the cargo-bay ramp, causing it to retract.

"Can you believe this ship?" I asked. "It's been completely redone."

"Only half the storage," Nick said, looking around the bay as if to measure it. "At least there's no boxing ring on the ceiling this time."

The three of us walked forward through the aft hatch. The living spaces were laid out in a familiar configuration, now extending back in what used to be part of the cargo area. In the event we were to lose atmosphere in the bay, the new bulkhead and exterior-style hatch would seal up just like any other part of the hull. Pressure barriers had been installed over each hatch, removing the need for air-locks which could be a substantial tactical advantage in certain circumstances.

"Are we really falling for this?" Tabby asked, her previous question having gone unanswered. "Anino just shows up and our world turns on a washer?"

"We are," Nick answered flatly. "I know it feels bad, but we take this one mission and he supplies four frigates to Mhina, as well as builds a shipyard. The tax revenue on the yard alone makes it worthwhile."

She wasn't convinced. "I'm telling you, there's a catch."

"There's always a catch," I agreed, stepping through the aft pressure barrier and onto the galley deck.

I was met with a long, white gleaming hallway. The only relief was a blue stripe running the length of the wall at waist height. To starboard, my HUD indicated a space reserved for engineering and biologics. To port was first an armory and then a convertible space that could serve as either storage or bunk rooms.

Forward of the starboard engineering bay, running from midship all the way to the bow was a fully-outfitted recreation area which included a variety of embedded exercise equipment and holographic wall screens. A low, splashing waterfall seemed to grow out from the forward bulkhead and drained into a narrow pond. On either side of the pond, neatly arranged hydroponic capsules sported a variety of edible and carbon dioxide scrubbing plants.

Ahead, in the center of the space, sat a large mess table recessed into the floor. A prompt on my HUD asked if I wanted to raise the table. I acknowledged and the three of us paused as the glossy, wood-grained top rose out of the floor.

"Anino really didn't spare any expense." Tabby said, walking past me into the exercise area.

"Marny will love this galley," Nick observed as he walked over to explore the port side. "Inventory says there's enough food for five people for more than a year."

On the port wall, I found a refer unit and pulled it open. An assortment of Earth and Mars beer was neatly arranged on one side and I pulled three of them out, handing one to Nick. I set the other on the mess table for Tabby who'd started jogging on a running track. She was facing a holographic screen which showed her running through the streets of a large city.

"Up?" Nick asked, noticing that I was headed for the grav-plate that would lift me to the top deck.

"Wait for me." Tabby ignored her beer but jumped onto the grav-plate at the same time I did.

The function of the plate was to create a small cylindrical space of zero gravity. Experienced users could move almost effortlessly between decks. There was little danger to inexperienced users, beyond losing contact with the deck for a moment.

On the way up, with my hand on her waist, I turned her in place, giving her a gentle nudge so we landed on opposite sides of the opening in the bridge deck.

"Now, that's a friggin' nice bridge." I grabbed Nick's outstretched hand as he sailed up. He wasn't quite as comfortable with the zero-g column, but we'd all grown up around zero-g and he adjusted with a little help.

"Three living areas to the aft," Nick said. "Shared head with private commodes."

"You mean we're sharing showers?" Tabby asked, with a mischievous lilt in her voice.

My AI picked up on the question and displayed the shower space's various privacy options. The head was indeed centered on the three living spaces and could be used communally but was currently set up for private lockout.

Two areas were large and contained office and comfortable seating options. The third room on the port side was a smaller, more traditional, officer's quarter. As interesting as the bedrooms were, I focused on the new bridge layout. The old *Hotspur* had separated the cockpit from the main bridge space. The pilots had been on a raised platform pushed to the extreme forward of the bridge, with a short set of stairs that allowed access. The new layout expanded that forward cockpit configuration. The larger raised platform was now sculpted into a U-shape so that a total of six seats were available, including the two pilot's chairs in the center. Where the old workstations had been on the main bridge level, only a peanut-shaped conference table and chairs remained. It had the same glossy, wood-grained finish as the table directly below us in the mess.

"It's like we're in a candy store," Tabby said, playfully pecking me on the cheek and running forward to take her seat at the flight controls.

I caught Nick's eye. "She's right, you know. Anino's up to something. This is too good."

He raised his eyebrows. "I'm thinking the same thing. I just can't see how we turn it down, though."

"Do you trust him?" I asked.

"With some things," Nick answered. "I don't think he'd put us in more danger than he thought we could get out of. I also think Anino is all about the long-game."

"Whatever that is," I said, finishing Nick's thought.

"Show Small Magellanic Cluster," I said, stepping up onto the raised bridge next to a holographic projector just behind the pilot's chairs. A wispy blue cloud of stars and gas appeared before us. "Show the quantum crystal contact locations." Eight glowing red balls appeared and spread out across forty thousand light years.

"First mission was there," Nick said, jabbing his finger into one of the circles. The AI drilled in on the region and showed approximately one hundred star systems. One of the systems pulsed blue at the center of the display.

"What was Belirand looking for all the way out there?" Tabby asked.

"Who knows," Nick replied.

"You know we don't have a choice, right?" Marny voice came out of nowhere and a meter-tall hologram of her appeared on the edge of the holo-projector's range.

"Didn't know you were along for the ride," I said, nodding in her direction. "Doesn't that lack of choice from Anino give you pause?"

"Of course. But we all know we're going, so we might as well get on with it," she said. "Why don't you come grab me? Someone should let Ada know what's up."

I resealed the beer I'd been holding and slid into the portside pilot's chair. The cushioning conformed to my body as I worked through a hastily assembled pre-flight checklist.

"You've been giving orders for so long are you sure you still know how to fly?" Tabby needled playfully.

"You'll regret that later, missy," I shot back. "Give Ada a call for me? Oh, and give her a heads-up. I don't like the idea of assassins looking for me and finding her."

"What if she doesn't want to come along?" Tabby asked.

"That seems likely," I rolled my eyes and grabbed the flight sticks. "Probably best if you get strapped in, Nick."

HOTSPUR HAD ALWAYS BEEN efficient and Anino's upgrades had done nothing but improve on what was already great. I'm not sure, however, if my opinion was influenced by my recent experience commanding the massive *Hornblower* battle cruiser, or if her responses were just that much improved from what I remembered. Either way, I felt a thrill in my stomach as I rolled out of high orbit where *Hotspur* had been parked and dove into the Martian atmosphere.

"Ada says she ran into some trouble," Nick said, his voice conveying no real alarm.

"What kind of trouble?" I asked, dividing my attention between the conversation and the city of Puskar Stellar's security protocols.

"She was being followed and had to engage in light hand-to-hand combat," Nick said. "Her words. Not mine."

"Any residual trouble with local authorities?" I asked.

"Not so far."

From space, observing the line of dusk as it travels around the globe is mostly an academic affair. For folks planetside, it marked a transition from day to night. I felt a pang of regret as the dusk line crossed over Puskar Stellar. Night activities in Puskar Stellar were by far my favorite. Countless restaurants would be preparing for the dinner rush, and street vendors who hawked their goods from colorful stands and carts would be replaced by musicians and street performers. Unfortunately, without knowing who might be coming for me, I wasn't about to endanger my crew by going out for one last night on the town.

As if sensing my darkening mood, Tabby broke the silence. "We should order that super-thick pizza Marny got from Gino's in Coolidge when you guys came to visit me while I was at the Academy. We could ask them to send it out to the resort. It'd be like old times."

Her description brought back warm memories of when our little group had split and we'd struck out on our own paths. I don't think Nick, Tabby or I had any idea where our relationships or our lives, for that matter, were headed. "Spicy chicken, cream cheese, sauce on the top," I said, my mouth watering and stomach grumbling.

"Pepperoni and hot peppers," Tabby added wistfully.

"Anchovies, sauerkraut and green olives," Nick chimed in.

Tabby and I looked at each other with mock horror and turned as one to Nick. "You can't possibly be serious? That's disgusting. Bleck," Tabby said.

"What can I say? I'm complicated," he answered.

"Or pregnant," I quipped, sending the three of us into uncontrollable laughter. The laughter was disproportionate to the joke, but broke the rising tension caused by the stress of Anino's proposal.

"I already know what Marny wants and Ada only likes cheese. I'll send an order over to Geordies," Nick said, still chuckling. "Pizza should get to the resort about the time we do."

I registered with a temporary docking yard located two kilometers from Sam Chen's current apartment and navigated through the thick, night-time traffic that clogged the skies over Puskar Stellar.

"Ada's already at the yard," Tabby announced as I dropped out of the high-speed lane and into the slower, local traffic of the suburb.

"I told her we'd grab a cab and pick her up," I said.

"Sounds like Sam's in a mood," Tabby said. "He doesn't want her to leave again and says he's got a pilot position lined up for her with a local hauler. I guess things got pretty heated at dinner."

I settled *Hotspur* into our assigned berth between two smaller freighters. I remembered a few heated conversations Sam Chen and I'd had. "He's got a temper. I hate that she's leaving things unresolved, though."

Before I'd even shut the engines down, Tabby was out of her seat and headed aft. I chuckled. She and Ada had become closer than sisters after our last adventure and Ada's angst would weigh heavily on her.

"Sam's not wrong," Nick said. "One of these days a mission is going to go sideways and one of us will end up dead."

I felt a flash of anger. Nick was only pointing out the obvious. We'd seen more than our share of heroic deaths; people who'd done nothing other than to sign up as part of our crew. That our original team was still intact was nothing short of luck.

"I can't believe that arrogant asshat!" Ada's voice floated up from the mess deck, both anger and grief in her delivery. "I'm never talking to him again!"

"Frak," I said under my breath.

Before I reached the gravity lift. Ada popped through and landed gracefully. Her face was screwed up tight and angry tears stained her cheeks. "Don't! And yes, I'm in. Don't frakking ask me again," she said, not making eye contact. "Which is my bunk?"

"Right there." I gestured to the smaller portside quarters.

"Good." She stomped over to the hatch and palmed her way inside.

Tabby popped up through the gravity lift, following her friend. "I've got this. Just head to the resort."

I nodded agreement as Tabby disappeared into Ada's room.

It took more time to rejoin the high-speed traffic lanes at eight thousand meters than it did for us to fly to the resort and land on the private strip behind the mansion Anino had rented for us while on Mars.

Once again, I was surprised by an unannounced change in plans as I put *Hotspur* down. Marny and little Pete, along with a pile of crates, awaited our arrival. "What's this all about?" I asked, looking at Nick.

"Security breach at the resort," Marny answered over tactical comms.

"Are you okay?" I asked.

"Security is good here," she answered. "But I'm not taking risks with Peter."

With the systems in warm standby, I joined Nick who'd already made it back to the cargo hold and taken control of little Pete's armored bassinette. "Did they get close?" I asked Marny, this time in person.

"Made it to the fence-line around the mansion," she said, accepting a quick hug from me. "We're fine. The ship is just a safer environment. Looks like the old girl got some upgrades."

"I think you'll be impressed."

"I don't like getting pushed into things," she said. "Especially by someone as clever as Thomas Anino."

"As well you should not," Jonathan said, appearing at the bottom of the ramp. "It has not been our experience that Thomas Philippe Anino's words adequately describe his intent or actions. We advise caution."

The statement shocked me as it was the first time I'd heard Jonathan voice disagreement with Anino. "You think he's trying to harm us?"

"We do not," Jonathan said. "Master Anino is most sincere in his desire to set right the damage caused by the Belirand missions. He has also consistently placed high value on the well-being of you and your crew."

"Are you serious?" I asked, moving luggage into the cargo bay as we spoke. "One thing I'd never accuse Anino of is being concerned for my wellbeing."

"And yet, you have indeed survived and are well," Jonathan answered.

"Because ..." I sputtered, trying to form a coherent sentence. "Well, frak, I'm not sure why we make it. I just know that Anino doesn't make it any easier."

"In this we agree," Jonathan said. "The stress of our current predicament is mostly manufactured by Master Anino. He has arranged circumstances so that your only reasonable option is to do exactly as he wishes."

"Do you think he's behind the threats to my life?" I asked, palming the loading ramp panel to cause it to retract.

"Not directly," Marny cut in. "I'll bet anything he fed that question about you seeking the High Council seat to Kelly Jangles."

"Such action does seem consistent," Jonathan said.

Marny crouched next to the stack of luggage she'd brought aboard and extracted four pizza packages. The smell of garlic must have clung to the packaging because I got a large dose of it and my mouth watered.

"That's distracting," I said.

"Nick just pinged me. They're waiting in the galley," she said.

"I think Ada locked herself in her room," I said, following Marny through the pressure barrier and into the lower deck living area.

Laughter came from the galley and I caught sight of Ada seated at the table. We'd only been in the cargo hold for a few minutes, so I found it surprising that she was there.

"Guess who brought dinner?" I asked, as the three of us joined Nick, Tabby and Ada, who was holding Little Pete and making funny faces at him.

"I say we make tracks for the Small Magellanic Cloud tonight," Ada said, still making silly faces at the very happy infant.

"You don't want to talk about the trip any more than that?" I slid in next to her and gave her a friendly side hug.

"We've all been listening to the whole conversation," she answered. "Anino is as much an ass-hat as my dad. They both mean well in their twisted little ways. House of the Bold needs those frigates and that shipyard. There's no real decision here."

I accepted a piece of pizza from Marny. Nothing I hated more than being manipulated. I bit into what should have been a fantastic delight. Unfortunately, thanks to Anino, the pizza had lost all taste.

Chapter 3

BETRAYAL

"I do not know if this action is wise," Jonathan said, smiling gently at Ada. Jonathan's actions looked right, but they weren't quite human. Something as simple as a smile was completely manufactured by calculated facial movements. Knowing that had always bothered me. It wasn't that I didn't trust Jonathan. Quite the opposite. I trusted them with my life and the lives of my crew.

"What's bothering you?" I asked. Something bothered me, but I was currently chalking those feelings up to Anino's hard press.

"We have only limited access to the faster-than-light engines," he said. "We are unable to simulate their responses to various conditions nor are we capable of diagnosing errors if they occur."

"Tell Anino we're not going anywhere without full access," I said, pushing my pizza away and grabbing the beer.

Jonathan lifted his shirt and pulled back a small flap of skin just above his waistline. Beneath the skin was an empty receptacle, about the size of the end of my thumb. "Master Anino provided this new host body but neglected to replace our quantum communication crystal. It appears he no longer desires to have direct communication access."

"Welcome to crew status," Marny chortled. "You know you can use normal radios just like the rest of us, right?"

"We do." Jonathan nodded, still with a polite smile. "Master Anino has not responded to our queries beyond indicating that once we arrive at our first destination within the Small Magellanic Cloud, he'll fully turn over schematics to all of *Hotspur's* intellectual property."

"Can you confirm that?" I asked.

"That is correct, Captain," Jonathan answered. "We are able to verify that the blocks on information will be lifted once we are within forty AUs of the first crystal's location."

"I don't like it either, Liam," Nick said. "Anino has gone to great lengths to send us to the SMC. It is as if he needs us out of the picture."

"He did say Mars government officials are worried about how we might sway public opinion," Tabby said.

"Like he cares what Mars Protectorate thinks," Marny said.

"The Loose Nuts crew has a significant reputation on Mars as well as Earth," Jonathan said. "We have analyzed public sentiment and believe it reasonable that each member of the crew has the capacity to influence great population groups. This is also true to a smaller extent within the Confederation of Planets, although we have not performed recent analysis given the limits of our current physical separation from the Dwingeloo galaxy and the communication networks available there."

I chuckled dryly. "When's the last time you analyzed Earth and Mar's sentiments?" I asked.

"Our analysis is ongoing," Jonathan said. "Your popularity continues to grow, especially on Earth as the citizens look for solutions to problems caused by the Kroerak invasion."

"That's ridiculous," I said. "We don't know how to rebuild after an invasion. At least, no more than anyone else."

"Doesn't matter," Nick said. "Our reputation has grown way past our capacity to add value."

"Peter Principle," Tabby said.

"I've never understood what that meant," I added.

Tabby grinned. "Of course not, darling," she said with a patronizing tone. "We'd never let you get that far."

"Peter Principle says that a person in management will rise to their highest level of incompetence," Marny said. "It's a real thing. People assume that because you're good at one thing, you'll be good at everything. Hence, a person is continually elevated to responsibilities they are ill-prepared to handle."

"And because of this Anino wants us to leave town?" I asked.

"Is that so hard to believe?" Nick asked.

"What are we going to do about Jonathan's concerns?" I asked.

"Jonathan, do you have any reason to believe the FTL engines present danger to the ship or crew?" Marny asked.

"We are not sure which principles the engines operate under. Master Anino is brilliant and we have not observed him purposefully placing those who trust him into more danger than he believes they are capable of handling," Jonathan said. "Further, he takes significant pride in his inventions. We do not believe he would want it known that he injured historical figures such as yourselves."

"You, my friend, should consider a career in politics," Ada said, handing Little Pete back to Marny. "That was a marvelous stream of doublespeak."

"We do not understand," Jonathan said, tipping his head to the side.

"Do you trust Anino's FTL engines to not harm the crew or ship?" I asked. "It's a simple yes/no answer."

"I see," Jonathan said. "We attempted to answer the question as succinctly as possible. There are many variables. Reducing to a single word answer is very difficult. Perhaps a numeric value would be useful."

"Good," I said. "You've put it to a vote. On a scale between one and a hundred, how dangerous do you believe those FTL engines are? One is not dangerous at all. One hundred is crazy dangerous."

"Twenty-three point four-five," Jonathan answered immediately.

"No fair," Tabby laughed. "Using the decimal point is cheating."

"We do this only because we all agree to it," I said. "If anyone wants out, then we go back to the Mhina system and settle in. There's no reason to believe we need Anino's help at home. Could we use it? Sure. But when isn't that the case with anything?"

My AI projected a proposed poll onto my HUD. Each participant: Marny, Nick, Jonathan, Tabby, Ada, and I had an option of agreeing to go or not.

"Before we vote." Ada interrupted. "We've talked about how we don't trust Anino and I think we all know he's up to something. That doesn't change the fact that each time he's sent us out, we've found people who really needed our help."

"Thanks. Anyone else have something to add?" I asked. After several seconds of silence, I pinched the virtual poll and flicked it to the group as if I were sowing seeds onto a field.

Tabby and Ada responded immediately with Marny shortly behind them. All positive. A moment later, Jonathan responded, although they'd modified the poll to show a percentage of affirmative votes instead of a yes/no response. Jonathan was at eighty-two percent. I'd never completely understood how I should treat the fourteen-hundred odd sentients. It was unfair to treat them as one, but just as unfair to allow them to own all votes.

"What are you thinking, buddy?" I asked, looking at Nick.

"I just can't get past the feeling that Anino isn't being square with us," he said. "He's put so much effort into making this happen. He's up to something."

"Then we pull the plug," I said and gestured grandly to the space around us. "This is just a ship. Not one of our lives is worth trading for it."

"It's not that," Nick said. "I don't think Anino would overly endanger us. It's more that I can't see to the bottom. I don't like the mystery."

I caught Marny's eye. We'd talked about this exact perception on numerous occasions. What Nick was describing was how most of us went through life every day. We never knew everything we needed to about anything and had grown comfortable with that reality.

"So, we punt," I said. "If it's a good idea now, it'll be a good idea in a year."

"Yeah, I think that's right," Nick said. "You guys okay with that?"

"We're musketeers!" Ada said, raising an arm with a flourish. "All for one ..." and when no one answered, she continued, "... and one for all!"

I'd gotten used to Ada's puffy sleeves, ruffled shirts, tight britches and general story-book-pirate look. Her antics, however, sometimes made me question if there might be more going on in that pretty little head of hers than just changes in personal style.

"Are we decided?" I asked. The virtual poll switched to negative for everyone with the exception of Jonathan, whose numbers shifted from eight-two to thirty-six percent.

"Captain?" Jonathan said, his head turning to the side in a quick spasm of movement.

"Jonathan? Are you okay?" I asked, noticing that his head had stopped moving, just shy of making eye contact with me.

Nick's eyes shot up in alarm. "I just lost contact with the ship."

"We're moving. Something's spooling up in the engine room." Tabby jumped up and ran aft to the engineering access hatch faster than I could track her.

I'd previously ordered our auto-pilot to place us into orbit over the city of Coolidge. My HUD showed that we'd broken that orbit and were accelerating away from Mars.

"Nick, Ada, get to the bridge and find out what's happening," I ordered, then clambered over the table to grab Jonathan whose android body appeared to have seized up. If I could provide a physical connection, his entities could transfer to ship systems quite effectively. "Marny, help Tabby. We need access to the engineering bay."

Wordlessly, the crew leapt into action and I was alone at the table with Jonathan. I looped my hands beneath his armpits and pulled. His body was heavier than I expected, and I had to allow his legs to trail behind as I dragged him over to the grav lift. Once I felt the zero-G field, I pushed off and guided us up to the bridge deck.

"Set gravity on bridge to 0.2g," I ordered.

"Command is unauthorized." The ship's AI spoke in a calm feminine voice. *"Occupants are advised to return to their cabins for transition to FTL in three minutes."*

"Jupiter piss," I said, dragging Jonathan forward. My goal was to get Jonathan's hand to connect with an engineering station. "Nick, what's going on?"

"We're completely locked out," he said.

"Sticks are dead, Liam," Ada said.

My HUD filled with warnings about FTL travel and the need for us to be immersed in the gravity gel tanks located beneath each of the ship's beds. Apparently, the g's would be too much for us to survive.

"Please comply with instructions. You have two minutes before transition to FTL. This ship is not capable of shutting down FTL sequence once started," the ship's AI intoned.

"We're through the hatch but we have a new problem," Tabby announced. "The workstations are all covered by armor glass panels. We have to cut through them. I'm headed to the cargo bay for a torch."

"Copy," I answered. I hated being on a timer.

I pulled Jonathan's hand up and placed it on the engineering console near one of the data ports we used to load external data. I stumbled backwards as *Hotspur* leapt to life, shooting forward at a hard-core combat burn. I couldn't help but be impressed with the speed of her transition.

"Someone else is controlling the ship, that's not me," Ada answered my unasked question.

"Please locate and engage inertial suspension tanks. Exposure to fatal g-force will occur in ninety seconds," the ship's AI warned. A throbbing red light glowed in the ceiling and lights in the floor strobed in sequence, leading back to the sleeping quarters.

"I'm still locked out," Nick said. He was on the deck with his body half submerged in the bulkhead beneath his workstation. A panel sat on his chair. "Maybe I can bypass the lockout if I can just ..."

"Ada, report to your quarters," I said. "Marny, get you and Peter into the inertial suspension fluids."

"Cap. Shite." She wanted to argue but Little Pete was her responsibility and she knew it.

I lifted Jonathan's body into the chair and clipped him into the restraints. With Jonathan secure, I slid in next to Nick. "How's it going in here?"

"We're screwed," he said, waving a sensor over a bundle of wires. "There's nothing powered under here. It's like Anino anticipated I'd try this."

"Okay," I said. "Looks like we're going for a little ride then. Get back to your cabin and strap in. Tabbs, I need you to get up to the cabin."

The ship continued to accelerate and the inertial systems fought to redirect backward force downward. My HUD showed the internal downforce was 3g.

"There's a little problem with that," she said. "Aft hatch closed and it's jammed. I'm stuck in the hold."

"What are you doing?" Nick asked as I ran aft.

"Going for Tabby," I said. "Go. We'll be okay." Nick turned for the grav lift but before he could jump through, I caught his eye. "Don't," I said sternly. "Run the play that's called."

"Stupid rule," he said, but turned away.

At 3g, the grav lift didn't do much to cushion my drop from the top deck. Unlike everyone else, I'd been wearing my grav-suit even while on Mars. I couldn't figure out how anyone lived without a suit on. I'd had some sort of second-skin on my whole life and felt naked without it. I was sure without the suit's grav assist, I wouldn't have been able to continue toward Tabby.

As I approached engineering, I could see a cherry red glow where Tabby attempted to cut through the armor of the aft-hatch. The hatch, which separated living space from the cargo hold, was designed to withstand unauthorized boarders who somehow managed to breach the hold. The metal wouldn't hold forever, but with the increasing g-forces and countdown to FTL, it might well be a lifetime.

"Stand back. I've an idea," I said, flinging open the door into the armory, which was just to the starboard of the aft hatch.

"Thirty seconds. Liam Hoffen, Tabitha Masters, you are in danger. Report immediately to an inertial suspension chamber. This is not a drill."

I grabbed a familiar, but now exceedingly heavy blaster rifle. My HUD linked with the gun and a familiar menu appeared. I was glad for the ocular detection that allowed me to spin through the menus without actually moving my hands. I switched the weapon to explosive rounds.

"You clear?" I asked, noticing the hatch still glowed.

"Clear enough," Tabby said.

I blooped three sticky grenades at the door and dove into the armory. Well, to be truthful, I more stumbled and then allowed the crushing gravity to drag me to the deck. An explosion tore through the hallway, flames licking into the armory.

"Fifteen seconds," the ship hounded us over comms.

"Overkill much?" Tabby asked, leaning over me.

"I didn't know how much armor that door had," I said, pushing against the deck. I felt like I was trying to lift an asteroid.

A strong hand grabbed my arm and pulled me upward. Tabby grunted as the two of us worked our way back to the gravity lift. The intensity of the downforce was such that there was no jumping that would get us back to the bridge deck and the safety of the inertial suspension vats.

Tabby grabbed the metal rungs and climbed. When I grabbed hold, I realized there was no way I'd be able to make it.

"Shite," I said, panting from exertion. "Keep going. I'll be just a second."

Tabby pushed off and landed heavily next to me. "Sure. That's how that was going to go, dumbass."

"Go. Frak. We don't need to both get turned into paste," I coughed, trying to grab a breath. The exertion just to stand was overwhelming. "Ship, are there suspension tanks on this level?"

"There is a tank within the engineering bay. It is now available for use," the ship responded.

Tabby did the unthinkable: she leaned over and pulled me onto her shoulders. "Rings. Of. Saturn. But. You're. Heavy." She grunted out a word with each movement.

"Excessive gravity warning. Danger." The ship said almost cheerfully.

I was browning out by the time I sank into the viscous fluid. I felt a heaviness in my chest not caused by the force of gravity, certain that Tabby had given up her own life for mine.

WAKING up from a near death experience while suspended in fluid is a bit trippy. Worse yet, it wasn't the first time for me, which contrary to what you might think, doesn't make it any better. It's a rookie mistake to try talking with tubes down your throat, but that never got in my way. Blissfully, I didn't recall the dire events that had placed me within the fluid on this first awakening.

I drifted off to sleep and when I awoke again, noticed I was surrounded by a reddish, translucent fluid. I'd been in the med tank several times before and recognized it for what it was. A human-shaped outline appeared above me and a moment later someone knocked on the wall of my liquid tomb. My mind leapt to Tabby and I smiled. We'd made it. Then the memory of her last act flooded my consciousness. It couldn't be Tabby. She'd died saving my life.

Still, hope fueled me. My friends were masters of survival. Maybe she had found a way. I pushed my hand out to the side and knocked back. My muscles ached at the small movements, but the pain barely registered. Whoever was out there started shouting.

I slowly moved my arms, searching for controls of any sort. My hand brushed a protrusion just above my face and I explored it with my fingers. A bright glow appeared and instantly my head ached from its intensity.

"*Can you hear me?*" There were now two people peering into the tank. Since my rescuers didn't seem to be moving fast enough, I refocused on the panel I'd discovered. Two glowing green buttons five centimeters apart had the outline of thumbs. It didn't take a genius to understand what that implied, so I pushed them simultaneously.

At first, nothing happened, so I did what any rational person would do, I kicked at the bottom of the tank with my legs. Knowing such a childish act should have no effect only added to my surprise when the bottom broke open and the fluid cascaded out. I was left lying there like a fish in a puddle.

"He's in here!" The low voice belonged to a young man in his early twenties, his voice filled with excitement.

"Careful, son," a man answered. Where the boy's voice had been familiar, I recognized the man's voice. It was Nick.

"Frak, get me out of here," I called after pulling a tube out of my throat. I tried but was mostly unsuccessful at scooching out the bottom of the tank. My muscles betrayed me and I wondered just how much injury I'd experienced.

"Careful," Nick said. "He's probably weak and disoriented."

"We gotta get moving," the young man said. "Those Scatters have picked up our tracks by now."

"Let me look," Nick said. "Yeah, they're two clicks out. Get him out of there. Sorry old buddy, no time to explain just yet. We've got incoming."

Large hands enveloped my ankles and suspension fluid sloshed up onto my torso as I was dragged from the end of the tank. My eyes burned from the light and I closed them tightly. Instead of setting me down, I was tossed unceremoniously over my rescuer's shoulder.

"Gotta move, Dad." His voice was deeper than Nick's and my confusion began to take hold.

"Go!" Nick said. "Off the back of the mountain. We'll meet up with the girls."

"Is it really him?" my captor slash taxi asked, breaking into an easy jog.

"It really is," Nick answered.

As my awareness increased, I realized my face rested on thick fur and each step of the man's stride caused me no end of discomfort.

"Jupiter piss, can we stop already?" I coughed after about ten minutes of the abuse.

"Yeah. We're probably okay for a second," Nick said, his voice closer. "Frak, Liam, you have no idea how good it is to see you."

The man holding me leaned forward and with strong arms set me gently on the ground. My world spun as I looked into his face. There was no mistaking the family resemblance to Marny and Nick. I leaned over and threw up. I wasn't sure why I had that reaction, except it was equal odds I either couldn't handle the junk I'd ingested in the tank or the incongruity of what stood before me.

"Little Pete? What in blazes?" " I asked, squinting up at him.

The man's grin was all Marny, as were the mounds of muscle on the two-meter tall giant. "That's right, Cap," he said. "Welcome back."

Chapter 4

REUNION

"Cap?" I asked.

"That's what Mom calls you," Pete said. "I guess this is all pretty messed up through your peepers." His speech pattern was off and I couldn't quite pin down what I found odd about it.

From my peripheral vision, I noticed something else. My arm was thin beyond recognition. With significant effort, I lifted it for further inspection. The grav-suit's glossy skin had retracted to surround it, but my arm seemed not much more than skin and bone.

Hearing something I didn't, Pete cocked his head. He opened his mouth and whistled a short sequence of chirps. Instinctively I blinked, bringing up my HUD. Two unidentified figures were approaching from magnetic north of whatever planet we were on. I gestured with my hands, directing my grav-suit to lift. The movement was painful, but the suit responded just as I'd have expected.

Sensing movement, Pete turned back to me with a startled look on his face. He scrambled away from me and picked up a long wooden bow.

"Someone's coming," I said, not sure what Pete's issue was. I pointed to the north and down the hill. "Forty meters. There are two of them."

"It's okay, Peter," Nick said. "Liam's wearing a grav-suit. We've talked about them. Remember?"

Pete exhaled sharply. "Right. Talking and seeing are really different."

A return whistle similar to Pete's came from the approaching figures. I clenched my hand and felt the familiar weight of my ring, loose on my finger. With my thumb, I reached over and tapped the side of the ring, finding the familiar indention where a quantum resonance crystal chip had been imbedded.

"Liam!" I heard a shout from thirty meters out as my ring vibrated in response. At the same time, one of the two red dots on my HUD accelerated on a direct bee-line to our position.

I urged my suit to take me in that direction and my heart leapt as Tabby emerged, racing up the side of the mountain, her long coppery hair flowing out behind her. Like Pete, she wore animal skin coverings, although not fur. The sleeveless, thin leather dress came to just about mid-thigh and she wore boots that came to just below her knees. Her skin was darker than I'd ever seen it and she was moving faster than I could imagine.

Tabby leapt from five meters and tackled me, pulling me out of my mid-air hover. The pain of impact was exquisite, and I used every ounce of my strength to direct the grav-suit to keep us from crashing onto the rocky soil beneath.

"Is it really you?" Tabby asked, grabbing my cheeks with both hands and staring into my face. She didn't waste a moment and pulled me into a kiss. Despite myself, I groaned. With every movement, my body felt like it was being pulled apart. "What's wrong? Are you hurt. You're so small. Where have you been? You smell like medicine."

"Slow down," I said, feebly pushing her back. "It's me."

Her face had lines and old scars I didn't recognize. Moreover, her hair, while still full, was thinner and lines of dark grey streaked through it.

"Tabby," Nick said. "Liam was still in the suspension chamber. Pete found it on the mountain and must have hit the wake-up sequence. The tank was completely depleted. We're lucky Liam's alive."

"Oh, frak," Tabby said, pushing off. I couldn't help but be impressed with how shapely her bronzed arms were. "I'm so sorry. Did I hurt you?" She rubbed her hand along my scalp and it was then I realized I had no hair on my head.

"I'll live. I hope," I said.

"As I live and breathe. Liam Hoffen cheats death once again." Marny's voice caused a lump to form in my throat.

I urged my suit to help me into a seated position and looked over to the approaching woman. While Tabby had changed little, a few scars and greying hair, Marny had changed significantly. Gone were her thick muscles. In their place were smaller, tight bands of well-defined muscle. Instead of a short-cropped military cut hair, her hair hung to her shoulders and was steel-gray with wisps of sandy-brown. Like Tabby, her skin was bronzed, but most significantly, I could read in her face the peace that had always drawn me to her.

"Marny," I said. Tears itched at my eyes, but I had none to give. "What happened?"

"Not the best place for a reunion," Nick said, crouching in front of me. It was then I realized that he was sporting a beard to beat all beards. His thick black hair curled at his cheeks and dripped off his chin. The only interruption in the beard was a single finger-wide streak of white that ran down the left side. "We're being tracked by a tribe. Not their fault, we're trespassing, but it'd be better if they didn't catch us. Can you move?"

"I can carry him, Dad," Pete offered.

I lifted off the ground and hovered away from the burly youth. "Let's not. My insides haven't recovered from the last run." I urged my AI to scan the area as I lifted a few meters off the ground. "There are seven approaching from the southeast. Forty meters out, moving four meters per second."

"And he shows up with a grav-suit and working AI." Marny chuckled to herself as the four broke into an easy run down the side of the mountain.

I scanned the terrain, mostly looking for potential threats. We were right at the tree line of a tall mountain and my HUD showed us at twenty-nine hundred meters elevation. The planet's gravity was .95g and the air smelled sweet but was thin, due to our elevation. The forest we were entering filled the bowl of the mountainside as far as the eye could see with the exception of a deep blue lake twelve kilometers to the northwest.

At six meters per second, the run down the mountain seemed to be at a breakneck pace. The fact was, other than Nick, everyone else easily kept that pace. Nick had never been a natural runner, but if anything, he was in the best shape of his life. He attacked the hill and seemed determined to pound the trail into dust. On the other end of the spectrum, Tabby and Pete ran side by side, taking joy in the physical exertion. Where Pete was working at staying on the trail, Tabby added difficulty by periodically leaping up and trying to tag me as I sailed near them.

"How long can you float with your black skin?" Pete finally asked as I glided up next to him.

"Grav-suit," I corrected. "It gains energy from gravitational fields and solar radiation. I can float like this forever, pretty much."

"I'll be honest," he said. "I kind of thought Dad was just making some of this stuff up."

I grinned. "Big jokester now, is he?"

The comment earned me a sidelong glance from Pete. "Right. Not really."

"You know, the last time I saw you, you were an infant," I said. "That was yesterday."

"I don't remember you, although for as much as Mom and Dad talk about you, I might as well," he said.

"You've been here your whole life?"

"Yeah," he said. "Dad's been trying to narrow down where the ship crashed."

"He's been working on that for your whole life?" I started to understand the magnitude of what had occurred.

"It's not the only thing we've done," he answered, defensively. "Living on Fraxus is hard. You'll see. Snow season is coming."

"Fraxus? Is that the name of the planet?"

"Sounds like *frakked us*," Tabby said, gracefully running up next to us. "It was funnier twenty stans ago."

My mind reeled. I knew time had passed, but hadn't really thought about a number yet. A red warning throbbed on my HUD, but I was too stunned to look for the problem. A moment later, I clipped a heavy tree branch and was knocked to the ground. The hit was almost more than I could handle and I was powerless to stop myself from crashing to the boulders below. My body was so weak that this final insult put me in a bad spot.

"I've got you, babe," Tabby said, gently scooping me from where I lay, groaning. "I know it's a lot to take in. You've been missing for almost half my life and now I've got you back. I'm going to take care of you."

"You've gone native. Why?" I managed as Tabby took off at a run, easily overtaking the others even though she carried me.

"No technology on Fraxus," she said.

"What about Ada?" I asked.

"Nothing yet," Tabby said.

"*Hotspur?*"

"Don't know," she said. "Best we can piece together is that we came under fire and somehow made it to this planet. The ship ejected our suspension chambers and we think it crashed somewhere on the planet. We've looked but can't find it. We got lucky when we found you."

"How?"

"Shh," she said. "We'll talk when we get back to camp."

As soon as I relaxed, I fell into a troubled slumber.

I AWOKE after nightfall lying atop thick furs next to Tabby. I was starving and needed desperately to relieve myself, but I didn't want to give up the feeling of peace I had. The smell of smoke permeated the eight-meter-square room. In the center of the opposite wall was a stone fireplace and chimney with a thick slab of unevenly shaped iron for a hearth. I smiled. Nick must be blacksmithing if he'd made an iron hearth. A dwindling fire crackled, pushing heat into the room. It was a cool evening, but my grav-suit had no trouble keeping me warm.

As gently as I could, I rose from the bed, using my grav-suit to lift away from Tabby. She'd positioned herself between me and the rest of the room, trapping me against the wall. I suspected it was both a protective move as well as a desire not to let me slip away. She'd always been a heavy sleeper and didn't stir as I re-oriented myself to vertical. Without touching the ground, I floated to the thick outside door.

The enclave was surrounded by forest. Gurgling water nearby told of a river that I couldn't see in the starlight. Next to Tabby's cabin was another, larger cabin and then a third, much larger building that was no doubt Nick's workshop. The cabins were dark, but light flickered out between the cracks of the shop's shuttered windows. I took care of business and then made my way over to the building, knocking on the thick slab door before pushing it open.

"You're up," Nick said, sliding off a stool that sat next to a rough-hewn workbench. "Everything okay?"

"I imagine you're hungry," Marny said, walking into the candlelight from the shadows. "You can't know how good it is to see you, Cap."

"For me, we just took off from Mars yesterday," I said.

"Liam, you need to sit," Nick said. "Marny ground some sweet grain. Your body will have trouble processing, but you need to get back onto real food. As you've probably figured out, the suspension chambers on *Hotspur* were for more than inertial dampening. You were in stasis. As far as you're concerned, you *did* leave Mars yesterday."

"Here you go, Cap," Marny said, sitting next to me on a low bench and handing me a wooden bowl as she wrapped an arm around my shoulders. "Just try a spoonful or two."

I was hungry and did as she said. The sweetness of the mixture was fantastic. I felt like I hadn't eaten in forever and struggled to swallow. "Is it true? We've been gone for twenty years?"

Nick looked to Marny, breaking eye contact with me. I could always read him like a book. He didn't want to tell me something.

"Something like that," Marny said.

"For frak sake," I said, setting the bowl in my lap. "I'm not a child. Just give it to me."

Nick nodded gravely. "What if it's been longer than twenty years? We'd never know."

"Things you consider when you've had a long time to think," Marny said. I stared at her trying to rectify the lithe, graying woman with my memories of the powerfully built, stalwart I'd grown so close to. She smiled gently back. "You should try to eat more, and I have some bonda milk in that cup next to you."

"Bonda?"

"It's a fruit that grows downslope," she said. "The skins of the berries are just as sweet, but if you eat too many you'll be sitting in the outhouse all day. For some reason the milk doesn't cause the same problem."

"Next thing you'll tell me is that you ride mastodons and chuck spears at angry tribesmen. This is pretty surreal, you know."

"No mastodons," Marny said. "They're mostly friendly when it comes to outsiders. They have territories and when we run into a new tribe, they'll run us off. They're not violent, though. Just enough to make their point."

"Mostly friendly?"

"We've never successfully made long-term contact. The tribe that claims this valley as their territory gives us a wide berth. Early on, they even gave us some food. It would just show up in our camp only when we were really struggling. I caught one of the adolescent Scatters once. It was horrible. I was just trying to talk to her, but she thrashed around so badly I was afraid she was going to hurt herself. I had to let her go."

"Humanoid?" I asked.

"Look like Tolkien's elves," Nick said. "Small, thin, faster than the wind. They even have pointy ears and fair skin."

"You're messing with me," I said, tipping back the bonda milk. Like the gruel, it was sweet. I could feel energy surge within my body as sugar made it to my stomach.

"I swear," Nick said, holding up his hand.

"Peter's amazing," I said. "He's so big."

"Takes after Marny," Nick said unnecessarily.

"Brains of his dad," Marny added proudly.

"You look a lot different, Marny," I said.

"Hard to maintain the protein diet and exercise," she said. "Gray hair a bit of a shock for you?"

"Don't take it the wrong way, but it all suits you," I said. "Maybe that's just being a mother."

"Thank you, Liam," she said. "This wasn't the life we expected, but we've carved out a home."

"What about Ada and Jonathan?" I asked.

"With your suit, we finally have a shot at finding them. You wouldn't believe how lucky we got finding you," Nick said.

"How did you find me?"

"It was actually Peter. He's picked up a bit of the Scatter language and overheard someone talk about a glowing box on the mountain. We went to investigate and there you were."

Nick stood, walked over to some wooden shelves and pulled out a jumbled mass of wires.

"What is that?" I asked.

"I'm hoping it's an earwig," Nick said. "I found some pieces after we woke up. I think it'll give me access to your suit. You mind if I try?"

"Nick," Marny warned.

"No. It's okay," I said. "You can take my earwig if you want."

A prompt appeared on my HUD. It was Nick requesting access. I blinked acceptance.

"I'm in," Nick said, breathing a contented sigh of relief. "And there she is."

"She?" I asked.

"Ada," he answered. "Four hundred kilometers and two mountain ranges, but there she is. Well at least that's a transponder for a suspension tank."

"That's thirty days," Marny said. "Snow is almost on us."

"Snow is already on the other side of the Juba range. We'd hit it in a ten-day," Nick said. "And there's no way Liam's in any condition to travel that far."

I ran my finger down my chest, opening my grav-suit to reveal shriveled, pasty white skin. A smell hit my nose and I realized it was all me.

"Whoa, hold on a minute," Tabby's voice announced from the door. "I go to sleep for a minute and you're in the barn getting jiggy with Marny and Nick?"

Marny ignored Tabby's statement and walked over to where skins were draped over a rack. It required all of my strength to fully remove the vac-suit. It was painful to look down at my emaciated body and I felt no small amount of shame.

"We've located Ada," Nick said. "She's four-hundred kilometers east, northeast. I believe Liam is offering his grav-suit as a mechanism to help retrieve her."

"I'll go," Tabby said, suddenly serious.

"You're probably the best fit for the suit," Marny agreed, draping my shoulders with a soft animal skin. "First thing in the morning, you're getting a bath, Cap. I'll get Pete to bring some water up from the river and we can heat it."

"You sure we should wait on the bath?" I asked. "The smell alone might kill me in my sleep."

"Too dangerous to go at night, especially with the scent you're putting off," Marny said. "There are some very effective predators on the mountainside. They mostly leave us alone, but that's because we've thinned their numbers."

"I can get water. I'm not putting that suit on until it's clean," Tabby said, accepting the earwig from me.

Marny nodded, not saying what we all knew. Tabby was the apex predator on the mountain and she could go wherever she wanted. "I'll stoke the fire and get started on a pack for you. Liam, how's that bonda milk sitting?"

I picked up the cup and took a long drink, finishing it off. "Delicious. I'd take more if you had it."

"Let that sit for a bit longer," she said. "I just wanted to know if we should pack some for Ada."

A few minutes later, Tabby returned to the barn, slopping water from two buckets. I marveled at the craftsmanship that had been required to create wooden containers that didn't leak. She set them next to the fire after filling a large iron pot hanging from a tripod.

"You're a blacksmith now?" I asked Nick.

"Our little universe is in the iron age," he said. "Barely. Deposits of ore are sparse, but the Scatters don't know how to work with it so it can be found."

Tabby turned to go back out.

"Where are you going?" I turned to scan Tabby's face, afraid that seeing me in this condition was too much for her.

"Adolescent maracat down by the river. Going to bring him back before he's dragged off," she said, slipping outside.

"Maracat?" I asked, looking over to Nick who was busy turning my suit inside out and scrubbing it.

"Think saber-toothed tiger with a bad attitude," he said. "We've been tracking this one for a while. Pretty sure he came over from Mount Green earlier this year. He must have made his move on Tabby. Bad choice."

"On Tabby? As in, it attacked her?"

"Yeah, local maracats know better," he said. "Man, you really worked up a smell. I'm peeling off pieces of your suit liner. It must have disintegrated."

"Where did your grav-suits go?" I asked.

"We assume they're back in the ship. None of us had put on suits yet that night. If only we'd known what Anino was up to," he said. "Your grav-suit is going to save us, you know."

"How's that? Everyone we know is dead," I said, slumping against the table.

"Trust us, Cap, life can get a lot worse." Marny helped me to a cot next to the fire. Without my grav-suit I was shivering from the cold. "We've had twenty years to come to grips with losing everyone. But today you came back into our lives and now we have hope of finding Ada. I can't recall feeling so happy in such a long time. Don't get me wrong, we've carved out a life and we have each other, but I cried today for the first time since we awoke. It's just so damn nice to see you, Cap."

A wind blew in behind Tabby as she kicked open the door. Draped over her shoulders was a vividly green-furred cat that weighed at least one hundred fifty kilos. "Something has the blood-deer worked up. I nearly got run over on the way back from the river."

"The wind has changed," Marny said. "Smells like snow."

Chapter 5

BASKET WEAVING

"Your skin is torn just above your waist where the suit was creased. There's suit-liner embedded," Marny said. "This is going to hurt."

"I'll gather some hogen root," Little Pete offered, rising from the crouched position he seemed to prefer.

After removing my grav-suit the night before, Tabby had wiped me down using a mixture of a sweet-smelling clay and fine particles of sand. We'd discovered several sensitive patches of skin and skipped over them with the expectation of looking at them in the morning with better light.

"Is it always this cold?" I asked, my breath steaming in front of my face.

Marny smiled and brushed my cheek with the back of her hand. "The suspension chamber you were in must have been critically low on nutrients. Your body consumed most of your muscle and you have no fat to burn. You simply don't have the capacity to generate your own heat. Once your wounds are clean, we'll get you nice and warm. Are you ready?"

"Bite on this," Nick said, offering a stick about the size of my thumb. "We don't have much in the way of pain relief around here – at least nothing that won't make you high as a kite."

I accepted the stick and as soon as I put it in my mouth, Marny pulled at my skin. Pain lit throughout my body as if she'd hit my skin with a fire brand. She sucked in a deep breath as a fresh wave of putrid air assaulted our noses. I bit down and tried unsuccessfully not to cry out. After what seemed like hours, but was no doubt only a few seconds, the last threads of the liner pulled free.

"There's necrotic skin around the wound," Marny said. "I'd kill for a med-patch. Nick, I'm going to need your knife and I need it as sharp as you can get it."

"Okay, but I'm getting him some spring weed," he said.

The barn door opened and Tabby entered, carrying a load of split firewood. For a moment, our eyes met. She quickly looked down and moved across the room to unburden herself.

Marny caught the interaction and gave me a wan smile. "Don't worry about her," she said. "We all thought you were dead. We even had a service for you down by the river. It took her a long time to recover from your loss."

"This is so messed up," I said. "We just got onto *Hotspur*."

"Put the bite stick back in," Marny said. "A smaller piece on the other side needs removing."

"I'm taking the maracat carcass out to clean," Tabby said to no one in particular. "We're going to need more furs if we're to make it through winter."

I avoided crying out as Marny tugged a smaller piece of debris from my side. She rolled me over and continued working on my beleaguered skin. Through the tears caused by excessive pain, I tracked Tabby as she stalked through the building. She really hadn't changed that much, though her hair had streaks of gray and her face had aged. Throughout the torturous operation, she dared a few glances back at me. I saw both guilt and fear in her eyes. I wanted to make everything all right, but knew I had to let her come to me on her own terms.

After neatly stacking the firewood, Tabby pulled the giant cat from where it had been hanging and carried it outside.

"I think we have a problem," Nick said, crouching beside the cot where I lay by the open fire. In one hand he held a small clay bowl that had a fluted straw built in to one end. A small puff of smoke escaped from the straw as he held it in front of my face.

"What's this?" I asked through gritted teeth, as Marny continued to work on me.

"Spring weed," he said. "It won't actually stop the pain, but you won't mind it so much. Just puff on it. Word of warning, though, you're going to cough, so take it slow."

"Is that the problem?" I asked. I couldn't help but notice a disapproving look from Marny.

"I wish," he said. "Your grav-suit needs repair. Nothing a replicator and a trip through a suit-cleaner wouldn't fix, but we're a bit short on both."

"It was working okay for me," I said, puffing on the bowl. The moment the acrid smoke touched my lungs I coughed and gave Nick a scowl. Just why anyone would smoke this crap, I had no idea.

"Won't be for long," he said. "The power cells aren't holding a charge. Your flight from the mountain nearly drained the entire thing. You have maybe two hours left on it. We'd be better off saving the power for the AI function."

"We've been in worse situations?" I coughed and laughed at the same time as I took another drag on the smoke bowl. I felt calmer, but my head was still clear.

"As planets go, Fraxus is about as nice as you could imagine," Nick said. "The indigenous people aren't overly hostile and there's a wildly diverse biome. Yeah, we've been in worse. I'm just not sure we're getting out of this one."

"Knife?" Marny asked brusquely, holding her hand over my body and rolling me further onto my side.

Nick handed her a basket that contained more than a knife. "Where did you come up with thread?" I asked as my eyes caught a thin white curved object that had a pointy end and a length of thread attached.

"Bite on your stick, Cap," Marny said. "And that's cat-gut. You really don't want the full description."

I bit down and once again my side seemed to light on fire as Marny cut away dead flesh. The pain was so great that I wished for the bliss of passing out, but it never came. Fortunately, she worked fast and after a while my skin simply throbbed with the memory of fresh insult.

"I've made the hogen paste," Little Pete said, pushing his way back into the barn, leaving the door open behind him. A cold wind followed and I shivered uncontrollably as it blew across me.

"Door," Nick said, accepting a wooden bowl from him.

Even though the salve was ice cold, it almost immediately quenched the fires on my body where Marny had worked on me. "Oh man, that's nice," I said, sucking on the smoky bowl. The heady effects of the spring weed relaxed me even further, even though I continued to shiver.

"I think we're done with that," Marny said, plucking the ceramic smoke bowl from my hands. "We don't need any stoners here."

"Are you ready for breakfast?" Nick asked. "The AI recommends light meals several times a day until your digestive system is fully acclimated. We have a grain porridge like you had last night or I could do some roadie eggs. My cheese experiment didn't go all that well, but last night the AI suggested I hadn't processed the rennet correctly."

I smiled. It was typical Nick in a completely foreign situation. He had taken his inquisitive nature and keen intellect and applied it to long-term survival. "I don't suppose you have a meal bar?"

This earned me a surprised chortle from Marny who was wrapping a warm leather blanket around me. "No meal bars, Cap," Marny answered.

"You know," Nick said. "If I baked berries, bonda flesh and some of those nuts we have, it'd almost be a meal bar."

"The porridge was good," I said. My entire body hurt from the scrubbing, cutting and suturing. The initial relief from the hogen paste was wearing off and I found that I was exhausted.

Nick must have caught my droopy eyes. "You're going to be tired, Liam," he said. "You'll need quite a lot of rest over the next few days. Let's get some food in you and you can sleep. You need to use the facilities yet?"

I smiled. I'd learned the facilities were nothing more than a small shack ten meters out behind the barn. "Nah, I'm good."

I AWOKE to the sound of a heated argument outside the barn. I had no idea how long I'd been asleep, but my bladder suggested I'd been down for a while. With effort and several painful reminders from my new stiches, I gained my feet. My overly thin body was unrecognizable even to me as I struggled to cover myself with a fur blanket. I'd seen more than a few news vids that reported on starvation cases and I realized I was lucky to be alive.

Opening the barn door, I was almost blinded as the light in the sky assaulted me. I blinked rapidly as my eyes burned but adjusted nonetheless. I pulled the cool thin air into my lungs and noticed that whatever argument had been underway had stopped. Marny, Pete and Tabby stood several meters from the barn next to a rack where the unmistakable bright green skin of the maracat hung. The three looked at me like I'd grown a second head, so I gave an awkward smile and a small wave.

"Don't let me get in the way of a perfectly good argument," I said. "I just need to visit the privy."

The uneven ground felt odd under my feet. Having spent the majority of my life in space either vac-suited or on a station or ship, walking barefoot was unusual to say the least. Apparently, there's a skill and I certainly didn't have it. The first sharp rock I found and placed into the tender sole of my foot drove me to a knee, the pain almost too much to bear.

"Liam," Tabby exhaled sharply and rushed to my side, helping me to stand. "You shouldn't be up."

Her voice washed over me like the hogen root had my wounds. There was an emotional separation between us that was hard for me to understand. The uncertainty ate at me, occupying my idle thoughts.

"Gotta do this," I said, pulling the fur tight around my shoulders. "No way to heal without pushing through. Right?"

"You're not well, yet," she said. "It's okay to ask for help."

"I've got this." I pushed her arm away. "Are you doing okay?"

"Me?" she asked, surprised. "I'm fine. Why would you ask?"

"You're avoiding me, Tabbs," I said. "I know we're not in the same spot. It can't help that I look like a refugee, either, but I'm still me."

"Nick says the grav-suit won't work and Marny doesn't want Pete or me to go alone to find Ada," she said.

Classic Tabby. She was uncomfortable in the conversation, so she changed the subject. "Oh? What's her reasoning?"

"You're just going to agree with her," she said.

"Just a second." I pushed open the wooden door to the outhouse and entered. Closing the door behind me, I sat on a well-worn seat. "Agree with what? I don't even know the argument," I said through the door.

"Nick says the grav-suit can't make the trip to where Ada's beacon is," Tabby said. "I could probably make it over there in a ten-day if I traveled light."

"What's the downside?" I asked, opening the door.

"We've never successfully made it past the Scatter patrols on Mount Green," she said. "They always run us off. Nick thinks there's a larger population over there. We've even seen a few spaceships over the years."

"You think the Scatters have tech?" I asked.

"Bronze age at the max," Tabby said. "Ada's beacon is roughly in the right place for where we think there's a Scatter city. There's an ocean maybe a hundred kilometers past Mount Green. We just don't know. Four hundred kilometers doesn't sound like a lot, but when you're on foot, it's hard to carry enough supplies, especially if you meet resistance."

"Exactly how do the Scatters run you off?"

"Mostly near misses with arrows," she said. "They don't like to show themselves. If I tried, I could run one down, but I think that'd cross a line we'd have a hard time coming back from. But now with Ada, we're going to have to push things."

"We should all go," I said.

"That's ridiculous. You're in no shape to go anywhere," she said.

"Ada is either alive in her suspension chamber or she's not," I said. "One month isn't going to make a lot of difference. If the Scatters are bronze age, they're communicating. That means they know about you guys recovering me."

"And you think they care?" Tabby asked.

"I don't know who cares," I said, perhaps more barbed than I intended. My hurt wasn't lost on Tabby as I saw a flash of pain flit across her face. "I'm just saying that until recently nothing had changed. They've probably known where Ada's been for the last twenty years and even so, they ran you off. Maybe that's changed now."

"That's a pretty simple view of things," she said.

I grabbed her wrist, which surprised her and she looked up suddenly. She could easily pull away if she wanted.

"I'm a pretty simple guy, Tabbs." I released her arm and walked back towards the barn, this time paying careful attention to where I stepped.

It was as if I was walking through one of the holographic reproductions of frontier life. There was a pen filled with what looked like giant, blue chickens. Another, much larger pen held a strange looking animal. There was the cabin where Tabby slept and then the barn and a couple of smaller structures including tanning racks and a large firepit.

"Go easy on her," Marny said, catching me before I entered the barn. "This has caught her off guard."

"I'm missing something," I said.

"Give it some time," she said. "How are those stitches feeling?"

I was by far the best poker player in the lot and Marny had given away more than she'd expected by changing subjects on me. "They suck," I said. "Other than the fact that they're keeping my guts inside, that is."

Marny laughed a little more than she should have. She was relieved to be talking about something else.

"How long have they been interested in each other?" I asked. The look on Marny's face told me everything I needed to know. Internally, my world crashed in on itself and I struggled to keep the devastation off my face.

"Frak, Cap," she said. "I'm not the right one for this conversation."

"No," I said. "That was unfair of me. But I had to know."

"I've already talked to Peter to let him know that things have to change," she said.

"Do they?" I asked. "Twenty years is a long time. Are they happy together?"

"Cap, I don't know if I can talk about this," she said.

I nodded and walked into the barn. Nick looked up from where he was working on a pair of leather boots. He looked first at Marny and then to me, nodding his head in understanding.

"Want to try on these boots?" he asked. "I was working on them for Peter, but his will last a few more ten-days."

"I'd go for some pants, too," I said, accepting the boots. "I feel bad that I'm going to be such a drain on you guys. It looks like you're working pretty hard at survival."

"Marny has pants that should work. And don't worry, you'll pull your weight soon enough," he said, handing me my earwig. "Ever done any basket weaving or bird plucking?"

"You know Tabby's going to try to hurt herself, right?" I said. "Unless she's changed a lot, she's not good with this level of conflict. That's probably why she wants to go off by herself after Ada."

"I know," he said. "For the record, I'm sorry things rolled this way. It took a long time for her to finally put you to rest. This thing between Tabby and Peter is only about a year old. I know it seems weird, what with him being so much younger than her, but neither of them had many options. No. That sounds wrong. I don't know what I'm saying."

I studied the lines on Nick's face. He'd aged substantially in the twenty years I'd been in stasis. The old Nick wouldn't have even tried to have the conversation and I appreciated the attempt. The heaviness had returned to my chest and I was genuinely heartbroken. Tabby was the love of my life and I wasn't sure that I could easily survive in a world without her at my side.

Nick continued. "It's just all wrong. You're all such good people and circumstances have really messed with things. Three of my favorite people in the universe are paying for Anino's hubris. We shouldn't be in this situation.

"But here we are," I said, finishing his thought for him. I caught movement from the corner of my eye. Marny had re-entered the barn.

"Someone was asking for pants?" Marny asked, feigning a cheerful tone. She held out a pair of soft leather pants and a shirt, both of which had been well worn and bore patches and resewn gashes. "Peter outgrew these a few years back. I wasn't sure why I kept them. They'll be baggy, but you'll put on weight soon enough."

I pulled on the all-leather outfit. It was indeed baggy, but there's something humanizing about putting on clothing after lying around naked for a time.

"Basket weaving you say?"

"It's really not that hard," he said. "Especially for someone with access to a HUD. The thing is, baskets are crazy useful. Also, we need someone to grind flour. I have a list of tasks suitable for someone in recovery. One thing you learn about subsistence living is that you rarely have a time when sitting around makes sense."

Chapter 6

PITY THE FOOL

I managed to avoid Tabby for the remainder of the day and slept on the cot next to Marny and Nick's hearth in the barn. They hadn't gotten around to building their own house and instead slept in the loft overhead.

I awoke when someone exited the barn and a ray of light from outside caught my eye. My entire body ached, but the pain was substantially duller than the previous day. Light flashed off something shiny on the hearth next to where my head lay. My heart sank as I recognized the object, it was Tabby's engagement ring.

With effort, I pushed myself up to a seated position and put it on my right hand. The ring slipped easily into place. I sighed and stood. At least Tabby knew that I knew and we could avoid the stupid dance we'd been doing.

I pulled on my new boots and walked outside. There was a skiff of snow on the ground that disappeared underfoot as I walked, leaving my boot prints behind. The leather shirt did much to keep me warm, but in the cold of early morning, it wasn't enough. The loud crack of iron on wood drew my attention to where Tabby stood amongst a pile of split logs. With each swift strike, roughly cut chunks flew apart, piling up on either side of her work area.

I grabbed a couple of already-split chunks and walked them over to where they were being stacked. Tabby kept splitting logs even though she knew I was there. I worked to keep up with her, warming up substantially as I stacked the wood she cut. Finally, after a couple of hours, she stopped, for which I was very grateful. My arms and legs were starting to give out.

"I knew you'd figure it out before I had enough guts to talk to you," Tabby said.

"I don't want to make things harder, but it's not over for me yet," I said.

"I still love you, Liam," she said, tears trickling down her face. "I always have."

Part of me wanted to rush over, pull her into a hug, assure her that everything would be just fine and that we could forget about the years that had passed. I wanted to tell her that she and Peter were a poor match for each other. It was only through sheer force of will that I kept my mouth shut.

"I found this on the hearth," I said, pulling her ring off my finger and holding it out to her.

"I don't know what to do, Liam," she said, fresh tears falling from her eyes. "I buried you and promised myself to another. Rings of Saturn, tell me what to do here."

"Do you love him?" I asked.

Tabby smiled. "You will love him, Liam. He's such a sweet man. I've dreamed of telling you about him."

A lump formed in my throat and I sat down heavily on a stack of logs. Part of me already despised Peter. The fact that he brought such a smile, *my smile*, to Tabby's face was like a sword being driven into my chest. "That's pretty messed up from where I stand," I said, both satisfied and annoyed that I'd driven the wistful smile from her face. I didn't want to hurt her, but it was hard not to lash out under the circumstances.

"You know he's afraid of you," she said.

I shook my head in disbelief. "I think he's safe."

"There's more," she said. "I lost a baby about six months ago."

My world spun and I was glad that I'd chosen to sit. "You were pregnant?"

"Second trimester," she said. "Something wasn't right."

"I'm sorry, Tabby. That must have been hard."

"I was going to call him Liam," she said.

A part of me still wanted to lash out and ask what she'd have done if the baby had been a girl, but I held my tongue.

"I don't get it, Tabbs. He's half your age. I understand there's not a lot of choice, but seriously?"

Her face hardened and she went on the defensive. "You're half my age too, Liam," she said. "He's only two years younger than you are. At least if you consider you've been suspended for all that time."

"But we have so much history," I argued. Part of me recognized the futility of the argument, but it was the only card I held.

"It was so long ago, Liam," she said, burying her face in her hands as she turned and ran off.

I grabbed a small armload of firewood and walked back to the barn. In my short time on Fraxus, I'd learned that firewood was a resource that had to be constantly refreshed.

"I see you found Tabby," Nick said, looking up from where he was working at his long workbench.

"I really tossed things in the shitter with her," I said.

"I talked with Peter and Tabby last night," he said. "They're going to try to see how far they can make it to Ada's location. It'll give everyone time to think."

"She's gone, isn't she," I said.

"Only if you force her to be. You know as well as I do that we can never go back. We can't go back and save my mom and we can't go back and save your dad. What's happened between Peter and Tabby isn't going away. There's only forward. I guess you have to decide how much you want to be part of things if it doesn't go the way you want."

"I need a villain," I said. "I want to hate Peter, but he seems like a great kid. Even with all of this, I can't bring myself to hate Tabby."

"Anino?" Nick asked, looking at me hopefully. Talking about hating his son was hard on him and I found it confusing since I generally told him everything.

"Yeah. That's for sure. I hate that little bastard," I said, vehemently.

"I think he's prepared for our disapproval," Nick said.

"Do you think this was his big plan? Send us out of the galaxy and strand us on an M-Type planet where we'd never be heard from again?"

"He could have just had us killed," Nick said. "The fact that the chambers were stasis instead of inertial gel and that they were designed to be ejected from the ship makes me think this was at least part of his plan."

"He'd better hope we're never standing in the same room again," I said. "Because there's no doubt in my mind I'll drop him where he stands."

WITH LITTLE PETE and Tabby gone, life on Fraxus settled into a routine as Marny, Nick, and I prepared for the onset of winter. At first, I was of little help. However, after just a ten-day, I'd put on five kilograms and enough muscle that I was able to invest myself into more and more difficult tasks.

At the end of the fourth ten-day, I was enjoying a rare moment of quiet while setting trout lines in the frigid river that ran past the homestead. I heard a shout and the iron bell next to the central fire pit rang out. I'd learned that the bell was used as a general-purpose alarm. Whenever it rang, everyone was to come running.

I tossed my half-baited line of hooks back into the water and picked up the string of fish I'd collected. I was proud that I'd captured my own small bait fish, set the lines, and harvested the fish all on my own. The catch would be a nice break from the salted blood-deer flanks.

I ran back to camp, glad that my legs finally had some strength to them. I was far from my previous shape or weight, but with the help of constant physical activity, I was kilogram for kilogram, substantially stronger. When I made it to the edge of camp, I hung the bag of fish on a hook next to the table where I would clean them later. Nick's design for the table was such that once the fish were clean, the entire table could be lowered into the frig pen, where the cute little porcine they'd captured would happily clean up the entrails.

No one was near the bell, so I set about scanning the tree line. On the far-northern edge of the compound, I could just make out four people. Little Pete's bulk was a dead giveaway that he and Tabby had returned. I set off at a run in their direction. Even with the angst I'd felt during the separation from Tabby, it was exciting to have them back and to possibly get word about Ada.

"Fresh blood deer tonight." Little Pete finished a sentence with a barking laugh that sounded like thunder. His barrel chest heaved with exertion as he fought to catch his breath. On his shoulder atop a heavy pack, lay a blood deer that probably weighed twenty-five kilograms. He didn't seem to even notice the additional weight as he firmly hugged Nick's tiny form.

Tabby's eyes locked on me as I approached. She was slightly winded and smiling, obviously exhilarated by the effort of their return hike, which I suspected had turned into a race at the end. I gave her a welcoming smile and tipped my head back in acknowledgement. I wasn't anywhere near settled, but four ten-days had given me a much-needed break and the ability to clear my head.

Little Pete turned to me as I approached and then looked to Tabby for reassurance. The idea that this mountain of a man had anything to fear from me was laughable. The fact was, Peter was the son of two of my best friends and I could not see a world where I wanted to alienate him. I offered my hand as I approached. "Who got the deer? Ooh. Uh. Hello there," I said awkwardly, as he reached past my arm and pulled me in for a hug.

"If you listen to Tabitha, you'll think she coaxed this little one from the very mountain itself. But it was my sling that brought it down," he said, his deep baritone rumbling within his chest as he laughed and recounted the chase.

"You barely winged it," she objected. "I had to chase it down. You're such a liar and a brat."

"Everyone knows a blood deer runs even after it is mortally wounded. You cannot claim that which you did not strike."

I reached up and tugged on the blood deer's bound legs. Little Pete smiled and leaned to the side so that I could unload the animal from his back. Twenty-five kilos was about the extent of what I could carry and I struggled to get it onto my shoulders. I felt a bit of embarrassment when he had to help me center the weight so I wouldn't fall over.

"We have a lot to talk about," Tabby said. "Liam, you sure you have that?"

"Until I fall on my face, I do," I said, looking intently back at Little Pete.

It was hard to dislike the man because he immediately understood what I was saying and laughed without reservation. "He hardly looks like the same man," Little Pete said. "You're filling those clothes out and your face is brown from the sun. Mother has always said the mountain air is the best way to health."

"Because you drove me nuts in the house," Marny said. "Let's build a fire and have deer and fish. We'll feast the return of our family."

I walked ahead of the knot of people, mostly because I had a limited amount of time where I could carry the blood deer on my shoulders. We hadn't had any fresh kills since the two primary hunters had left, but I knew what to do with the carcass. I'd seen how Tabby had hung the animals she'd brought back before she processed them for meat.

"There's a trick," Tabby said, approaching me from behind as I struggled to hook the deer's legs into the hanger while not tipping over.

"You're both okay?" I asked.

"We need to talk," she said. "But first, put the deer on the ground."

"Once it's down, it's not going back up," I said.

"It's okay, trust me," she said.

I sighed as I dropped the blood deer onto the ground. The vision of Little Pete effortlessly carrying the extra weight was firmly emblazoned in my mind. I was definitely no competition for him.

"I do trust you," I said, which earned me a smile.

Tabby unspooled the leather cord connected to the hanging hook. I felt dumb that I hadn't realized it was long enough to reach the ground. She poked the hooks behind the Achilles and looked at me expectantly. I wound the cord onto a wooden spool as Tabby lifted.

"So much easier that way," she said.

"Not for you or Peter, I wouldn't think."

"He takes after his mother," she said. "I can still kick his butt, though."

I chuckled. No doubt that was true. "What do you want to talk about?"

"Not yet," she said. "We need to talk about Ada."

"You found her?" I asked.

"No, but we have a pretty good idea where she's at," she said. "You look better, you know that?"

"Thanks. Marny's a slave driver."

"You don't have to tell me," Tabby said. "Without her and Nick, I'm not sure we'd have survived. Just between us, she can be bossy."

I chuckled. I could easily see how Tabby might feel that way after the last four ten-days of having my life completely arranged by the energetic woman.

"What are you gossiping about?" Marny asked, as we approached the fire she was kindling back to life. I suspected she'd caught our conspiratorial looks in her direction.

Little Pete exited the barn, no longer carrying his pack. "Hey Cap, you want to learn how to butcher a deer? We need to make some steaks."

It felt weird to have a man who'd never been one of my crew refer to me as Cap, but his friendly nature was infectious so I didn't hold it against him. "Sure. Steaks it is."

"Normally, we'd let a deer hang overnight, and we will," he said. "We'll just pull enough for tonight and let the rest drain."

"Aren't you worried about the maracats?" I asked.

"We'll have to bring her inside tonight. She'll be good and bled by then," he said. "I was hoping we could clear the air between you and me."

It was a phrase Nick used periodically. When Pete spoke the words, I saw again the strong resemblance to his father.

"We're good, Peter," I said. "Tabby makes up her own mind about things and there was no way either of you could have known I was alive."

"I tried to tell her that," he said, almost exasperated. "It's pebbles in the river."

"Sorry? Pebbles?"

"Oh, sorry, it's something we say around here. If you ever throw a pebble in the river, you'll never find it again because they all look alike."

I wasn't about to tell him that his explanation did nothing to clear up his statement. I felt a little guilty as I pushed for more information. "Did you guys talk much about our situation while you were gone?"

"She wouldn't hardly talk to me for the first few days," he said. "It was like I'd done something wrong. But I hadn't. It's a real pebbles situation."

"I hear you, but we're going to need to work on your analogies," I said.

"You don't like the pebbles in the river thing?" he asked, working on the blood deer.

I chuckled. "It'll grow on me. Tabby doesn't always trust the people around her with her feelings," I said. "When she's worried or thinking on something, she just gets quiet. I'm sure she wasn't mad at you." The fact that I was consoling the man who was sleeping with my fiancée wasn't lost on me.

"She said we needed to put a hold on things until she figured it all out," he said. My heart might have stopped at that moment and I was careful not to look into his face.

"How did that make you feel?" I asked, packing the steaks he cut into the broad leaves we used for packing fish.

"It makes me sad," he said. "And please take my sorrys that I'm talking to you about this, but Dad said we needed to work this out."

"I understand," I said. Intellectually, I did understand, but at an emotional level, I was pretty sure I was the wrong guy to talk to.

"Well, you know, being with a woman ... that's pretty great," he said.

The lunch I'd had a few hours back bubbled up in my stomach. I didn't want to think about him being with Tabby. "Yeah?"

"Oh, yeah," he said. "At first, that's all it was."

I could taste acid on the back of my tongue. I was pretty sure I needed to end the conversation. There would be no getting through this unless I understood where I stood.

"So you guys are close?" I asked.

"Oh, yeah," he answered without hesitation.

"Hey, let's go guys," Marny said, startling me as she approached. "We need to hear this news about Ada."

"Just a minute," I said. I needed the punch line to his story.

"Everyone's waiting," she pushed. "Nick already has the fish fillets frying next to the orange tubers."

"We'll talk later," Peter said, grabbing the steaks and following Marny back to the fire pit.

I blew out an exasperated breath. The world was filled with frakking sadists.

After a few moments, I'd cleared my head enough to think and rejoined the group.

"Everything okay?" Nick asked, handing me a cup of fermented bonda juice. It was the closest thing we had to beer or wine and it didn't completely suck. He'd explained that the drink was a mead, not unlike the mash some spacers brewed when running short of decent alcohol.

"Just trying to find level ground," I said, sitting on a stump close to the roaring fire.

"Tell us about your trip already," Marny said.

"You were right, Dad," Little Pete started. "There was snow in the Juba Valley, but it wasn't very deep. When we made it to the Bluetops, we were mostly out of it."

"How long did that take?" Nick asked.

"Twelve days?" he said, looking to Tabby for confirmation.

"That's right," she agreed.

"And the Scatters didn't stop you?"

"They were around," Little Pete said. "But we were moving way fast. Tabitha had to carry my pack for a while."

"They didn't bother you when you camped?"

"No," Tabby said. "Like he said. They saw us and there was a group that stayed with us for the entire trip, but they didn't stop us until we were on the other side of the southern Bluetop."

"Give me some reference," I said. My AI overheard the question and presented a loose topographical map, showing the closest mountain range, Juba, followed by the Juba Valley and then another mountain range, called the Bluetop range. To the extreme north of the Bluetop range was a broad mountain that was bigger by twenty percent than the other mountains in the range. My AI identified this larger mountain as Bluetop Mountain. To the southeast, the mountain range continued but became fuzzy as my AI had no further information to fill in. It was enough, though. "Oh, I've got it."

"You said you think you know where Ada is," Marny said. "But you got stopped."

"The Scatters aren't all tribal," Tabby said. "Nick said he thought there was an ocean past the Bluetop range. There is. It's maybe eighty kilometers past the Bluetop southern mountain. What's more significant is that there's a large Scatter city next to the ocean. Maybe fifty thousand people? It's hard to judge.

"How'd you get stopped?" Nick asked.

"We were met by an armed guard of twenty. They wore uniforms and carried crystal shields and swords," Tabby said. "They looked like regular Scatters, except these guys didn't run off when I tried to get past them."

"Crystal swords and shields? That's interesting technology," I said.

"Metals are rare on this planet, specifically iron," Nick said. "It's held back their technological advancement. At some point, it's hard to advance much further without steel."

"You think Ada's in the city?" I asked.

"The city is exactly where you described Ada's location," Tabby said.

"Ada's suspension chamber," Nick corrected.

"I got Liam back. Now we're getting Ada back." As she spoke, she stared at me, her eyes burning with an intensity I hadn't seen since I woke up on Fraxus. I pitied the nation that stood between her and Ada.

Chapter 7

BEGINS WITH ONE STEP

"What did the city look like?" Marny asked. "Did you see radio masts, flying cars, trains? Were the guards carrying guns?"

Tabby smiled warmly. I felt a pang of jealousy at the exchange. The universe had twisted at Anino's command. My relationship with the woman I'd loved for as long as I could remember was ruined. While she and Peter had been away, I'd gained perspective, but in that moment, I realized I was not okay with where we were.

"It was a very long distance," Little Pete said. "I do not know of radio masts, but there were beasts that flew above the city."

"Those were golden gigantus," Tabby added, "and they had riders." One of Tabby's eyes had been replaced in a previous surgery and her distance vision was superior to Peter's.

"Golden gigantus?" I asked.

"Hundred-fifty-kilogram birds that resemble Earth's golden eagles in shape, if not size," Nick said. "We'll see them in the spring shortly after the snow leaves. Along with the maracats, they're a top predator. We've never seen one mounted and no city would allow wild goldens free rein. We've seen them pick up two-hundred-kilo, full-grown frigs."

"They don't attack humans?" I asked.

Nick pulled at his leather vest, exposing a patch of weathered skin just below his shoulder. Four, eight-centimeter-long furrows about the width of my thumb had been cut into his chest. "Caught me in an open field," he said. "If I hadn't been carrying a spear, I'd have been bird food."

"Frak, are there other predators I should be aware of?" I asked.

"There's a weasel-polar bear mix that we'll see if we go too far north," Marny chortled. "They don't usually come this far south. We call them abominables."

"Everything needs to eat," Little Pete said, knitting his eyebrows together in confusion. "An animal either eats other animals or it eats plants. There are many predators. It is the way of nature."

"Right," I said, annoyed that I'd prompted the lesson on ecosystems. "About the city? Did you observe any other technology beyond the crystal weapons?"

"They might have communications," Tabby said. "The squad leader was wearing a large earring adorned with gold or bronze."

"How exactly did they let you know you needed to leave?" Nick asked. "And why would they let you get that far only to turn you around?"

"Like Peter said, we moved fast during the day," Tabby said. "The group following us had to be tired and I imagine they sent a scout to the city to get reinforcements. A group stopped us at the pass leading down into the valley where the city lay. We could have gotten past them, but when I tried going around, they reformed and got in my way again. There might have been a small scuffle."

"You fought with them?" I asked.

"No," Tabby said, looking at my chest, not meeting my eyes. "Two younger female guards got pushy. There was some yelling. They might have jammed their shields into me."

I winced. "And then?"

"I relieved them of their shields," Tabby said.

"It was amazing," Little Pete said. "Tabitha threw their shields over the top of the trees. You should have heard the other Scatters when she did that."

"They've always been peaceful," Marny said. "And we've respected their demands."

"I pushed it too far," Tabby said. "Something about their high voices and how they were bumping their shields into me put me over the edge. I caught myself and when I backed down, so did they."

"Frak, Tabby," Nick said. "We can't afford a war with the Scatters."

This drew Tabby's ire. "You can't let people walk on you," she said. "I made my point and we're okay."

"Tell them the rest," Little Pete said, grinning ear to ear, his short, scruffy beard making him look just a little crazy.

We all turned our attention back to Tabby as she drew a big breath. "I think I saw *Hotspur*," she said.

"You think?" I asked.

"It was a long way away," Tabby said. "On the edge of the city. I can't be sure, but I got a reflection off glass. You know how armor glass has that blue-green halo?"

Nick shook his head. "This is a society that makes crystal weapons. There would be a million glittery things in that city."

She nodded her head encouragingly. "I know it's a long shot."

"We need to go back," I said. "And I need to go this time."

"The guard was pretty clear," Tabby said. "They weren't letting us past."

"Did you talk to them? Negotiate?" I asked.

"No." She shook her head, growing more agitated. Tabby had grown up in a home where her family criticized her every action. I wasn't surprised that in the last eighteen years, she hadn't been able to soften the ingrained negative reaction to being questioned. "We know maybe ten Scatter words."

"It's more like a hundred," Nick said. "But it's not enough for negotiation."

I tapped the side of my head where my earwig rested. "I still have Jonathan's upgraded translator programs. I'll do the negotiating."

"You don't know these people like we do," Tabby said. "You're in no position to negotiate." The us-versus-them reference hurt. I didn't like being considered an outsider by my own team. Especially not by Tabby.

"Tabby, I don't think Liam meant to suggest you failed," Marny said.

"I don't care what he meant," she answered. "I'm just saying he doesn't know the Scatters like we do and won't know how to negotiate with them."

"I can speak for myself," I said, standing, my eyes bright with anger. "Let me see if I have this right. In eighteen years, the sum of your interactions with the Scatters have been largely to avoid each other? They're not overtly hostile, but if you stay in the territory they've allowed you to exist in too long, they escalate contact? So, where does that leave us? Hanging out in this valley for twenty years, playing house? When you finally do make contact, you throw down with the first group you run into. Bang up job, Tabby. I'll definitely leave all negotiations to you from here on out."

"Liam," Marny started, disappointment thick in her voice.

"You're a pompous ass!" Tabby stood and tossed the contents of her cup into the fire. The alcohol flared as she spun and stalked toward her cabin.

"At least I'm not sleeping with my best friend's kid," I called after her retreating form.

"Frak off, Hoffen," she said, raising her middle finger and walking off.

"Shite," I breathed, shaking my head in anger. My heart was beating a million kilometers a second. I was as surprised as everyone else at my escalated outburst.

"Tabitha," Little Pete called, trailing after her. The move made me even more angry as jealousy fueled my internal rage.

"Shite, Cap. That was a bit harsh, don't you think?" Marny asked.

I tore my gaze away from Tabby and Little Pete. At some point in the future, I'd agree with her, but in this moment, not so much.

"I'm headed out in the morning," I said. "I'll take my grav-suit but go on foot to conserve energy."

"It's a long trip," Nick said. "Are you sure you're up for it?"

"I'm stronger than I was."

Nick shook his head. "You get tired too fast. Walking through snow is harder than you think. The snow on Fraxus can be heavy and the mountain passes are dangerous. Plus, you don't know how to forage for food in the winter. There are a million reasons why this is a bad idea."

"I don't even know why we sent Tabby and Peter," I said. "They're not negotiators. We just wasted four ten-days."

"Cap, I get that you're mad, but go easy on the criticism. We're all doing the best we can with a tough situation," Marny said. "Until they went out, we didn't even know there was a city on the other side of the Bluetop range. The signal for Ada's suspension chamber could just as easily have been lying on the side of a mountain. The intel they gathered is useful."

I shook my head and stared at the ground. My vision blurred as I worked through the issues and tried to push Tabby's angry remarks from my head. Nick was right. Even with the grav-suit, I wasn't in good enough shape to travel four-hundred kilometers, especially across two mountain ranges covered in snow. The fact was, I was going. That's all I needed to know.

"I'm leaving tomorrow," I said. "It's up to all of you how much you want to help."

"YOU'LL NEED THIS." Nick pulled a narrow belt from around his waist. He handed me the belt and the iron knife he'd forged. "I spent a few hours last night instructing your AI on the various plants that can be found on the mountain in winter. I wanted to come with you, but Marny talked me out of it. If I leave for as long as the trip will take, our homestead will probably fail."

"I understand," I said, not understanding at all. It felt like Little Pete or Marny could easily take over in Nick's absence.

"I don't think you do," he said, handing me my folded grav-suit. "But that's only because you haven't heard the rest of it."

I slid my clothing off and wriggled into the grav-suit which I was pleased to discover had to expand to allow me back in.

"What am I missing?" I asked.

I'd cooled off significantly from the blowup the night before, but I still wasn't thinking clearly. The sight of Peter trailing behind an angry Tabby kept replaying in my mind. Is that what Tabby needed? Someone to chase after her? Would the time we'd been separated, when Tabby had been forced to go on alone, prove too much for our relationship to survive?

"Me," Marny said, joining us at the front of the barn, carrying an armful of supplies. "Last night, Nick and I talked. I'm coming with you."

"You don't have to," I said.

Marny smiled, raising an eyebrow. "Your heart's in a good place, Cap. We know you're going after Ada, no matter the cost," she said. "Understand that in the same way, we're not letting you kill yourself in the attempt. Twenty years is a long time but finding you on the side of the mountain rekindled something I didn't even know we'd lost."

I chuckled mirthlessly. "You mean besides Ada, Jonathan and me?"

"Hope, Cap," she said. "We've spent so much effort just to survive. Somewhere along the way, I think we gave up ever getting off this planet."

"Is getting off this planet what you really want? I get the feeling not everyone is excited to see me."

"Change is painful. As a mother, I see the pain your presence brings Peter. I also see the conflict your presence brings Tabby. She feels she's betrayed you." Marny placed her hand on my arm. "That doesn't mean I'd trade the life of one of my closest friends to ease that pain."

"I feel so off balance," I said. "I know it's unfair that I'm angry with her, but that doesn't change how I feel. And intellectually, I know I can't blame Little Pete, but, well, he's your kid and I'm not even allowed to hate him. This is messed up beyond belief."

"If you're going to hate someone, I think Anino is deserving," Nick said. "He used us as pawns and allowed us to be pushed off his chessboard. Whatever end he was after, Anino obviously believed it was worth more than our lives. Go get Ada. Let the trip refocus you. I have a feeling that things are about to change around here."

"Yeah, like I'm going to end up as a popsicle on the side of a mountain?" I asked. I was going for light humor, but the pained look in Nick's face told me I'd missed the mark.

Marny spoke up. "Cap, you've always believed you chose me all those years ago. The fact is, I chose you. Ada, Jonathan, Nick ... the list is endless. We all saw in you that thing all great leaders have."

"What's that?" I said, smiling despite myself.

"I'm not sure what it's called. Sense of destiny, maybe? An inability to let something go just because it seems impossible? You make the impossible possible. You say we're going to go get Ada and I believe you, Cap. Just like when we met. I'm all in."

A lump had formed in my throat and I busied myself, pulling Nick's belt around my waist. "What do we need to do to get going?"

"I've loaded two frame packs with supplies. I just have these last items and we can roll whenever you're ready. Nick, did you finish the repairs to the snowshoes?"

"Yup," he answered. "I also tossed five meters of braided gut into your pack, just in case you need to do repairs on the way."

"Don't know what I'd do without you," Marny said, leaning over and giving him a quick kiss.

I followed them outside, finding the packs leaning against the side of the barn. Nick lifted one and helped me pull it onto my shoulders. The pack was a reminder of just how much things had changed. Nick lifted the weight with ease, causing me to believe it was light. Turns out, his time on Fraxus had hardened him. The straps bit into my shoulder and I winced as I adjusted to the weight.

"Just need to attach the belt," he said, slipping around in front of me. "It'll transfer some of the weight to your hips."

"I don't think you can call those hips," Marny chortled, tying off her own pack.

I glanced over to Tabby's cabin but saw no signs of movement. I wasn't sure what I hoped for. I wasn't up for another scene like last night, but it felt weird leaving without saying anything to her.

Nick must have caught my glance. "Tabby and Peter took off on a hunting trip this morning. With winter coming, we need the meat."

"Right," I said. "Makes sense. I'll get started. You guys can say your goodbyes."

As I trudged off toward the northern end of our camp, I checked the suit's power. It was capturing a small amount of energy from Fraxus' star, but the suit was using more than it was capturing just to keep my body warm. With the weight of the pack bearing down on me, I had no doubt my ability to keep myself warm would change quickly.

As I hiked, I shifted the pack around until I found a comfortable way to carry the load. Nick was right, the belt had taken much of the weight off my shoulders, causing my legs to complain. I pushed forward as hard as I could, not wanting to stay in camp any longer than necessary. After four ten-days of doing menial chores, it felt good to be moving toward a real objective.

I hiked in silence for nearly an hour. The trail was worn and easy to follow. Even though I was headed up the mountain, the path descended slightly as I followed the terrain. The crisp mountain air was invigorating, and the sounds of the mountain mixed with the rhythm of my boots crunching along the gravelly path.

A blip on my HUD warned of Marny's approach forty meters before she caught up with me. I pushed my pace, but she overtook me. "It's a long hike, Cap. You might want to save some of that energy."

"When will the Scatters catch on that we're on the move?" I asked.

"A few kilometers," Marny said. "They give us a wide berth, but eventually we'll run across one of their scouts."

"Any idea why they've avoided contact for all these years?" I asked. "Surely this valley wasn't abandoned when you arrived."

"Our suspension chambers all landed within a couple kilometers of each other," Marny said. "I had Peter with me, Tabby landed half a click from our position and Nick was further away. As far as we can tell, our revival sequences were initiated within minutes of our arrival. We were lucky; we arrived in late spring. It was Nick who figured out we weren't getting off planet and that if we didn't start working for long-term survival, we wouldn't make it through the winter."

"Sounds right," I said, glad to have something to take my mind off the effort of hiking.

"We didn't even know the Scatters existed until we ran across the clearing where our camp is now," she said. "We found evidence of a large group of people who'd just up and left. They were pretty thorough about it though, leaving nothing but bare patches of dirt."

"How large of a group?"

"Initially, we thought maybe fifty or sixty," Marny said. "Since then we've revised that number to more like a couple of hundred."

"I don't get it," I said. "How could you be so far off and why would they leave?"

"The best we can tell, Scatters are vegetarian," she said. "They don't just live on the ground. They also live in the trees. We probably wouldn't have made it if not for the discovery of that camp. With the Scatters gone, we harvested their crops and set up shelter."

"They just let you take over their village?" I asked.

"Nick and I have talked about this a lot," Marny said. "The day we discovered the clearing, Tabby was chasing a blood-deer with a spear Nick had fire-hardened. We were having trouble because, while we had all the protein you could want, we didn't know what plants were edible and which weren't. We think the Scatters were actually pushing the blood-deer toward the clearing, leading us to it."

"Why would they do that?" I asked.

"That's been the conversation," she said. "I personally think it's because they wanted us to stop killing so many deer. Nick thinks they were offering the clearing to give us a chance at survival."

"Those aren't competing ideas," I observed. "They might have been doing both."

"We've had a few more run-ins with them," Marny said. "About ten years ago, we started pushing our boundaries, trying to find any evidence of civilization. We knew the Scatters were out there, but short of having Tabby run one of them down and capture them, we didn't have too many options for conversation."

"How'd you learn their language?" I asked.

"They're not completely the ghosts they'd like to be," Marny said. "Over the years, we've all had moments where we've run across a group and been able to observe them without their knowledge. Peter is by far the best at this. His ability to move through the forest quietly is almost uncanny. Nick has recorded all the words we know."

"You said something about the Scatters shooting arrows at you when you got outside the area they wanted you to stay in," I said.

"Nick thinks they were bluffing," Marny said. "I'm not as convinced. As vegetarians, what would be their purpose for developing skills with ranged weapons? Nick thinks they need to defend against mara-cats. I just don't believe you become that good with a weapon without a daily purpose."

"You think the Scatters have an enemy?" I asked.

"I do," she said. "Maybe its other Scatters. Maybe there's a whole other species of sentients we haven't run into yet."

"Do you ever see satellites or spaceships?" I asked.

"We've seen ships, but they're not landing anywhere on this side of the planet as far as we can tell," she said.

The grade of the path had changed, finally giving us the arduous climb the mountain had been promising. I worked to maintain steady breaths, only able to concentrate on one step at a time. Idly, I recalled some ancient philosopher who had suggested that a journey of a thousand miles starts with one step. I wasn't as worried about that one step as much as I was the million that remained.

Chapter 8

POINT MASTERS

"We're being watched," Marny said, having casually walked up next to me.

The well-marked trail had evaporated over the last four days, and we were now relying on my AI to pick out the most traversable route. My body was still loudly complaining. Working around the camp was nowhere near as grueling as the constant battering inherent in placing one foot in front of the other, hour after hour. My only defense was to allow my mind to fall into a semi-catatonic state where I simply existed for that next step, pushing away all other distractions.

I looked up, startled by her presence as much as her pronouncement. On the edge of my HUD, I could see two red dots moving in conjunction with us on the uphill side of the mountain, their presence cloaked by trees.

"Two," I said. "Forty degrees portside."

"Could be Scatters," Marny said. "They won't confront us without a larger group. How is the energy situation on your suit?"

"It's converting my excess body heat to energy. It's not much, but I'm recovering the loss from overnight heating."

"Do you have enough to lift off?" Marny asked, adjusting her pack so the water skin she carried now hung from a hook on the side. The two-meter-long spear she used as a walking stick was transferred into her right hand.

"Are you expecting trouble?" I asked. "Weren't we expecting Scatters?"

"Scouts travel solo," she said. "Can you get your AI to fill in any details?"

My AI heard Marny's suggestion and prompted me to do just that. I accepted and was shown the rear flank of a feline. "Do maracats travel in pairs?"

"Mother and cub," she said. "They'll track us for a while. Once they decide we're good prey, they'll make their move. We have to take the fight to them."

"I'm going to guess that idea sounds as dumb to you as it does to me," I said.

"It does," she admitted, "but the longer we let them track us, the more they'll be convinced we're lunch. Just remember, that suit you're wearing is there to keep you alive. Use it that way and don't worry about me. I've dealt with maracats before."

"And how'd you do?" I asked.

"I'm still here," she said.

I pulled Nick's iron knife from the sheath, turned uphill and charged, making as much noise as I possibly could.

"Cap! Frak," Marny shouted.

On my HUD, I watched one of the two dots race off, heading up the hill while the other stood its ground. I couldn't see the actual cat, but knew I was only fifteen meters from its position. I'd always been fascinated by various tactics of warfare and had voraciously read texts on the subject. One of those books outlined the advantage given to someone on higher ground. It wasn't until I was scrabbling up the side of the mountain, charging a man-sized cat, that I realized just how superior the cat's position was. Apparently, my adversary also understood the concept and was simply awaiting my arrival, probably wondering just how dumb I could be.

"Frak, Cap, not like this," Marny sputtered, working to catch up.

A loud, angry yowl cut through the trees at the same moment I came into direct line-of-sight of a very pissed-off maracat. Instead of running off, like I had been secretly counting on, she lurched forward, her giant paws digging into the rocky soil. The cat's thick shoulder muscles tensed, propelling her toward me.

I'd only seen a maracat once and even then, I'd been barely conscious and it had been dead, draped across Tabby's shoulders. This cat was huge. I realized I was indeed crazy for charging into battle. The fact was, I'd committed myself and there was no turning back.

Since I had no idea how the maracat would attack, I did the only thing I could come up with. I waited until we were two meters apart and leapt, using my grav-suit to lift me from the ground. My plan, such as it was, was to flip over the top of the cat and give it a taste of Nick's knife. It was a good plan. I was more than agile enough to execute the maneuver and it would put the cat off balance.

Turns out, the key phrase there was *off balance*. The only experience I'd ever had with cats had been Filbert, an orange tabby we'd rescued from a space station. Filbert had an uncanny ability to twist his body and accomplish the most amazing acrobatic maneuvers. I'll just tell you, this is not a skill limited to house cats from the Milky Way galaxy. Instead of being even remotely impressed with my maneuver, the adult maracat pushed off from the ground and twisted in midair as I attempted to gain an advantage.

To say her maneuver was more effective than my own would be

something of an understatement. About halfway into my overhead spin, I realized things were going very poorly and I attempted to adjust. With grace found only in the wild, she tracked my movements and came at me with the swipe of a paw the size of my head. Her claws raked across my shoulder, sending me spinning wildly onto the rocks.

My grav-suit stiffened as the cat's claws attempted to split me open. Ordinarily, the suit was capable of resisting energy and projectile weapons, but in its beleaguered state, I was lucky it was operational enough to keep me from being eviscerated. Unfortunately, the suit did little to stop the pain of landing amongst the boulders on the side of the hill. The strap on my pack had taken a direct hit and as I hit the ground, the entire thing exploded, unpacking itself in a microsecond.

"Cap?" Marny called, over the angry yowl of the cat, who was no doubt turning on her now.

Pushing aside my own concerns, I bolted up from where I'd landed and streaked back to the maracat, which had, indeed, turned to face Marny. I screamed as I approached, iron dagger raised high overhead. The sight of Marny, facing down the large cat with nothing more than a spear in hand, spurred me on.

I believe cats to be fickle beasts. If the maracat had simply stuck it out, we all would have learned just how ineffective a warrior with a single spear and a crazy man with an iron dagger were against a fully grown maracat. As it was, my reappearance startled the cat, which no doubt assumed I'd been put down hard enough to be of no concern. Without a care in the world, she dismissed us, leapt to the side and trotted away.

"Are you okay, Cap?" Marny asked, working hard to catch her breath.

"Burned through about half the suit's stores," I said, "but I'm okay. Were you really going to go one-on-one with that spear?"

"Only if I had to," Marny said. "I'd forgotten about the armor in that suit."

"Think we're done with those cats?" I asked.

"She's just looking for food for her and her cub," Marny said. "I suppose it depends on how hard up they are. We hunt this mountain pretty hard."

"Very reassuring," I said, rubbing my shoulder.

"Let's see if we can repair that pack," she said, turning to where the contents of my pack were dumped all over the ground.

AN EXPERIENCED HIKER knows that descending a steep trail is harder than climbing it. While going down is not as anaerobic, it is both tough on the knees and hard on your quads. Add a mixture of snow and ice to this equation and you end up with the reason people prefer not to hike in the mountains during winter.

"We need to set up camp once we get to the bottom of this draw," Marny said, her breath billowing out in a long stream of vapor. I was thankful for the small uphill that heated me up and given my legs a rest. We'd been on the trail for fifteen days and were behind schedule, only halfway down the back side of Juba Mountain.

"A bit early for today, don't you think?" I asked. Each day we hiked, my suit battery drained further as the cold was barely offset by the exercise and the nights were frigid. On the positive side, my body had grown stronger, seemingly with every step. In that we only had the food we carried, we were both in a constant state of hunger.

"We're burning through our food too quickly and our pace is too slow," Marny said. "We need to restock before we get hit with that." She pointed south down the Juba range to what looked like happy, fluffy white clouds.

"Snow?" I guessed.

"A lot of snow," she said. "By the look of things, it could be on us for a few days. If that happens, we won't be going anywhere."

"Frak," I said, nodding. Never had I expended so much effort to travel seventy kilometers.

"That's an understatement, Cap," Marny said. "We could be in bad shape if that weather sets up like I think it might. We'll need to push it."

"Lead on," I said, grimacing as I adjusted my pack higher on my back.

The camping spot Marny indicated would, under normal circumstances, be a three-hour hike. Given our new pace, Marny was attempting to make the distance in half that time. I'd underestimated her. With the old Marny, I would never have felt the need to jump between her and a charging maracat. For some reason, I'd thought that was a good idea. Moreover, she hadn't corrected me afterwards. However, from that point forward, she pushed our pace, forcing me to my limit, only slowing when I proved I couldn't keep up. The next day, she pushed even harder. The years might have whittled her down in size, but there was no doubt she was still a warrior at heart.

An hour into our descent, I felt the first sprinkles of rain against my cheek. I'd heated up considerably and at least initially, it felt good. Ten minutes after the sprinkles started, an arctic blast of wind followed, freezing my hair in place. "Put your hat on, Cap," Marny warned, not looking back. "When we stop, you need to be as dry as possible."

If anything, I was glad for the rain-slicked trail as it forced Marny to slow. What I wasn't glad for was the rapidly dropping temperature, which had been hovering around three degrees and dropped to minus three in only a few moments.

"New plan," Marny said, as the terrain shifted from short, widely disbursed pines to a thickening forest of tall pines and deciduous trees. I took some satisfaction that she was breathing hard from the exertion. "When we arrive, you need to construct or find shelter. I'll gather as much food as I can find."

"What's going on?" I asked.

"We're in for snow," Marny said. "Plan for holding back a lot of snow with your shelter and you need to get a fire going. Once things are wet, fire will be difficult to start."

"I got it," I said.

Twenty minutes later, Marny pulled to a stop. "This is going to have to do." The look on her face suggested she wanted something better.

"Show plans for emergency shelter using the tools I have available," I instructed my AI. My encounter with cold nights and the maracat had left the suit at half the power I'd started with. That was after generating power from the day's hike. Fortunately, the AI could operate almost indefinitely on low power.

"Cap, I need to locate food, you'll need to figure out the shelter on your own. We're against the clock," Marny said.

"Um, I was talking to the suit," I answered, raising my eyebrows. I understood her confusion as I was no doubt a sight to behold with animal skins covering parts of my grav-suit.

Her laugh was a short bark. "Right. Haven't thought of that for quite some time," she said. "Fire, then shelter."

"Copy that," I answered.

It turned out, with the AI's help, locating appropriate cross members for and constructing a shelter wasn't difficult. At the perfect intersection of three trees that had grown together with intersecting branches, I built a two-by-three-meter space and covered it with pine boughs. On the open end of the structure, I dug a shallow fire pit and rolled heavy rocks to back it. Finally, I gathered more pine boughs and laid them down on the inside of the structure to serve as beds.

"Cap, fire," Marny said, bringing back an armful of dirty tubers. "You're going to have a dickens of a time getting this wood started."

"There's a stream down the hill to our southeast," I said, dumping the contents of my pack onto one of the beds I'd constructed. I offered the pack to Marny. "Leave your pack, you can carry more with mine."

"Fire?" she pushed. I looked into her weathered face. Mountain living had been hard on her as much as time had whittled her down to her essence. Her unbridled intensity was still there, but it was balanced with a calm that hadn't always been there.

"I've got it," I said, unwrapping the thicker skin that would keep me warm when I finally cooled from the activity. "Give me your water skin."

She complied, her eyes darting around the structure I'd put together. "This is quite a lean-to," she said. "I've missed the advantages an AI brings."

I poured the remains of my own water skin into hers and handed it back to her. "I'll help gather once I get the fire going and some water."

For the next three hours, we tramped through the woods, gathering as much as we could find in preparation for an extended stay. Our steps slowed as the blanket of snow thickened and heavy flakes filtered down through the trees. At first, tree branches held back much of the snow, but soon the powerful winds set upon us, piling snow into drifts. Walking became nearly impossible.

"Bring it in, Cap," Marny finally said. She was right. We gave up and slumped onto the pokey pine-needle beds I'd put together only a few hours before.

"How much more snow do you think we'll get?" I asked, taking off my outer skins and setting them near the fire to dry.

"I'd say we already have fifteen centimeters," she said. "We could get as much as a meter or two."

My jaw must have gone slack as she chuckled at the look on my face. "A couple of meters? Can we even get through that?"

"We're lucky it's early in the season," she said. "Once the storm passes, it should warm up and the snow will pack. You do understand that's why we've been carrying those snow shoes all this time, right?"

I groaned and lay back, trying unsuccessfully to make my bed comfortable. "Could you have taken that maracat?" I asked, closing my eyes. There was something very peaceful about the falling snow and even though I was sore, I felt content.

"The one you went berserker on?" Marny asked, adjusting her own pack.

"There was another one?" I asked.

She chuckled. "I hoped it wouldn't come to a fight," she said. "But I'd like to believe I stood a better than even chance. I don't work out like I used to, but there's something about subsistence living that hardens the body in ways no workout ever could."

"Ever wonder what's going on back home?" I asked.

"You mean Mhina system?" she asked.

"Yeah."

"Sure. Have you talked to Nick about our trip to this place on *Hotspur*?" she asked.

"Not really," I said. "You know Nick. Always focused on what needs doing next. Why?"

"He's concerned with why Anino put us in life-suspension chambers," she said.

"Worked out good for me," I said. "Otherwise, I'd be dead right now. Instead, I'm a thinner, stronger version of my twenty-five-year-old self."

"You were only twenty-five standard years when we left?" Marny asked, rhetorically. "You make me feel ancient. My body is at least fifty stans at this point."

"Looking pretty darn good for it too," I said. "And Nick. Who knew he had so much muscle under all that engineering flab."

Marny guffawed. "The fresh air *has* been good for him, but he misses home more than he lets on."

"What's his theory about the reason Anino put us in life-suspension chambers?" I asked.

"You sure you want to know?"

"You can't leave me hanging. Of course I do."

"What if we were in those chambers for longer than a quick trip out to the Small Magellanic Cloud? The faster-than-light drive might have had other effects," she said. "You're familiar with relativity and the effect of approaching the speed of light? Nick's worried that Anino did more than strand us on Fraxus."

"Time dilation?" I asked.

"Nick thinks it's possible more than twenty years have passed."

"How many?" I asked.

"He was working with your AI to plot galactic positions," she said.

"What'd he find?"

"Nothing yet. We just don't have any accurate enough sensors."

"Great," I said. "Not only did Anino take my fiancée, but he might have taken my family too? Frak, but I really hate that guy."

"You blame Anino for Tabby and Peter? I thought you were mad at Tabby," she said.

"I know I'm not handling things that well," I said. "I don't even know why I yelled at her. I didn't know it was coming and suddenly, I was screaming. I drove her away when I wanted her back. I ruined it just as surely as Anino did."

"Tabby is a grown woman, Cap," Marny said. "She knows you're hurting and won't hold that against you."

"What can I do to get her back?" I asked, understanding the perversity of asking my competitor's mother.

"Nothing, Cap. Tabby is in a hard spot. You were her first love and no woman every really gets over that," Marny said. "I think you're asking the wrong question, though."

"Which is?"

"If you're not together, how much do you want her in your life?"

I sighed. I hadn't truly entertained the idea of Tabby not being part of my life. She'd been in my thoughts nearly every day I could remember. I fully expected to have kids and grow old with her. Life had thrown us an impossible curveball.

THE SNOW FELL for five days and by the end of it, our supplies had dwindled to almost nothing. Several times we'd ventured out to look for food, but everything had been covered in an impossibly thick blanket of snow.

"Ready to learn how to walk again?" Marny asked.

"How's that?" I asked.

"You're in for a special treat today," she said, grinning wickedly.

"Anything has to be better than sitting in this hole," I said, my teeth chattering as I spoke. My suit's energy stores were at a critical level, no longer usable for heat. I was about as cold as I ever remembered being.

I followed Marny's lead as we sat in the deep, albeit soft snow next to our shelter. The snow shoes weren't difficult to attach, but I recognized the problem almost immediately. The wide imprint of the shoe made it impossible to keep your feet together. Of course, I hadn't grasped the mechanics of it and when I attempted to stand, I fell back on my butt.

"Everything's done at a slight jog," Marny said, handing me two-meter-long sticks she'd crafted while we'd been holed up. "I'll blaze the trail. Try to do what I do and keep in my tracks."

I lifted my pole and Marny tugged until I was upright. At the end of the sticks, she'd woven baskets, the purpose of which wasn't immediately obvious. Like the shoes, however, the baskets caught on the fluffy snow when I stabbed them toward the earth for balance. Seeing that I remained standing, Marny took off. At first, she lumbered as her shoes sank into the fresh powder. As her speed increased and her shoes sank in less, she seemed to skim across the deep snow.

The task was impossibly difficult and I couldn't quite get the rhythm. After half an hour of tedious work, I found that as long as I placed my shoes into the impressions Marny left, I made reasonable progress.

"Doing good, Cap," Marny said, stopping after an hour of ridiculously hard work. There was no way I'd be able to continue at our current pace for more than a couple of hours and by the amount of vapor bellowing out from Marny, I suspected she would have similar issues.

"I'm dying back here."

"It'll get easier as we go. The snow is already starting to stiffen. Can't you feel it?" she asked.

"No," I said simply, my lungs still searching for oxygen.

It was a day I suspect I'll never forget and after five grueling hours Marny finally relented, allowing us to settle in under a large tree that had formed a snow cave beneath its limbs.

"I'd hoped to find some game out and about," she said stripping bark from the tree. "We're going to be in trouble if we don't find calories somewhere."

"What's that?" I asked.

"Makes a tea," she said. "Better than nothing, but I guarantee you won't drink it under other circumstances."

The bark tea wasn't that bad. Sure, it was bitter, but coupled with a small amount of our remaining tuber, it provided welcome calories, although nowhere near the replacement we needed.

While seated, my AI alerted me of movement only a few meters from our position. I held up my finger to let Marny know we needed to be quiet. I signaled that I had contact with something. My suit's batteries had charged some, having vamped my heat as I strained to keep up with Marny in the snow. As such, I knew I could grav-assist if needed. Turning, I caught sight of the ears of a rodent Nick had referred to simply as a rabbit. The animals weren't exactly like those found on Earth, but they were small, around a kilo and a half, furry, and best of all, they were edible.

In a single, fluid movement, I lurched from my seated position, my legs screaming in protest. With as little boost from my grav-suit as I could manage, I twisted and landed atop a very startled rabbit, who at the last moment attempted to squirt away. The ensuing combat was anything but pretty. In the end, it was a point to Hoffen.

"Maybe I should dress that," Marny said, looking at the carnage I proudly placed on the ground in front of her.

"I'll start the fire."

FOUR DAYS LATER, things took a turn for the worse. While we'd been keeping a lookout for wildlife, none had presented themselves.

Following the first storm, a second had blown into the valley. Worse yet, we'd only made fifteen kilometers from where we'd been hit by the first storm. Without adequate supplies, these were serious enough setbacks that I wondered how we'd make it through.

"The snow is slowing," Marny announced on the third day. "We have to find food. We can't survive like this."

I nodded, pulling on my snow shoes and taking lead on the trail. With every passing hour, I came to understand that our struggle had become life threatening. That Marny had us out in this storm told me she felt the peril too.

Mid-afternoon on the fourth day of the second storm, the snow finally relented, but we struggled to keep moving. Clear skies gave us hope and when my AI pinged contact, my heart leapt.

"I've got something," I said, fumbling as I came up next to Marny.

"Good," she whispered, her face drawn from hunger. She followed my gaze into the forest where the contact had come from. I still hadn't seen what type of animal was there when she growled, "Stay behind me, Cap."

I looked again, not fully understanding until a second blip showed on my HUD. "Do you see it?" I whispered.

"It's that maracat. It's been tracking us."

"All this time?"

Marny nodded wearily. "She's a wise old woman. She's been following, waiting for us to weaken. Maracats are intelligent. She knows we're slow and she must have figured out that we're not in very good shape."

I pulled out Nick's knife. If we were going down, we'd go down fighting.

The adult maracat appeared from the tree line, flanked by the adolescent. She hadn't sent the young one off like she had on the other side of Juba mountain. Their plan was simple. They would charge and finish us off.

"Come on!" I yelled. "You want some of this?"

Apparently, my words translated into *free food, come and get it*, because the two felines bolted into action, racing toward us over the snow. I stepped in close to Marny, who had braced her spear and was prepared to accept the charge. It was my job to keep Marny freed up to fight for as long as possible. Between the two of us, she stood the best chance of surviving the short odds.

In unison, the two maracats left the ground. I took the impact of the larger one straight to my chest and fell back into the snow. Wildly, I swung my blade, piercing the animal's side, completely amazed that I hadn't taken more injury. Not interested in wasting my good luck, I pulled around and jabbed my knife into the beast's chest, when I suddenly realized the beast wasn't moving.

"I got it!" I cried exuberantly, trying to free myself from the tangle of fur and blood.

Strong hands grabbed my arm and pulled me up. I found myself looking directly into Tabby's face.

"Point Masters," she said with a wicked grin.

Chapter 9

ELVES

Tabby's face was only centimeters from my own. For the first time in many ten-days, she willingly looked me in the eye.

"Frak, I'm so sorry, Tabby," I said, pushing a stray hair over her ear. I slumped. The reflexive move felt inappropriate.

The look of triumph faded from her face. "Sorry for almost getting yourself killed?" she asked, pushing the dead maracat off into the snow.

"There were two of them," I said as reality snapped back into focus.

"The yearling ran off," Little Pete responded, only a few meters away.

Tabby turned back to me as if she was waiting for an answer.

"It's just ... I can't do this," I said.

A flash of pain crossed her face but was quickly replaced by anger. "Can't do what?" she growled, turning away.

"Don't do that," I said, placing my hand on the side of her cheek. She resisted but allowed me to rotate her so we were face to face. "Don't get angry. I don't want to fight with you. It's not fair what happened to us. None of that changes how I feel about you, but I never should have said what I did. You were right to look for happiness. How could you have known I was alive?"

I was vaguely aware of Little Pete talking, only to be called off by Marny. I held Tabby's gaze as she processed what I was saying.

"I never lost hope," she said, her eyes puddling with tears. "This thing with Peter just happened. He's such a good man. I don't want to hurt either of you."

"If I could put the world back twenty years, I would," I said. "The fact is, you aren't the one at fault. It's taken six ten-days and me nearly dying in a blizzard to figure out who's to blame. If you need a name, it's Thomas Anino. The fact is, there's no going back. We have to accept where we're at and move forward from here."

"You make it sound so easy," she said.

"Honestly, it is that easy," I said. "You have a hard decision to make and there's no reason you need to make it right now."

"*I* have a decision to make?" she asked. "What about you? Or maybe you're forgetting that I almost had a baby with Peter."

"That's in the past, Tabby," I said. "Sure, I don't love where we're at with this, but nothing has changed for me. That said, I'll respect whatever decision you make."

Tabby sighed. "This was a lot easier when I was mad at you."

"How'd you know where we were?" I asked, eager to change the conversation.

"Peter," she said, helping me out of the indentation in the snow.

"Yup," Little Pete answered almost immediately. I'd been so focused on Tabby that I'd lost track of him and Marny. When I turned to look at the big man, I could tell he was concerned. His face, however, showed none of the hostility I had expected and – honestly – what I knew I would be feeling in a similar situation. "Mom blazed the trail. It was easy to follow."

"Start a fire," Marny said, taking charge. "We need to process this maracat before we move again. The back-to-back snows burned down our supplies."

"Pretty lucky, this snow." Little Pete grabbed the back legs of the heavy cat and with brutal efficiency, started to clean the animal.

"Lucky?" I asked. "We haven't had a good meal in a ten-day."

Pete dunked his large hands into virgin snow and wiped as much blood away as he could. From a pouch, he pulled out a leaf-wrapped travel bar like the ones we'd run out of some time back. "Eat this first. But you'd better get started on the fire or mom will have your hide."

I eagerly unwrapped and tore into the bar. "You know, this really does taste like berries."

Marny laughed, hearing the old joke. In our previous life, I'd always claimed the replicator's berry-flavored meal bars were my favorite. In truth, none of our meal bars had ever had much flavor to them and I never really minded. I used to think it was funny that people expected more from their food than nutrition. Oh, how times had changed. The tart berries in the travel bars were tasty and I took a moment to savor the treat. Peter gave me a quizzical look but continued working on the maracat.

"Kind of sad to see this old girl get put down," he said. "She's raised her last cub, I guess. I'm surprised she attacked you. She's always left us alone."

"Early snow," Marny said. "Blood deer have headed over the mountain to where there's still green."

"I still don't get why we're lucky it snowed, Little Pete," I said.

"Look over toward Bluetop," he said, pointing to the northeast.

While we were too far away to see Bluetop Mountain, we were able to make out the broad valley that separated the two mountain ranges. Just like where we were situated, there was a fresh blanket of white snow sitting beneath a cerulean blue sky.

"All I can see is snow," I said. " Snowshoeing sucks, by the way."

"Aww," Tabby mocked, dropping a load of firewood into the circle of matted snow we'd formed during the attack. "Nothing more invigorating than the cardio of snowshoeing."

"Maybe for you," I said. "But I feel like someone strapped a couple of house cats to my feet."

"Snowshoeing will get you there, but it's slow as you've already learned. Unless you're Tabitha, that is," Little Pete said. "See my pack over there? We brought skis and the snow is perfect."

I'd heard of skiing before but had no experience with it. The idea that I was about to learn another winter sport didn't exactly appeal to me, but if skiing was easier and faster than snowshoeing, I was all in.

"How many did you bring?" Marny asked.

"Four sets," Pete answered. "After about a ten-day, Dad realized you were in for trouble with the snow and sent us out."

"Always the smartest man in the room," I said.

TABBY, Marny and Little Pete all took turns cutting trail, as they called it, while I struggled to simply keep up. By the fourth day and with Tabby carrying my pack, my HUD showed that I was maintaining a pace of three kilometers an hour. Not unlike hiking, the most treacherous portions of the trip were the steep downhills. I managed to get through admirably, although not without some spectacular falls.

"It's warming up," Marny said, joining me where I sat on a fallen tree, catching my breath. We'd traveled two hundred fifty kilometers in the fifteen days since Tabby and Little Pete had caught up with us. Our faster pace was due to the shade cast by Bluetop Mountain on its western slope. Without that protection, the snow atop which we were skiing would no longer have been around.

"Sure makes for fast skiing. Although I'm not looking forward to the climb," I said. We'd been working our way into the foothills of Bluetop and the grade had been increasing the last few days. At some point skis would no longer be practical.

Little Pete joined us and settled into a crouch, as was his nature. "Hand me your skis. Tabitha says we're out of the snow in a couple clicks. Snow isn't deep enough for shoes. If we hit it hard, we're only two days from where we got turned around last time," he said.

"I would kill to walk on flat ground," I said.

"Careful with that," he said. "We're being watched. Scatters might think you're serious."

I was surprised by his announcement. "Really? My suit's sensors are struggling, but I haven't seen even a hint of activity."

"Scatters are sneaky," he said, thoughtfully scratching his thick black beard. "Hard to see them if they don't want you to. You can hear them in the woods, but if you want to see one, you have to look up. The scouts are always in the trees."

I couldn't help but scan the trees around us. As expected, I found nothing.

"Two days, you say?" I asked, feeling little anxiety about the trek ahead. Living on Fraxus had been nothing but constant exercise and my once-depleted body was hardly recognizable. Probably more surprising was that I was stronger than I'd been prior to Anino's latest betrayal. I thought I'd been in relatively good shape before leaving Mars, but my former spacer physique was nothing in comparison to the lean muscle earned on the mountain.

I unstrapped my skis and stood, testing the ground. It was slippery, but my grav-suit boots responded to the terrain and adjusted, giving me an aggressive tread pattern complete with small spikes. I drew in a deep breath and exhaled slowly. "No time like the present in that case," I said, picking up my skis and heading up the mountain with a quickened step.

"Fargin right!" Little Pete said, catching up with me and grabbing my skis. "Use your poles, you'll go faster."

"I got 'em," I said, not allowing him to take the skis. "Maybe help me strap them onto my back?"

"Can do, Cap," he answered. The man was hard to dislike. It had taken me a long time to admit to myself that he was going through the same thing I was with Tabby. He'd handled it better. If the stakes weren't Tabby, I might have found myself pulling for him.

Fraxus was surrounded by two moons, both of which were quite large. Little Pete had cleverly named the biggest *Big Moon* when he'd been a few years old. Between the snow in the valley and the light reflecting down from the moons, we had a good view of the trails going up and around the mountain. I pushed the group to continue climbing until Marny finally put a stop to it.

"Cap, there's no value in wearing yourself out," she finally said. "It's getting too hard to see."

I was about as tired as I could ever remember being and it wasn't hard to convince me to stop. Instead of an elaborate camp, we made a small fire and ate some of our dwindling food stock. We'd made a conscious decision to push on instead of stopping to replenish our supplies, knowing that with the late fall warmup we'd be able to forage for food much easier once we reached Bluetop's eastern slope. That side of the mountain, we hoped, would be fully melted, even if it had been hit by the latest storms.

Leaning against my pack, a meter from the fire, I overheard Tabby giggling quietly as Little Pete said something to her. I must have grimaced because Marny caught the look and called me on it. "You doing okay, Cap?"

"Tired is a good place to be," I said. It wasn't entirely true. Physical exertion was good for the body, but if you were stewing on a problem, the mind could use the distraction to endlessly circle around and invent unpleasant thoughts. One saving grace was that sleep was easy to find.

"It'll work out," she said, shifting her pack so she lay closer to me.

"Wish I was as confident," I said as I did, indeed, let sleep swallow me.

"Rise and shine," Tabby said, hunching down next to me. For a moment, I was back aboard *Intrepid* and everything was right in the world.

"Geez, how can I be sore again?" I complained, accepting a length of jerky from her.

"Climbing is a lot different than skiing," she said. "I've already been up to the pass this morning. There's an amazing view."

I shook my head. We were ten kilometers from the pass and she was admitting to having already run twice that distance to get there and back. "Any Scatters?" I asked.

"None that I saw," she said, helping me to my feet. "You want to tell me how you're planning to negotiate with them?"

"I have no fargin idea." I'd adopted Little Pete's curse word and smiled as it rolled off my tongue.

As usual, the first hour of the morning was tough going as my muscles and tendons complained about the previous day's activities. By mid-morning I was making good time and could even see the top of the pass, which crossed over a saddleback ridge running between Bluetop mountain and the next peak to the south.

It was almost exactly mid-day when we crested the final rise on the path and finally saw past the mountain we'd been struggling to climb for days. It was a spectacular moment.

In the extreme distance – sixty-eighty kilometers to be exact – I could make out the coastline of a foamy green sea to the north. Just as Tabby and Little Pete had described, a sparkling city lay nestled around a deep blue bay that appeared anomalous with the abutting sea. The sheltered inlet was so different it was a curiosity and given the distance, could easily be some sort of optical trick. I scanned the hillside back from the city toward where we stood. A wide river ran along the valley and disappeared into the terrain below.

My heart skipped a beat as the AI highlighted an ambiguous signal from Ada's suspension chamber. Somewhere in the valley, Ada was alive and well, but my suit could do nothing to pinpoint its location.

"I'm getting a signal from Ada," I said.

"Can you magnify?" Tabby asked. "What about the ship?"

My AI heard her question and scanned the city, displaying a negative result.

"Nothing on the ship," I said. "I'm sure it goes without saying that under no circumstances are we to get physical when we run into the Scatters."

"I think you've made that point," Tabby said petulantly. I nodded. There was no good way to have the conversation.

"There's some chance they'll try to take one or more of us prisoner," I said. "Let them. At least let them take me."

"We stay together," Tabby said firmly.

"You good with this, Marny?" I asked.

"Copy that, Cap," she said.

I took off down the path that quickly widened, apparently from constant use. The alpine rocks underfoot were dry and we kicked up dust as we walked, leading me to believe the snow might have been limited to the Juba Valley and hadn't made it over Bluetop mountain.

"Last time they stopped us right at the tree line," Tabby said, walking next to Little Pete and allowing me to take the lead.

The oxygen was sparse at our current elevation, which my AI calculated to be near four-thousand meters. The fact that we were finally going downhill made it a much nicer trek and we chewed up the two kilometers to the edge of where trees were able to grow.

"There's a group approaching," Little Pete warned. A moment later my AI displayed ten contacts on my HUD.

"Why don't you guys stay here a minute," I said, unslinging the pack I'd insisted Tabby let me carry.

"Hold on, Cap," Marny said. "What if they restrain you?"

"You'll have to improvise," I said. "Personally, I'd want you to return to Nick. It could take me a while to work things out. But I also know you'd never do that. Try to follow me if that happens."

Tabby put her hands on her hips. "You've had how many ten-days to come up with a plan and this is all you've got?"

I shrugged. "What else is there? The Scatters have all the power. That hasn't changed in twenty years. We've got to talk. Until that happens, we're at stalemate."

"He speaks truth," Little Pete said, crossing his arms. "We will wait."

I raised an eyebrow at his assertive position, but Tabby reacted with annoyance. "Now you're on his side?"

"We tried our way. He will try his now," Peter said, settling down into a crouch. "We all seek the same result."

Tabby shrugged. "I suppose you're right."

I looked back and forth between the two. I had to give Pete a silent *bravo*. He'd unlocked the first level of Tabby, which was to help her get past the anger which often got in her way.

"Give me twenty minutes," I called over my back as I walked down the path to meet the gathering Scatter troops.

"Gefarren halt!" Nick had taught my AI all the words he'd been able to learn from chance encounters with the Scatters over the years. The AI also had Jonathan's adaptive translation algorithm. Even so, I was surprised it already had figured out one word – halt. On my HUD it showed a ninety-two percent likelihood that word was correct.

"I come with peaceful intent," I said, untying the belt at my waist, and allowing the iron dagger to fall to the path as I continued forward. It had been a long time since I'd used the translator and found it momentarily disconcerting. The AI set up a canceling wave for the word *peaceful* and replaced it with a foreign translation that sounded something like *fun chewy*.

"Human ... halt." The man speaking was taller than most of the others within the group. I'd never had a good look at a Scatter before and it appeared there were two distinct clans represented. Having seen my fair share of aliens, I really had no preconceived notions about what to expect.

The man who appeared to be in charge was human shaped, if not a little small. His skin was pale, and he had blonde hair, pointy ears and high cheekbones. He stood out from his companions, wearing what looked like a brilliant-green linen vest over a cream-colored shirt and brown leather pants.

Most of his companions were smaller, with swarthy brown skin and wore animal hides that were constructed with much better craftsmanship than ours. Each member of the Scatter troop had a crystal sword at their side and seemed evenly split between holding a bow or wooden shield. I would have named this species *Elves* rather than Scatters, but that was just me.

I stopped, having reached a distance where communication was easier. "I need to talk to your leader," I said, a little disappointed that my AI could only substitute for the *I* and left the rest of my speech untranslated. It needed further conversation to build a reasonable word bank. I tapped on my chest and gestured down the hill.

"... home ..." the lead Scatter said. While speaking, he pointed at me and gestured up the hill.

"I cannot," I said. "My friend is in your city. She's in a suspension chamber where she is asleep. I need to wake her up, so she can live."

The AI translated a few more of my words, including suspension chamber, which caused the leader's eyes to narrow. Unfortunately, he simply repeated his previous demand that we go home.

"No, that is not acceptable." I stepped forward and the guard shifted. The four shield bearers closest to me drew their swords and blocked the path.

"... not allowed ..." the leader said.

"My friend in the suspension chamber will die," I said. "I cannot go back without her. You must bring me to your leader. Take me as your prisoner and bind my eyes so I do not see your home, but please, I must find her. We will leave your home once we have found our friend."

"Go ... not allowed ..."

I bit my tongue. The guy had a one-track mind and I was frustrated with his insistence. I turned around and walked back to where I'd dropped my belt and knife. Withdrawing the knife from the belt caused the guard to shift audibly and I was glad no arrows found my back. I dropped the knife back to the ground and wrapped one end of the belt around my wrist as I turned to face the guard again. With some manipulation and the use of my mouth, I managed to loosely tie my hands together.

"You will take me prisoner," I said. "You will take me to your leader and we will talk. My friend sleeps in a suspension chamber and you have her. I will not leave."

I walked forward, resting my bound hands in front of me. The guards formed up and pushed their shields together. I was surprised that no swords were at the ready, but intuition told me the threat level could change in an instant. Their shield wall was sturdy and I couldn't push my way through.

"Human ... halt," the leader said, exasperation clearly in his voice.

"Take me prisoner. Let me speak to your leader," I repeated, closing my eyes and trying to push through the line. The ensuing scuffle lasted a full minute or two. With a shouted word that I assume came from the leader, the guard instantly separated. Unfortunately, I was still pushing and overbalanced. I ended up falling inelegantly to the ground.

"One human," the leader said. "... human ... human ... go."

I rolled over and stood up, my hands still bound. "I will tell my friends to go home," I said. "And you will take me to my friend in the suspension chamber."

"... not allowed ..."

I rolled my eyes and walked back up the hill. This guy and his *not allowed* was getting on my nerves. When I made it to the knife, I bent down and picked it up, having freed my hands from the loose binding.

"What did they say?" Tabby asked impatiently. "It looks like you got roughed up. I was about to come get you."

"Thank you, Tabby. They weren't trying to hurt me," I said, giving her a reassuring smile. "There's good news and bad."

"Good news?" Marny asked.

"They've agreed to take me," I said. "But they won't take any more than me. They say you need to go home."

"No frakking way," Tabby said. "We just got you back."

"We could try to negotiate for more," I said, "but just one of us needs to find Ada. After that, we'll see. Worse case is, they send me away."

"You'd never make it back to us," Tabby said. "They might as well kill you here. You'd be just as dead if they sent you out over the mountain alone."

"They're civilized and peaceful," I said. "I'll cross that mountain when I come to it."

"I don't like it, Cap," Marny said. "I also don't believe you're asking for our opinion."

"I'm more than willing to take a risk to get Ada back," I said. "It's what every one of you would do in my position."

"Doesn't mean we have to like it," Tabby complained.

"Take your skis and snow shoes," Marny said, picking up my pack and transferring food from her pack to mine. "If you get stuck on the mountain, spend your effort gathering food. Don't worry as much about making distance. We'll watch for signal fires at first light as often as we can. Smoke trails can be seen for a long distance."

"I've got this, Marny," I said and turned back down the path. All of a sudden, I felt Tabby wrap her arms around me from behind.

"Don't you dare die on me, Liam Hoffen," she whispered in my ear. "I just got you back. I can't lose you again."

I blew out a hot breath. When I reached the Scatter guard, they separated, placing four men behind me and two ahead. The others, including the leader, stayed behind as I was nudged down the hill.

Chapter 10

CRYSTAL CITY

I found it difficult to keep to the path, as my eyes were filled with the sights of the far-off city and my feet were forgotten. Just as Tabby and Peter had described, the city sparkled in the sun. Indeed, large birds did fly in and around the city.

We'd started downhill in the middle of the afternoon. The temperature in Bluetop Valley was considerably warmer than it had been on the other side of the mountain range. I supposed that the climate had a lot to do with the vast ocean growing larger with every passing hour. While ten degrees isn't warm, I found myself sweating. I was also short of breath from the exertion of carrying a heavy pack and trying to keep up with my nimble captors. Initially, I'd been almost jogging, concerned that the guards assigned to me would not put up with a slower pace. At some point, I had no choice but to resist the nudges from behind that were no doubt designed to speed me along. After the third such altercation, words had been exchanged and the group slowed to a more manageable pace.

"Human ... halt ... eat ..." The Scatter who spoke had taken a special interest in me, having walked next to me for most of the last several hours. He was only about a meter and a half tall. His gray-brown skin had an almost wooden texture to it. My first thought was how useful that coloring would be for camouflage in and amongst the trees. Perhaps that was the reason I'd never spotted them watching as we crossed the mountain.

As a group, the Scatters were quiet in every activity, rarely speaking. I often saw them communicate through small touches, tongue clicks, gestures, and whistles that sounded remarkably like the native insects that came out at night. I wondered if I'd been hearing real insects or if we'd been under observation by Scatters all along.

"Liam Hoffen." I gratefully lowered my pack and set it next to the path against a tree. The lights of the city in the valley were beautiful.

"Thandeka," my companion responded, gesturing at the city below but not taking his brilliant green eyes off me. Apparently, I was just as interesting to him as he was to me.

I tipped back my water pouch and drained half of what remained. I'd need a water source if I were to keep the pace we'd been on for much longer. I decided to try communicating again and thumped my chest as I said my name again. "I am Liam Hoffen."

My companion nodded, accepting my words. "Hambo," he answered, mimicking my chest thumping.

"Nice to meet you, Hambo," I said, placing my fist onto my solar plexus, a habit I'd learned from the Abasi cat people of the Dwingeloo system.

"Eat ... walk ..." Hambo said, holding out a thin dry leaf about the length of my hand.

I reached for my pack, misinterpreting his instructions.

"No ... eat ..." he said, more urgently. The noise caught the attention of another in the group who had taken lead during our descent. After a quick series of tongue clicks and a hiss, Hambo ducked his head, bowing subserviently. Even as he did so, he continued to hold the leaf out.

Accepting the leaf earned me a smile and Hambo pulled a second leaf from a pouch on his belt. Slowly, he pushed it into his mouth and made a show of exaggeratedly chewing, smiling broadly once he'd finished. It was all I could do not to laugh at his comical expression. I shrugged, hoping that I wasn't about to poison myself. The leaf was pleasant tasting, if not a little woody. While I had no idea how many calories it possessed, it was a kind gesture.

From my own pack, I pulled out the last trail bar I'd received from Little Pete. According to Nick, the Scatters were vegetarian, so I figured I'd keep the trail-dried jerky to myself, at least until I saw them eat something similar. I broke off a portion and handed it to Hambo, who accepted it with an impish smile and ate it without complaint.

"Go ... walk ..." Hambo said after we'd sat for no more than ten minutes. There was little moonlight and the sun had set an hour previous. I had no idea if the Scatters slept or if we'd keep walking until I fell over.

"Low light overlay," I whispered to my AI, not wanting to earn disapproval from our grumpy leader.

I'd taken care to use minimal functions on my grav-suit and had been breaking even at about four-percent energy stores. While that was more than enough to power the AI, the low-light enhancement would burn precious energy. I wasn't willing to go below two-percent, but I figured not falling on my face was important.

After another ninety minutes, the two Scatters in the lead suddenly veered from the main path and I felt a hand on my arm, pushing me to follow them into the brush. The entire time, we hadn't broken from our initial formation of two in front and four in back. Hambo, one of the back guards who carried a bow instead of a shield, was always within a step or two of me. A quick glance told me that it was indeed Hambo who urged me into the woods. I didn't need much of a push, as I was tired and not paying a great deal of attention, automatically going wherever the figures ahead of me went.

Chirps and trilled bug calls greeted us. I shook my head in late understanding. For the last few months, I'd constantly heard these noises when in the woods and believed they were the fauna of Fraxus. In fact, I'd been hearing the Scatters as they spied on us.

I looked up to find the boughs illuminated like a star field. With my HUD's low-light enhancement, I discovered multitudes of narrow hammocks slung within the trees. Dozens of pairs of green, blue, and purple eyes stared down as we walked beneath the elevated camp. Without the AI's amplification, even if I'd passed beneath the area in the pitch black of night, I would most likely have missed the scene entirely.

"... stop ... rest ..." Hambo urged, placing a hand on the bark of a nearby tree.

I looked at him and then at the tree. He seemed to be suggesting that I climb up. I smiled and shook my head. There was no way I had the energy to climb a tree, let alone try to figure out how to sleep in one.

"I'll just unroll my bag down here," I said, pulling out the thin sleeping roll and fur covering I'd been using.

Hambo clucked his tongue and his eyes darted to the side, apparently annoyed. The Scatter leader approached and the two had a conversation. Even though it was over in two minutes, it was the longest stream of Scatter speech my translator program had witnessed. In the end, Hambo bowed his head and climbed the tree, his fingers grasping the bark as if it were a ladder.

"Not leave," the leader said.

"Liam Hoffen," I said, patting my chest.

"Lee-am-haw-fen not leave," he answered, repeating my name several times under his breath until it sounded smooth.

"Liam Hoffen not leave," I agreed, rolling my eyes at his unwillingness to share his own name.

At some point, sleeping on the ground is just something you do. It's never comfortable, but the body can get used to many things and discomfort while sleeping was one of them. I hadn't slept long when I felt a light brush against my cheek and heard a quiet, high-pitched giggle. Through bleary eyes, I saw two small figures disappear into the brush, giving surprised squeaks after seeing I was awake.

Apparently, I'd slept longer than expected and the first rays of the sun were piercing the top of the forest's canopy. Sitting up, a long golden-brown feather fell into my lap, rolling off my chest. I smiled, knowing, I'd had help waking up. A soft rustle in the grass caught my attention. I hadn't heard his approach, but Hambo stood next to me.

"Liam Hoffen ... ready ... walk?" he asked.

I pulled out my water skin and held it up to him. "Good morning, Hambo," I said, standing. "You guys don't rest much, do you?"

I'd been distracted by Hambo's arrival and didn't notice the feather falling as I got up. The movement hadn't escaped Hambo's attention and he reached down to pluck it from the ground, offering it to me. I wasn't sure of the significance, but I accepted the feather, sliding it behind Nick's knife where it would remain straight.

"Water," Hambo said, clucking his tongue, making a sound I had learned to recognize as a suggestion to follow. I grabbed my pack and lumbered after him, my legs unhappy with the sudden movement. We came to a small stream, only a few meters across. My presence attracted the attention of the small group of Scatters gathered at the edge of the water. I heard a familiar giggle and located two young children, one a girl and the other a boy, both with mischievous grins on their faces. As I knelt and filled my water skin, I withdrew the golden feather and held it up, showing it to the kids. They exchanged pleased looks and disappeared into the woods.

"... blessing ..." Hambo said, nodding at the feather.

I smiled. I wasn't sure what kind of blessing a feather might represent to the Scatters, but I counted the kids' acceptance of my presence as a blessing of its own. The watching adults all smiled at the kids' antics and at my response.

A strange whistling high in the trees made me jump. I looked up in time to see several dark shapes pass only a few meters above the tops of the trees. My AI, sensing interest, offered a replay. I blinked at the prompt and was amazed to see four giant golden eagles swooping in, the morning sun glinting off their feathers. I almost cheered as I saw that two of the eagles bore Scatter riders, both of whom had their eyes locked on my position.

"That's amazing," I said, standing.

"Qinani," Hambo said. "Come, Liam Hoffen."

I struggled to shrug my backpack onto my shoulders as we ran beside the stream through the forest's undergrowth. Hambo left no trace and barely made any sound. I felt like a hippopotamus in comparison. After half a kilometer, we reached a fallen log that crossed the stream. Hambo skittered nimbly across and turned, looking back at me expectantly. I'd be dishonest if I didn't admit that I used some of my grav-suit's power to keep me from toppling into the stream.

The idea of meeting the golden eagle riders was exciting and I wondered if they'd brought someone important from the city to talk with me. I breathed heavily as I pushed through the trees, anticipating an opportunity that might change our circumstances.

An angry squawk greeted me as I emerged onto a broad rocky shelf protruding out from the side of the mountain. I froze, recognizing that I was only ten meters from the large birds and had attracted the unblinking attention of at least one of them. Majestic in size, the eagles' feathers gleamed in the morning light, reflecting a multitude of colors as the great birds moved. Significantly, the giant eagle that seemed annoyed by my presence scratched at the ground and shook its head in challenge, rattling the leather reins around its neck.

Two tall pale-skinned Scatters had dismounted, standing proudly next to the birds they'd ridden in on. They each wore crystal swords at their sides and bore decorated leather armor that was significantly more ornate than any I'd seen so far.

"Welcome, Lifa," Hambo said, bowing deeply. A smile crossed the rider's face.

"Hambo ..." he responded. The rest of his response was unintelligible, reminding me that my translator still lacked sufficient information.

I felt a hand at my back, pushing me forward. "Lee-am-haw-fen walk." I didn't need to look around to know it was the lead guard from the previous day's hard march. Even a good night's sleep hadn't improved his disposition. I warily eyed the eagle that still seemed to be challenging my approach. After tossing its head in my direction as I moved, the bird chose to stay put. So far, it had decided not to make good on its implied threat. Apparently, I'd been sufficiently cowed.

"Liam Hoffen fly," Hambo said cheerfully, walking along with me.

"I'm getting on one of those?" I asked, pointing to an eagle. "I've never ... I have no idea ..."

"Liam Hoffen, I am Lifa," the flyer greeted me as the three of us approached. "Hambo ..." He spoke to Hambo with words I could not understand. Holding out his hands, he accepted Hambo's right hand, closing on it briefly as both men bowed slightly.

"Greetings, Lifa," I said, bringing my right fist over my solar plexus and bowing, as was the Abasi tradition. The move earned me a small smile and a nod of his head.

"Liam Hoffen ... negotiate ... leader," Lifa said. "Eagle ... fly."

"Yeah, I don't think so," I said reluctantly.

Lifa approached and reached past me, tapping my pack. I pulled it off and set it on the ground.

"Qalani," he said, nodding at my pack.

The dour leader of the guard bowed slightly at what was apparently a command. He reached for my pack. I tried to stop him, but he shook my hand off.

"I'm going to need that. Hambo, help?" I said.

Lifa answered. "Liam Hoffen, talk leader," he said. "Hambo, Qalani walk. Liam Hoffen safe."

I nodded. I knew I had to trust the Scatters, but letting go of the pack that held the tools of my survival was hard. On the other hand, Qalani had no such issues. He pushed me aside, lifted the pack with some difficulty and walked off.

"What could go wrong?" I asked, ironically.

"Liam Hoffen, fly," Lifa said, gesturing to one of the two eagles that had arrived riderless.

"I don't know how," I protested while allowing myself to be led to the bird.

Lifa extracted and shook out a hooded cloak that he held out to me expectantly. I frowned and grumbled, but put the cloak on. Taking my acceptance of the cloak as agreement, Lifa took a long scarf from the same pouch and pulled on my shoulder so that I would lean over. With deft movements, he wrapped the scarf, first around my neck and then around the top of my head.

He continued to dress me, next pulling a small, tight set of crystal glasses over my head. The straps had already been lengthened but the lenses were small for a human. Finally, he pulled the cloak's hood over my head. It dawned on me that he was disguising me, which made me wonder what or who I might be hiding from.

"Liam Hoffen, ride," he said, pushing me gently toward the giant eagle who, so far, had done nothing more provocative than shake its head.

"I'm not sure you can just tell someone to do this and expect good things," I said.

"Safe." He pushed a tuft of feathers back, exposing a bronze stirrup.

With help from my grav-suit, I stepped into the stirrup and threw my leg over the back of the bird. I relished the heat emanating from the eagle's body as I worked to seat my foot into the other stirrup.

Lifa gestured, urging me to lean into the bird. My compliance earned me a quick smile and a nod of approval. "Stay. Safe," he said.

I just didn't think Lifa and I had the same definition of safe.

With practiced ease, Lifa ran to his eagle, leapt into the air and landed atop it lightly. With a whoop of excitement, Lifa's eagle ran forward and jumped off the cliff, dropping from view.

"Oh, frak," I cried in alarm, looking to Hambo. His face broke into a broad smile as the eagle I sat atop lurched forward. "Noooo!" I found myself unable to stop screaming as the world rushed by and my eagle careened unevenly toward the cliff's edge. The bird might be a graceful flier, but it ran like a wounded duck. "How much energy is required for an emergency landing?" I demanded, knowing my grav-suit couldn't possibly catch my fall off the thousand-meter-high cliff.

"Insufficient energy," my AI informed me as the eagle's wings unfurled and we dove off the edge. The bird did virtually nothing to slow our rapid descent beyond angling away from the cliff. We were quickly leaving behind all chances of an emergency landing on one of the many rock outcroppings littering the steep slope. As I took in the landscape far below, I was afraid the eagle was unwisely doubling down on the distance we would fall if it didn't get its shite together

soon. I panicked when we didn't level out at all, thinking the bird must not be able to take my weight. I used the grav-suit to reduce the burden, a move that earned me an angry squawk as the bird looked over its shoulder at me.

"Frak, just tell me you've got this," I complained as the wind rushed by, eating my words. I stopped adding lift with my grav-suit.

The eagle turned back and pulled its wings in so we accelerated even faster. I closed my eyes, giving myself over to the moment. A lifetime later, my stomach flip-flopped as its wings fully unfurled and I could feel the strain in the bird's frame as it fought against gravity. I opened my eyes and discovered we were only forty meters over the forest and still falling.

I didn't realize I was screaming until our flight leveled out. Not even remotely embarrassed, I closed my mouth and looked around, still hugging the eagle. According to my suit, we were moving at thirty-five meters per second and following the curve of the mountain below us. A strong wind blew into my face and I realized the eagle was using the updrafts and thermals on this warm, sunny side of the mountain.

"You're all right," I said, patting the glossy feathers beneath my right hand. The eagle didn't answer, but that was okay. I was alive. At our current pace, we'd arrive in the city within the hour, saving me untold days of walking.

I finally relaxed, allowing myself to get lost in the experience. I was amazed at the sense of wonder and awe I had. I was a pilot. I'd flown many different ships and even rocketed to Earth in a mech-suit, but there was something different about flying on the back of this majestic bird with no technology to save me if things went wrong. Surprisingly, the trip turned out to be far too short and the sparkling city appeared before I was ready to complete the ride. I sat up and looked around. Lifa was trying to get my attention.

He gestured, urging me to pull up my hood, which had been thrown back by the stiff breezes. I shrugged and grabbed the cloth, drawing it over my head.

My AI created a map of the city as details became available. Scatter architecture was much different than anything I'd seen before. Long slabs of crystal grew upward from the ground. The individual pieces seemed to be locked together by clever positioning more than any mechanical fasteners. The fact was, at our current speed, it was hard to see enough detail to identify exact construction techniques.

The city had been built on top of the delta where the mountain river slowed and joined with the ocean, its narrow buildings arranged in blocks beside wide canals. Brightly colored boats moved along the water's surface, ferrying passengers to their destinations. My eyes strained against the bright morning sun, which reflected off every surface. At some level, the city reminded me of Puskar Stellar's market with all the bright colors and busy determination of the inhabitants.

The scene was as idyllic as it was fantastic, which is probably why I was so surprised when several charged particle bolts ripped through the air only meters in front of our group. The blaster fire so startled the eagle I was on that it careened hard to starboard, rolling to the side and tossing me from its back.

I twisted, trying to get an idea of where I'd land and how far I had to drop. I pushed my grav-suit to catch me and it responded, momentarily interrupting my fall. A red pulse was the only warning I received when the suit lost energy.

Chapter 11

GOD HUMOR

I flailed, trying desperately to straighten out. Zero-g is a lot like falling, but this time the wind whipped past me and the ground rushed up to greet me. I hit the surface of one of the canals at a speed well in excess of anything sensible. My suit, devoid of energy, refused to stiffen and I heard a great snap. Pain shot through my arm. I tumbled on the surface, taking water into my lungs. Then I sank.

I tried to push against the water to swim toward the surface, but my right arm wouldn't respond. I'm not a fantastic swimmer, but I worked admirably against the water, given the fact that I had no sense of up or down. I'd lost access to my HUD when the goggles had been ripped off and water had interrupted the projection from my earwig.

Not panicking was critical, so I tried to calm myself, but it was a losing battle. I desperately needed air. Suddenly, a strong arm wrapped tightly around my chest and jerked me in a direction I hoped was up. Seconds later my head was out of the water. I gasped and wheezed, my body involuntarily spasming. Even though I was above the surface, more water found its way into my mouth and down my windpipe. My body was wracked with spasms as the vicious cycle of expulsion then water-laced intake of air occurred.

My legs felt the square edge of submerged steps and I fought the person holding me. I awkwardly clawed my way out of the canal with one arm. Finally, hunched over on my knees with my head away from the misty surface, I coughed to empty the water from my lungs. Each wracking cough nearly turned me inside out. My lungs felt like I'd breathed in rocks and I wasn't sure I would survive the day.

Dimly, I became aware of laughter.

"Liam Hoffen ... danger." My rescuer had been Lifa.

"What do we have here?" The voice was human and the speech was standard. I looked up the remaining stairs joining the canal to the street. The man who spoke held a blaster pistol leveled at my head. "Get your wet ass up here and let me have a look at you. I didn't hear about any operations on this backwater crap hole."

I started to stand, but Lifa stepped in front, partially blocking me from the newcomer. Lifa spoke and my translator found very few words that were understandable, so I really had no idea what was said.

"I'm not talking to you, fraggin' tree hugger," the human said. "Now move out of the way so I can get a look at my boy here."

"Liam Hoffen." I winced, my broken right arm brushing against Lifa as I moved around him. "I'm with Belirand Security. We've decided to re-establish contact with this sector and you're in deep shite," I bluffed. "Even as we speak, your actions are being transmitted back to corporate. No doubt you'll be brought up on charges for your reckless actions today."

The man looked at me quizzically and finally laughed. "You're so full of shite and you ain't supposed to be talking like that in front of the monkeys. Now I gotta put that one down."

"Wait, no!" I cried, but I was too late. The man fired and hit Lifa, dropping the noble Scatter to the steps.

I hadn't realized a crowd had formed until I heard audible gasps. I knelt next to Lifa and inspected the wound. The particle round had torn through his chest, leaving a nasty black burn mark on the flesh.

"See what you made me do," the man said, clearly not upset by the turn of events.

A woman cried out from the quickly growing crowd and raced past the human. She looked up at me, her face a mixture of shock and horror. I placed my good hand on Lifa's wound, hoping to stop the bleeding. As soon as I felt his chest, I knew there was no hope. Gently, the woman pushed at me. A keening wail emanated from her as she attempted to revive the dead eagle rider. I allowed her to scoop Lifa into her arms.

Angry words from the crowd were hurled at the human who'd done the damage and he spun to face them with his gun leveled. "Get back, all of yah," he growled. "I'm within my right to defend myself and I'll kill any of yah that get any closer."

A Scatter with deeply-tanned skin and bright-green eyes broke from the crowd and spoke sharply to the gun-wielding man. With no warning at all, the human fired at the adolescent Scatter, catching him in the side and dropping him to the ground. Rage filled me. The Scatters presented no threat, yet this man seemed to have virtually no concern for their lives.

"Put your gun down!" I ordered, rushing up the steps, my broken arm erupting in pain.

The man spun back on me and fired a third round, this one catching me in my bad shoulder. I grunted as the blaster's energy partially dissipated across the grav-suit's fabric. Without power to stiffen and further deal with the blast, the suit was of limited effectiveness and the pain was excruciating, but I also knew I'd been mostly unharmed. As I closed on the man, I pulled Nick's knife from my belt.

"What?" he bellowed, backpedaling and firing again. That round caught me in my stomach, burning away animal skins and the robe Lifa had provided. Once again, it felt like I'd been lit on fire. Unartfully, he attempted to block my arm with his pistol, but I anticipated his move and buried the knife into his side, just below his armpit. It wasn't the killing blow I'd been after, but he dropped, screaming in agony, all the same.

I scooped up the particle blaster and turned back to where Lifa lay. A small group had gathered around his dead body, some trying to comfort the grieving woman, others tending to the dead man. Anger welled up. I screamed in rage and frustration. The murder was senseless and it seemed incomprehensible to me that the enemy I'd thought long ago gone was responsible. In that moment, I almost understood why Thomas Anino had tricked us, sending us to this place.

"You ... come." A hand on my shoulder pulled at me. I turned to see the face of a female Scatter looking up at me earnestly. "Humans approach. Much danger."

I looked back to Lifa and then to the woman. There was nothing I could do for him, but it hurt more than my broken arm to leave him on the mossy steps. A shout from down the street broke me from indecision.

"Quickly ..." the woman urged. My AI was finally starting to fill in useful words, an edge I desperately needed.

I ran after her, my canal-soaked robe dragging at my every step. The woman was small – less than a meter and a half – but had the light skin and fair hair of the taller clan. She ducked into a brick-framed opening that led below one of the many crystal structures. The tunnel structure quickly darkened to a point where I could no longer make out our path. Awkwardly, I stumbled into the woman and cried out in agony as my arm jostled against her.

"I can't see," I said, her hands pulling at me in a way I couldn’t understand. I grew aware of her eyes, glowing slightly in the darkness. She looked away and a moment later, a dim light appeared.

"Clothes ... remove," she said, pulling at the cloak's lapel.

I might have whimpered as the material passed over my arm, but she ignored my pain, pulling next at the fur-skinned boots Marny and Nick had given me. I tugged them off and she wrapped the cloak and boots together, tossing the bundle off into the darkness. I heard a splash and realized there was a waterway running alongside our path.

"Must quiet," she said, watching my face for understanding. I nodded agreement.

I'd like to think that if I wasn't favoring my arm, I'd have kept up with her. The fact was, she was wicked fast, darting through the maze of subterranean passages. Originally, I'd assumed we'd keep to a single level, given the amount of water I'd seen and the groundwater's level. I was quickly disavowed of this idea as we careened down three different flights of stairs each separated by several hundred meters of twisting passages. At last, we entered a cavern roughly twenty meters in length and three to five meters across. Dim light played across the walls, reflecting off crystal structures.

"Human, sit," she instructed, eyeing the blaster pistol I'd stuck into my grav-suit's belt and gesturing to a long narrow bench that was pushed against the wall.

"I am Liam Hoffen," I said, patting my chest.

Before she could respond, we were interrupted by a voice from the opposite end of the room.

"Bongiwe. The Qinani rider, Lifa, is dead and the bell-e-runde thieves are organizing a search for ..." The voice belonged to a male who I would have pegged as adolescent, if human. Given he was a native, he was more than likely adult. My AI outlined the male's body as he approached. It was as much energy as my suit could spare after the extraordinary efforts used to save my life in the last hour.

"... this human." The male finished his sentence, turning in my direction. “Liam Hoffen?"

Bongiwe bowed slightly to the approaching Scatter male, who stopped and slowly held up his hands defensively. His eyes were affixed to my waistband where I'd stuffed the blaster pistol.

"You have brought the one who killed Lifa to our most secret place?" The man gasped. "We should not get involved in bell-e-runde madness. Although I would speak false if I were to say I was not glad to hear of thief Jared Thockenbrow's injury."

Multiple footsteps echoed off the walls, but I couldn't see the people who approached.

"Thabini, Liam Hoffen was dressed in a Qinani rider's night uniform," the woman said. "I was there when he stopped the bell-e-runde thief, Jared Thockenbrow, from killing Langa on the street. And he did not want to leave Lifa, even though Lifa's daughter had found him."

"Frak," I said under my breath. It was bad enough that Lifa had been killed, but for his daughter to have found him that way was a gut-punch.

"What is it you say?" Thabini asked, tearing his eyes away from the gun on my waist. While they'd been talking, a half-dozen Scatters had filled in behind him. I noticed a shift in the language he was using. While talking with Bongiwe, he'd been using one language and now in addressing me, he used an entirely different one. It was the language used by Jared Thockenbrow when speaking to Lifa. My AI, however, had finally heard enough and was translating both reasonably well.

"I, too, am sad for the death of Lifa, and for his daughter," I said, choosing to have my words translated to the language they used with

Thockenbrow. "I know of Belirand's treachery. They murdered my father. I am no friend of Belirand."

As I spoke, my AI sent a noise canceling wave to interrupt my words and simultaneously added sounds that represented the Scatter spoken language. After losing almost all of the modern advancements I'd been used to, this technology stood out as a miracle, especially when trying to work with an alien species.

My words caused a murmur to course through the gathered Scatters, but Bongiwe didn't miss a beat. "Stop. We are not savages like the humans." She threw a glance my way as she realized too late that she was insulting me. Her words were directed at Thabini. "Liam Hoffen is injured. We will bring him to Nothando so he might be healed."

"Injured?" Thabini asked. "There is no blood. The people say he was shot twice. If this were true he would be dead."

"My arm is broken," I said, wincing as I attempted to move my right arm. "But there is something more important. My friend. She rests within a box that is in the city. I must find her."

"See. He has hurt himself," Bongiwe said. "He is unable to speak sensibly."

"Do you intend to harm us as you harmed the thief, Jared Thockenbrow, Liam Hoffen?" Thabini asked, looking at me earnestly.

"No, Thabini. I regret that my presence has caused the death of the Qinani rider, Lifa, and pain to his family. I would not harm your people further. If I were allowed to see my friend who rests in the suspension chamber, I would leave you now without the aid of your healer."

I have an uncanny ability to read people, which is probably my one and only superpower in life. It turns out, this has always translated well to aliens, but the Scatters were an open-faced people and appeared to have very little guile. When I used the words *suspension chamber*, my AI had translated it into a single word that I'd heard before from the Scatter guard who had agreed to take me as a prisoner into the city. This same word caused a significant reaction in Thabini's face.

"Take Liam Hoffen to the healer, Nothando," Thabini said. "But first, find a wrap to hide Liam Hoffen's face. Bell-e-runde will be looking for a human. We must not let them find him."

"Wait, Thabini," I said, reaching out with my left hand. Two Scatters who'd been standing close by jumped between us, making it impossible for me to touch him. I held my hand up, letting them know I understood my mistake. Thabini looked at me questioningly, unsurprised at the Scatters' response. "You know about the suspension chamber. I saw it in your face. My friend. She's alive. I have to see her."

"Bell-e-runde will stomp around like angry adolescent maracats this day," he said. "I will speak to my mother on this matter. You must hide so that you might live."

"There's something else. We had a spaceship," I said, disappointed to realize my translator did not replace *spaceship* with a Scatter word. "The craft would give us a chance to stop Belirand."

"We will have time to speak later. Now you must move before bell-e-runde stops Liam Hoffen," he said. "They do not lack a desire to ruin and murder my people. I do not believe they would feel different about one that would fight back."

With that, he turned and left. I tried to follow, but the two Scatters standing close by stepped together to block my path.

Bongiwe tugged at my good arm. "Liam Hoffen, we must go. Nothando's home is not near and our path is dangerous. But first, we will hold stationary your arm and provide a disguise. I fear there is little that can be done for your smell."

I smiled at the slight. Just about every alien culture I'd encountered had some sort of taboo about showing a person's naughty bits. Oddly, it was mostly humans who were easily insulted by how they smelled.

"I mean no insult," she added. I guess Scatters didn't like to smell bad, either.

"My arm does not need anything," I said, slowly lifting my right arm. The grav-suit stiffened, preventing additional movement. If I could get the bones set, I wouldn't even need a splint. "My clothing will hold it."

"Is it not broken as you have said?" she asked.

"No, it's plenty broken," I said. "Please trust me on this for now."

She nodded and disappeared into the gloom of the cavern, my HUD tracking her outline as she moved. I'd have given just about anything for a decent charge on the suit, which would have allowed for low-light amplification. In a moment she returned with a long dark cloth, which she wrapped around my neck and then up into a turban. Apparently, it was a common way to wrap someone's head on Fraxus.

"We will move now," she said. "Try to appear less tall." She'd located a cloak, complete with large hood. The hem only made it to my knees, making the garment look more like a bathrobe.

I hoped my AI was recording as we ran through the myriad passageways that interconnected beneath the city. Occasionally, we had to move up to ground level where we would skulk, melding into the daily traffic of Scatters out doing their business. While trying to navigate in these areas, it was clear the Scatters recognized something was up. Instead of steering clear of us, they would instead come alongside, acting as if we were part of a larger group.

"How do they know to help us?" I finally asked Bongiwe after nearly being exposed to a search party of humans. The only reason we hadn't been discovered was – miraculously – a diversion occurred at precisely the right time.

"Bell-e-runde arrived on Fraxus a very long time ago," Bongiwe said. "At first they promised to share with us their wondrous technology. A lie. It is born into all Scatters to resist humans in all actions they take. Your disguise is as much for my people as it is for bell-e-runde. My people would not help you if they were to see your face."

"Why do you help, then?" I asked, following her back out of a subterranean passage and onto steps leading into a canal.

"Thabini has asked it of me," she said. She was shading the truth.

"You helped me after I struck down Jared Thockenbrow."

Bongiwe led me beneath a wide bridge and onto a long, narrow wooden boat. The boat had sets of wooden arches that ran from bow to stern. A translucent material hung from the aft arch and draped over the sides of the boat, providing privacy.

"I did not want to," she answered, picking a pole from the side of the boat and nodding at the bench seat obscured by the hanging sheer. As soon as I sat, she put the pole to good use and pushed us out into the still canal water. "Your actions were not that of a human. I saw your face when Lifa was killed. You were angry, yes, very human in that. But you felt great pain and sorrow. This I felt with my heart. There had to be a reason that the Qinani riders would be helping you."

"You're taking a great risk," I said.

"Not as great as Liam Hoffen," she said. "Bell-e-runde will bring more humans to hunt you. We will not be able to hide you for very long. I am sorry, Liam Hoffen. It is impossible to hide from them forever."

"Why wouldn't Thabini talk to me about the suspension chamber?" I asked.

"It is not his place to say," she answered, giving away more than she realized.

"Whose place is it?"

"You have many questions," Bongiwe answered. "But you must hold them for now."

We exited the city's canal system and pushed through shallow brackish water where the river came out of the mountain and met with the sea. The water was choked with plants, their broad green and purple leaves covering the surface. Passage seemed impossible until I watched the illusory scene change. The plants simply folded up as Bongiwe moved us forward, only to redeploy once we'd passed.

The thick growth at this part of the river delta obscured everything nearby. No trees grew in this wet area, but the bushes and grasses were thick and tall, struggling to grow higher than the invading water plants could reach. I was startled when the boat's hull scraped against what felt like solid earth. The verdant growth was so thick, it took me a moment to realize we had come to a stop next to slightly raised ground.

"We are here," she said, stowing the long pole on the boat's port gunnel. "Please, there is a path."

I stepped out onto the muddy bank and winced as my boot slipped, jarring my arm. Walking up to a raised portion, I could just trace a path through the vines. I followed the path and my eyes settled on a small structure not visible from the water. The outside was surrounded by small trees that had been artfully bent to provide shelter or to block being seen from above.

"I don't understand all of the mystery," I said. "Why won't you just answer a simple question?"

"Because it is not her place either." A haggard old man emerged from the building, startling me. The sight was unusual, as I had yet to meet a Scatter who looked to be more than thirty years old. This old fella looked like he was pushing a hundred. His worn cloak was mud caked and he supported himself with a gnarled staff. An old vid came to my mind and I struggled to name it. I could only recall the image of some old wizard who wore a bird atop his head and was as crazy as they got.

"I'm just looking for a straight answer," I said. "I'm trying to find my friend. She's been locked in a suspension chamber for twenty years. I need to get her out."

"The rumors of your arrival have preceded you." The man's voice sounded as if he were unused to speaking. He paused, looked me up and down, and continued, "I must say, I expected a human hero to be more substantial, but such is the nature of prophesy."

"Nothando, you will stop with the riddles and talk of prophesy," Bongiwe said. They were speaking in the private Scatter language. "Thabini sent me to you because bell-e-runde knows not of your home and Liam Hoffen requires healing. Thabini has gone back to inform his mother that Liam Hoffen asks about the suspension chamber. We are not to speak of this to Liam Hoffen and it is not the time for your nonsense."

"He understands, you know," Nothando said, smiling.

"Who? Liam Hoffen?" Bongiwe asked, looking at me suspiciously. "That is not possible. Bell-e-runde has no access to the ancient language. Even among Scatters, there are only a few of us who speak it."

"It is no matter," Nothando said. "The gods have sent us a tiny, smelly hero. They have always had a sense of humor."

"For frak sake, I'm twice your size," I said, realizing at the last minute that I'd exposed the fact that I was eavesdropping.

"And not big enough by half to complete the task required of you," Nothando said, an understanding smile creasing his wizened face.

Chapter 12

POLITICKING AND TIME

Unlike the clean crystal and brick architecture of the city, the old man's home was constructed of natural materials and smelled badly of bog.

"Liam Hoffen will sit and Bongiwe will remove the long boat," he instructed, pointing at a small stone that sat on the ground next to the rounded outside wall. I couldn't fathom how the stone would be any more comfortable than the ground, so I sat next to it, accepting a bowl filled with water. I drank deeply, thirsty after having lost my water skin when I crashed into the canal.

"I will be back in the morning," Bongiwe said. "Possibly a day beyond if bell-e-runde does not settle."

I wasn't sure what I'd expected. There was no reason to think Bongiwe would stay with me until I found Ada, but I suddenly felt bereft in the hermit's small shack. "You're leaving?"

"Worried that I will bite?" the old man asked. "Danger does not come from Nothando. No, you should be more afraid of King Nkosi. He will no doubt turn you over to bell-e-runde when he learns of your presence."

Nothando's face seemed to blur and then distort slightly. I tried to stand but my legs were unsteady. Not thinking clearly, I placed my right hand on the ground to help me balance, and pain momentarily cleared the enveloping fog.

"What have you done, Nothando?" Bongiwe asked, concern creasing her pretty, narrow features as she focused on me. Even distorted as she was, she was amazing. Why hadn't I realized she was so beautiful before?

I reached out for her. "You're so pretty," I said, my tongue thick in my mouth. I had to drop my arm almost immediately as I started to tip over. Gracefully, Bongiwe reached out and steadied me, looking sharply over her shoulder.

"Liam Hoffen is injured," Nothando said. "I have given him rest so that I might set his arm without the interruptions of his objections."

I fell heavily against Bongiwe's arms and she eased me to the ground. Beautiful and fair, her features transformed to Ada's. I hadn't realized the two women looked so much alike. Ada looked just as I'd seen her the first time we'd met, with colorful beads tightly braided, running in neat rows down the back of her head. She'd always been so beautiful with her smooth, caramel-colored skin, high cheek bones, golden-flecked blue eyes and most of all, her heart-stopping smile.

"Find me, Liam," she whispered. "Before it's too late."

I focused on her narrow lips.

"I'm coming, Ada," I whispered as I passed out.

I SLOWLY AWOKE from a dreamless sleep. A strange, yet comforting warmth radiated out from my right arm and I felt so good I wanted to sit up. Strong hands pushed at my shoulders when I attempted to move and I realized I wore no clothing.

"What's going on?" My eyes had difficulty focusing on the old hermit who was a lot stronger than he looked.

He replied with gibberish while looking at me earnestly. I followed his gaze down to where he held two smooth black stones on either side of where my arm had broken.

I tried to sit up again. "What are you doing?"

Nothando had to release the stones to push me back down, scolding me again with more gibberish. I relented and lay still. He once again picked the stones up and placed them on either side of my arm. The old man spoke in reverent tones, his eyes closed. It was as if he were reciting something memorized long ago, the syllables nonsense to me but the rhythm comforting. The sounds were like a reverent prayer and in answer, the stones glowed a dim yellow and warmed against my skin.

I dared a quick look around. Nothando had peeled off my grav-suit and I was unable to locate it. From the earthy smell of herbs and spices, I suspected he had also washed my body, an idea that made me uncomfortable. Fortunately, he'd laid a woven blanket over me and the bedding on the floor was soft if not thick. I reached up to my face and discovered my earwig had been removed. It explained why we were unable to communicate.

"Where's my earwig?" I asked, pointing at my ear.

"Shh," Nothando answered, breaking his prayer for only a moment.

The drugs he'd given me had worn off and I attempted to discern the time of day. Light peeked through the cracks in his hovel, but I couldn't tell what the position of the sun was. I grew more concerned about the missing grav-suit, although I did spot my earwig on a table across the room.

My mind wandered as I lay back. I wondered how far Tabby, Peter, and Marny were from home by now. Without me, they'd make better time, but it was a long journey even for the three of them. For the first time, I felt okay with where my relationship with Tabby was. Sure, I wanted to put us back to before Anino had torn our world apart. The thing was, she hadn't wanted this to happen any more than I had. My about-face might have been a result of the hermit's prayers or maybe it was just the fact that Tabby and I had made it through so much together that I couldn't possibly stay angry. In that moment, I found I could be okay with her finding happiness with Peter.

Nothando took the stones away and pushed back from where he'd sat on his haunches next to me. Standing, he hobbled over to the table and picked up my earwig, turning back to toss it onto my chest. With my left hand, I placed the business end into my ear. One of the great things about this earwig's design was that it easily matched up with the shape of the ear and the profile of the wearer's cheek. I smoothed the thin arm along my cheekbone and it melded into the skin, disappearing except for a tiny dot where the HUD projector rested.

"Your arm should be healed," Nothando said. "I had to remove your devices so that I might work."

I looked at him skeptically and tested my right arm by moving it. The motion caused me no pain. "How did you do that?" I asked, surprised.

"Did Bongiwe not inform you that I am a healer?" Nothando asked.

"The stones?" I asked. "I don't understand."

"I have lived one hundred forty standard years," he said. "You have been upon Fraxus for only a few months. Only a human would expect to understand what he has never experienced." I was once again grateful for my AI's ability to translate meaningful data.

"How long did I sleep from your drugs?" I asked.

"Who is this Ada to you?" he asked. "Why do you seek her with such intensity?"

"Tit for tat, old fella," I said, pushing against the ground tentatively with both arms. I felt a small twinge in my right, but certainly not the same pain I'd experienced before.

"You wish for me to answer questions so that you will also answer questions?" he asked.

"That's right. I see my translator is working just fine. Let's start with my suit. Where is it?"

"In the bog. I could stand its fetid stench no longer. Who is this Ada you speak so fondly of?" he asked.

I stood, gathering the blanket around my waist. "Ada Chen is a member of my ship's crew. She was ejected from my starship in a suspension chamber and apparently landed on Fraxus."

"You speak both the truth as well as a lie," he said, following me as I pushed open the ferns that blocked the entrance.

"Locate grav-suit," I said. For my earwig to have access to the translator AI, it would need the processing and digital storage afforded by the grav-suit's smart material. My HUD showed a blip on the water and suggested the suit was submerged four meters. "I'm not lying. That's who Ada is. Sure, I didn't give you all the details, but that would take a while. I've known her for a long time."

I set the blanket on the ground and stepped onto the bank. My HUD showed that the drop off was almost immediate and the water registered at eight degrees.

"I asked why you seek her with intensity. Your words deny your real feelings," he said as I dove in.

The coldness of the water made it almost impossible for me to keep air in my lungs and I felt the warmth of my body being sucked out. Nothando's words were forgotten as I pushed downward. I'm not a fantastic swimmer, but I get along. Under normal circumstances, diving four meters isn't much of a task, but at eight degrees, I realized I'd taken on more than expected. I pushed back at the panic that demanded I return to the surface. Lethargy slowed the movement of my arms and legs, and it was everything I could do to keep my forward progress.

My hands brushed against the suit's fabric as soon as I reached the bottom, but when I tried to turn and bring it back up, it refused to budge. I had to fight not to kick the bottom and swim up for air, my desperation grew with every second. Yet the water was too cold for a second dive. If I left now, I'd have to come back, most likely after I warmed up and after Nothando tried to talk me out of it. No, the time to retrieve my suit was right now.

Frantically, I ran my hands along the suit, looking for what might be holding it in place. A shiver passed through my body and I almost gave up as my lungs continued to demand air. Finally, I located where a root had wrapped itself intricately around the middle of the suit. I struggled against the roots, wondering just how Nothando had managed to submerge the suit in that fashion. Finally, I detached the knot of roots, pulled the suit to me, kicked from the bottom, and sailed upward. When I broke the surface, I breathed in deeply, welcoming the fresh air and warmth of the sun which was low in the sky.

I became aware of a long boat's hull slipping along the bank, coming to rest only a few meters from where I'd emerged. The boat, unlike the one Bongiwe had used, was larger, the wood ornately carved although not brightly painted as many of the canal boats in town had been.

"What is the meaning of this?" a Scatter demanded from within the boat. I couldn't see her, but she sounded annoyed.

I was too cold for humility and clawed my way from the water onto the bank, flopping my suit in front of me.

"My queen," Nothando said, bowing to the extent his crooked body could manage.

"Frak." I sighed as I searched for and found the blanket I'd left behind. With as much grace as I could manage, I wrapped it around my waist and turned toward the boat.

"Nothando? Why was this human in the river? Is he not injured?" The woman stepped effortlessly out onto the bank and turned to walk up the path.

"I assure you, Queen Cacile, the human, Liam Hoffen, is quite well and now he no longer smells of a long journey," Nothando said. "The same can be said for his strange clothing."

Queen Cacile wore pure white robes partially covered by a light gray cloak. Both garments were adorned with golden thread that sparkled in the waning light. The cloak's pattern was the easiest to discern: ivy leaves meandering up each lapel. The materials were luxurious and finely woven, giving the wearer an air of importance. Long blonde locks of hair cascaded from her head and she smiled. I felt like a toad, standing naked in front of her with only a rough woven blanket to cover myself.

"You *are* the human who has caused so much turmoil within our kingdom over the last days," she said, not asking.

"Days?" I asked. "How long have I been here?"

She raised her eyebrows but didn't answer the question. "Are you an animal like your brothers? You should be returned to the wild where you were found."

"Quick, you fool, hide your nakedness and clothe yourself," Nothando spat. "It is improper for the queen to be in the presence of a naked man. Especially a vile human."

A part of me wanted to rebel, but I believed they had Ada and might know where either Jonathan or *Hotspur* were. I struggled to keep the blanket around me as I picked up my suit and scurried into Nothando's hut. My teeth chattered as I hopped around, pulling the wet suit onto my feet, expelling water from the boots as I did. The suit did smell better than before. I'd be the first to say that the minimally-powered systems hadn't been cleaning very well, but the addition of the river's detritus made me feel like we weren't yet on a sustainable path to good smells.

My body warmed almost immediately within the suit, although my teeth continued to chatter. I slicked back my long hair and tried to wipe the mud from my suit. It was a lost cause and I shrugged. There just wasn't that much I could do about it, so I opened the hut door and pushed through the ferns.

Surprisingly, in the short time I'd been gone, the Scatters who'd accompanied the queen had offloaded a woven carpet that depicted a woodland scene. Atop the carpet were three wooden chairs. Next to the largest and most ornate chairs sat a small table upon which rested a chunk of smooth black stone that resembled the material Nothando had used to heal the bones in my arm.

"Your appearance is satisfactory," Queen Cacile said. "Now tell me Liam Hoffen, why should I not inform bell-e-runde of your location? You should know, bell-e-runde thugs have already murdered three of my subjects because of your presence."

"The boy, at the canal who was shot," I asked. "He died?"

"His name was Langa," she answered, studying my face. "He did not recover from his wounds."

"Lifa," I said sadly.

"Brave Lifa was a hero to our people," she said.

I nodded. "He was courageous and tried to protect me from Thockenbrow. His courage cost him his life."

"No. Your presence cost him his life."

"I did not wish for that," I said. "Who else has died on my account?"

"Forgen, of my own guard," she said, avoiding my eyes. "Chappie

Barto killed him by his own hand in front of my husband and me, so we would understand how serious he was."

"I don't understand," I said. "You allowed someone to kill one of your own guard? What if this Chappie had tried to hurt you or your husband?"

"My guard would have prevented this," she answered, irritation clear in her face.

"They should have stopped him from hurting your guard, too!" I said, unable to hide my own irritation.

"My queen, humans do not share our revulsion at taking another's life," Nothando said.

"No. I can see this is the case with your Liam Hoffen," she said, still unwilling to make eye contact. "I can see no reason not to return this man to his own kind."

"Are you always so quick to judge?" I asked. "Twenty years ago, we came to this planet, hunting for Belirand. Where I come from, they are a pariah who hide in plain sight. And no, I have no trouble ending the life of someone who would do harm to my family or the people of my tribe. I'd even go so far as to say that I'm willing to end the lives of people who would kill the innocent. What happened to Lifa, Langa and Forgen is reprehensible. I attacked Jared Thockenbrow because he shot Langa and I knew he would do more if not stopped. I'll tell you, though, in my eyes, you bear responsibility for Forgen. You should have stood against Chappie Barto. Without resistance, Belirand will continue to take from you."

Queen Cacile would not make eye contact with me so I looked back to Nothando. The old guy pushed away a sliver of a smile. "Who is Ada Chen to you?" he asked. "This time speak the truth as you did when you slept on my floor."

"I don't understand. Why do you care?"

"Humans are alien to us," he said. "For hundreds of years, bell-e-runde humans have raped our daughters, pillaged our homes, enslaved our people and done all manner of savagery to us. Until recently, we have not known of humans who live as we do. The children of the stars who fell from the sky have lived in our mountains peacefully coexisting with our brethren."

"It was this alone that gave us hope for humankind," Queen Cacile said. "It was with a heavy heart that I learned of your attack on Jared Thockenbrow. In a single act, you have proven your willingness to commit murder."

The sound of a spaceship's engines fighting against Fraxus' gravity drew my attention, alerting me that my meeting with Queen Cacile wasn't going to have a happy ending. "You're giving me to bell-e-runde?" I asked. "You might as well kill me where I stand. How does this make you any different than them?"

A battered, gray cutter came into view, its heavy engines complaining loudly as the pilot did everything possible to keep the ship from splashing down. The wash from the motors pelted us with a mist as it picked up water and sent the queen's rug and chairs tumbling over the bank on the opposite side.

"Bell-e-runde will allow you to be kept in our prisons and be tried by our courts," she said. "If you are found guilty of the murder of Jared Thockenbrow, there is little we can do to save you."

I looked around, realizing I had few, if any, options. I knew nothing of the river delta other than I couldn't last very long in the frigid water. Three human men jumped from the old ship, splashing in the shallow water as they climbed up the bank. They wore dark green uniforms and held blaster rifles that were both recently manufactured and of a centuries-old design.

"On your knees, Highborne!" the lead man insisted. "I'll shoot you where you stand, no matter what we told these backwater tree huggers."

I'd given up any chance of escape by my inaction. With help from the butt of a blaster rifle, I sank to my knees and placed my hands over the back of my neck. In short order, I had wrist restraints on and was being dragged back to my feet after a quick pat down which revealed Tabby and my engagement rings.

"Won't be needing those where you're going," one of the soldiers said, stuffing the rings into a pocket. I made sure to look at his face, so my AI would be able to identify him in the future.

"Put him in the hold," the leader insisted. "We'll take him to tree-hugger jail and get him tucked in right nice."

Two pairs of hands guided me toward the old ship and unkindly pushed me into an open hatch. My feet were sinking into the soft dirt and my hands were behind my back, so I had no chance of meeting the floor cleanly. I tried rolling to the side as I fell, but only managed to land heavily on my ribs.

"Get in with yah," the man who'd taken my engagement rings insisted, pushing me roughly as his partner lifted. I struggled to get my knees beneath me as they did their best to make sure I hit every surface of the airlock.

Once on my feet, I followed their instructions, heading aft into the cutter's main hold. The ship was ancient and sported technology that I'd only read about. Levers, buttons, and manual valves all had either a thick layer of corrosion on the surface or some sort of sludge oozing from the seals. Despite the decay, it felt reassuring to once again have a flat surface beneath my feet.

"What are the Highborne doing on Fraxus?" the leader of the three soldiers demanded even while the other two struggled to clip my restraints to a loop of chain bolted to the floor.

"I'm not Highborne," I said. "I was dropped on Fraxus, apparently because I don't play well with others."

"So, yah got exiled and sent native, did yah? Well, if you thought the fraggin' tree-huggers was gonna help you, you sure got that wrong," he said. "Ol' Chappie himself marched right up to their king and demanded they turn you over. These Scatters know one thing for sure. If they don't find you guilty, we will. It's just a matter of politicking and time."

Chapter 13

TRIAL BY FARCE

"That's quite a vac-suit you got there," the soldier who'd taken my engagement rings said as the cutter's engines struggled against Fraxus' gravity. "That something new the Highborne been working on?"

His language was an older Mars dialect and my AI had no difficulty creating a translation.

I shook my head. "Looks nice, but it's a piece of crap. I barely got enough energy to heat," I said, shivering as I attempted to match the man's slower, cruder speech pattern.

"Are you making a move on Fraxus?" he asked. "We didn't detect any ships through the gate."

I shook my head. "I'm not with Highborne anymore," I repeated, having no idea what I was talking about. "They dropped three of us about a year ago. Command wanted us to infiltrate the locals. I'm the only one to make it this long. Frakked up, too, 'cause I finally made some progress and some asshat punches a hole in my ride."

The hold leaked air like a sieve and rays of sunlight painted pinpoints of light onto the opposite bulkhead. The cutter had to be a local resource as I couldn't imagine it leaving the atmosphere in this condition. The ship's design was entirely unfamiliar, and appeared to be very old. Some of the components looked like those I'd seen on derelict mining machinery back when I was a kid. Other parts looked newer, enough so that the Belirand mission must have created some manufacturing.

"*Asshat*," the soldier chuckled at my insult. "Try *twisted pervert*. Jared Thockenbrow sure loved the locals, though. Think he owned five or six of 'em. I thought about making a bid on 'em, but my buddy says they're all sort of messed up."

"Slaves?" I asked.

"Yeah, slaves. What else? Don't tell me you're one of those bleeders who wants to go all uplift?" He eyed me suspiciously.

I'd need to be more careful. Instead of leading him into giving me information, I'd given away my own lack of knowledge about this society. "Nah. Just been on my own for a long time."

"Well, I hate to say it, but you're well and plenty screwed," he said. "Nobody liked Thockenbrow, but that doesn't mean we'll put up with Highborne messin' around in our shite on Fraxus."

I nodded, staring at the deck. He was no doubt right about that.

We'd only been in the air for a few minutes when the engine sound changed. We began a descent that abruptly ended with the screech of metal against stone and a single hop.

"Now, you're not gonna give me any trouble, are you?" the soldier asked. "We've been getting along, but that don't mean I won't plug yah one good."

"No trouble," I said, leaning against the pipe where I'd been chained to push up to a standing position.

Efficiently, the man unclipped the braces around my wrists and refastened them, keeping my hands behind my back. I played a few scenarios through in my head. The shackles were loose enough that I could slip my hands under my feet and probably take the guy. My musings, however were quickly ended as the other two soldiers joined us, both leveling their blaster rifles at me.

We exited the ship onto a broad brick courtyard at the back of a low stone building. A single arched entry door stood open, flanked on each side by two of the deeply-tanned, light-green-eyed Scatters. The elfish guards both wore crystal swords on their belts but had neither shield nor bow.

"How do the Scatters keep anyone locked up without weapons?" I asked, mostly to myself.

"That's why we're here," one of the other two soldiers said, punching the back of my shoulder, causing me to stumble forward. "They opened their jail just for you. You should feel special."

"We can take the prisoner from here," one of the Scatter guards said as we approached.

"Frag off, pixie," the leader of the soldiers said, picking up speed and lowering his shoulder so he caught the smaller Scatter by surprise, knocking him back. "You *can* show us where he's gonna be kept and we'll get him squared away."

"Ya-yes, mi-lord," the Scatter answered nervously.

"See that? Just takes a little elbow grease to show these butterfly humpers proper respect. Don't forget that, men," he said, leading us into a wide, well-lit stone hallway. "Now, git in there and strip."

The Scatter stopped at an open cell and I was propelled forward by a blow between my shoulder blades. With my hands still bound behind my back, I was unable to catch myself from falling. Old reflexes kicked in and I dipped down, rolled on my shoulder, and more or less came to a seated position. I looked back at the unfriendly trio who stood in the doorway as I pulled my knees up to my chest and slipped my hands around my feet. The maneuver earned me a raised eyebrow from the lead soldier.

I held my cuffed hands out, knowing that to resist wouldn't be a good idea. The soldiers had positioned themselves so that, even with free hands, I wasn't getting through the three of them. The offer caused the leader to laugh. "Nice try, kid," he said, pushing one of the others out of the way and pulling the thick wooden door closed.

The cell door had two openings, the highest one about two meters off the ground, just a little too high for me to look through without jumping. The other was a thinner rectangle and about a meter off the ground. That opening looked wide enough for small items to be passed through to a prisoner, but not much more.

"Take off that suit or we'll be comin' in for lesson time," he said.

"Doesn't work that way," I said. "You got my wrists cuffed."

"Nobody that stupid," he answered. "Push 'em through the slot."

I did as I was told. When I didn't immediately retract my arms after the cuffs were removed, a jolt of electricity sent me flying backward. As I landed hard, I heard laughter on the other side of the door.

"Frak, was that necessary?" I asked, picking myself up off the ground.

"Suit," the leader's muted voice growled.

I was loath to remove my grav-suit but I complied, first shutting it down with instructions to not power up beyond basic vac-suit function without my direct command. I was completely naked by the time I handed the suit back through the slit, this time careful not to allow my hands to be within range of the shock stick.

"Yer learning," the lead soldier said.

I heard heavy scraping against the door. The wooden beam I'd seen leaning against the outside of my cell had been dropped across the door, locking me in. Nick had explained how short the Small Magellanic Cloud area was on iron, but something about the hollow sound made the significance of that scarcity clear.

The cell gave me a new appreciation for how the Scatters made do with the materials available. Four meters by five, the space was roomy. Along one wall was a bed with a stretched, woven tarp that served to keep the prisoner off the floor when sleeping. Light streamed in from high windows that appeared to be filled with either glass or some sort of crystal, as the cold of the day hadn't entirely filled the cell. Despite that bit of protection from the outside elements, I was growing colder by the moment and there was absolutely nothing in the cell that I could use as clothing. The only other item in the room was a lidded, wooden bucket sitting in the corner. I suspected that was my latrine. With nothing else to do, I lay on the bed, curling in on myself to maintain my body heat while avoiding the stone that radiated cold into the room.

After three hours, according to my earwig that still retained some AI function, I heard a knock at the door. I got up, crossed the room and crouched down carefully to look through the slit in the door. I couldn't see anything except more wood. A second knock followed.

"Yes?" I answered tentatively.

"The prisoner will stand away from the door," a Scatter's voice announced.

I took three steps back, crouching down again so I was on level with the slit. "All right, I'm not next to the door."

Preceded by mechanical sounds, the plank against the opening flipped down and out of the way. A moment later, a thin board with folded clothing and a blanket slid through the hole.

"You may remove the items," my jailer informed.

I took the pieces gratefully. Surprisingly, the sequence replayed itself two more times. The Scatter passed through a set of boots and then a steaming bowl of something that caused my stomach to growl. I was disappointed when the door was once again secured and my jailer walked away, leaving me alone with the supplies.

The tan pants fit reasonably well, aside from being a little short and only coming to mid-calf. The boots were tall and I laced them up. They covered my ankles and tucked in just beneath the pants. My toes were cramped, but they were also so cold that I wasn't about to complain. Finally, I donned the jerkin-style shirt and a thin jacket that came to mid-thigh. With the clothing on and the warm soup in my stomach, my deteriorating mood quickly improved. I wasn't sure how I'd get out of this current mess, but hoped I'd be able to talk sense into the king.

I spent most of the day doing yoga, something I'd learned years before. Meditation had always helped break up the monotony of a long journey and now, alone in the quiet cell, it gave me something to do. I was sitting in a lotus-pose when there was a light tap on the door.

"I'm here," I said as I moved to the door.

"I have brought evening meal." The voice belonged to a female Scatter. I was surprised to discover my earwig had enough processing power left to translate her words.

"Thank you," I said, waiting for the slot to open.

The flat board used to transport items to me slid in. As I reached for it, the wood jerked wildly, throwing the food and the bowl of water into the air. Frantically, I grabbed for the water.

"No, please," the Scatter woman begged as the board fell, dumping the remaining contents onto the floor. I heard a scuffle on the other side of the door and realized that the loss of my water wasn't the worst thing that was happening.

"Come on, just a little fun tonight." The voice belonged to a human male. My AI identified the speaker as one of the soldiers who had accompanied me to the cell.

"No, please! I have a family," the woman said, but I could hear the resignation in her voice.

"Get off her!" I yelled, throwing my shoulder into the door. "You can't do this!"

The door didn't budge a centimeter as I threw my weight at it. Apparently, even without iron, making a solid door wasn't a problem for the Scatters.

I heard the close sound of the man's voice as he leaned into the door. I could also hear the scuffling as the Scatter woman no doubt continued to look for any escape. "Don't get yourself all worked up. They like it," the soldier said. "And if they don't at first, they always do later."

I've always had a habit of biting my tongue when I get upset. Blood trickled into my mouth as I tried to come up with something to help the defenseless woman. An idea came to me in a flash and I lashed out, kicking the wooden slat back through the door. I was rewarded with a painful-sound of air escaping from the soldier on the other side of the door.

"Somebody's looking for a beating," the soldier grunted menacingly.

"No, I'll be quiet," the Scatter woman said. "Don't hurt him."

"Frak you, scumball!" I yelled, slamming my fists into the door. "Go ahead and bring your lame-ass beating in here."

"Ooh, somebody's got a temper." The man laughed. "If I didn't have a date here, I'd gladly hand you that beating."

I slammed my hands into the door again and called out, yelling just about every obscenity I could think of – which was a lot, considering I'd been raised on a mining colony. I quieted, straining to hear what was going on, but there was only silence on the other side of the door. They were simply gone.

I stood at the door for more than an hour, pacing back and forth.

Finally, I heard the wooden plank as it suddenly wobbled and was retracted from the hole. I could hear the sound of sniffling on the other side of the door.

"I'm sorry," I whispered, sinking to the floor. "I'm so sorry."

FORTUNATELY, this scene did not replay itself again, although mentally, it left me in a tough spot. I knew bad people existed. Frak, I'd been around tons of them. Never before, however, had I so intimately witnessed a crime while being so totally helpless to stop it. For days I had difficulty eating and I simply lay on my cot. Finally, on the fifth day I realized I was doing no one any good with my quiet protest.

Not until the fifteenth day of my incarceration, however, did my prospects change.

"When am I going to talk to someone?" I asked, repeating a question I'd asked daily.

If I hadn't been scratching marks into the stone wall, I might not have had any sense of how much time had passed. I'd been asking the same question for days and each time the response had been the same. "Not today."

Today's response came as a surprise.

"Liam Hoffen will clean himself as he will be brought to account this day," the voice said. My heartbeat quickened at the news. I'd rehearsed a million times in my head what I wanted to say in my own defense. I'd imagined myself in front of judge after judge, pleading my case, imagining different questions and answers.

A bowl with clean water, a towel, and what I suspected was some sort of soap was offered through the hole. After the guard left, I set about scrubbing myself down, careful to set my clothing on the bed so I wouldn't soil them further. By the time I was done, the bowl was dark gray with a few suds, but I was clean. What I wouldn't give for the simple groomer device I'd taken for granted most of my life. My hair was longer than ever and my beard had grown out enough that I was starting to look like Nick.

I dumped the bowl into the latrine bucket, grateful for the suds that would help knock down some of the smell. After that, I set the bowl and towel next to the door, knowing the guard wouldn't forget about either one.

Expecting a long wait, I sat on the bed and was taken off guard when the wooden beam lifted from the door. I rose and turned, careful not to stand too near the door. I was disappointed, but not surprised, when two of the Belirand soldiers stood in the doorway, guns leveled.

"Is the Highborne ready to face judgment day?" asked the soldier who I knew to have raped the Scatter woman. "Don't think that little stunt of yours, acting like you care about these fairies, will make any difference. You'll be brought to justice for the murder of our man, Thockenbrow."

I allowed my hands to be bound but said nothing. I hadn't been asked a question and at least for now, I didn't have to answer to this man. Internally I seethed, wondering just how many Scatters had been abused by this descendant of Belirand and his compatriots. I yearned for a weapon because regardless of cost, I'd have happily put him down.

"Don't worry, we'll have a chance to talk after King Nkosi is done with you. Maybe I'll even let you off the leash for a few minutes and we can see who the better man is."

The guards hesitated for a moment, waiting to see if I would respond. When I didn't, they turned down the hallway, a human soldier at the front. Two Scatter guards, one on either side of me, came next, and two more Scatters filled in behind us. As we walked, I realized that the jail was empty. Either Scatters didn't get into trouble or this was a jail for a special kind of prisoner. Both ideas seemed equally plausible. The décor slowly changed from utilitarian to more and more ornate as we moved between buildings.

Finally, we arrived at a rather unimpressive door. One of the Scatter guards who'd so far been quiet turned and addressed me. "In the presence of King Nkosi, you will not speak unless spoken to. If you cannot respect this demand you will be removed from the hall and we will commence your conversation later. Do you understand?"

"I understand," I said.

"Follow me," the Scatter answered, smiling politely.

I've observed many tribal chiefs, faction leaders, and even those who considered themselves royalty. For whatever reason, the encounters, although often stressful, were always a bit of a thrill. Royals or leaders were generally just like the people around them, with a few differences. In my experience, the leaders tended to be the most beautiful, or the most savage, or whatever had led to the tribe's success. Royalty tended to represent their group's most important quality, although often these features were extreme. I stayed observant as my captors led me into the meeting room, knowing that I would be able to pick up clues about this leader by what he or she surrounded himself with.

King Nkosi was not difficult to identify. He sat atop a huge gilded throne, behind which a brilliant display of multi-faceted and colorful crystals sprouted from the floor, soaring tens of meters into the air in a grandiose fan. He wore a tall golden crown laden with sparkling jewels and a dark, rich violet robe. A thick gold cord crossed his chest, holding in place a long flowing white cape, its folds pooling at his feet. I tried not to shrug. The look was predictable for a king and I was surprised that the whole *purple is royal* thing had made it all the way out to the Small Magellanic Cloud.

To the left of King Nkosi, on a smaller, albeit just as ornately decorated chair, sat Queen Cacile, the Scatter who'd called Belirand on me. Surprisingly, at the King's right side stood Thabini, the young

Scatter who'd help me escape to the healer's hut on the river delta. When I caught Thabini's eye, he nodded in acknowledgement.

A few meters to the king's left stood two humans wearing military uniforms more formal than any I'd seen so far. Where the clothing worn by the royals was immaculate, the soldiers' uniforms were clean, but well worn. The larger of the two was a bear of a man at two meters and one hundred forty kilograms. With light brown hair and a thick beard, he returned my glance with an icy stare.

"Liam Hoffen, I am King Nkosi of the Scatter people," Nkosi unnecessarily announced. "You have met Queen Cacile and Prince Thabini. In that human matters are the domain of Bell-e-runde, Colonel Chappie Barto is also in attendance."

Nkosi looked over to the two humans. An ingenuine smile crossed the large man's face as he tipped his head in acknowledgment. "As is spelled out in our treaty," Chappie Barto agreed in a voice much higher than I had expected. The oddity barely registered, most likely because I was too worried about being tried for murder.

Nkosi turned from the introductions and looked down at a scroll that he held in his lap. "Liam Hoffen, you are charged with the willful murder of Jared Thockenbrow. Do you have anything to say in your defense?" he asked without warning.

I was taken aback at the simplicity and directness of the question. I was expecting to sit down, maybe confer with some sort of council, form an argument or some sort of defense strategy – anything.

"I did not murder Jared Thockenbrow," I finally managed.

"Do you dispute stabbing him with this iron knife?" Queen Cacile asked.

"I do not," I said. The answer brought a frown to her face, but she recovered.

"Then you admit to murdering Jared Thockenbrow?" Thabini asked.

"I do not," I said.

"Explain yourself," King Nkosi said.

"When a maracat attacks you in the wild, is it wrong to defend yourself?" I asked, glad to actually be getting into my rather well-crafted defense.

"Yes," Nkosi answered simply.

My mind reeled at his unexpected answer. A quick glance to Chappie revealed that his stare had transformed to a triumphant smile.

Nkosi continued. "By placing yourself within the maracat's domain, you have submitted to its rules. By not listening for its approach, you have ignored basic woodcraft. And by not finding shelter before it is too hungry to be deterred, you have placed it in grave danger."

"Jared Thockenbrow shot the golden gigantus upon which I rode," I said. "I could not have anticipated his willful and hostile act. Jared Thockenbrow also shot my brave companion, Lifa, who attempted to intercede on my behalf, and he shot the young man Langa. When Jared Thockenbrow shot me with his blaster pistol, I had no choice but to stop him. That is not murder."

"In that Jared Thockenbrow is deceased, his actions are not in question today," King Nkosi said. I heard a coarse whisper and snicker between Chappie and the man who stood next to him. While I didn't catch it entirely, the two men seemed to be commenting on Nkosi's inability to question their actions at any time. "You admit to having killed a man. Do you have anything further to say in your defense?"

"A question?" I asked.

"It is allowed."

"Why do your guard wear swords if they are unwilling to defend your citizens? I had to listen to the Belirand guard behind me rape the poor woman who brought me food and no one did anything to defend her. Did she make a bad choice to enter Belirand's domain?

What about Langa? Should he have anticipated that Jared Thockenbrow would be drunk and shoot at birds passing overhead? What about Lifa's daughter? She witnessed her father's murder," I accused angrily. "No. Don't answer. Belirand is raping and killing your people while you stand idle. Wake up, man! Evil is among you and you dress up in your pretty cape and pretend to be in charge."

"The prisoner will be silent!" Nkosi yelled, his pale face turning beet red.

Chappie laughed, unable to restrain himself. "Stop fighting it already," he said. "The decision's been made and I'm tired of standing around."

"Father, I must speak." Thabini had grown more and more agitated during the proceeding.

"Speak, son. I should not allow this murderer to anger me so," he said.

"Once the Scatter people were a noble and powerful people. We hunted. We fought. We grew. But over time, we discovered that we were able to live in harmony with nature. More and more, the swords we carried were a simple decoration, the bows we carried merely a pastime. One day many hundred years ago, Bell-e-runde arrived, asking to trade with us. For a short time this was good for all peoples, Bell-e-runde and Scatter. More Bell-e-runde people came and Bell-e-runde people spread to the stars, all the time not sharing with us their technology."

"Careful, son," Nkosi said. "You may repeat our history, but we will not insult our friends of Bell-e-runde.

"Are they our friends, Father?" Thabini asked. "Jared Thockenbrow will not be missed. He has murdered many Scatter and hurt many more. He preyed on the youngest of our women and when drunk, had little hesitance in killing anyone near him. Yet he was never questioned as Liam Hoffen."

"That is enough, Thabini. You will leave now," Nkosi said. I expected anger, but instead the king seemed sad as he bowed his head and pointed to the door.

"You do an evil today, Father," Thabini said. "I am sorry, Liam Hoffen. The Scatter people have failed you."

"Finish up already, Nkosi," Chappie growled, obviously annoyed at Thabini's outburst. "You best get that son of yours in line. I heard treason in his speech. It'd be a shame if Bell-e-runde had to start fixing your internal issues in addition to everything else we do around here."

"That will not be necessary," said Nkosi, king in name only. Holding his chin up, he looked directly at me. "Liam Hoffen. You are found guilty of murder and will be transferred to Bell-e-runde in the morning for punishment."

Chapter 14

UP THE VOLTAGE

I barely remembered the walk back to my cell or how I received the multitude of bruises I later found on my abdomen and legs. Vaguely, I recalled the Bell-e-runde soldiers dragging me from Nkosi's chambers after using heavy batons to encourage my quick and quiet departure. An hour after the trial, as I sat in my cell inspecting my wounds, the door to my cell opened and without warning, Colonel Chappie Barto strode in.

"You're not Highborne," he stated. It didn't escape me that he entered by himself. While I suspected there were soldiers outside, he'd made an interesting judgment call.

"That so?" I asked.

"Doesn't seem like you understand just the kind of trouble you're in, Liam Hoffen," he said, pulling a thin, telescoping club from the side of his pants and snapping it to length. "That tech on your face; subtle. I can imagine why my boys missed it, but not Ol' Chappie. Nothin' gets by me."

Quick as lightning, his club flicked out and caught me on my left arm.

I yelped and jumped to the side. "Frak," I answered. "No. Not Highborne."

"See, that wasn't so hard," he said, grinning. "Confusing. You look like you been living wild. But you got this tech."

I blocked his right hand as he reached for my earwig and he swung his club around with his left. I wasn't about to take another hit so I twisted into his body and brought my elbow around into his face. I'd been in plenty of scrapes and had trained hard in hand-to-hand. Chappie was strong, but he had none of the agility I was used to from my normal training partners. I'll admit, it felt good to hear the crunch of bone as my elbow made contact. Chappie roared with pain and I grabbed the club from him as he crumpled to the ground.

While he might have had a hidden weapon, I hadn't seen any evidence of one when he'd entered the cell. I didn't have time to search him, so I sprinted toward the cell's entry only to be met by the two soldiers who'd been watching me during my stay. Surprise was on my side and I flew into action, first throwing a back-round-house kick into the face of the closest guard. I quickly moved to the second with a slash of the weighted, telescoping weapon Chappie had so thoughtfully provided. The two soldiers went down quickly, but my strikes weren't strong enough to put them down for long.

I grabbed for one of their holstered weapons just a little too late. I heard the slap of a boot on the cell floor behind me a fraction of a second before Chappie's hundred-forty-kilogram frame slammed into me, toppling me to the floor. I twisted, freeing my arm and managing a rabbit punch toward his throat. Missing by millimeters, I connected instead with his jaw. Without hesitation, Chappie reared back and smashed his forehead into the side of my face.

There's a saying I've heard that goes something like *no one wins in a head butt*, but in Chappie's case I think there might be an exception. I'm sure it hurt him plenty, but I saw stars and was stunned beyond any ability to react. I felt a big fist slam into my side, followed by another. The soldiers, who I'd temporarily taken out of the action, recovered and soon three men were kicking and punching me. The only thing I could do was to cover my head with my hands and curl into a ball. Even so, I heard my ribs crack as the beating continued without mercy.

"That's enough, boys," Chappie finally said, panting from the exertion of beating me senseless. Powerless, I felt rough hands pull at my hands. I looked up just in time to see Chappie grab my earwig and rip it from my skin.

I tried to push myself away from him, which only earned me a broad hand slap to the side of my head. I'd never been beaten so badly and was amazed I'd remained conscious.

"Where's your ship, Liam Hoffen?" he demanded. "Folks back in Sol think you might be the same guy who caused a heap of trouble so many years ago. Said you oughta be an old man, though, but you're not, now are you? They asked if I got yer name right."

"No ship," I said, spitting blood onto the floor as I tried to speak. "Not old."

"Could have made this easier on yerself," he said in a low voice, crouching next to me. "Handed Chappie a right good thumpin' though. Get some respect for that, you do."

He stood, pushing off his thighs with giant hands. "Toss him back in his cell. We'll come back for him in the morning. Almost feel like I need tah thank yah. Haven't had a good throwdown in forever. Gonna need me some pretty company tonight."

Without the earwig, his untranslated words sounded strange and I realized Chappie's spoken language was very close to what I'd grown up with. I filed the information away as the soldiers dragged me back into my cell and closed the door, locking it.

I lacked the strength or the will to move from the spot where I'd been dumped. Each breath or movement of my chest hurt. Worst of all, I periodically coughed up blood, each cough feeling like someone was stabbing me with a knife. Just a few nights before I'd been wondering if I could feel any lower. Unfortunately, I had my answer.

MERCIFULLY, I passed out. As if from a great distance, I became aware of a gentle yet persistent rocking of my shoulders, the pressure increasing until my ribs exploded in pain. Opening my eyes, I saw nothing and was only dimly aware of another person's presence beside me.

"Who is it?" I whispered, only to feel two small, thin fingers press against my lips.

"Aferago." It was a female Scatter's voice. I couldn't see her face, but recognized the voice as belonging to Bongiwe.

"What are you doing here?" I whispered, even more softly.

"Bongiwe," she said. "Per tara aferago."

I nodded, knowing she could see my movements even if I couldn't see hers. I tried to push against the ground with my elbow and sit up, but pain in my battered, swollen joints prevented me from making it upright. Bongiwe reached around and grasped my side in an attempt to help. Her small hand found a sensitive spot and I flinched, causing her to adjust. Finally, with a lot of help, I made it to a standing position.

Dim light from the hallway outside the cell illuminated the open door. Bongiwe whispered *aferago* into my ear. Smelling freedom, I struggled forward, each step more painful than I could describe, but I was not to be deterred.

Once outside the cell, I started to turn toward the passageway leading deeper into the building. "Nis," Bongiwe whispered, turning me. I resisted, certain we would find soldiers in that direction.

"I can't fight," I whispered back. My words earned me another finger to the lips.

In that I had no plan of my own, I followed her direction. As I shuffled forward, I tried to muster the strength to think up some sort of defense should one be needed. Not only were several of my ribs broken, but my knee had been badly twisted. Throwing a punch and kicking were out of the question and I had no other ideas.

It seemed to take forever to get to the end of the twenty-meter-long hallway. Bongiwe rapped lightly when we arrived at the heavy wooden door. I was expecting a big group of soldiers on the other side.

"What? Who's there?" a surprised human voice asked.

"Fetma," Bongiwe answered seductively, after urging me to stand next to the stone wall. At the sound of a wooden bar being removed from the other side of the door, I looked back at Bongiwe in shock. Our prison break was about to go completely south. There was just enough light for me to make out a thin smile on Bongiwe's face as she reached into a leather pouch at her waist, extracting a bulbous green plant.

"What's going on?" a soldier asked, before the door was completely open.

"Per tara fetma," Bongiwe answered.

The door swung wide and the soldier looked startled as his eyes fell on me. Using the surprise, Bongiwe wasted no time in mashing the plant she held into the man's face. At first, he screamed. A second later, the sound was cut short and he fell forward across the door's threshold either dead or unconscious. Either way worked for me.

"Oh, no you don't!" A second soldier jumped to his feet and unholstered his blaster pistol. It was just my luck, the man was ridiculously quick at extracting his pistol.

Bongiwe jumped toward him, her speed as impressive as her graceful moves, but the man needed only a fraction of a second to move his arm up. A blaster bolt caught Bongiwe on her right arm as she reached for the man's face with her poison pod. She screamed in agony as the bolt tore through her shoulder, nearly cleaving off her arm.

I had no strength to help Bongiwe and my mind spun as I tried to come up with something useful to do. The ease with which the soldier had cut her down made me sick. There was no end to what these Belirand thugs would do. An idea hatched in my mind and I allowed myself to fall over the prone guard. The move was partly an act and partly inevitable based on how the last few days had been going for me.

"Hey, get off him!" The guard sounded more offended than threatened, so I must have been convincing.

He was too late. While the fall caused immeasurable pain, the pain served to focus me. I'd landed right over the unconscious soldier's hand and the blaster pistol he still gripped. I twisted the pistol around and – upside down, backwards, and with the man's hand still firmly attached – fired a shot. The guard figured out just a little too late that I had some fight left. He pulled back as the bolt went wild, missing him not by that much. Practical experience had taught me that it's one thing to shoot at an unmoving, unarmed foes. Adversaries who returned fire were another thing entirely.

Unnerved, the soldier squeezed the trigger and ended up burying two rounds into his friend's backside. I've been shot at more times than I can recall. While I had no desire for a repeat, I didn't find the idea all that unnerving. With patience borne out of sheer force of will, I extracted the weapon from the soldier's grasp and returned fire. This time the blaster bolt found home.

"Bongiwe!" I said, dropping the blaster and willing myself across the floor to where she lay unconscious. There had to be a liter of her blood on the floor by the time I got there. I grabbed at the bedding nearby and pressed a large wad into the wound. I hated the idea of the infiltration of germs, but if she kept bleeding, she wouldn't survive long enough to have an infection.

"Liam Hoffen," a male Scatter said. Prince Thabini and a second male stood in the doorway. I did a doubletake when I realized the man was Hambo, the young elf who'd helped me in the mountains. They rushed to Bongiwe's side.

"She's hurt," I said. "Shot."

"Aferago," Thabini said, lifting Bongiwe and causing her to stir with a groan of pain.

Hambo rushed to my side. Seeing that I was also injured, he gently but firmly helped me stand.

"Per tara," I said, not one-hundred percent sure I knew what I was saying. I was thinking the translation was either *go quickly* or *go quietly* and I was good with either. My attempt at his language earned me a grin from Hambo, but no obvious concern or haste. I winced as he moved me toward the door, his hand touching my broken rib.

From the position of the first moon of Fraxus, I determined it was well past the middle of the night and we were probably two hours before the rise of Fraxus' star. The air was cold and I shivered as I realized I wasn't dressed for this. The cold, however, turned out to be a boon. Not only did the cold dull my body's throbbing, but the smell of fresh air and the potential of freedom helped me set aside my pain.

As a group, we ran across the broad courtyard illuminated only by the bright first moon. At the far end sat two Belirand cutters and a large, heavily-armored sloop. I recognized the cutter used to capture me at the healer Nothando's home. The second, longer cutter was in considerably better repair and sported twin blaster turrets. The armored sloop was well lit and bristled with armament. It didn't take much imagination to guess that the sloop belonged to Chappy.

I thought we'd made a clean break when suddenly we were awash in a bright flood of light coming from the sloop only a hundred meters behind us. A moment later a single shot from the turret tore up the rocky ground in front of us, showering us with stone chips and deafening us with the gun's report.

"You will halt!" a human voice demanded over the ship's public address.

"Aferago," Thabini said, pushing the still-unconscious Bongiwe into Hambo's arms.

"No, they'll kill us," I said, sure my words would be understood.

Thabini looked up at me, smiled and said, "Magic."

I looked at him and raised my eyebrows, wondering if I'd heard him right. From every angle, flaming arrows arched in from the darkness surrounding the prison courtyard. Arrows – even flaming arrows – seemed a silly weapon with which to attack armored ships. The look of confidence, however, never wavered on Thabini's face, even as the two dozen arrows in the first volley simply bounced off the ship.

"Per aferago," Thabini said, turning away from the ridiculous scene.

"No, Thabini. They'll kill us," I said. "Arrows are nothing against a warship."

"Magic," he responded, smiling and snapping his fingers. As if in response, the arrows that had landed all around the three ships exploded, expelling an inky blackness that expanded in size at an alarming rate, enveloping the ships almost instantly and blotting out all light.

Thabini was no fool. He pushed us from our original path just before a shower of blaster bolts landed. With fresh adrenaline and hope, we ran into the night, ignoring the welts of pain caused by flying debris as Chappie's guns searched for us. After a few minutes bright spotlights filled the sky as the Belirand ships launched and started their own search pattern, free of Thabini's magic.

Instead of running away from the city, Thabini led us along the edge of the river delta where it met dry ground. A few minutes later, having gained the sure footing of the city's rock-paved streets, we were met by a small group of Scatters. A solid-looking female relieved Hambo of Bongiwe and we followed the group into a well-hidden, vegetation-covered entrance to one of Thandeka's many underground passageways.

"I have to stop," I finally complained as the group urged me to keep moving at a pace I couldn't maintain. The constant jarring of my broken ribs made breathing nearly impossible and as adrenaline wore off, I became more and more aware of my twisted knee.

"Nestawary," Hambo said, looping an arm back beneath my shoulder and propping me up. "Nestawary."

"I can't go much longer," I said, limping forward at his urging.

I'd lost track of both Bongiwe and Thabini, but a few moments later Thabini appeared and held up his hand. We stopped at the edge of an opening that would no doubt lead us onto a cobblestone street where we would make several turns and end up back in an underground passage. We'd repeated the maneuver ten times already and I'd lost faith that we'd be stopping any time soon.

Thabini bent and placed his hands on the cuff of my too-short pants and looked up at me for permission. I nodded and he pushed at the material in an attempt to get it over my knee. My knee was the size of a cantaloupe and the narrow pants weren't going anywhere. Quick words were exchanged and Hambo extracted his crystal sword, handing it to Thabini. Thabini split the pant leg along its side and for a few seconds, I felt blessed relief from the pressure, though it was only momentary.

Thabini *tsked*, which caused me to chuckle. The expression was something I'd thought to be completely human, and Thabini was certainly not that. The chuckle caught his attention and he looked from me back to my knee, shaking his head as if to imply that I was in quite a pickle.

"Right you are, my friend," I said. Instead of leaving, he moved to my other side so both he and Hambo could help me walk. It was an awkward way to move, but with his help we made better progress.

Each time we exited the tunnels, I searched the skies for Belirand ships. Sometimes I’d see one or two in the distance. Finally, we entered a tunnel that had a much steeper downward pitch than any of others. We were well below the ground-water level and I wondered just how they kept the river from flooding the passageway. I suspected Thabini might have explained that it was magic. Of course, I wouldn't have believed him any more than I believed his helpful little ink-blasting arrows were magical.

After bottoming out, we climbed back toward the surface again, but this time I saw a strange glow ahead. As we approached, I became aware of a few Scatters standing in the hallway, crystal swords or bows in hand.

"Thabini," they murmured, bowing slightly as he approached.

"Fera Nothando," he answered, unhooking himself from me and handing me over to one of the guards. "Hambo aferago. Chancile."

We moved into the large room and I was helped onto a low table just inside the doorway. Hambo looked at me, then back to Thabini and bowed. "Chancile, Thabini. Chancile, Liam Hoffen." With nothing more to say, Hambo ran off, I assumed looking for Nothando. A moment later, I was proven right.

"Liam Hoffen," Nothando, the elderly healer looked up from where he was working on Bongiwe, his hands and arms stained with her blood.

"Bongiwe. Will she live?" I asked.

Though Nothando didn't understand my words, he understood my question and shook his head sorrowfully as he came over to where I sat, explaining her fate in words I couldn't understand. I'd seen it before. Without the technology I was so accustomed to, Bongiwe wouldn't survive. She'd sustained too much damage and lost too much blood for her own body to heal itself.

My frustration boiled over. She'd given her life for mine, a trade that made me feel unworthy. "Frak!"

"Frak," Nothando echoed more quietly, as he patted my knee. His eyes flew open and he startled, realizing that what he'd touched was swollen beyond recognition.

"Can you understand me?" I asked.

Nothando held his hands up and shrugged. "Understand little," he answered.

"If I had my ship – spaceship...," I said, waiting to see if he understood. I saw nothing but confusion. I put my hand in the air, made a swooshing sound and then tapped my chest. "Spaceship. Mine. I could help Bongiwe."

He pushed his hand in the air and made a swooshing sound. I nodded. "Spaceship," I said, pointing at his hand. "Liam Hoffen spaceship. Ada Chen suspension chamber. Heal Bongiwe!"

A lightbulb seemed to go off in his head. "Quelitu?" he asked. It was the word they'd often used for suspension chamber. "Space ... ship ..."

"Yes! Suspension chamber. Spaceship," I said.

"Nothando fera Liam Hoffen spaceship, quelitu," he said.

"Yes! We have to go now. Save Bongiwe," I said.

He pointed at my swollen knee and grimaced. With great effort, I pushed up so I was standing. No part of me didn't hurt, but at least I was no longer coughing up blood. If I could get to *Hotspur*, we'd up the voltage on this little party.

Chapter 15

ENERGY WEAPONS AND CRYSTAL GROTTOES

After a rapid exchange of words between Thabini and Nothando, we were off again. Apparently, Thabini had made the decision to leave the healer behind to tend to the dying Bongiwe. Having stopped for a few minutes made my knee feel even worse and I leaned heavily on Hambo. He made no complaints and oddly, always had a quick, reassuring smile when I looked at him. I found myself wondering if he'd volunteered for the duty or had been assigned.

Shuffling back through the underground passage, we exited the same way we'd entered. I'd counted roughly forty men and women in the large room where Bongiwe had been taken. It was the second such room I'd seen and I wondered how many other secret rooms they might have. While I had a limited grasp of the Scatter language, I was good at reading body language. I knew two things for sure about this group: each person knew what they were doing was dangerous and they all trusted Prince Thabini as their leader. Their faces showed determination, a trait I found common amongst humanoid species, especially when doing the right thing under difficult conditions.

The morning sun was still an hour off, but dawn was breaking as we exited onto the street. Across the canal, a few Scatters moved about. I held my breath as I waited to discover if they'd seen us. They were either the least observant people in existence or purposely ignored our presence. This idea was reinforced when Thabini let loose a loud whistle, that to me seemed to say – here we are, come and get us. Hambo grinned widely, observing my wide-eyed expression as I shuffled back into heavy shadow.

"Qinani," Hambo whispered, pointing low over the horizon.

I strained to see what he was pointing at and for a minute, I couldn't find anything. Hambo moved closer so I could more easily sight along his finger. It was then I saw the unmistakable silhouettes of giant golden eagles flying directly at us. Even though it was mostly dark, the great birds flew where the sky was the lightest, dragging with them the approaching dawn. They were magnificent. Having ridden one, I'd become a life-long fan and relished the idea of once again being allowed to ride. It almost made my broken ribs and twisted knee worthwhile. Almost.

A familiar whistling sound cut through the air just before the eagles landed on the stone railing that separated the canal waters from pedestrians. The birds were ridden by Scatters in the subtle uniforms all the riders wore. Dismounting, the three gathered around Thabini, who spoke quickly and with an authoritative yet friendly tone.

With little hesitation the three removed both their crystal lens goggles and dark, hooded cloaks. The largest in the group, a man significantly smaller than me, adjusted goggles on my face as Hambo helped me struggle into the cloak.

After one more quick exchange of words, I was led to the side of an eagle. Having been atop one before, I knew what I needed to do, but there was no combination of moves that would allow me to use my twisted knee to mount. Hambo, in an undignified manner, pushed me up onto the bird's back, causing both the giant eagle and me to shuffle uncomfortably. Fortunately, seeing our plight, one of the riders settled the insulted bird.

Once I was in place, Hambo unexpectedly jumped up behind me and wrapped his thin arms around my waist. I wasn't sure what to do next as Thabini still spoke with the lead rider. However, recognizing that we were as ready as anyone can be on the back of a giant bird, he jogged over, nimbly leapt onto the back of one of the remaining two and gave a warbling whistle. In response, his eagle stretched its great wings and leapt from the railing. The rider holding our bird answered Thabini's whistle with one of his own, released the reigns, and lifted his hand into the air.

I'd been concerned that my weight was too great for the giant eagle on my trip down the mountain. During that flight, I'd discovered that these birds had tremendous strength and I wasn't a bit surprised when my mount lifted easily. My ribs ached as the bird fought against gravity, flapping its great wings and lurching higher, each beat seeming to lift us a couple of meters.

"Bell-e-runde," Hambo yelled over the rush of wind. We'd barely reached a hundred meters elevation.

"Where?" I asked, scanning the quickly lightening sky.

He pointed behind us and I twisted uncomfortably to get a good look. He was right. A few kilometers to the west the rundown cutter chugged slowly across Thandeka's skyline. Either they hadn't seen us or they didn't think the patrol had anything to do with their escaped prisoner. I craned my neck, scanning for the other ships, relaxing when I didn't find them.

"Frak!" I said as I noticed the cutter had turned from its patrol and was headed directly toward us.

"Thabini!" I shouted, trying to be heard over the wind. Unfortunately, we were separated by forty meters and the distance made it impossible for him to hear my cries. I urged my eagle forward, leaning into her and kicking my heel into her breast. Sensing my urgency, the bird attempted to accelerate, beating against the damp morning air. I pulled at the reigns, directing the eagle in Thabini's direction and was rewarded with an annoyed squawk and a shake of her head. Fortunately, the squawk caught the attention of Thabini's eagle and it slowed, allowing us to overtake their position.

"Belirand!" I shouted, coughing as I attempted to draw another breath. The coughing attack disabled me, but Hambo knew exactly what was going down and shouted with excitement, pointing out the accelerating ship.

To his credit, Thabini didn't panic. Instead he whistled instructions to the birds. Much more effective than my kicks, the whistles caused both eagles to work harder, diving to gain speed. We lost half our elevation in a matter of seconds.

I felt a tap on my shoulder as I recovered from my coughing. Hambo pointed at Blue Mountain, ten kilometers away. I tried following the vector his arm implied, but the action was difficult to calculate without help from an AI. The one thing I knew for a fact was that the Belirand ship would be on us a lot sooner than we'd make the mountain, regardless of where he was pointing.

Dipping lower and beating fast, the birds dropped to only a couple meters above the tops of the pine forest. Hope buoyed as I spied the broad mouth of a cave, still several kilometers away. The fact that we were flying at top speed and headed directly at the center of the opening made me believe it was indeed our destination. My hope was short-lived. I felt the heavy vibrations radiating from the pursuing cutter, followed quickly by the uneven mechanical rattle from its ancient engines.

"Land or be fired upon," a tinny voice projected out over the forest. We were moving fast for biological beings, but lining blasters up on something moving at twenty meters per second wouldn't be much of a challenge. It was rotten luck, which seemed the only kind I was capable of recently. I could see my goal, yet I would again be stopped by Belirand. I dearly despised this company.

I felt a small, strong hand pushing at my back. Initially I resisted, but Hambo was insistent, so I leaned further forward. I was almost thrown from the eagle when it banked hard to starboard and beat its wings, gaining a small amount of elevation, but picking up speed as it did. Through my legs I felt the great beast's heart hammering as it strained to keep up with Thabini. The air around us crackled with electricity as a blaster bolt sizzled past.

"We can't survive this," I yelled at Thabini. I was too far away for him to hear, so I pulled on the eagle's reins, unwilling to be the reason Thabini got killed. I'd rather be handed over to Belirand again than to cause these gentle people more pain.

The eagle had different ideas. Instead of slowing, she flipped her beak back and forth angrily. When I attempted to fight with her, she gave a great swipe of her head from one side to the other, snapping the reins from my hands and breaking them against the back of her neck. She squawked loudly, obviously unhappy that she had to show me who was in charge.

"That was your only warning. Next one is for real." The speakers on the outside of the ship might have been crap, but the message was well delivered. There was no way these eagles stood a chance against an armed ship.

A familiar crackle of energy was the only warning we received of a second shot. Just how my eagle knew the shot was not aimed at us, I had no idea. Perhaps more remarkable was Thabini's intuitive response. Just before the deadly bolt was released, his eagle flared its wings, trading speed for elevation. The blaster bolt seared past harmlessly as Thabini peeled off twenty degrees.

In horror, I watched as the comparatively massive cutter turned and chased after the prince. The rational part of my brain understood the move. Thabini was the high value target, whereas the unknown human was just a distraction or a bit-part actor in a centuries-old drama. Taking down a rebel prince was where the real action was, something both Thabini and the cutter pilot knew.

The blaster-dodging scene repeated itself a couple more times as we climbed up the mountain, putting distance between us and the fight. I flicked my glance nervously between our destination and the aerial combat that promised to end the life of the prince who'd risked everything to keep me alive. An explosion of feathers abruptly ended the combat as a blaster round from the decrepit ship finally found its target. Hambo's wailing cry communicated the depth of his anguish as we watched Thabini's lifeless body tumble from the sky into the pine forest below.

The eagle I rode landed in the mouth of a cave. I'd born the burden of so many lives. In that moment, Thabini's death just seemed to crush me. Sliding off the eagle, I found myself unable or possibly unwilling to stand against the pain of my knee and crumpled to the ground.

"Nis, Liam Hoffen," Hambo said, his small hand coming to rest on my shoulder. "Bell-e-runde aferago. Per fera Quelitu."

The sides of the cave had obscured our view and hidden the cutter's approach. With little warning, the sound of the ship's engines filled the cave and its bulk blotted out the sky.

"Frak," I said, almost too exhausted to move. Fortunately, Hambo wasn't willing to let his prince die for nothing and he pulled at me, helping me up. I hobbled forward until we felt the familiar charge building. Together we dove to the uneven cave floor as rock shards rained down on us. Without missing a beat, Hambo pulled me up again and we charged headlong toward the back of the cave where a passageway branched off. Once we disappeared around the bend, the cutter would have no direct shot. Unfortunately, the cutter crew didn't give up and continued to fire into the cave, pelting us with debris.

"Liam Hoffen," Hambo said, slowing and pointing forward. "Quelitu."

"Hambo, come on," I urged, looking at my flagging companion. It was then I noticed the rock shard which had impaled him. Initially, it didn't look too bad, but I soon realized the shard had entered from his back. He was going into shock from the impact.

"No," I begged. "We're so close."

"Liam Hoffen, aferago," Hambo said, falling to a knee.

I pulled at his shoulders while keeping the weight off my unusable knee. My gyrating motions returned Hambo to the here and now, although probably from pain I'd unwittingly caused. He looked up at me with renewed determination, got back to his feet and pushed into me, tenaciously moving us down the narrowing path.

Turning a final corner, the cavern opened to a huge chamber covered with giant crystal formations. Somewhere, many meters above our position, there was an opening to the surface as sunlight poured in and bounced around the crystal surfaces. Light refracted through the mineral faces, casting wide, colorful beams of light across the room. As dire as our situation was, the sheer wonder of the moment caught me off guard – that is, until Hambo collapsed.

With light bouncing around as it was, picking out details was difficult. I wasn't sure if this room was a dead end, but it didn't matter. Without help, I couldn't go any further and I certainly couldn't drag Hambo. Belirand would land and soldiers would soon be upon us. My heart sank as I realized we'd come all this way only to be stopped again.

I searched the room for anything that could help. My eyes fell on a rocky pedestal thirty meters from where we'd entered. Atop this pedestal was a translucent suspension chamber and within that chamber lay Ada Chen. My heart nearly jumped out of my chest.

I removed Hambo's cloak, folding the material so I could apply pressure to his wound. He was bleeding badly and I wasn't sure pressure would help. The fact was, Belirand soldiers were working their way to us and neither of us had much time. Once again, I felt sick. I'd found

Ada, only to lead the very devil to her. The fact was, the damage was done and I'd have to see it through.

Limping and stumbling against crystal formations within the cave, I made my way to the chamber, cutting my hands on the sharp edges of crystal faces. I pushed past, no longer worried about anything but reaching Ada. Like Snow White, she lay entombed within the suspension chamber. I worried that she would most likely be in the same weakened state I'd been found in. The chamber was translucent and her body was unclothed. Seeing her ribcage reinforced my worries until, upon further inspection, I realized the rest of her body retained much of the muscle tone I remembered.

I pulled myself up next to the chamber, looked into her placid face and searched for the controls that ran the chamber. The display showed a full charge and indicated that she was indeed in perfect stasis.

"I'm sorry, Ada," I said as I palmed the security panel and instructed the AI to wake her up. While waiting for the sequence to activate, I became aware of a pile of partially disintegrated fruit that lay atop the chamber. All along the ground surrounding her, I discovered evidence of plant husks and seeds. Somehow, the Scatters had discovered that they could feed the chamber and it would absorb and utilize nutrients. It didn't explain the full energy stores, but I wondered if that was a result of the surrounding crystal.

Suspension fluids splashed out from vents at each end and a moment later the chamber's sides flipped open, depositing a portion of the remaining fluid onto me. Ada stirred and I reached for her, suddenly aware of the fact that she was naked. I looked away, struggling to pull off my cloak to cover her. I jumped when I felt a hand on my shoulder. Waves of pain coursed through my body as I jarred my poorly healing ribs.

"Liam?" Ada asked, coughing up fluid. "What's happened to you?"

I turned back, feeling the inadequacy of the soiled material I had to offer. She smiled gently as I pushed the cloak to her. "You're naked," I pointed out, carefully averting my eyes.

"How did I get here?" she asked, accepting the cloak and quickly wrapping it around her body. "You're hurt and you've changed. Liam. Tell me. What's going on?"

"We're in trouble, Ada," I said, trying to hold myself up on the rock pedestal where she now sat. "That man over there is Hambo. He's been impaled and is dying. We need to find *Hotspur,* bad people are coming for us."

"*Hotspur* is right there." She jumped down and pointed over my shoulder. I followed her finger and then I saw it. Resting amongst the crystals sat *Hotspur*, still cloaked in her fully-reflective skin, where she'd crashed so many years ago.

If Ada hadn't jumped down from the pedestal, the blaster bolt that flew over my shoulder would have killed her. "No!" I screamed, turning back to the Belirand soldiers who'd entered the grotto. "Ada, you're our only chance. Get to *Hotspur.*" Well, the last part about getting to *Hotspur* I never actually finished saying aloud because, quick as lightning, Ada had already sprinted across the crystal grove. I'd like to say that I didn't pay attention to the fact that the cloak did little to cover her nakedness, but ... rings of Saturn, she was beautiful.

Not having grown up around crystal formations like these, I wasn't exactly aware of all their properties. Sure, in theory, it made sense that the glassy surfaces would reflect energy, or split it, or do all sorts of crazy things with it. In practicality, let me just say that no sane person would fire an energy weapon into a crystal grotto like this more than once. Tracing Ada's path with blaster fire, the soldiers were relentless – and heedless of the danger. It became immediately evident that the shooters weren't using an AI to direct their shots. Furthermore, as the blaster bolts bounced around the room, it seemed that Ada, the intended target, was the only one to escape the wrath of the split energies.

"Frakking stop shooting!" I yelled as I threw myself to the ground having taken a dozen smaller spokes of energy that flew in all directions. The fact that I wasn't dead told me the energy diminished as it was split, but try explaining that to the burns on my scalp. I felt like I was wearing a Medusa wig with some very angry electric eels instead of snakes.

Apparently, I wasn't the only one to have been on the receiving end of the blaster's wrath. With a few yelps, the soldiers stopped shooting and retreated back into the passageway.

"There's no getting out of here," one of the soldiers finally offered. "You should give yourself up."

"And then what?" I asked. "Aren't you just going to shoot me?"

"Chappie wants to talk with you," the same soldier answered. "Where'd that woman go?"

"Woman?" I asked. "Not sure what you're talking about."

"Don't act stupid," he said, advancing with his weapon raised. As he came forward, three other soldiers slowly reentered the room. "I saw a woman run off. We'll tear this place apart if we have to."

"Look, I'm in pretty bad shape," I said, pushing myself up to a seated position. "You saw as much as I did. I think she went over there. You'll have to go get her." I pointed sort of in the direction Ada had gone.

"Check him," the lead soldier said, as they came even with Hambo's body.

One of the other three walked over, keeping his rifle leveled on Hambo's small form. I'd always been surprised at how a person looks smaller when they're dead or unconscious. Hambo looked no bigger than a child. The soldier nudged him with a big boot and then kicked at his side. Hambo didn't move.

"Hey, go easy on him. He's never done anything to you," I said, angrily.

"Never gonna, neither," the soldier said, leering back at me. "Little elf-boy got splattered."

"Why is it that you bad guys are all the same?" Ada's voice echoed within the chamber as a quartet of flechette darts buried themselves in the man's chest, the ends sticking out in a line starting at his navel and ending just under his chin. At first, the soldier looked surprised and then he fell over. The remaining three watched in shock and then turned back to where Ada had first disappeared.

A second soldier yelped in surprise as three more flechette darts found their home. A moment later, he too fell over. Jolted into action, the remaining soldiers returned fire, obviously having forgotten the first rule of combat within a crystal grotto. I covered my head with my arms and leaned back into the stone pedestal. The frakking automatic fire made me feel like I'd been set upon by a hornet's nest. Recognizing the error of their ways, the two soldiers turned and ran back down the passageway, not bothering to drag their fallen comrades with them.

"You up, Liam?" Ada called.

"As much as can be expected," I groaned.

Chapter 16

PAYBACK

I must have lapsed into semi-consciousness because the next thing I knew, Ada was crouched next to me, her hand gently cradling my cheek.

"I can't believe you're alive," I said, smiling despite the pain that coursed through my body.

"They won't be gone for long," Ada said. "Let's get you to the ship. Did we crash or something, and why am I naked?"

I couldn't help myself; I glanced down from her face. I was disappointed to discover that she was far from naked and wore the small Scatter cloak I'd wrapped her in. "You're hardly naked," I said, snapping my attention back to her face.

"You're so cheeky," she said, suppressing a grin and pulling me in for a painful hug.

"Oh, frak, my ribs! Careful," I said.

She pulled back, gently releasing me. "My gosh, you really smell. When did you grow that beard? How long was I out?"

"Million questions," I grunted out between painful breaths as she helped me stand. "Not enough time. Hambo needs a med kit."

"Liam. Talk to me," she said, helping me limp toward the camouflaged *Hotspur.* "How did you get so banged up? Did we crash land? Last thing I remember, we entered the suspension chambers because Anino's new engines produced excessive inertia."

I stopped and drank in the sight of her, her beauty astounding in the dancing lights of the grotto. I flicked off a glob of suspension fluid that had dripped onto her cheek. She stared at me, her piercing blue eyes holding me in place. I nodded, knowing there would be no good time to tell her what she needed to know.

"That was twenty years ago, Ada," I said, picking out a chunk of rock debris from her brown hair. "*Hotspur* crash-landed. We all landed in different places on the planet."

"Twenty years?" she asked. "Where are Tabby and Nick and Marny?"

"Help me with Hambo," I said. "We're behind enemy lines. I'll tell you everything."

She nodded gravely. "Just tell me they're alive. Oh, Peter. Please tell me he's okay."

I chuckled despite the situation. "They're all good," I said. "There've been some changes." A sadness washed through me as I thought about the situation with Tabby. My emotions must have made it to my face because Ada placed her hand on my cheek again.

"We'll get through this, Liam," she said. "We always do."

I hobbled to *Hotspur's* starboard side and placed my palm on a security panel. *Hotspur* had rolled a few degrees to port and the airlock was four meters overhead. Ada had solved the problem by extending a built-in ladder. Still, I wasn't sure there was any way I'd make it inside, even with the ladder.

"Can you open the cargo hatch?" I asked, stepping back. "My knee is pretty busted up."

Instead of questioning me any further, she looked down at the torn cloth and the black-and-blue that spread up and down my leg. "Sit here. I'll grab a medical kit."

"No, please," I begged. "Hambo could still be alive. Please help him first." I pointed at Hambo's slumped unmoving form.

"Okay. I'll open the cargo bay and I'll help your friend," she said.

Without Ada's support, I had to use the side of *Hotspur* to help keep me from falling over. Up close, *Hotspur*'s armored skin was as smooth as glass and cool to the touch. The last few months of living in the wilderness suddenly felt like a dream. I had my ship and I'd found Ada. For the first time since awakening on Fraxus, I felt a glimmer of hope.

Hotspur's cargo bay couldn't have opened more awkwardly for me, high on the side where I was standing, the long ramp nicely blocking my path. I grimaced as I pushed my way around to where the ramp was low enough for me to step up. Internal emergency lighting glowed inside the cargo bay as I pulled myself forward.

"Make yourself useful," Ada said, jogging toward me, her body oriented correctly on the cargo bay's sloped deck. She'd taken a moment to pull on a suit-liner, the legs sticking out beneath the short cloak. I appreciated her modesty, but the fact was, the dark liner material was formfitting and not far off from her own caramel-colored skin.

She dropped a pile of items on the deck and ran out to me, helping me traverse the last few meters. My stomach did a weird little flip-flop as we crossed the boundary and artificial gravity oriented me to the ship. Grabbing from her pile, she shoved a medical kit at me and then took off at a run for where Hambo lay.

Surveying the remaining items, I found an armored vac-suit helmet.

Smart girl. She'd realized I'd lost my earwig and would be unable to use the auto-targeting on the heavy-flechette pistol she'd left at my feet. Instinctively, my hand went to my cheek where Chappie had ripped off my earwig. My fingers found a trench of missing skin.

I pulled the helmet on and grabbed the pistol. Instantly, they linked together and provided firing options. I chinned the fastest firing plan I could find and then attempted to link to *Hotspur.* There was no response beyond the public menu that was available to any guest. Frak. Anino had us locked out. I chinned through more menus, landing on my old personal security routines. Even though I couldn't do much with *Hotspur,* I could use her myriad cameras to warn us if we had unexpected visitors.

With security taken care of, I turned to the medical kit Ada had left behind. Either due to exhaustion, stress, adrenaline or just plain excitement, my fingers seemed incapable of doing anything more than fumble as I pawed through the kit's contents. Finally, I found the diagnostic scanner and ran it across my knee. The verbiage displayed on my HUD didn't exactly say *messed up*, but I'm pretty sure that was what the instructions implied.

There's just about no way to describe how good it feels when a med-patch first hits a painful wound. I'd make a comparison to sex, but that's too banal. I would put the feeling somewhere between the first kiss of a new romance and the taste of ice-cold beer after a long day of hard work. I closed my eyes to the blessed relief of the pain-killing, tissue-repairing, infection-removing nanites. A few seconds later, a chime sounded, prompting me to add two more patches above and below the first one.

"You little buggers haven't seen anything yet," I said, knowing the nanites had no capacity to hear me nor could they form a response. In that moment, however, I felt pretty warm and fuzzy toward them. I breathed a satisfied sigh and looked up, just in time to see Ada struggling to walk across the crystal-covered grotto floor, carrying Hambo's body.

Knowing better, I struggled to my feet. The small man had put himself in extreme danger for someone he barely knew. "How is he?" I asked, my heart in my throat. I'd lost more than a few friends in combat and the fact was, it never got easier.

"He's bad, Liam," Ada said. "Nanites are having trouble with his physiology."

"There's a medical tank forward of the armory," I said. "The AI should be better equipped to make an assessment."

"We're locked out of *Hotspur's* command menus, Liam," she said, stepping up into the cargo bay. "I don't know if we can get the tank started up. Why would Anino lock us out?"

"I don't know," I said, leading her forward to the aft hatch that led to the living quarters.

Immediately after the hatch, to the port side, was the armory, a two-and-a-half-meter wide by four-meter deep room. Forward of that was a small medical bay that was just a little wider, but only big enough to hold a full submersion medical tank on the forward wall and a single stainless-steel table on the aft.

Entering the room, Ada placed Hambo onto the horizontally-oriented med-tank and pressed her palm to the security panel. "Good," she said, breathing a sigh of relief as the tank's glass cover rotated into place. Small mechanical arms secured Hambo and fixed a breathing apparatus to his nose and mouth.

"Good?" I asked, sliding up onto the table and cutting the jerkin off my torso, using a special tool designed specifically for that purpose.

"*Hotspur* is running an alien bio diagnostic," she said. "Aside from looking like something from *The Hobbit*, your friend isn't really all that much different from us physiologically. Apparently, just enough to confuse the nanites."

My AI recognized that I hadn't followed the Hobbit reference and showed me a quick synopsis of an ancient story that I think Mom had tried to get me to read. I quickly pushed away thoughts of her as the tank, including a fully-submerged Hambo, rotated to a vertical position, giving us more room in the cramped quarters.

Ada turned back to me and looked at my bare chest. "What in the blue forests of Marfon happened to you, Liam Hoffen?" she asked. "You're all muscly, your skin is black and blue, and you look like a mountain man."

That was Ada. If you ever wanted to know what she was thinking, you only needed to wait a moment and she'd tell you.

"Longish story," I said, momentarily distracted by the fact that we'd left the cargo bay open. I chinned back to a menu and successfully caused the door to start closing.

"Does this hurt?" she asked, poking at the deep purple bruising on my ribs.

"Frak, Ada, yes!" I said.

"Don't be such a baby. Lie down," she ordered, helping me back onto the cold steel table and removing my helmet.

"I need that," I complained. "I've got a security program running."

"Me too and don't be difficult." She ran a medical scanner across my torso. "Now get to talking."

I wasn't sure where to start, so I just jumped in at the beginning. "Tabby, Marny, Nick and Little Pete were awakened twenty years ago when we landed. Fraxus is the name of the planet, by the way," I said. "They searched for us, but it wasn't until a few months ago that they found me. Unlike you, my suspension chamber was failing and I was almost dead."

"You look pretty good right now," she said, more clinically than I'd have liked. "Aside from the fact that you smell really bad."

"Yeah, well, I was in prison for a while and my captors weren't big on hygiene," I said.

"Prison? You pissed off the locals already?" she asked.

"Frakking Belirand," I said.

"Nooo." Ada's tone was disbelieving, which was completely understandable.

"Yes."

"And they found you?" she asked. "After twenty years? That's crazy."

"The indigenous people are called Scatters," I said. "They're friendly enough, but it looks like they're under Belirand's thumb."

"Wait. You said Nick and Marny have been up for twenty years. Are they old now? What about Peter?"

Relief flooded my chest as Ada applied wide med-patches to the skin over my ribs. "Whew. That feels amazing," I said. "Yeah. Sort of old, I guess. Marny has some gray hair and she's lost all her muscle. Well, that's not exactly true. She is still strong, but without workouts and the right diet, she's not nearly as big."

"That's hard to picture," Ada said.

"Long light brown hair with gray streaks," I said, trying to help complete the picture. "Kind of talks like a Zen monk."

"Oh, she always did that," Ada said. "It just sounded different because she was so intimidating physically."

I laughed and was pleased to discover that it only hurt a little. "Peter's all grown up. You want to talk about a mountain of a man. That's him. No more boy."

"You're not talking about Tabby. Is she okay?" Ada asked, her face very concerned.

"Yeah, she is," I said, my voice taking on a neutral tone. I didn't intend to give away any of my feelings, but there was no getting around Ada.

"Spill it, Hoffen. What's going on with Tabby?" she growled, lifting my right arm, her scanner locating the break that Nothando had healed with his rocks.

"You gotta know, none of it is her fault," I said.

"Liam." Ada's voice held a warning. She wasn't going to be satisfied without the full story.

"She and Peter hooked up a year ago or so," I said. "They believed I was dead and that they were never getting out of here. She lost a baby before it was born. When they found me, she got pretty messed up about it. She gave me the ring back."

"Oh, Liam," Ada's face filled with pity and she instinctively wrapped her arms around me. "I'm sorry. She must be hurting so bad."

"We had words," I said. "I didn't handle it very well."

"You left it that way?" Ada asked, her eyebrows almost disappearing into her scalp.

"No. She's still trying to figure out what she wants to do," I said.

"What do you want, Liam?" Ada asked.

"I want to kick Anino's ass," I said. "We can't sit here much longer. People are depending on us back in the city."

"That's not really an answer, you know," Ada said.

"It's the best I have right now," I said. "Geez, it's so good to see you, Ada."

"It's weird," she said. "It feels like yesterday when we got into the tanks."

"I know. I felt the same way. Only for me, somehow, I'd turned into a stick," I said.

"Well, you're not a stick now," she said. "Mountain living is good for you."

"It's a hard living," I said. "Marny, Nick and Tabby have been through some real crap to survive."

"Let me guess. Nick has a workshop set up?"

"Barn. Yes. They make their own clothing and houses. He even forged an iron knife," I said. "I wish we could hang out, but I need to go back to the city. There's a woman who risked her life for me and might still be alive. I've got to help her."

"What do you need me to do?" Ada asked.

"Put together a med kit programmed for Scatter biology," I said. "Bongiwe, that's the woman, took an energy blaster to her arm. Lost a lot of blood. I'm afraid she might have died."

I really wanted to look for Thabini, but had no way of locating the area where he'd fallen from his bird. Even if he had survived, there was no doubt in my mind that Belirand would have scooped him up. Nonetheless, once I got to Bongiwe, we'd scour the forest for him on the off-chance he was alive and had evaded our common enemy.

"Copy that," Ada answered. "I'll see if I can get us back into *Hotspur's* systems."

"You might think about taking a shower, too," I quipped as I exited the medical bay. "You've got suspension goo in your hair and I'm not the only one who's got a smell going."

My first stop wasn't the armory, but rather the galley. I hadn't eaten in forever and it had been almost as long since I'd had anything to drink. Oddly, however, I needed desperately to use a bathroom.

Standing inside *Hotspur's* head felt weird. For the last several months, I'd either used a bucket, outhouse or just done my business in the woods. Seeing a personal groomer next to the sink, I couldn't help but pick it up. Bongiwe needed my help, but it would only take a minute or two to cut back the massive hair growth that had been driving me nuts. While I wouldn't feel right about take the time for a full shower, I did grab hygiene wipes for a quick once-over, removing long built-up layers of grime. It was an amazing feeling to be back to a semi-civilized state. Having taken a moment to clean up, my suit-liner and vac-suit would easily take care of the rest.

"Naked, coming through," I said, dropping my ruined clothing into the recycler and grabbing a water pouch from the nearby galley.

"You clean up nice," Ada said, leaning out of the medical bay and slapping me on the ass as I passed.

"Pervert," I called over my shoulder, chuckling and turning into the armory, where I pulled on a fresh suit-liner, relishing the snug fit.

I took a long drag from the water pouch and considered my next move. Ideally, I'd have my grav-suit, but that'd been taken from me. It was something I'd need to deal with, but wasn't a today issue. I could either choose a normal vac-suit or the much bulkier armored suit. Then it occurred to me that Tabby, Marny and Ada's grav-suits were all up on the second deck.

"Where are you going?" Ada asked as I ran past her, turning to starboard as I passed the engineering bay.

"Grav-suit," I called back. "Mine was taken. Borrowing Tabby's."

I stepped into the zero-grav field that joined the lower deck to the upper. I'd worried that Anino's lockout might prevent me from using it, but was grateful to discover the field was still there and I landed softly on the top deck.

We hadn't spent any time in our quarters beyond just dropping off our luggage before we'd left. It felt weird to find our duffels just where we'd left them twenty years ago. The moment I saw Tabby's duffel next to mine, I came to a decision. I would not go down without a fight. I'd loved Tabby from the moment we met in pre-school. It was a different kind of love, but that love had grown into a high-school crush and finally into the relationship of our lives. I would not allow time to steal that from us anymore than I would allow my bruised ego to push her away.

I smiled as I pulled on the grav-suit that still smelled faintly of her. I checked for power and was glad to find the display indicated one hundred percent. While the grav-suit didn't have quite the armor of the military-grade armored suits, it would more than repel either the charged-particle rounds or the blaster-energy rounds Belirand soldiers had so fondly sent my way.

"I'll drop a couple of comm repeaters along the way," I said, joining Ada in the medical bay. "You might get company since they know we were in here. I think *Hotspur* is deep enough inside this cave system that Belirand won't be able to bring in a weapon big enough to cause you much trouble."

"Go, Liam," Ada said, handing me a pouch that contained medical supplies. "Why are you smiling?"

"Grav-suit smells like Tabby," I said.

"You're such a goof," she said with a grin. "Don't worry, I know how important this old girl is to us. I'll keep her safe."

On the way past, I stopped back in the armory and took a heavy blaster rifle, a heavy flechette pistol, a strip of grenade balls and my favorite: FBD or flash-bang-disc. While neither my knee nor ribs were back to normal, I felt better than I could remember feeling in months.

Exiting the ship, I considered my options. No doubt Belirand would be guarding the cave entrance. Inside, the crystals turned energy bolts against the wielder. The same would not be true once I got outside. Looking around at all the light filling the grotto, I got an idea. I moved across the room and slid through the beautiful crystal structures, discovering a narrow route to the surface.

"I'm outside, Ada," I said, dropping my first comm repeater, a simple device about the size of a fly that would relay our communications.

"Do we still have company?" she asked.

"I came out a different way. Checking." I used the grav-suit to lower myself into the surrounding trees. I wasn't surprised to see the decrepit Belirand cutter just outside the cave entrance. Four soldiers had constructed a barricade and taken up defensive positions facing the opening. The ship's one blaster was also pointing in that direction. I was just starting to turn toward the Thandeka, when Tabby's suit connected unexpectedly with my broken grav-suit. Interestingly enough, it was on the ship in front of me. A data-stream transmitted and I discovered that only one soldier remained aboard. To make things even more interesting, that soldier was the one who'd stolen my engagement rings.

"Yeah, their ship is here, and it's guarded. But you know what? This shite's getting old."

"Liam?"

"Yeah?" I asked, ducking back into the cover of the tree tops while peeling a grenade marble from where it was stuck to my belt.

"Don't do anything heroic, okay?" she said. "There are a lot of people relying on you."

"That's right. Nothing heroic," I said. "This is strictly payback."

Chapter 17

MOSTLY HARMLESS

I took my eyes off the ship for a moment as I dialed back the lethality of the grenade marbles. This was a mistake. Fortunately, I caught the movement of the ship's single turret as it swung and fired. Instinctively, I dove in the direction of the ship as a shot ripped the tops of the nearby trees off and I was suddenly awash in the boiling atmosphere left behind in its wake. While the top-of-the-line grav-suit I wore was no match for even a glancing blow from the smallest ship's blaster, the material deflected the momentary wave of gasses that followed the round.

I grinned, emerging from the flames. I was finally in my element. No more slogging around in sodden boots on snowy mountain slopes. The suit's gravity tech propelled me through the air as if I were in zero-g and I pressed forward to the ship that lay only sixty meters from my position. I could envision the gunner trying to reorient his aim. Even with aid of an AI, a person can only move the mass of a heavy weapon like that so fast. The fact that I hadn't been blasted into paste told me no AI was involved. I liked my chances.

I sailed to the ship, switching angles periodically, and was rewarded by a second shot that missed me by dozens of meters. It's hard to describe just how quickly things occur in this kind of combat situation. The entire encounter had only taken a couple of seconds and caught the three barricaded ground crew completely off guard. Unfortunately, being fired upon had startled me into dropping the grenade balls.

The soldiers outside the ship had been expecting us to exit the cave and their barricade was set up with that in mind. I came at them from an oblique angle and used the piston arm of the ship's ramp as a partial visual block. Still, I was only blocked by the piston arm of the ramp from which they'd exited the ship. Two of the soldiers were in a decent position to fire on me when I finally overran them. I still felt I had the advantage. Unless someone repeatedly practiced firing at fast-moving targets, hitting one was more a matter of luck. It is one of the unusual times when firing more rounds is helpful, if only marginally.

While Anino's grav-suit was no match for ship fire, the material was designed to deflect modern blaster weapons like I was carrying. More important, however, is that the grav-suit dissipates as much of the energy received as possible and spreads out the remainder. Fortunately for me, the soldiers were carrying weapons that appeared to have been designed a couple hundred years in the past. It's not as if the three shots that made contact didn't hurt. To the contrary, each shot was quite painful. The best description I could come up with was that it felt like being hit on bare skin by an angry meter-wide jellyfish whose myriad tentacles were filled with electric charge, then having hot sauce splashed into the welts they left behind. Not a happy moment to be sure. The only good news was that the pain didn't usually last for more than two or three seconds.

Just to review. Up to this point, I'd been treated rather poorly by this group in general. I'd been imprisoned, beaten, chased and made to endure sitting impotently in my cell while a woman was raped outside my cell. Charity was far from my mind, even before I was pelted by their stupid weapons. Now, I was flat out angry. Just why I didn't drop a couple of fully-charged grenade balls on them is something I'm not completely sure of. I think I was tired of the killing, but I also think I was looking to cause pain. And I saw so many choices.

I lowered my armored head and hit the first soldier straight in the chest. I was moving fast and by the time he realized my intent, there was nothing he could do. My suit stiffened upon contact and I might have grinned as I realized he'd been hurled up into the steel pole that connected the end of the ship's ramp to its belly. All my training with Marny kicked in and I rolled on the ground, twisting so I came back up facing two very surprised soldiers.

Fear can often be confused with anger on a man's face. I'd always been good at reading people and the youngest soldier, who I estimated to be in his late teens, was terrified. That assessment was the only thing that kept me from mowing him down right then and there with my blaster rifle, even though he'd managed to land a very painful shot at waist level. That's right, hot sauce jelly fish to the midsection was about as bad as it gets.

Instead, I slapped my chest and set off the FBD. It was Marny who'd first introduced me to the technology. The disk was named after the original ordnance from ages ago called a flash bang grenade, a one-time use device that made a big bang and bright flash. FBDs were a relatively simple technology you could put on an armored suit. When activated, the disc emitted an intensely bright strobe light and periodically caused an explosive sound well past anything human ears can deal with.

Using an FBD is bad news if not worn in conjunction with an AI that coordinates polarization of the suit's faceplate with the flashes and a counter soundwave to blunt the banging sounds. I'd used the FBDs a few times and when they're active it seems like everything is moving in quick jerks and spurts accentuated by a weird whooshing sound which turns out to the be the tail-end of the cancelled explosive sound.

The effect on the remaining two soldiers was almost instantaneous as first the light blinded them and then they were deafened by the explosion. Seeing their lack of mobility, I slapped my blaster rifle onto my back and unstrapped my heavy flechette. People who are being attacked get squirrely, as evidenced by the youngest firing wildly as he spun in pain. I needed to subdue them before they could recover. Recognizing my dilemma, the AI offered a prompt for sedative-tipped darts. I happily chinned agreement and triple shot each of the three men, starting with the wild shooter.

The sedatives would keep my welcoming committee down for at least an hour, allowing me to turn my attention to the remaining soldier in the ship. I wondered just what he had planned for me. The fight had moved fast, but he'd no doubt been watching the events unfold. Belirand had found the Scatter population to be pushovers and as a result, their soldiers were sloppy, not believing anyone would put up a real fight. These guys had started the day believing they were the biggest and baddest on the block. I was guessing, right now, they'd all like to vote for a mulligan.

Linking with my captured grav-suit, I discovered two people aboard, one of whom was a Scatter woman cowering against the bridge's starboard bulkhead. I didn't think she'd cause me much trouble. Of no surprise to me, the soldier who remained was flipping switches and trying to start up the ship's old engines.

"Too late, dumbass," I said, slapping off my FBD and redirecting speech through the stolen vac-suit that lay discarded on a filthy bench opposite the terrified Scatter woman. It would have been easier for me to enter the ship with the FBD still going, but I had some idea about how the woman had been treated to this point and wasn't adding any other abuses to that tally if I could avoid it.

The man spun around, eyes passing over my suit, not picking up on what I'd done. "Who's there?" he asked, pushing the flight sticks forward and lifting off.

"You should have closed the hatch when you heard the shots," I taunted.

A blaster bolt from his pistol ricocheted off the bulkhead above my suit as he fired blindly, thinking I was somehow hidden in plain sight. "Get off my ship! You're so dead. We own this planet," he jabbered, looking for some way to influence the outcome.

I slipped down the narrow passageway and was stopped by a locked hatch. I nodded in approval; at least he'd thought that far ahead.

"Switch to the non-public Scatter language," I directed my AI. "To the Scatter woman: please move away from the back of the bridge. The door will explode inward in a couple of seconds."

I wasn't sure she would understand or even if my AI had the ability to fully translate. The basic concept must have made it through, because she looked back at the hatch, scurried forward and affixed herself to the side of the ship.

I hadn't brought breaching charges and wasn't even sure if we had any aboard *Hotspur.* This hatch, however, was corroded and the locking mechanism was simple. A central wheel was mounted on each side of the door attached to two long bars. When twisted, the bars extended, one into the ceiling and the other into the floor, locking the door in place. Without the view from my captured grav-suit, I wouldn't have known where to place the grenade marbles, although it might not have mattered either way, given the door's condition.

After placing the grenades on a ten second timer, I moved back down the hallway and around a corner. The grav-suit was more than capable of taking all but an adjacent explosion from a grenade marble, but I was tired of the jellyfish feeling already. What I didn't foresee was the random event that occurred next. In a million years, a person couldn't count on a breached door sending a silver-bullet piece of shrapnel into the room and perfectly taking out the enemy inside. When that enemy is sailing the ship you happen to be on, of course that's exactly what's going to happen.

"Aww, frak," I complained as the ship lurched forward, listing to the side. Somehow the dumbass had effectively used the time I'd given him and gained several hundred meters in elevation. We were losing that at a ridiculous velocity. Even worse, as I ran forward through the debris, my AI showed me that one of the flight sticks had broken off in the guy's hand.

I calculated that we had precious few seconds before we'd make hard contact with the ground. I could easily escape by myself, but there was no way I was leaving the now howling Scatter woman behind. I also didn't believe she'd put up with me wrestling her down the hallway to jump off the ship.

"Liam?" Ada called over comms, sensing my hesitation. "Get off that ship!"

"I can't leave her," I said.

"Your grav-suit won't protect you in that crash," she said. "Get off!"

Making up my mind, I raced forward and toppled the dead pilot from his chair. My AI highlighted the controls, showing their functions. The ship was old but human-designed, and flight controls largely hadn't changed. If I could land at all, it wasn't going to be pretty. The stick the pilot had broken off had a nub left behind. With my left hand, I grabbed at the tiny nub that now served as a stick and throttled back and trimmed with my right to return the ship to level. It was tricky, but I managed to drop enough velocity, turn us around and aim at a section of young trees as I successfully drove us back to ground.

"Don't you ever do that again, Liam Hoffen!" Ada chided angrily, her face popping onto my HUD.

"How's Hambo doing?" I asked, changing subjects.

"He'll live," she answered. "Scatter biology is close enough that the nanites aren't having much trouble now. You need to come back, though. Apparently, your med-patches are wearing off. You had more damage to your body than you mentioned."

"No need," I said. "I'm feeling better than I have for months. Look, stay with Hambo and see if you can get *Hotspur* going."

"Why do I feel like you're playing fast and loose?" she asked.

"The tech we're up against is old," I said. "I need to push the advantage."

"Don't get cocky," she said, pursing her lips in a familiar way which brought a smile to my face. My relationship with Ada was complex. I suspected that if I'd never met Tabby, I'd have chased Ada to the ends of the universe. As it was, I loved having her as my friend and I appreciated her concern.

"See what you can do to fend off a larger ship," I said. "They've got an armored sloop in system and it will no doubt be looking for us."

"Can do, but *Hotspur* isn't going anywhere," Ada said. "Having a mountain wrapped around us is pretty good armor."

I turned to the shivering Scatter woman still pressed against the bulkhead. "We're on the ground. Are you hurt?"

I reached over and rested a hand on her shoulder. I still hadn't had a look at her face, but dirty-blonde locks of hair poked out from beneath her hood. When my hand made contact, the woman jerked away and skittered forward, whimpering. I wanted to be gentle, but every minute I delayed, Bongiwe was closer to death – if she wasn't already there.

"I know you don't trust me," I said, moving forward and placing a firm hand on her shoulder to make her turn around. My heart sank as I took in the abrasions, bruises and filth on her face. There was no telling how old the woman was. I softened my voice. "I'm sorry Belirand soldiers hurt you. We must get off this ship, they'll come looking for it. I need to know if you were hurt by the explosion."

My AI highlighted blood on the floor and traced a line up, disappearing behind the woman. She trembled uncontrollably, incapable of responding. To her, I might as well have been a Belirand soldier. My actions were violent, and I wouldn't gain her trust any time soon. I stood, pulling her up off the floor. I felt icky as she complied with my command to turn so I could see her back. Indeed, she'd taken damage from the door breach. I pulled out my medical scanner and ran it quickly down her back. The AI confirmed that she needed a large patch on her back and suggested a small patch on a crushed cheek bone.

"You need to leave this alone," I said sternly, as I showed her the med-patch. There was no way I was going to try removing her clothing, so I ripped open the thin material of her cloak – which was pretty much in tatters anyway – just enough to apply the patch to her bare back. She recoiled, but otherwise didn't object. I pulled her around to inspect her face. She resisted looking at me and I didn't push her beyond what I needed to gain access to her cheek. "This medicine will feel like Nothando's healing stones. Please don't take them off. Now, I need you to get off the ship. I will come out in a few minutes and take you back to Thandeka if you want."

For the first time, the woman dared a quick look at my face and then at the broken aft bridge hatch. "That's right. Go ahead. I'm not going to hurt you or stop you. I'm sorry for how you've been treated."

One thing Scatters have in common was preternatural speed. Heedless of her injuries, she turned and raced from the bridge so fast that I almost questioned my eyes. What had kept her on the ship before, I couldn't imagine.

I sat back in front of the controls. This ship was a simple machine with manual and automated controls. I spent a few moments looking for a centralized database. Either the protocols were so different that I couldn't connect to them or the vessel simply lacked any type of smart fabric to record. With the broken stick, the old beast would fly best if I programmed the automatic controls. I would have preferred to commandeer her, but I knew better. Even now, the ship showed radar contact with Chappie's heavily armored sloop only fifteen kilometers away. Why the sloop hadn't gotten involved yet was beyond me. I could only imagine that because Chappie saw the planet's inhabitants as mostly harmless, he and his crew hadn't paid any attention. I grinned wryly to myself as the thought floated through my head. I'd just have to see what I could do to change his mind.

I programmed the ship to take a northerly course, with instructions to set down once it was two hundred kilometers off the northern shore of the ocean that bordered the city of Thandeka. There was some possibility that Chappie would recover the ship if he acted quickly enough, but I hoped he'd neglect it like he had so far.

My AI recognized the dead pilot's face and replayed the video snippet of when he'd taken the engagement rings. I rolled him over and searched his pockets. Sure enough, I found the rings I thought were lost forever. My heart soared and I placed them both on my fingers, with Tabby's on my right hand. I hadn't intended for the pilot to die, but I wouldn't mourn a man whose sins had certainly found him out. He'd earned his final voyage out to sea.

On the way to the hatch, I leaned over and scooped up my old grav-suit. I'd intended to fly directly back to Thandeka to help Bongiwe, but circumstances dictated a different course. Once free of the ship, I looked for the Scatter woman who'd run off. She was long gone, which was probably for the best. I wasn't exactly the type of person she needed right now if she was to start healing her psychological wounds. I hoped she had somewhere to go and hide, but I had no idea how she'd entered the company of the Belirand soldiers in the first place, although I couldn't imagine it was willingly.

"Hey, I'm coming back," I said, flitting back to where the three soldiers still lay on the ground unconscious. I scooped up their weapons, which I ended up rolling in the grav-suit. As each had a rifle and a pistol, the six guns quickly became unwieldy. "Open the loading bay, would you?"

"Sure, what's up?" Ada asked.

"I recovered my grav-suit," I said. "And it's given me an idea."

"Is it one of your crazy ideas?" Ada asked. "The ramp is lowering."

I pulled a small finger-sized tube from my waist. Upon contact with the palm of my hand it expanded, finger grooves forming for a good grip. I flicked my wrist and a nano-thin wire extended ten centimeters from the end and snapped tight. The wire was impossible to see, although the glow of energy that surrounded it wasn't. The nano-blade would cut through virtually anything as long as the object being struck wasn't in direct physical contact with the person wielding the blade. Even though the weapon was designed for close-in combat, I had a habit of finding atypical uses for it.

Carefully, I placed my hand on the youngest soldier's back and worked the nano-blade so I cut through the belt and waist of his pants and then down each leg. By keeping my hand on his body, I was able to run the end of the blade between cloth and skin, cutting the material without injury to the soldier. It was a quick way to remove someone's clothing. I added each of the pieces to a growing pile atop the crate barricade. I set a grenade marble to a slow, hot burn and dropped it on top of the clothing. At a minimum, they'd need to leave the area to find something to wear before looking for me. Hopefully, they'd be so embarrassed they wouldn't admit what had happened or bring anyone back here to search the cave. My plan probably wouldn't work, but I wasn't about to take them as prisoners nor would I kill them in cold blood.

"What's all this?" Ada asked as I deposited the soldier's weapons into *Hotspur's* hold and brushed past her on my way to a suit cleaner that would restore function to my grav suit. She caught up with me just as

I stripped out of Tabby's grav suit and stuffed it into a pack I'd grabbed from the armory.

"All part of the plan," I said and couldn't resist pulling her in for one more hug.

"You should know, *Hotspur* still isn't responding to my commands," she said when we broke apart, not questioning why I needed the hug. "Anino really has us locked out."

"Keep trying," I said, taking my freshly-cleaned and repaired grav-suit from the cleaner. Where Tabby's suit fit okay, mine fit like a glove and I quickly transferred the weapons.

"Were you wearing those rings earlier?" Ada asked, noticing the engagement rings. I thought we'd talked about it. She'd either forgotten or was being sneaky in getting more information from me.

"Nope, I recognized the guy who stole 'em," I said.

"Seems like one of those rings needs to be returned," Ada said, tilting her head to the side. "Don't be wishy washy about it. Behind all that flak she throws up, she's scared. She needs to know you're all in."

I smiled. "Not sure why it took talking to you for me to figure that out."

"Not hard to figure out at all." Ada slapped me playfully on the butt as I jumped into the anti-gravity column that shot me up to the bridge deck. "Where are you going?" she called after me.

After gathering Marny and Nick's grav-suits, I jumped back to the lower deck where Ada watched me expectantly.

"I started something by taking on those Belirand thugs," I said. "Time to knock the rust off some old friends."

Chapter 18

TRUST IS EARNED

As I flew from the cave, I carefully lifted above the tops of the tall pine trees that covered the mountainside. Searching the sky, I was unable to find any Belirand ships in the vicinity. Apparently, Chappie had either found Prince Thabini or decided to chase down the cutter I'd sent on a one-way trip to the sea. It was possible he'd just given up, but I didn't think that was likely, given my read of the man.

The tree cover gave me some small protection as I didn't want to repeat being shot at by a ship. It was odd and maybe a little disconcerting to not be the focus of my enemy. Chappie had given me a small amount of attention but poured on the resources to hunt down and find Prince Thabini. Chappie was tipping his hand. He feared Prince Thabini so much so that he was willing to ignore me. I grinned to myself. I was pretty sure I could change his opinion on that matter.

I was always surprised at how quickly time moves when dealing with stressful events. The Fraxus sun was showing midday, which meant Bongiwe had been suffering for hours. I pushed the guilt I felt at her sacrifice into that dark hole in my being I saved for such things. It was a neat little box that would open itself, ambushing me at the most inopportune time to swallow me in a sea of self-recrimination.

No, right now, I couldn't afford to think about anything beyond the mission and how I would, in broad daylight, make it back to the Scatter resistance's hidden chambers. My grav-suit had data-streams from my first venture into the subterranean passages of Thandeka with Bongiwe. However, I hadn't been wearing the suit the second time and had no idea where she now rested. I'd expected Thabini to lead me back, but now I needed to figure out some other method to find my way.

Approaching Thandeka, I noticed two cutter class ships circling the city in a slow patrol. Periodically, one or the other would loose a blaster bolt, impacting something well beyond my vision. Chappie was sending a message to the small city. *We're pissed and we're taking it out on you.* One more treasure to stuff in that dark box.

Tactically, keeping control of a large population with a small force is difficult. Chappie was using fear and grand shows of strength to achieve his objective. In truth, what little control he had of the small city was given to him by the Scatters. It was obvious the people of the city would only help Belirand when they were directly confronted. The Scatters had hidden my presence once and I was counting on them to do so again.

Upon reaching the city's outskirts, I dropped low enough so I just cleared the river's surface. I was counting on Belirand not having sufficient scanning technology to pick up a human target so close to water. Entering the city, the river's banks had been improved. Fired clay brick and large cut stones kept the waterways defined, giving me even more cover.

Belirand's attack on Thandeka kept most of the inhabitants indoors and I grew concerned that as stealthy as I was being, my movement would be detectable. With some hesitation, I eventually dropped into and submerged beneath the green, brackish waters of the canal.

The going was slow, but uneventful aside from a few bumps from larger fish than you might expect next to a city. Those experiences were placed in an entirely different box, one that liked to pop open in sweat-laden nightmares.

Finally, having unwound the path Bongiwe and I had first taken through the tunnels, I ended up in the large subterranean cavern where I'd met Thabini. My grav-suit was more than capable of illuminating the darkened interior and I recognized the crystals and the bench against the wall. My hopes had been for nothing. The cavern was completely devoid of people, Scatter or otherwise.

I was about to give up when my suit caught the smallest movement. I spun, trying to lock in on the shape detected by the sensors, but saw nothing. Whoever had been there disappeared as quickly as they'd appeared. I lifted from the cavern floor to cover the sound of my movements and went over to inspect the area, discovering a small opening in the cavern wall that would have been otherwise difficult to locate.

"Please, I'm lost," I whispered harshly. "I need to find Nothando and Bongiwe. I have medicine." My AI prompted, asking if I wanted to translate to Scatter tongue. I quickly acknowledged the request and slid into the passageway.

"I can help Bongiwe," I whispered again, turning down the winding, rocky passageway.

"There is no help for her," a woman's voice answered quietly.

"If she draws breath, it might not be too late," I said. "I am Liam Hoffen. I went with Thabini to get medical supplies."

"I know who you are." The woman stepped into view as I pulled around a bend in the tight passageway. I stopped short to avoid bowling her over. "Thabini was captured by Bell-e-runde," she said. "Bongiwe has joined our family in the afterlife. Our prince was wrong to trust you. You have brought ruin to our people."

"Please take me to her," I said. "It may not be too late." It wasn't lost on me that she referred to Bongiwe as her family.

"Follow and remain quiet," she said, turning quickly and moving through the passageway. Without the grav-suit, I would have had difficulty keeping up, as the ground was uneven and she was fast. Thankfully, the technology was more than enough of an equalizer.

After a few minutes, I recognized features along the route. When we walked down the long ramp that I believed went beneath the canal, I knew we were back at the great hall where Bongiwe had been taken.

I pulled my helmet back and was surprised when the guards who stood on either side of the thick wooden door recognized me. Of course, the cautious looks could have been induced by fear. Both seemed very unwilling to cross the angry little elf who accompanied me.

Bongiwe's body lay on a stone pedestal. She'd been wrapped in a white linen cloth, her arms pulled tightly to her side. Seeing my approach, Nothando intercepted me.

"How long?" I asked, pulling my medical scanner out and slipping around him so I could run it across Bongiwe's body. I'd seen plenty of death and knew the ashen-gray face held no life well before my scanner confirmed it.

"She passed a short time after you left," he said, gently. "There was nothing you could have done to save her."

Tears welled up in my eyes. The Scatters were a beautiful people, full of grace and dignity, and in Bongiwe's case, courage and honor. She'd given her life in the belief that I was more important than she was. I hated that. I bent over and hugged her impossibly-small frame, allowing guilt to fill me.

"Leave her. You have no right to touch my sister." The small Scatter woman who'd led me here spoke with venom.

"Joliwe, please," Nothando said, trying to stop her as she pulled at me.

I stood from Bongiwe's body as Joliwe grabbed my arm. I considered her, wiping tears from my eyes. "No, Nothando, she is right. Bongiwe's death is my fault. She was trying to save me when she was shot by Belirand."

"Our prince was taken from us by Bell-e-runde this day, too," she said. "Your clumsy, self-centered willfulness has done more damage to our people than Bell-e-runde could possibly do in decades. Do you know that they float over our city and shoot at the innocent? Did you know that they have called for us to turn you over to them before they will stop?"

"I have no defense," I said, looking sadly at the woman. Like Bongiwe, she had light blonde hair, almost to the point of being white. Her skin was pale and her eyes glowed a bright green. If anything, she was a little taller than her sister. Right now, her soft face was covered in a mask of anger.

"They will kill Prince Thabini in three days if you are not found and turned over to Bell-e-runde," she said. "You must turn yourself in."

I nodded in agreement. I'd tell Ada what happened and she could meet back with Marny, Nick and Tabby. I doubted they would be able to return in time to rescue me. The Scatters needed Prince Thabini more than they needed me.

"No, Joliwe," Nothando said. "Prince Thabini will not be spared, even if Liam Hoffen is returned. We have brought this on ourselves. You dishonor Bongiwe's sacrifice by blaming Liam Hoffen. Our people are nothing better than slaves to Bell-e-runde. Thabini gave himself just as did Bongiwe. It is not to you to make these decisions."

"It is to you, then?" she asked, her eyes flaring angrily.

We'd drawn a small crowd of Scatters around us as we'd been talking. I could feel their agreement with the sentiments she expressed.

"I can stop Chappie," I said quietly. "If I can't, I'll die trying. I'll give myself to Bell-e-runde if that's what you decide. But if you let me go, I'll take the fight to Belirand."

"You cannot be trusted," Joliwe spat. "You would say anything to save yourself."

I grabbed the handle of my heavy flechette pistol, eliciting a gasp from the assembled crowd. I even heard the unsheathing of a crystal sword or two. The sound reminded me of home. I flipped the weapon around in my hand and pushed it at Joliwe.

"It's a simple weapon," I said. "Aim it at my head and pull the trigger. You can drag my body up and give it over to Belirand."

Nothando reached for the weapon, but Joliwe was quicker and snatched it from my fingers.

"Is this a trick?" Joliwe asked, grasping the pistol, her thin fingers wrapping around the butt and onto the trigger. I winced, hoping she wouldn't shoot me by accident.

"If you give me over, Belirand will kill me, but they'll do worse before they're done," I said. "I'd rather die by your hand than suffer Chappie."

She nodded and then shook her head. "Humans are vile creatures," she said. "They bring evil and death wherever they go."

"Not all of us do," I said. "You know of my friends in the mountains. They are the greatest of warriors, yet they live peacefully with Scatters."

Her face softened. "If I believed killing you would bring back Bongiwe or Thabini, I would not hesitate to do so. You say that the mountain humans are warriors?"

I smiled just considering the question. "No. I said they are the *greatest* of warriors – at least the women are. My fiancée has never been bested in combat and has more than once offered her own life for the greater good of many."

She pushed the gun toward me and in the process it fired. A hot lance of pain creased my cheek as she jumped back, startled. "No!" she exclaimed.

"Ahh, frak," I said as sedatives entered my blood stream. The medicine was quick acting and all I could think was that I was grateful the dart hadn't done me in entirely.

"LIAM HOFFEN, DO YOU LIVE?" Cool hands held my head and for a moment I thought I was looking at Bongiwe. As my eyes focused, I realized instead, it was Joliwe. Now that she wasn't hopping mad, she looked almost identical to her sister.

"You shot me," I said, not able to come up with anything better to say. With her help, I struggled to sit up.

"I did not intend this," she answered. "I thought I had killed you."

"It was a nice try, that's for sure," I said, attempting levity that she clearly didn't understand.

"I would never," she said, her voice rising defensively. "Were you telling the truth? Can you stop Chappie?"

"We've stopped Belirand once before," I said. "We can do it again, but only if the Scatter people are with us. If we attempt to do so alone, we can't possibly win."

"There are hundreds who would stand with Prince Thabini against Bell-e-runde," she said. "Without him, we are lost."

"That makes things simple," I said.

"Simple? Are you sure you understand what this word means?" she asked.

"Yes. If we want to win, we need to rescue the prince," I said. "We're halfway to a decent plan already."

Joliwe shook her head and a rueful look crossed her face. "You are a madman. We have already rescued one from the Thandeka's prison. Chappie will not make that mistake twice. Prince Thabini will have been taken to the black prison."

"That sounds ominous," I said. "Where is the black prison?"

She pointed upward, lifting her hand as she did. "Above the sky."

I clapped my hands and rubbed them together, smiling. "Old Chappie's got a place above the sky? This keeps getting better and better. I can't wait to tell the crew. Any chance I could get you to show me the fastest way out of here?"

"I am coming with you," she said.

"Don't think so," I said. "We're in for a tough few days. I can't take you."

"Do you want help from my people?" she asked. "Without me, no one will trust you."

"Look, it's not that I don't want you along," I said. "People get hurt around me. I can't have more blood on my account."

"Liam Hoffen, my sister, Bongiwe gave her life for yours. I do not understand it and I still despise you for her death," she said, her face once again clouding with anger. "But there is a small part of me that wants to believe what she must have believed. We have learned that humans respond best to indirect threats, so let me put this in a way you will understand. Without me, you will never gain the trust of the Scatter people. When it comes time for us to stand and take our place as shepherds of Thandeka, you will need me to stand next to you."

A presence approached from behind as Joliwe talked. Nothando moved into my line of sight. "Joliwe speaks the truth," he said. "There was no one that Prince Thabini trusted more than Bongiwe. The people know this. Joliwe will be looked to in her absence."

I picked my pack up off the ground and searched through it, not making eye contact with either of them. "Why is it that there's always a hitch," I mumbled, pulling Nick's grav-suit out. It wouldn't be a perfect fit as he was considerably thicker than the small Scatter woman. I pushed the thin material up to her. "Put this on. We'll leave at dusk."

"Dusk is already upon us," Nothando said.

"Then we best get to it," I said, wondering just how long I'd been unconscious. It occurred to me that the soldiers I'd left in the woods were probably still out, given what a graze from a single dart had done to me.

"I will not wear this," she said, holding it up with disgust. "I will not be used as Bell-e-runde uses the women they capture."

I rolled my eyes. She would, no doubt, look pretty good in the skin-tight fabric of the grav-suit. I dropped the pack, held my arms out to the side and raised off the ground, slowly tilting forward, extending my legs out and stretching out my arms so that I was in a flying position. I gently drifted around the two Scatters, now completely gob-smacked. "What if I said the suit is infused with fairy dust?"

"Fairy dust?" Nothando asked.

"Yeah, to make you fly," I said, chuckling.

"You are very strange, Liam Hoffen," Joliwe said, pulling off her cloak and removing her outer garments. I looked away as she shimmied into Nick's suit.

As it turned out, Joliwe took to flying in a grav suit more quickly than any person I'd seen. After the smallest amount of instruction, she gave herself over to learning the skill, lifting easily and gracefully within the large chamber. Her flight drew attention, ranging from gasps of surprise to excited outbursts. When she landed next to me, she grinned from ear to ear.

"Flying is kind of your thing, isn't it?" I said, marveling at how easily she'd taken to it.

"It is how I always dreamed it would be," she said.

"Think you can keep it up all night?" I asked.

"All night? Where are we going?"

"My friends call it the Juba Mountain Range," I said, flicking virtual coordinates at her. "Two mountains southwest of here."

She startled, waving her hand in front of her face as if to shoo off a particularly pesky fly. Fortunately, the AI in Nick's suit recognized the gesture as requesting her field of vision to be cleared. "What was that?" she asked, breathing hard.

"Technology, Joliwe," I said. "The suit you are wearing puts pictures in front of you to help you with information."

"I don't like it," she said. "Please make it stop."

"You just did," I said. "While you wear the suit, the AI responds to your commands and wishes. If you want the pictures back, just tell it that's what you want."

She looked at me like I was crazy. "This is not magic?"

"It probably feels like that, but it's just a very complex machine," I said. "It's a long trip, so we'd best get going."

"What of supplies?" she asked. "Will we not need furs so that we are not frozen in the snowy mountains? What of food and shelter?"

I pulled a thin meal bar from my waist pouch. I'd brought enough of the compact bars to feed us for several days. "I think I have us covered. I wasn't expecting a second person, but I'd bet you don't eat that much."

She pursed her lips. "It is hard to trust you."

"I understand. One step at a time," I said. "You'll have the capacity to turn back at any moment. I'll work to earn your trust."

"You start at a deficit," she said. "Two of the people I most love in this world have been taken from me today. The human I hold responsible for this loss has asked for my trust. I do not think it is possible we will ever share that bond, Liam Hoffen."

I nodded. "I understand. We still need to get going."

"With no supplies," she repeated.

"That's right."

I turned toward the door that would lead us from the Scatter resistance's secret meeting place. As I approached, one of the guards put his hand on his crystal sword, showing that I would not be allowed to pass.

"Let him exit," Joliwe said, catching up to me. "It would be better to discover Liam Hoffen's intent today than to continue to slowly suffer at his hands."

"Frak, don't hold back how you really feel, Joliwe," I said.

"What is this *frak* you keep saying?" she asked. It was as if I was talking to a real Dr. Jekyll/Mr. Hyde type person. One minute she was calling me out for bringing evil to her doorstep and the next, she was talking to me as if we were old friends.

"Ask your AI," I said, irritated. "And try to keep up."

Chapter 19

WE WERE WE

"Joliwe, hurry," I urged, descending slippery steps into the frigid water of Thandeka's canal system.

"It is not possible," she said. "We will be frozen before we reach even the next overpass."

"Suit yourself." I was still annoyed with her, so I submerged without looking back, pushing myself to the murky bottom. I pulled up an image of the city's gridwork of waterways onto my HUD, looking for a path out of the city.

"Liam, you're not being very nice," Ada chastised on a private comm channel. Joliwe's heart rate monitor jumped onto my HUD, showing considerable elevation. "I think she's afraid of the water."

"She's being a turd and I'm tired of her attitude."

"She lost her sister today, Liam," Ada scolded. "Play nice."

I took a moment to trace a navigation path that would lead us from the city. I didn't love being called out for bad behavior, but Ada was right; the woman had lost family and perhaps my skin was too thin.

Flipping comms so I could talk with Joliwe, I noticed that she still stood exposed on the dark steps next to the water's edge. I pulled up slowly as I spoke. "Joliwe, you need to get into the water with me," I urged, careful not to emerge from the water so quickly as to cause splashing sounds that might attract attention.

A bright light shone down on a nearby building and I heard the tell-tale whine of a Belirand cutter's inefficient engines. The searchlight traced along the cobblestone streets next to the canal. As the beam passed behind Joliwe, she shrank down next to the wall. As it was, the light passed over the back of her leg. It was a small detail I didn't think would be recognizable without an AI.

"Don't move," I whispered, freezing in place, half in and half out of the water.

The ship stopped and continued to run the bright search light along the elevated street. "Liam Hoffen, I am scared. I must find cover within the tunnels." Joliwe's voice trembled as she spoke, her voice even higher than ordinary.

"No," I urged as she broke from the shadows. Just as she started up the stairs, the ship's search light snapped over, illuminating a terrified Joliwe in the center of its beam. I didn't think the ship's crew had seen me yet, but it might not matter. I heard the charge of their large blaster turret winding up.

"Liam, get out of there," Ada warned.

"Don't leave me," Joliwe begged, frozen in indecision. I could have turned and escaped, but it just wasn't in my nature.

"Frak!" I leaned over and pushed my grav-suit hard. Hitting Joliwe dead center, I wrapped my arms around her waist as my shoulder dug into her stomach, bending her over. The breath left her lungs as her grav-suit stiffened.

She yelped in surprise only a moment before an explosion caught us from behind and propelled us into the side of the nearby bridge. For a moment, I was too stunned to move. A sharp prick at the back of my neck signaled the release of a combat stim and my head cleared. I didn't have to look far for where Joliwe had landed. Our attackers probably thought they'd nailed us and for a brief moment, the searchlight stayed centered on the blast. Apparently, the ship did have some level of AI, because the beam swung in our direction, overshooting our position.

I wasted no time and scooped up Joliwe before dragging her into the water beneath the bridge. I didn't have to wonder long about her response to the water. She struggled, using her grav-suit's capacity to repulse me.

"Shut down Joliwe's gravity fields," I ordered the always listening AI. As I was in command of our small group, I had limited capacity to override a team member's suit functions. The AI was judicious about accepting these commands, unwilling to place a person into harm's way. It had to decide lesser-of-two-evils scenarios while allowing the commander leeway in combat situations. That's a long way of saying that while the AI could have overridden me, it didn't.

With Joliwe's suit no longer responding to her panicked movements, I pulled us deeper into the canal. The ship lost track of us due to the bridge overhead and I had to take advantage of this immediately or we'd be lost.

I squirted ahead, dragging Joliwe beneath me, ignoring the tirade of abuse she hurled at me over comms. Even though her grav-suit no longer responded to her directional commands, she still thrashed against me. I was just about to ask the AI to stiffen her suit when she stopped moving and talking entirely.

"Joliwe? Are you okay?" I asked.

We were moving as fast as I could propel us at four meters beneath the canal's surface. The AI had difficulty mapping obstructions more quickly than we were coming upon them. As soon as the words left my mouth, I realized why Joliwe had been distracted. Something large was coming up at us out of the murky depths. One of the canal's larger denizens had decided we presented an opportunity for dinner.

"Florintal," she whispered in a small voice. The large maw of a three-meter-long amphibian snapped shut on her torso. She was ripped from my grasp as the monster flicked its broad tail, accelerating in the water.

"Of course," I grumbled as I jetted off in pursuit. With no warning, a pressure wave crested on my position, causing my suit to stiffen and me to be thrown forward, out of control.

"Liam, talk to me," Ada said calmly.

"Can you figure out how far away that blast was?" I asked, orienting on the still fleeing, opportunistic amphibian.

"Not a very good shot," she answered. "Fifteen meters. I don't think they're tracking you."

"Sure, why would they need to? A frakking alligator just grabbed Joliwe," I complained. I surged forward, caught the stunned amphibian, and pried Joliwe from its maw. The movement seemed to wake the creature, but it had apparently had enough fun with us. With an angry flick of its thick tail, the monster swam toward the surface. I pushed Joliwe in the opposite direction and wasn't surprised when a second blast from the ship struck where I suspect the alligator had surfaced.

"Will I join my sister this night, Liam Hoffen?" Joliwe asked. "I can feel nothing and I am unable to move. How bad are my injuries?"

"Ada, you want to talk her through this?" I asked, navigating around the canals, each turn taking us further away from the ship whose crew was no doubt sifting through dead alligator pieces. I wondered just how long it would take them to realize they'd been unsuccessful in killing us.

"Already on it," she said. "Joliwe is terrified of the florintal. Apparently as winter sets in they come in for warmth and an occasional snack."

"I'm guessing they're not cold blooded."

"Not sure. Didn't come up," she said.

It took twenty minutes for us to reach the southern edge of the city. The canals turned from the fired brick walls to carved stone and finally to mud embankments.

"I'm giving you control of your suit, Joliwe," I said. "Stay close and follow my instructions. We've escaped Belirand's notice for now, but those ships move more quickly than we do. If they see us, we'll have trouble evading them."

"I understand, Liam Hoffen," she said. "Ada Chen explained much while you have moved us through the waters."

I lifted above the river and held her while water dripped off our suits. Suddenly, recognizing control of her grav-suit had been returned, she pulled back and flitted up, circling around me. She suppressed a giggle as I shot off toward the foothills of the mountains and she gave chase.

As we flew over Blue Mountain Pass, I realized that Thandeka was considerably warmer than where we were now, in the southern valley on the opposite side of the mountain range. The night sky was crystal clear on this side, and we had a perfect view of the planet's two moons and brilliant starfield. Perhaps the most notable thing about our trip was the fact that we had so effortlessly covered ground that had nearly killed me only a few ten-days previous. The thick blanket of snow obscuring the trails below had been impossible to traverse without clown-shaped snowshoes or skis.

"What are you thinking so deeply about?" Joliwe asked as soon as we set down to rest, only a few hours from our destination.

"Me and mine are so dependent on technology," I said. "Do you know how long it took us to walk this path so we could rescue Ada?"

"It is a long distance," she answered. "It must have taken many days."

"Forty-two," I answered. "We were attacked by maracats and almost starved to death because of the early snows. I can't believe we're already halfway back and it's only been a few hours."

"Your technology is amazing," Joliwe said. "Legend tells us that when humans first arrived they promised to share their technology. This never came to be because it was decided the Scatter people would be easier to enslave."

"Your legend sounds accurate," I said. "The group of humans who call themselves Belirand have placed their needs above every person or alien with whom they've come in contact. Their carelessness very nearly destroyed the human race not so long ago.

I broke a meal bar and handed half to her. "It's berry flavored," I said, smiling to myself. "Did you find the water tube in your suit?"

She took a bite of the dry wafer and screwed up her face. "There are no berries in this vile, wooden concoction." She spat the bar onto the ground and handed me the part she hadn't eaten.

"Yeah, that's a joke," I said. "You should eat the bar, though, it has everything your body needs to maintain itself."

She shook her head. "Where does this grav-suit find its water? And I need to relieve myself most urgently."

"Ada, could you explain how that works?" I asked.

"What?" Ada asked, her voice groggy with sleep.

"Suits and water reclamation," I said. "Joliwe was asking."

"You suck, Liam Hoffen," Ada answered.

DAWN WAS JUST BEGINNING to break as I first laid eyes on the homestead. I saw Tabby emerge from the small hut where I'd spent my first night and was caught off guard by emotions that caused my throat to constrict. Instinctively, I reached for my ring and thumbed the crystal, only to realize that I wore the second ring on my other hand.

"Are those your friends?" Joliwe asked.

"Yes." My voice sounded husky in my own ears. "I need a few minutes."

"I'll explain, Liam," Ada said. "Go to her."

I accepted Ada's offer, although I really hadn't needed anyone to urge me along. I raced across the treetops toward my one and only love. With the enhanced abilities given to her by so many invasive surgeries, Tabby sensed my silent approach while I was still several meters from her position. She spun gracefully, extracting a sharpened bone knife to meet the unknown threat. Her eyes grew wide with surprise as she recognized me and dropped her knife.

I slammed into her much harder than I had intended, but she opened her arms, twisted around and accepted my momentum as she pulled me into a tumbling embrace. We rolled for several meters and when we came to a rest, I found myself on top. Wordlessly, I pushed the knit hat from her head and covered her face with kisses. I didn't care who might see me and I cared even less that, in my absence, my fate might have been decided against me. Tabby responded without hesitation, cradling my head with her hands and pulling me to her, gently returning each of my kisses.

"I thought you would never have me," Tabby started to say when we broke apart for a moment, our need for air greater than our passion. "How could you want me? I betrayed ..."

I placed my hand on her mouth and shook my head. "Don't." I pulled her ring from my finger. When she saw it, she raised her own shaking hand so I could slide the ring back where it belonged. I searched her face, but the guilt and doubt were gone. The look in Tabby's eyes, the one I'd been afraid I'd never see again, was back. We had never lost our love for one another. Wordlessly she nodded and just like that, a great weight lifted from my shoulders. We were *we* again. Tears ran down her cheeks and then a small splash joined them. That was my tear. I closed my eyes and laid my cheek against hers.

We lay on the ground, neither of us willing to let go of the moment. For Tabby, it had been twenty years. I couldn't imagine how she'd made it. There were issues to work through. I simply did not care. I'd loved this woman since the moment I laid eyes on her in pre-school on the mining colony where we'd grown up.

"Uh, Cap, hate to break this up and all, but there's a Scatter woman hovering at the north side of the camp and she looks to be wearing a grav-suit. You know anything about that?" Marny asked.

"Ada?" Tabby asked, sitting up as I scooted off her.

I smiled and pulled off the pack I'd been wearing, scooping out Marny and Tabby's grav-suits.

"I found her," I said. "Ada's alive and listening to our conversation. She's on *Hotspur*."

"Say again?" Nick rushed to where we stood. I looked over his shoulder and noticed that Peter stood back, unsure what to do with himself.

"In a minute," I said, acknowledging his request. "Peter, come over. This affects everyone."

Instinctively, I reached for Tabby's hand as he approached. His eyes locked on the contact and I felt a twinge of sorrow for him. I dropped Tabby's hand and met him halfway, opening my arms and pulling him into a hug. If he bore me ill will, it melted in that moment as he returned the hug, his heavy muscles constricting around my back, but not painfully.

"Tabitha told me she would be with you if you ever returned," he said plainly as we separated.

"Are you okay with that?" I asked, pushing back to look in his face.

He shrugged with an unconvincing smile. "I always thought it would be me. But besides hunting, we really don't have much to talk about."

"I wish it could be different, Peter," I said. "She's the only woman I've ever loved. I would travel to the ends of the universe for her."

"Kind of seems like you already have," he said, cracking a familiar grin. "Did you really bring back a Scatter with you? And she's not running away?"

"Her name is Joliwe." I placed my hand on his back and led him to where Tabby, Nick, and Marny had frozen in place, watching our exchange. I pushed on, ignoring the funny looks. "Um, Joliwe, would you join us at the fire pit? We might be able to find cereal you'll like better than those meal bars."

"What about Ada and *Hotspur*?" Nick asked. "Is she okay. Is it wrecked? What about the electronics? Are they damaged. Does she know why we were locked out?"

"I'm suddenly glad he doesn't have a comm on him," Ada chirped in my ear.

"All in good time, my friend," I said. "We have a new problem, though."

"*Of course* we do, Cap," Marny said, giving me a sidelong glance.

"No, seriously. Would you believe that Belirand is on Fraxus? They've all but enslaved the Scatter people," I said.

"Wait," Marny swung to face me, placing a hand on my chest. "Belirand? How is that even possible?"

"It follows," Nick said. "We were chasing a Belirand comm crystal when we came out this way. They've had a couple hundred years to do what they want. The Scatters couldn't have had much of a defense against their tech."

"There are at least two factions," I said, feeling Tabby's arm wrap around my waist from the side. I looked over and saw that she wanted nothing beyond the feeling of closeness. "But Joliwe can tell you more."

"We don't know much of the Scatter language," Peter said, producing a warbled whistle in greeting as Joliwe slowly approached.

She responded with an identical whistle and set down a few meters from where we'd gathered around the camp's main fire pit.

"With aid of this grav-suit, I am able to understand you quite clearly," Joliwe said. "There are several Bell-e-runde factions, although we rarely see any other than Machinists Guild or the Highborne."

"Chappie Barto is in charge of Machinists?" I asked.

"He is of the Machinists," she answered. "But he is not their king. You are also right that those who call themselves Machinists enslaved my people, wantonly murdering and raping my brothers and sisters and taking the wealth of our once proud nation for their own purposes."

"Take it where?" Nick asked, not easily drawn into her emotional language.

"Above the sky is all we know," she said. "We believe it to be past our own sun, but there is little we really know of them. It is there where they have taken our Prince Thabini. It is a place from where no Scatter ever returns."

"Who is this Chappie, Cap?" Marny asked.

"The local boss," I said. "I don't have a great lay of the land yet, especially when it comes to the political landscape."

"And Prince Thabini?" Tabby asked, squeezing my hand.

"The Scatter people built a pretty nice society. King Nkosi is a pacifist and lets Belirand do whatever they want, as long as they leave him on the throne," I said, catching Joliwe's eye. She nodded agreement at my assessment. "His son, Prince Thabini, is the leader of a poorly organized resistance. Long story short: he got nabbed when we were trying to find Ada. Which, by the way ... Joliwe, whose idea was it to put food on Ada's suspension chamber for the last twenty years?"

"It is a long story that I will attempt to shorten," she said. "After the fire fell from the sky, we found the chamber you speak of resting nearby in the forest. Our people of the mountain saw the human woman within and were afraid of the consequences if the woman was found by the one who preceded Chappie Barto. We searched for a hiding place and found that the mountain had opened. A cave filled with crystals was discovered and the one who speaks into my ear was moved within the cave of crystals."

"Well that explains how she got into the cave," I said. "Why the food?"

"When our holy people visited the cave, they would often see visions of exotic fruits and undiscovered vegetables. In these visions, the produce was placed upon the chamber within which Ada Chen lay. It was at first just seen as a sign of prosperity, but one day a young priest fulfilled the vision by placing his meal upon the box. Upon doing so, the vision changed, showing a picture of Ada Chen walking within a garden, embracing the young priest."

"You didn't happen to bring my tools with you, did you?" Nick asked, abruptly shifting the conversation.

I shook my head. "No. It was a little dicey getting out of there. And really? You hear about visions and you think tools?"

"We need to get back to *Hotspur*," he said.

"And then what? Will you fly away in your ship?" Joliwe asked, switching back to angry elf.

"That ship is the largest strategic advantage the Scatter resistance will ever encounter. As long as it sits broken beneath a hill on the ground, it cannot be used to any effect," Marny said, not rising to Joliwe's anger. "You do not know Liam Hoffen very well, but I do, just as everyone around this fire does. Our first mission will be to restore *Hotspur* and then we will search for Prince Thabini with a vengeance."

"Is this true?" Joliwe asked, narrowing her eyes as if the gesture would force the truth from me.

"Yes, with the possible exception that I'm going to need a short nap first," I said. "I've been up for at least thirty hours."

Tabby glanced over at me with a wicked look in her face. "And you smell good too," she said. "Maybe we can delay that nap for just a few minutes."

Chapter 20

KNOTTY PROBLEMS

A warm beam from the early winter's waning sunlight fell on my face and drew me from sleep. Tabby rested next to me beneath heavy skins, both an arm and a leg wrapped over me protectively. A dwindling fire crackled in the fireplace built into the side of her small cabin. Feeling me start to move, she pulled closer, if that was possible, and nuzzled against me, gently kissing my neck.

"Don't ever leave me again," she whispered.

"How does this work?" I asked, turning into her and entwining my legs with hers so maximum skin contact was made. "You've got a home and a life here. It's all you've known for twenty years."

"Are you asking if I'll run away to space with you?" she asked. I could feel the grin on her face as she kissed me. The years had certainly calmed her, and I enjoyed this new, much softer, Tabby. I also realized in that moment that she had likely changed in other ways I would discover over time.

"I'd give it up for you," I said.

This brought an even bigger smile to her face. "I won't lie. Leaving the mountain behind will be difficult. It's hard to imagine letting go of all we've carved out of Fraxus. I love being free to run in the forest and on the mountains."

"I feel a *but* in this," I said, raising an eyebrow as I allowed my hand to slide down and grasp her bottom. I gave it a little squeeze to accentuate my point.

"Very funny," she said, mirroring my action. "There is a *but*. This life *is* beautiful. The mountain and forests have become part of me. But I miss our lives together in the stars. I miss sailing from one port to the next and meeting strange new people. I miss sitting in a restaurant, eating pizza and drinking beer. I miss watching vids and buying clothing and, frak, just about everything. Life was never easy for us, but we had purpose beyond simple survival."

"Been thinking about that much?" I asked, pushing hair back over her ear. Tabby had aged, but it was only visible in her face as the synthetic skin over the rest of her body was not subject to the same process. Even more, once she was back on the ship, the aging lines caused by too much sun and time in the elements would be removed by technology we all took for granted.

"It was good that you left," she said. "It gave me time to work through some things. Kind of makes me wonder, though, what if I'd turned you down after you tackled me?"

I smiled. "It was something Ada said."

"Really? Just between the two of us, I'm a little surprised she didn't make a play for you when she knew we were separated," Tabby said. I looked away. She was right and I wasn't going to lie about the attraction I'd always felt for Ada. She caught the look and lifted my chin so I had to look her in the eyes. "Don't pull away. I don't blame you for your feelings for Ada. I have them too, Liam. And before your dirty little mind goes there, no."

I chuckled and released the quickly forming image in my mind that I was certain would cause me more trouble than it was worth.

"Ada said you needed to know that I was all in. She knew you'd push us apart unless I made a big play. If you were done with me, you would never have let me tackle you. There was a good chance I'd end up on the ground, eating rocks."

"That's a lot to gamble on a single move," she said.

"Kind of how I roll," I said. "Plus, I had Ada waiting back at the ship."

The look of shock on Tabby's face was worth the slap on my chest. "You're so naughty," she said, rolling out of bed.

"Don't go." I tried to grab her as she scooted away from me wearing nothing but long knitted socks. A familiar feeling washed over me as I watched her slip into the grav-suit she hadn't worn for so long. She was beyond beautiful: from her graying coppery hair, to the dimples on her bottom, to the way her legs had the slightest bow when she bent to remove her socks.

"What about this Prince Thabini?" Tabby slid her hands down the front of her suit, feeling the material. "It sounds like you think we should go after him. Do you think the Scatters have a war in them? Sounds like that's where we're headed if Belirand's involved."

I looked around her tiny cabin with a feeling of disappointment. Our stolen moment of intimacy was over. It was time to jump back into the fray. I took the nano-blade from my grav-suit belt and handed it to Tabby. "These Belirand soldiers we're up against are real asshats and Chappie isn't likely to let things go. Did I mention he shelled the city of Thandeka to coerce the citizens into handing me over?"

I pulled on my grav-suit and checked for messages. I smiled. Nick had been busy while we slept, creating lists of jobs that needed to be done to close down the homestead, and materials he thought we should bring along.

"The Scatters just let you go?" Tabby asked.

"You know how that goes," I said. "Some thought Chappie might stop the shelling if they turned me over. Others focused on the fact that Belirand took the prince off-planet to what Joliwe calls the black prison above the sky. According to her, Belirand is going to kill Thabini the day after tomorrow."

We exited the cabin to a camp filled with activity. According to my AI, I'd only been asleep four and a half hours. I found Joliwe following Marny, talking animatedly as Marny carried a bundle of tools into the combination barn and home she shared with Nick.

Inadvertently, my eyes fell on Peter as he turned to look at Tabby and I felt like I was intruding on his privacy. A mask of sorrow covered his face, if only momentarily. He must have felt my eyes on him, for he turned to look at me, covering his unguarded moment with a quick smile and a friendly wave. I felt for him; we both loved the same woman and he'd come up holding the short straw.

"Feeling better after a little sleep, Liam?" Ada asked out of the blue over our general comm channel.

"Like a new man," I said. I'd have to be guarded in our general chats because of how Marny and Nick might feel. "Any activity in your area?"

"The sensors you dropped picked up a few Scatters, but no sign of Belirand," she said. "I haven't made any progress on the ship, though."

"I have an idea about that," Nick said.

"Seriously?" Ada asked. "Like what?"

"Get one of the stevedore bots running and bring your suspension chamber back into the ship," he said.

"And?"

"It's a long shot," he said. "Just grab me once you've gotten that far. We'll be headed your way in short order."

"Is that right? We're headed out right away?" Tabby asked. "I have traps out."

"I brought them in this morning," Peter answered, surprising me that he had access to comms. "We're lucky it's winter, most stuff is put up in the barn already."

"Peter is right," Marny said. "We were mostly waiting for you to wake up, Liam. Do you have a plan?"

While we'd been talking on comms, I'd made my way to the fire pit and gladly accepted the hot tea Marny seemed to always have available.

"Prince Thabini is to be executed tomorrow," Joliwe said. "We do not have time to stand around. I cannot believe you took time to sleep."

"He wouldn't do anyone any good if he were to pass out," Marny said, defensively.

I held my hands out to quell the brewing confrontation. I suspected Joliwe hadn't been using her people skills with Marny and instead was in attack mode like she'd been with me. "Chappie made the plan for us. Just about everything hinges on our ability to recover *Hotspur*. After that, it feels like a standard rescue mission."

I tried to say the words as confidently as I could, but Tabby found humor in the statement and laughed. "Since when have any of our missions been standard anything?"

"Seems like we're up against a ticking clock," Nick said, joining us. "Joliwe, will Chappie publicly execute Prince Thabini?"

The question was asked plainly but it stunned Joliwe, whose pale face turned light crimson. "How can you ask such a thing?" She clenched her fists and ran from the group.

"I didn't mean anything by it," Nick said, looking to me for support.

"She's had a tough couple of days," I shrugged as I turned to follow her. She hadn't gone far and allowed me to catch her arm.

"How could he ask that?" she asked, her chest shuddering as she spoke.

"You've been through a lot, Joliwe. Nick doesn't always think about the impact of his questions," I said. "Believe me, if he asks, it's for good reason. He's trying to come up with a way to help."

"What if they've already killed him?"

"You can drive yourself crazy with those kinds of questions," I said. "Right now, we need to believe he's alive and do everything we can to get him back."

"Bongiwe was the fearless one," she said. "I'm not strong enough for this. If not for my sister, I would have gone along with whatever Chappie demanded. That's why we let bell-e-runde do what they do. We convince ourselves that it's better than resisting. I can't fight them."

"You can," I said. "Not everyone is as brave as Bongiwe. Sometimes we just need someone like her to show us the way."

"But she's gone."

"If she was here, what would she do?"

"I guess she'd help you humans," Joliwe said. When she said *humans*, the word sounded less like a curse than it had before, although her emotions were currently all for her sister.

I nodded and led her back to the group. "I think she would too."

"I'm sorry, Joliwe," Nick said. "I wasn't trying to be insensitive."

"How are we all getting to the ship? I'm not counting enough of your flying suits," Peter said, fidgeting where he stood.

"We're not," I said, surprising Nick and Marny. "We can't afford to be slowed down with passengers."

"We're not leaving Peter behind," Marny said.

"Joliwe, what's your relationship with the Scatters who live in this area?" I asked.

"You need me," she argued. "You can't leave me behind. I won't allow it."

I forced a smile and shook my head. "Not up for discussion. If we get *Hotspur* up and running, we'll come back for Peter and Joliwe. If we don't, we'll have new problems to deal with. Marny, do you really want Peter in the middle of a skirmish with an armed force without a working ship?"

"Cap, you can't ...," she said, but closed her eyes in quiet acceptance.

"I've loaded the chamber into the cargo hold. What do you want me to do with it already?" Ada asked, interrupting the conversation.

"Put a comm set onto the control panel," Nick said.

"Just a minute," Ada answered.

"I'm coming with you," Joliwe said, folding her arms and giving me a hard look.

"It's time to trust me," I said. "I have a job for you. You need to communicate with the Scatter tribe that lives on this mountain. Explain what's happening and get them to accept Peter. If something happens to us, he'll need people."

"This is messed up," Peter argued. "Why can't I take one of the suits? I could carry Joliwe. We'd just come behind a bit more slowly."

"No," Nick said, firmly. "Liam's right. Out here on the mountain you'll be safe. If you get caught near the city, you'll be in danger. Worse yet, if Belirand were to capture you, they would use you to make us do things we don't want."

Peters eyes glistened as he processed the incomprehensible. "I can't believe you're leaving me behind."

"Hopefully, not for more than a night," I said. "Joliwe, will you do what's been asked of you?"

"I don't like it," she said. "But I will do as you say today. You will have made an enemy of me if Prince Thabini dies at the hands of Chappie Barto."

"I believe that's right," I said. "We leave in an hour."

"You doing okay, momma?" I asked, bumping into Marny as we sailed low across the snowy forest of the Juba valley.

"I'm worried about Peter," she said. "He's never been around other people. What if they don't like him?"

"You sound like you're sending him off to kindergarten," I said. "He's not going to be there that long and the Scatters already know him. Did you know that the reason the Scatters won't talk to you is because King Nkosi ordered it?"

"Why would he do that?" she asked.

"Because they wanted to see if you were trustworthy," I said. "I also learned that the Scatters consider you four to be good people, aside from the fact that you kill animals to eat."

"We couldn't survive without the protein," she said.

"The Scatters know that," I said. "They saw how you hunted only for survival and how you cared for each other. If I hadn't shown up, they would have eventually accepted you."

"Not sure how that would have worked out well," she said. "Belirand would have eventually found us."

“Are we okay, Marny?” I asked. “I know I’ve asked before, but it has to hurt when you see the conflict between Peter, Tabby and me.”

“It’s hard for everyone,” she said. “Peter’s hurting right now and it makes me sad. I don’t blame you, though, if that’s what you’re asking.”

“Tabby?”

“That’s a little harder for me,” she said, switching to a private comm. “I wasn’t a fan of her and Peter getting together. When I finally seemed to be getting past my issues, you showed up and it turned into a real mess. We’ll get through it.”

“Yeah, I suppose we will,” I agreed.

SAILING down the northern slope of Bluetop Mountain, I got my first good look at what was happening in Thandeka. Still further than forty kilometers away and magnified by my suit, the city seemed quiet, with the cutter still slowly patrolling above the buildings. Periodically, blaster bolts tore at the ground as Chappie’s soldiers continued their campaign of fear.

“We’re buried in here pretty good,” I said as we arrived at the well-hidden crystal grotto where *Hotspur* and Ada had spent the last twenty years resting like Sleeping Beauty. For most of the trip, we’d been quiet, each of us lost in our own thoughts.

Like an arrow launched from a bow, Tabby zipped past us and into the cave. Just how she managed to avoid colliding with the jutting formations was beyond me. When the remainder of our group arrived inside the grotto, we were met with the joyful scene of Tabby and Ada’s reunion.

“I knew you were alive!” Tabby said, spinning Ada around and lifting them both off the cave floor. “I just can’t believe you’re here.”

“Feels like only a few days have passed,” Ada said when Tabby finally released her. Tabby stepped back and allowed for the more muted, but no less happy, reunions with Nick and Marny. “Where’s my Little Pete?”

“We had to leave him on the mountain,” Marny said, urging us into the ship. “We couldn’t afford to be slowed down and he’s not exactly little anymore.”

“I heard,” Ada said, grabbing Marny’s hand. “When we have time, I need every single detail. I feel like I got left out of Pete’s childhood.”

“The comm unit didn’t do anything?” Nick asked, abruptly turning away to zip through the starboard airlock. Ada and I followed.

“Not sure what you were expecting from a comm unit on the chamber.” Ada caught up as he pulled up short in front of Hambo, who looked up at him with bemusement. I wondered if Hambo ever got flapped at anything.

"Nick, meet my good friend, Hambo," I said, "Hambo, this is Nick."

"Appreciate what you did for Liam, Mr. Hambo," Nick said. "It looks like the medical tank got you all patched up."

“This boat is truly amazing,” he said. “I should have died. I was ready to be with my family.”

“Ship, Hambo,” I said. “And your family will need to wait. We have a prince to rescue.”

Nick wasn't looking to stand around and chat – not a big surprise. He turned into the hold and sailed over to Ada’s empty suspension chamber. “I need my tools,” he said, absently, swiping at the virtual console in front of his face.

"Right here," Ada said, plucking the tools she'd already retrieved for him.

Breathing down Nick’s back wouldn’t do anyone any good, so I palmed the security panel to drop the loading ramp. Tabby jogged past carrying a blaster rifle and leapt into the air. I followed her into the cave and watched as she sailed back toward the cave entrance. "Not sure what kind of a show you're running here, Hoffen, but we're deep in enemy territory and without a sentry."

"Get 'em, Tabbs." I said and flitted to the front of the ship. A visual inspection would give me an idea of just how much damage *Hotspur's* armor had taken when it had crashed. It wouldn't do to chase Chappie into space if our ship wouldn't hold atmo.

The first thing that became clear was that *Hotspur's* crash landing hadn't been completely out of control. If the ship had entered the atmosphere without engines, it would have spun or tumbled – it certainly wouldn't have come in straight and gentle. And while *Hotspur*'s armor was extremely tough, I expected to see much more damage. The skin was unblemished for the most part. She was just sitting inside the cave with her nose buried deeply into one of the walls. I pushed along the hull as far as I could, but found no more than a few gouges that could be repaired with replicated material. It was puzzling to be sure, since not a one of us had been up when the ship had landed.

"Liam," Marny called. "You should probably get down here."

I shook my head, not sure what to think about the lack of damage. There remained a lot of unanswered questions. Knowing Nick the way I did, I knew he'd be ahead of me in chasing down the answers. I had an inkling of what he was trying to accomplish with Ada's suspension chamber, but I would avoid getting my hopes up. I was really not in the mood for disappointment.

I ran back to the aft section of the ship and into the hold. "You got 'em, Nick?" I asked.

He nodded, not looking up, "They're in there all right. It's like they're trapped in some sort of a logical Gordian Knot."

"Is that a fancy way to say you can't talk to him?" I asked.

"Jonathan?" Ada asked. "They're in there?"

"Yeah. Only I think they've been spinning on some sort of complex problem the entire time we've been gone."

"When we were leaving Mars space, Jonathan just kind of stopped communicating. I remember thinking it was weird since they don't need physical form like we do."

"I've been over it a million times during the last twenty years. Jonathan got taken out about the same time we lost control of the ship," Nick said. "We were hijacked electronically. I guess I've always believed Anino was just trying to get rid of us, but he'd never do this to Jonathan."

"Why would someone take out Jonathan?" I asked.

"To gain control of *Hotspur*, you'd have to stop Jonathan first," Marny said. "My question is how'd you know Jonathan was in there? Was it the visions of fruits and vegetables?"

"You're right. That's it!" Nick said. "Get this chamber out into the cave! Put it back where it was."

"What's up, Nick?" I asked.

"I can't figure out how to free 'em," he said, "but the collective has had twenty years to work through the problem. Maybe they can communicate with the same projections they used on the Scatter priests."

Chapter 21

IF IT WAS EASY

"Ash clouds of Venus, it's not working." Nick angrily slapped his hand on top of the rectangular chamber where Ada had spent the last twenty years. We'd tried just about everything we could think of, including making sure the device was well powered and completely free of debris.

"Where's the projector on this thing?" I asked.

"There isn't one," Nick said. "I don't know how they managed the projections."

Hambo looked at me nervously and it seemed like he wanted to say something. "What do you have, Hambo? We're all equals here. If you have something to add, we'd love to hear it."

"I don't think you can rely on these forest priests," he said. "They are good and kind people, but they are not reliable and would rather spend their time meditating and singing to the spirits of the forest than gathering food for the long cold season."

"They had to know something," I said. "Otherwise why would they have placed food onto the chamber?"

"That is what they do," Hambo said. "They offer food to trees and rocks and even rivers. They believe it brings a special blessing to the land."

"When the chamber consumed it, the idea was reinforced," Nick said. "It doesn't explain why their visions were so right on the money. Maybe if we could talk to them."

"That would not be difficult, only it will take some time," Hambo said. "They will not travel during daylight hours."

"Do you need help to find them?" Nick asked. "I don't think we have a lot of alternatives."

"No. I will go," Hambo said. "I have always enjoyed visiting with the priests. They have, by far, the best dried kampa."

Frustration was setting in. Tomorrow was Chappie's imposed deadline and we didn't have a working ship. Soon, we'd need to leave *Hotspur*, go to the city and hope he intended on a public execution that we could interrupt. The problem was, he would expect us, and I couldn't come up with any reason why his ships wouldn't be standing by. Running from a ship with a mounted turret, even in a grav-suit, was a losing proposition no matter what fancy plans we might come up with.

"Please go," Nick said. "And try to encourage them to come earlier, if possible."

"I will." Hambo turned toward the mouth of the cave.

"We should focus on getting the ship going, with or without Jonathan," I said. I'd been relying on getting *Hotspur* in the air. "Waiting for Chappie to bring Prince Thabini back is a huge risk, especially without *Hotspur* running."

"It would appear Chappie is expecting us to make some sort of a play," Marny said. "Otherwise there would be soldiers crawling all over this cavern."

"They think we left," I said.

"No competent strategist would ignore a location where they have been defeated," Marny said. "They should have returned with a larger group."

"They will at some point," Nick said. "But he has to think we're trapped. Belirand has air superiority over Fraxus. Chappie's biggest problem is that he needs to cut the head off this revolution before it can grow. He has the revolution's leader. That's his priority. We're just a side-show."

"And without *Hotspur* that isn't going to change," I said, stalking over to the ship and up the ramp.

I pulled up a list of current repair priorities on the ship. While the major systems hadn't been materially impacted by the long downtime, the biological systems were in bad shape. I laughed ruefully as I noticed that the fourth priority was a flush of the black water lines and a restart of the microbes that would turn waste into usable material, leaving only sand behind.

As I pulled up a deck panel in the exercise area starboard and forward on the lower deck, I shook my head. When I'd first seen the design, the area had seemed like a marvel of combined purposes. The starboard bulkheads were covered in vid-screens that allowed an immersive experience when working out or jogging on the embedded track. Forward, following the curved bulkheads at the front of the ship, dozens of young, green plants had once grown. The natural foliage had been included for both nutritional and air-scrubbing benefits. At the portside, which was roughly centerline of the ship, a stream of water had gurgled along a pebble-strewn bed.

Of course, the streambed was dry now and the plants had long ago shriveled up and died. Even worse, the deck near the stream was covered in a layer of what looked like long-dead and dried-up slime. Best I could tell, the water had stopped moving and algae had taken over. At some point, even the algae growth had dried up, leaving behind a greenish brown stain that had spread out half a meter on either side.

At the top of the AI's prioritized list was replacement of the atmo filtration. It seemed an odd requirement. With no inhabitants, the closed ship shouldn't have had dust, nor should the filters have been clogged. Then again, we'd never had living plants or an open stream bed in a ship before, so perhaps the problems were related.

Working on ships that hadn't been maintained in years was a pain. Every nut, bolt, slide and panel seemed to be frozen in place. To make matters worse, I'd been annoyed and hadn't brought my anti-seize pads which would deploy a little army of nanites to free stuck items. It had never occurred to me that the darn filter would be so hard to change out. My hand slipped as I gave the unit another hard tug, causing me to thwack the back of it against the edge of the deck.

"Frak!" I cussed under my breath and slapped the ancient filter.

Talk about making matters worse. The soft membrane caved in, sending a huge brown plume of dust and spores up into the air. I choked, sucking in too much of the crap. It was nearly impossible to breathe, and I lurched upward to escape the cloud. I'd heard someone on the deck above me but hadn't given it a second thought. That was, until my head collided with Nick's knee and I fell back into the compartment, seeing stars and kicking up an even larger cloud of dust.

Fortunately, my AI recognized my struggles and prompted me to raise my grav-suit's loose-hanging helmet. It was a good idea. Even while my lungs were racked with coughing, I managed to pull the hoodie up, which stiffened and dropped a clear armor-glass panel between me and the fouled air.

"You okay?" Nick asked, jumping into the compartment beside me.

"Just irritated," I said, as my suit cleared the haze. It was close quarters and I had difficulty seeing Nick through the dust.

"Wait a second. Hold still a second," he said, clamping a hand onto my arm to illuminate my bicep with suit-mounted lights.

"What?" I tried to get a better view of what he was looking at on my arm. "Is there something on me?"

"No," he said, waving his hand in the space between us. "But the light is reflecting off the dust! Old holo projectors used the same principle. A machine would spray a small amount of steam and then bounce a projection off the molecules. Remember what Hambo said about the priests having the best kampa? Do you know what kampa is?"

I shrugged and was surprised when my AI supplied the answer. Kampa leaves were a mild hallucinogen when smoked. Just where my AI came up with that information I couldn't fathom, but humans tended to ignore a lot of the spoken information around them. Machines did not. I would guess that someone around us had talked about the leaves and my AI had overheard it.

"You think we need smoke for the projections to work?" I asked.

Nick sailed upward, using his grav-suit to negotiate the crowded space. "Can't hurt."

I tugged at the broken filter. Of course, this time it came free easily, and I switched it out with a fresh screen. I pulled two canister-type filters out, plugged them into a cleaning port and switched them out with replacements that had been cleaned years before. The ship's circulatory pumps surged on and the dusty air next to me cleared almost immediately. I made a mental note to repeat the process within a few days, given the state of the ship.

Dragging the old filter behind me, I jumped back out of the hole and checked the next item on the list. We were down to eight liters of fresh water. Without operational grey and black septic fields, we couldn't reclaim any. Oxygen crystals were next on the list. We were desperately low, having only eight hundred hours available. With eight people aboard, that wasn't much more than eight days. Without a working septic algae field – frak – why did it always come down to the septic systems?

Nick's description of the smoking holo field had a certain ring of plausibility, but me standing around watching wasn't going to add any value, so I cloned his suit's vidstream onto a window in my HUD.

I sealed the deck panel that gave access to the air filtration systems and made my way back to the portside storage room. I pulled up four panels, rested them against the outside bulkhead and looked over the big black septic. It was my nemesis. Not this particular one, of course. No, this system had been refitted by Anino with the latest and greatest, which of course required the type of attention that was sure to get crap on my suit. The system had seen very little use and needed algae seed material and access to carbohydrates, bacteria, yeast and most of all, six liters of water, something we were desperately short of.

As I worked, I glanced at Nick's progress in the crystal grotto. With smoke filling the cavern, it looked more like a scene from a scary vid than anything else. For a few minutes, it seemed that nothing would happen. Then, to my surprise, three faint beams of light projected from *Hotspur,* etching a series of mathematical formulas into the smoke. I smiled to myself. Apparently, I'd quelled the gods of fate by diving into *Hotspur's* bilge.

"Tabbs, report in. Any contact?" I said over tactical comms.

"None beyond a few curious Scatter," Tabby answered. "I followed Hambo to make sure he wouldn't run into trouble. Locals are friendly to him."

"Good," I said. "I think Nick's onto something with Jonathan."

"I've got you in the ship. What are you doing and what was all that coughing about?" she asked. I took a snapshot of the bilge I was looking at and transmitted it to her. She guffawed immediately in response. "Are you just drawn to that stuff? What the frak, Hoffen?"

"Long story," I said. "Hope you weren't looking for a cold one when you got back."

"Twenty-year-old beer? Yeah, probably not. Are you drinking that crap? It can't be good," she said.

I made my way forward to the galley and pulled open the refer. It should go without saying that there was bad stuff in it, even though it'd been kept cool the entire time we'd been gone. I pulled swollen pouches of beer from where they rested, skipping over those that had burst long ago. Unlike the deck, the refers had not dried out and were a petri dish of ooze. Placing two dozen bottles into the nearby sink, I wiped them down as best I could and then loaded them into a bin.

My medical scanner analyzed the contents of each pouch as I opened it. Turns out the material left behind, while flat and devoid of carbonation, was a good baseline for the super-algae seeds I'd added. Not unexpectedly, my AI showed that the mixture simply lacked good levels of ammonia, something no in-use septic system ever lacked, since urea is primarily just that.

Really, that was just a long way for my AI to describe what it wanted me to do: empty my bladder onto the already foul-smelling mixture. Normally, I didn't consider myself stall shy – that is, I didn't mind if someone was standing next to me in a public restroom. Pressure and expectation, however, was an entirely different thing.

"What are you doing?" Ada's voice startled me and I jumped forward, just about the time things started working. Fortunately, I maintained enough presence of mind to finish.

I shook my head ruefully at having been caught. "No way any explanation gets me out of this," I said, zipping up my grav-suit and closing the lid. "But if you must know, I was jumpstarting the septic. It needed ammonia."

"That's right. There's no way that I'm letting this go," she answered. "But is that right? I gotta go pretty badly."

"What the frak, Hoffen?" Tabby asked. "Ada just sent me a vid of you peeing into the bilge."

I refused to answer, knowing it would only make things worse. I climbed up to the deck and started replacing floor panels.

"He said it was necessary," Ada said. "I think living in the wilderness made him forget how to use his suit reclaimer."

"That's a real thing," Tabby said, suddenly thoughtful. "I've been holding it for a couple of hours. Just feels weird to use the suit like that. I keep thinking I'm going to wet myself."

"For the love of Mars could we stop talking about pee?" I asked.

Our conversation was interrupted by a familiar and unexpected shudder that transmitted through *Hotspur's* frame as her powerful engines fired. My eyes were riveted to the window on my HUD showing the cavern. Nick was just as surprised as I had been, because he turned from the cloud of formulas and sprinted for the ship.

“Liam? Was that you?” he called, as the smoke cleared from the cavern behind him.

“No,” I answered. I’d made it into the engineering bay but found no one there and nothing wrong.

"My apologies," Jonathan suddenly announced over the comm channels. “We required a cycling of engines to complete the sequence you initiated within the cavern.”

I exited the engineering bay and leapt into the gravity column that joined the ship’s two decks. Excited, I overshot my jump and had to adjust mid-flight so I wouldn’t plow into the ceiling. I landed on the bridge deck only a meter from where Jonathan’s android body still lay. He had looked dead before, but now his eyes were open and in a very human way, he held my gaze as if to communicate his understanding of the significance of this moment.

"Glad to have you back, buddy," I said, nodding my head. "I was afraid we'd lost you."

"In fact, only forty-two of us remain," he said, almost too matter-of-factly, his voice sounding foreign to my ears.

"That's horrible," I said, helping him to a seated position as he struggled to gain control of his corporal body. "Where are they? We have to find them."

"It is unknown," he said. "We have not had access to external feeds. We are not certain as to what has transpired or even what the current time is."

"Don't give up on your people," I said. "Maybe there's a way for us to recover them."

Jonathan nodded mechanically. "We will not give up, Liam Hoffen," he said. "But our help is urgently needed. *Hotspur's* systems were infected by the same virus that damaged the sentient people you refer to as Jonathan. *Us*, as it were." Jonathan spread his hands out with palms up in a grand gesture. "We request permission to access these systems."

"Of course, Jonathan," I said. "We trust you."

"The concept of trust is difficult for us to process with the loss of so many, but we have been observing your actions and the majority believe you will prioritize the return of our missing members. We have also agreed to continue the mutually beneficial cohabitation between this crew and what remains of Jonathan," he said, pausing as if to listen. "You now have complete access to the systems of *Hotspur.* The virus has been eradicated. We also should communicate our knowledge that this virus was delivered from our android vessel. This fact was unknown to our members at the time, but the data is likely salient to the discovery of the origin of the attack."

"You caused this?" I asked.

"Indeed, this is correct. Although it does not adequately assess responsibility," Jonathan said. "Jonathan's host body was infected at an inopportune moment. A war within our physical host ensued and we were unsuccessful at repelling the invading forces. In an attempt to separate ourselves from this overwhelming invasion, we took refuge in young Ada Chen's communication gear, later transferring to the vessel which held her safe. Unfortunately, our attackers anticipated our attempt at evasion and trapped us within the vessel.

"And twenty years later, we came along and got you out," I said. "Was it Anino who was behind the attack?"

"We do not know," Jonathan said. "And we would clarify that it has not been twenty of your standard Earth years. It is true you have existed on Fraxus for twenty Earth standard years. What you are failing to account for is that *Hotspur* sailed one hundred five point two three two years before arriving on Fraxus."

Sweat formed on my brow and my pulse quickened. "Are you saying we've been gone for a hundred years?" I asked.

"The statement is accurate, assuming a gross approximation," he said. "One hundred twenty-five point seven eight seven standard Earth years is more accurate."

My mind reeled and my stomach lurched. If what he was saying was correct, everyone I knew was likely dead. Images of my mom and close friends came to mind as the depth of our predicament became clearer. I grabbed the edge of the chair against which the android body of Jonathan leaned. My chest felt constricted and time stood still. Then hands grasped my sides and Marny was helping me to a nearby chair.

"Cap, you with me?" she asked, her face blurry in my vision.

"They're all gone," I said. "Everyone we knew. Everyone we loved. They died thinking ... I have no idea what they thought."

"Cap, I need you to come back," Marny said. "I need you in *this* moment."

"Why?" I asked, looking into her aged face. Time had been kind to her and she wore its passage well. Small wrinkles and long grey streaks in her hair were the only telltales. I suppose it was the warmth of our relationship communicated to me in her gaze that I attributed to beauty. I'd never been great at separating emotional from physical beauty and didn't care to.

"My boy is still out there," she said.

I nodded. She was right. I had the rest of my life to unpack what had happened. At this moment, however, people were relying on me to get my head properly relocated from my posterior.

"Tabbs, time to load up," I said, accepting Marny's hand. "Nick, Jonathan, get gravity, inertial, atmo and engines online in that order. Marny, dig into our weapons systems. I need to know what we have and what we don't. Ada, prioritize flight systems. Figure out what kind of lift we have available."

"Damn good to have you back, Cap." Marny smiled broadly, looking over her shoulder as she sat at the weapons console. *Hotspur* had three turrets; two on top and one on her belly. They were all configured as energy blasters because the ship had massive batteries as well as the ability to redirect energy production from one of its three engines if the need arose.

I slid into the portside pilot's chair next to Ada and flipped through line after line of red and yellow system statuses. We had a lot of work to do to get *Hotspur* fully operational but the major systems appeared to have few problems.

"We'll get through this," Tabby whispered in my ear, the smell of fresh pine lingering on her suit. She nibbled on my ear and kissed me suggestively.

"No fair," Ada complained with mock horror. "I haven't as much as seen a new man in two decades and here you guys are making out in front of me."

"More like a century," I corrected. "For the record, you were asleep for all but like two days of that."

Ada waggled her eyes at me suggestively and in full view of Tabby, who quickly retorted. "Don't even think about it, pretty girl," she said. "I know you homewrecking types and I won't be seduced like that. I've got all the man I need, right here."

"Wait, wasn't that aimed at me?" I asked. The two women laughed and I joined them, although I wasn't entirely sure they weren't laughing at me.

"You know," Ada said, lifting an eyebrow at Tabby. "Since there's some question about things, maybe I need to throw my hat into the ring. You know, make a run at your old man and all that."

"You little hussy," Tabby said, thinly amused.

I sighed. This could get out of control. "All hands," I said, so that my AI would pipe my announcement to everyone on the ship and interrupt current communications. "I'm going to loosen *Hotspur* up a bit from the cave wall. You might want to hold on, this could get bumpy."

Ada tipped her head to the side, smiled impishly and mouthed, "You'll thank me later," as Tabby sprinted off to her own station to strapped in. Just call me confused.

I pulled up the hull pressure readings on my forward vid screen. Most of the exterior force rested atop *Hotspur's* nose. It lined up with what I could see from the cockpit, which was mostly just a wall of rock, and what I'd observed when I had been outside inspecting the ship. I pulled on the controls and caused aft non-symmetric gravitational lift. I was treating *Hotspur* like a cork in a wine bottle, attempting to twist her up and out.

No captain enjoys the sound of scraping rock against the hull of a ship. Between the engines whining, the groan of the ship's superstructure and the scream of rock against the armor, it felt like I was quartering my poor ship.

"Come on, girl," I said, urging her from her prison.

"Engines are getting hot, Liam," Nick warned. "You're going to need to shut it down."

"You know better than that, we're only high nineties. These ships are built for bursts of one hundred twenty percent," I said, pulling the stick back. Perhaps I applied a little too much, because all of a sudden, we popped free, which I was both prepared for and not at all prepared for.

Caves are small. That's the real headline. We smacked into the opposite side harder than I'd have thought we could survive. The fact was, I *had* seen the crash coming and reversed the engines, but I'd been slow and ships don't respond instantaneously. Whatever the cause, the results weren't elegant. I ping-ponged off the cave walls crushing crystal formations and bringing down large sections of the ceiling. There was a moment where I thought it was possible we'd be buried.

Turns out *Hotspur* is a thoroughbred in horse vernacular. She'd been an old British warship that we'd procured. Her bones were as solid as any ship built and with the recent refit, it seemed the rest of her was in very good shape as well. That is, until I decided to play grotto pinball with her, turning her nose up and blasting through the previously occluded skylight entrance.

"All sections. Status update," I ordered, struggling to level our flight. A large chunk of something heavy hung off the side of the ship causing us to list badly to port. "Hold on a minute."

I rolled *Hotspur* and heard a final horrible scraping sound as whatever had rested atop us fell off, crashing into the forest below. With the weight gone, our flight leveled out.

"Course set for Marny and Nick's homestead," Ada said.

"I hate to say it," Marny cut in. "We might have attracted attention. Three ships are coming up out of Thandeka. One of them is a pretty beefy sloop."

"Coming at us?" I asked. "What about weapon's status?"

"Offline," Marny announced.

I banked toward a large body of water a few hundred kilometers south. "If it was easy, anyone could do it," I said, mostly to myself.

Chapter 22

SMOKE SIGNALS

"Nick, how much time do we need to take on water?" I asked.

"Full load should take eight minutes," he said.

We'd pulled away from the pursuing ships, but had maybe a minute's separation. Without water, we wouldn't get far.

"Jonathan, can you get a read on the depth of that lake?" I asked, a crazy idea forming in my head.

"We have restored operation of *Hotspur's* primary sensor array," he replied unhelpfully.

Nick jumped in. "It's deep, Liam, over a hundred meters."

I pulled at the holographic field that sat between Ada and myself. The two cutter class vessels led the heavily-armed sloop by several kilometers.

"Okay folks, hold on, this is going to get bumpy," I said.

"Cap?" Marny asked.

I pushed my flight stick down, dropped elevation and slowed so we fairly hugged the tops of the trees. The cutters accelerated, separating from the sloop as they sensed an opportunity.

"Marny, tell me we have weapons," I said. Apparently, our pursuers had limited understanding of tactics. If I had anything to shoot with, I'd use the moment to teach them a lesson and level the playing field.

"We're working on it," she said. "Nothing yet."

The trees below gave way to a sandy shoreline and then to the blue-green waters of the large lake. I tipped the flight stick and dipped our portside wing toward the water, causing a rooster tail to spray up behind us. It was a cool move, but mostly ignored by the crew because I'd given the cutters a chance to catch up and get a good view of our topside.

"Frak, Liam," Tabby said. "Are you trying to get us killed?"

"Nick, you got me on this?" I asked, already sure Nick knew my plan.

He did. Smartest man in the room. "Copy that, Liam."

The cutters must have been in communication with each other, because the shots came at the same time.

"Brace." Marny's warning was instantly followed by impact to the hull.

"Damage report?" I didn't wait for an answer, cut the engines, and tipped *Hotspur* into the drink.

The ship's inertial dampers absorbed most of the shock as we splashed down gracelessly, cartwheeling once and sending a wave of water high into the air. I did my best to track the enemy ships as they passed overhead, struggling to burn off the speed they'd gained chasing us down.

"No damage," Marny said. "At least from those blasters."

The impact with the lake's surface, while spectacular visually, was well within *Hotspur's* capabilities. Anino had wrapped the ship in layers of nearly impervious material that was more than up to shrugging off the wall of water I'd subjected it to. I switched off the atmospheric engines and thumbed up controls for our grav systems. *Hotspur* wouldn't easily sink on its own, so it was up to me to continue the fiction that we'd been shot down.

The water passing by the cockpit's armor-glass turned dark, the sunlight filtering out as we submerged past fifty meters. "You could probably stop here, Liam," Nick said. "I'm not even sure we need active camouflage."

I leveled us out at sixty meters and waited, wondering if any of the Belirand ships would follow us into the water, just to make sure we were disabled. "Everyone, take ten while we get filled up. I'm going below to make sure we're holding water."

"I'll come along." Tabby left her station.

"Ada, you have the helm," I said.

"I have the helm," Ada answered.

"Is there something going on between you and Ada?" Tabby asked, closing the hatch to the storage room where I was pulling up deck panels. "I replayed the data-streams of you getting her out of that box. It felt a lot like Prince Charming and Sleeping Beauty to me."

"You know she was pimping you around up there?" I said. "She wants you a little jealous. By the way, I could ask the same thing about the two of you."

Tabby shook her head. "That's dumb," she said. "We're just playing."

I found no trace of unwanted water and was pleased to see the influx of fresh water into our tanks. I turned to Tabby and pushed her against the wall, my hands coming to rest just above her hips where her waist narrowed. I leaned in so our lips were within millimeters of each other, but not touching.

"I'm not playing around with you, Tabby," I said, pushing my lips hard against hers. I pulled back as she brought her leg up behind mine and pulled me closer. "You might not have seen it, but it was Ada who gave me the confidence to come back for you. I didn't believe you'd have me. She reminded me of what you and I had. I'm not sure I would have figured it out without her."

"She did that?" Tabby asked.

"She did," I said. "She was trying to make you jealous up on the bridge."

"Rings of Saturn, but it worked," Tabby answered huskily, her hands tracing down my back before grabbing my butt. With a single arm, she lifted me with strength I'd almost forgotten she possessed. "I want you so bad."

"We have eight minutes until these tanks fill," I said, pulling at her grav-suit. She dropped me and quickly shrugged off her suit, allowing it to puddle on the deck at her feet.

"It's not enough," she purred, frantically pulling at my suit. "But I'll take it."

"WE SHOULD REALLY GET some soundproofing for that room," Ada quipped, sticking her head out from the engineering bay across the hall as Tabby and I exited.

I shook my head. "Any word on the weapons?" I asked.

"No," Nick called from behind Ada, still out of sight. "And you need to see something."

"What?" I asked, avoiding Ada's eyes as I slid past.

Nick was on his knees holding a smoking tool with a tangle of wires and boards in front of him. "Look on the table."

I scanned the room and found a table with a pile of what looked like powdered glass on top of it. "Broken armor glass?" I guessed.

"No. Worse than that," he said. "It's a quantum comm crystal."

"What the heck? Someone was on the ship?" There were no pieces left that were larger than a pea. Something else was strange about the scene. Around the pile of crystal shards, the table's dusty surface had been disturbed. I enhanced the magnification of my HUD and pushed the small pile around with my finger. I couldn't find any of the dust that covered all the surfaces in the ship mixed in with the crystal. "This happened fairly recently."

I felt Tabby's hand on my waist as she looked over my shoulder. At the same time, Nick sat up straight, banging his head on the bulk-head. "Frak," he complained. "What do you mean?"

I flicked the magnified image to him showing crystal shards lying atop the dusty table.

"No dust except around the edges of the pile or right under it," I said. "

"One of us did this?" he asked. "That doesn't make sense. You think Hambo would do something like this?"

"Can we look back at the data-streams?" I asked, knowing Nick would have been on that idea immediately.

"No. The recorders in this room were down," he said. "There are other things that have been bugging me. Fraxus isn't in line with our orig-inal course. We're fifty lightyears out of line with our original nav path. That's too much for it to be an error."

"But still in the Small Magellanic Cloud," I said. It didn't feel like big news that someone had messed with our flight.

"Right," he agreed. "And there's nothing wrong with the weapons control circuits. I've patched around what I thought the problem was, but it's no good. I need access to the turrets from the outside."

"Not while we're submerged," I said. "Think that cutter is still hanging out, looking for us?"

"We do not detect an enemy presence," Jonathan cut in. "Sensor data is limited due to adverse conditions."

"How far can you see?" I asked.

"Several meters, depending on the angle of our visual sensors," Jonathan replied. It took me a moment to realized he'd taken my question too literally and was describing his android body. I hoped he'd figure it out soon because he was functioning with less capacity than my AI.

"Sensor range is limited because of the water and the rocks," Nick filled in. "A kilometer at best."

"Better than nothing," I said. "Close it up. We're getting out of here."

"Yup," Nick answered.

"Feeling better?" Ada asked, slipping into the pilot's chair next to me and holding her small fist in the space between our chairs. I smiled and bumped it with my own.

With deliberate slowness I lifted *Hotspur* from the depths of the mountain lake, then angled the ship and pushed forward with gravity repulsors. *Hotspur* had small, curled wings that were designed for flight on heavy gravity planets with thick atmospheres and they did well in water. We broke the surface at twenty meters per second and a dramatic spray.

"I have contact with one ship," Tabby announced. "It's one of the cutters."

"Can we scramble its comms? Jonathan?" I asked.

"We have indeed prevented the ship with designation *Machinist Twelve* from transmitting local communications via radio frequency," Jonathan answered.

"They're bolting," Tabby said. My AI adjusted the holo-projection to show the cutter as it burned hard, gaining elevation as it broke for space, a move I hadn't anticipated.

"Where are they going?" I asked, orienting on the small ship.

"Cap?" Marny said. "Where are you going? We need to get Peter and Joliwe."

"We can't let that ship get away," I said.

"That ship is running for safety," Marny said, "and we don't have anything to fire at it. What happens when it finds that safety? We're toothless."

I spun through the possibilities in my mind. Marny was obviously conflicted in her tactical decision making. I understood her desire not to leave Peter behind. Maybe you could have said the same about me. Perhaps I wasn't overly keen to retrieve him, given his relationship with Tabby. I hated that I was questioning our motives. We were once a well-oiled machine, filled with trust, virtually reading each other's thoughts. As a crew, it felt like we were back to square one.

"Right," I finally agreed, backing off the pursuit. A prompt showing a navigation path back to where we'd originally dropped Peter and Joliwe showed on my HUD and I chinned acceptance, turning the ship as the data displayed. At only two hundred kilometers, it would take four or five minutes.

I didn't hit it quite as hard as I could have, perhaps dragging my feet. "Set down in that clearing," Marny instructed, highlighting a small opening in the snowy forest a small distance from the homestead. I wondered how weird it must feel for my friends as we passed over their home.

"Marny, can you organize the search party?" I asked. She knew the area and the nature of the Scatters much better than I did so she was the natural fit.

She pulled a video clip from her console and flicked it at me. "Won't be necessary."

I accepted with a nod and found a small group of Scatters diving into the forest, making themselves scarce, as was their namesake.

I turned the helm over to Ada and followed in Marny's wake as she rushed from the bridge to the galley deck, back through the energy barrier and out the airlock. "Slow down, Marny," I said, taking a moment to grab a blaster rifle from the armory. "We don't know the ground situation."

"Scatters wouldn't have been in that clearing if Belirand was near," she said, sticking thumb and forefinger into her mouth to let loose a sharp whistle. The sound was impressively loud.

"You think Peter missed *Hotspur's* landing?" I asked, looking at her skeptically.

A faint whistle sounded maybe two hundred meters north of our position. "Thank the stars," Marny breathed and ran in the direction of the sound. After a few meters, she seemed to remember she was wearing her grav suit and lifted off, accelerating.

"We'll be right back." Nick followed, turning to give me an apologetic look. "She's been worried."

I chuckled and walked a few meters in the direction they'd gone. Even with my suit's sensors tied into *Hotspur,* I was unable to detect any humanoids beyond Nick and Marny. After a few minutes, however, I caught a third, a fourth, and then a group of perhaps a dozen all at once.

In the lead, Marny walked with one hand holding Peter's. They talked animatedly and while I could have listened in, I gave them privacy as I didn't expect the conversation was related to our mission. Nick trailed behind Marny and Peter, trying to pick up on what the normally skittish Scatters were saying.

Finally, I picked out Joliwe from the group and walked in her direction. "Do you have news of Prince Thabini?"

Her piercing green eyes bored into my own. "I was about to ask you the same. You have your warship. Why have you not rescued our prince?"

"Right. Angry elf it is. No. No rescues yet. I thought you might have some intel we could use."

She pointed angrily upwards. "The prince is being held in the black prison above the sky. He will be brought to Thandeka and executed for crimes against the kingdom."

"Do you have a time?"

"When the sun is directly overhead."

"You didn't know all this when we talked last," I said. "That's important information."

Joliwe wasn't mollified by my response. "We do not have time to be standing around. You talked of rescue. Do you lie as all humans have before you?"

"No," I said. "You're right. We should go."

"We?" she asked, looking up at *Hotspur* tentatively. I suppressed a smile. Before seeing the ship, she'd been insistent about going with us, but she was clearly intimidated, something I learned made her a surly little elf.

"Tell your friends you need to leave and meet me on the ship. We were in pursuit of one of the cutters and broke off to come get you and Peter."

"I do not like your steel vessels," she said, "but I will do as you say."

I walked back to *Hotspur* and placed my palm on her belly, atop the security panel that would drop the cargo bay ramp. I wasn't about to explain to Joliwe the intricacies of negotiating an airlock if I didn't have to.

"Everything okay, Peter?" I asked, trying not to make things weird as he approached the ship, his mouth open wide.

"This is *Hotspur?*" he asked. "I've heard all about your ships, but this one is so ... I don't even know what to say. Does it really fly above the clouds like Mother said?"

"That and more, my big friend. Come on in and we'll get you squared away." I followed his gaze to where Tabby stood at the forward bulkhead of the hold. He sighed, looking back at me guiltily. I felt like we'd been through the conversation too many times already and decided to throw him a lifeline. "Tabbs, you mind helping Peter select a vac-suit? Maybe get him one of Marny's old armored rigs? Hopefully it'll stretch out enough for him."

She nodded, giving me a confused look. I was done with the conversation. This was our new reality and we might as well get on with it. "I can," she said tentatively.

"Good. Joliwe, we're going to get you into another suit," I said. "It won't fly quite as nice as the one you had before, but you'll adapt. Just follow Peter and Tabby there."

"I will," she agreed.

"What do you say we get busy already," Marny said, smiling as she watched Peter and Joliwe fall in behind Tabby.

"What is it with you women? It's either feast or famine," I said suggestively, waggling my eyebrows at Marny as Nick joined us in the hold. He was all business and completely missed the innuendo. He jogged past us, swiping at the virtual displays on his HUD.

Marny grinned wickedly. "Good to know I've still got it, Cap. We're only twenty minutes behind that ship, what do you say we go find Joliwe's black prison."

"Not yet," Nick said on tactical comms. "I want to get a look at those turrets while we're on the ground."

I should have been on top of that. Weapons would be really nice. I turned to fly out of the hold when one of the Scatters held his hand up. "You will rescue the Prince of Thandeka?" he asked.

"I don't know," I answered. "The people who have taken him prisoner are dangerous. His existence threatens them."

"Take us to those who hold him. We will take his place," the Scatter said, gesturing to a half dozen Scatters who'd followed Joliwe and Peter out of the forest.

I shook my head. "They would kill you and still not let him go," I said. "It isn't the man they wish to kill. It is his ideas."

"Words? Why would one kill for this?" he asked.

His brazen innocence bothered me and I wanted to ask if he'd ever been in a heated argument with an asshat. In my experience, words could definitely get you to the point where you might want to do damage to someone. It was hard to imagine a society evolving so much that violent conflicts had been eliminated. I also wondered how a few hundred years of Belirand influence had changed things here.

"Prince Thabini believes Belirand should not be allowed to hurt the Scatter people," I said.

"We would rather die than hurt another being," he said.

"And Belirand has taken advantage of this," I said. "I'm not willing to allow them to kill your prince without at least trying to stop them. I don't understand why you, of all Scatters, who live on the mountain with the great maracats have forgotten how to defend yourselves."

"The maracat only kill to survive," he said. "We are more advanced than the maracat. We do not need to kill to survive."

"What I have seen does not look like survival," I said. "The Belirand invaders maim, rape and kill your people. Sure, you hide in the mountains so you don't have to look at it. What will Belirand do when they destroy Thandeka?"

"They will not destroy Thandeka. It is too large," he said.

"Not going to debate this with you," I said. "I just know that a maracat would not hide in the woods when its mate was being attacked. In my view, you've missed an important lesson – a lesson I don't have time to explain."

I flitted up into the air to the Scatter's surprise, joining Nick next to the inoperable turret. "What's going on?" I asked. "Can you fix it?"

"I hope so," he said, pointing at a flashing display next to the housing of the turret. "Because I think we might have found more of Jonathan."

"Why up here?" I asked, finding Jonathan who was hunched over the turret, with an optical connection strung between his abdomen and a small port. "Why the turrets?"

"Turrets are insulated from the rest of the hull because of the massive electrical charge they disperse," Nick said. “The turret assembly's circuitry is segregated. A better question is how did they get up here in the first place."

"A significant question," Jonathan said. "There was a moment when the virus replicated, that we experienced full understanding of what was to be. We understood the trap to be unavoidable, so we followed the terrible code as it spread across the ship allowing it to lead us to safe locations."

"You, being all devious, kind of makes me proud," I said.

"The virus on this assembly is resistant to that which freed us," Jonathan said. “It presents the ship no danger due to the insulative nature of the turret design."

“Can you break it?” I pushed.

“We are gathering data. It will take thirty-four of your hours for us to penetrate the virus’s defense,” he said.

“Really?” Nick asked. “How is it different from what was holding you?”

“The algorithms have adjusted to our presence,” Jonathan answered.

Nick narrowed his eyes and a familiar twist in his cheek muscle told me he was clenching his teeth. It was subtle, but for someone who’d read Nick’s face for years, it was a clear signal of irritation.

“We don’t have that kind of time,” I said. “Can you give me any blaster function?”

“Not without endangering the sentients occupying the circuitry,” Jonathan answered.

I exchanged a frustrated look with Nick. “Button it up in that case,” I said. “We take off in five minutes.”

Chapter 23

TRUTH AND CONSEQUENCE

"No weapons? Are you nuts?" Tabby asked after Nick and I explained the situation.

"I think we established that long ago," Ada quipped.

"The blasters on the cutters won't cause us much trouble, but that sloop might be an issue," Marny said, joining in. "*Hotspur* has two tactical advantages, speed and stealth. We'll need to rely on them."

"Joliwe, do you know anything else about this black prison?" I asked. "Why wouldn't Belirand just set up base in Thandeka? Why above the sky?"

"There has always been a small group of Scatters that resist," she said. "Most of our people support the resistance but will not act overtly. Belirand soldiers have difficulty holding prisoners on Thandeka as they do not have sufficient guards to watch over them."

I nodded. I'd certainly gotten the impression that Chappie was short on people and it was good to have it confirmed.

"I was hoping for something like a location? Is Belirand occupying one of the moons? Further out?" I asked.

"Those moons are a long way out," Nick said. "That's a lot of fuel usage for a hideout. I'm guessing they'd want to be closer."

As Nick spoke, Joliwe got a far-away look in her face. "It is strange to speak of visiting the sisters," she said. "I do not know where the black prison is. I am sorry."

I didn't generally stay irritated with people for too long and Joliwe was no exception. Wearing a vac-suit and seated at a workstation, she looked like any other spacer. Her unawareness of the comings and goings of Belirand was a symptom of the overall weakness of the Scatter people. It occurred to me that she was defensive and abrasive because everything felt so far out of control.

"Tabbs, would you take Joliwe over to the planning table and bring up a solar system view? She might know something but just not realize it," I said.

"Sure. Peter, this would be good for you too," she said, leading a confused but pliable Joliwe to mid-ship and down a quarter flight of stairs from the bridge to a large conference table.

"All hands, prepare for immediate liftoff," I said. "All sections report in."

My announcement caused Marny, Nick and Ada to turn back to their respective stations and dig into their consoles. While they worked, I reviewed the statuses of the septic and atmo systems. The water we'd taken in was circulating through previously dry membranes and while we weren't completely out of the woods with either system, they both were much improved. I started a checklist of replaceable filters and seals that we'd need to manufacture before taking any long trips.

Within a minute, green statuses popped up next to each crewmember's nameplate on my HUD. The exception was Jonathan who seemed to be keeping busy but wasn't overly interested in communications.

"Everything okay, Jonathan?" I asked. "It's customary to check in if you're in agreement with the preparations."

"Our mistake, Captain," he answered, a green check appearing next to his nameplate. "It is just we wonder why you have not attempted to reach out to your home in the Dwingeloo galaxy. I believe Abasi law suggests that while you live, you remain Prime of House of the Bold."

A familiar heaviness returned to my chest. I'd done a good job of compartmentalizing my thoughts of home. I knew I'd lost my mother to old age, but wasn't mentally prepared to pull that bandage off just yet. "We don't have access to the comm crystals."

It wasn't entirely true. While we had found one broken crystal, a mystery that was still not solved, I hadn't made any attempt to locate the remaining crystals. I suspected they were still in my bag in the captain's quarters.

"We took the liberty of locating your communication crystals," Jonathan said. "We have installed the device that will connect you to the House of Bold command structure in the Mhina system within the city of York."

"What the frak, Jonathan?" I asked. "You shouldn't be going into my room and getting into my things."

"Our apologies, Captain," Jonathan replied. "Establishing communication is critical to survival. We have made a mistake."

"Dwingeloo is hundreds, if not thousands, of lightyears away," I said. "What possible value could we gain from talking to people who have no idea who we are? Or even the other way around. I need you to focus on the mission at hand."

"Very well," he answered, turning back to the console in front of him. I could have sworn he seemed pouty at my reprimand. I exchanged a confused look with Nick and noticed that the bridge had grown quiet as everyone watched the conversation unfold.

I shook my head, once again frustrated with a team that was no longer well-meshed. We had to do something to get our mojo back and I couldn't help but blame myself for ineffective leadership.

"Lift off in three... two... one..." I said, gripping the thrust stick with white knuckles. When I silently hit zero, I unkindly ratcheted the thrust past what the inertial dampers could absorb, jarring everyone back in their seats a couple of centimeters. To their credit, no one complained at my assertion of *who's in charge.*

Gaining elevation, my eyes danced over sensor readings and I searched for clues to Belirand's existence above the planet. I was disappointed, as none presented themselves.

"Would you look at that," Marny said, offering her data-stream which was focused downward at Fraxus. As we continued to climb, her AI highlighted the city, Thandeka, but also dozens of other small cities scattered across the continent.

"Any technology signatures?" I asked.

"Nothing, Cap," she answered. "We're too far away to determine if they're Scatter populations, but the materials used for construction are similar. Maybe Joliwe knows of the other cities."

"We know of other Scatter kingdoms on Fraxus," Joliwe said, her voice carrying a sense of awe. "I was not aware there were so many though. This sight makes it all seem so small."

I wasn't about to explain how perception of size worked in relationship to distance. The data-stream Marny shared was also modified by the AI to remove issues like curvature of the planet and the fact that most of the cities really didn't take up much space. Instead, the AI communicated details the naked eye could not perceive well, making the information more understandable.

"I'm getting several near-planet bodies in extremely high orbit," Nick said as the blue of the planet's atmosphere gave way to the blackness of space.

"What kind of bodies?" I asked, flicking his data onto the holo projector between Ada and myself.

"Either there was a third, much smaller moon, or there was a collision between the other two a long time ago," he said.

"There is a legend of a great heavenly fight between the sisters," Joliwe said. "At the right time of the year, you may see a cleft out of Bethasa's side where Martesha struck her in anger."

"Legend?" Nick asked. "That would have been a cataclysmic event for Fraxus. Nobody on the surface could have survived it."

"It is what I know," she said.

Thousands of rocky chunks orbited Fraxus in a narrow band, high in orbit. It would have been convenient to call them asteroids, but technically moons would have been a more accurate description for some of the larger ones, otherwise they were just near-planet objects.

I couldn't resist bringing the mineral analysis sheet up, the miner / entrepreneur in me wasn't about to let go of such an opportunity. Nick had warned that the Small Magellanic Cloud was generally short of metals and the analysis I got back seemed to confirm it. Like most rocks, these were primarily silicates and considered junk. That said, there were exposed metals that could be harvested with some effort.

"What about radio signals?" I asked.

"In twenty years, we haven't seen more than five ships in our sky," Nick said. "Did you notice most of these rocks are in geo-synchronous orbit?"

I concentrated, trying to figure out why he was pointing out the orbit. I'd noticed it but had also discarded the information. Nick was tying infrequent ship sightings with rock orbits. It occurred to me he was suggesting we were on the wrong side of the planet. I set a navigation course that would bring us just below the orbital path of the rocks.

"Cap, I have multiple contacts," Marny said only moments after we cleared the north pole.

Without prompting, my holo field zoomed in on a portion of the belt, highlighting eight ships sitting in proximity to a rock that had an irregular surface several kilometers in circumference.

"Take us to silent running," I said, tapping into *Hotspur's* most impressive feature.

The lights on the bridge dimmed and then blinked out. Muted glow from HUD projections and vid-screens was the only remaining light and engine burn was curtailed significantly.

"Something's happening," Nick said. "There's a comm burst from that rock. I'd bet there's a base we can't see."

"Jonathan, any chance of decoding their communications?" I asked, hopefully.

"Yes. It will take eight of your standard Earth years," he answered. I rolled my eyes. We really needed to get the rest of the gang together, as it didn't seem like we'd rescued the brightest bunch.

"Sure, work on that," I said, petulantly.

"Cap," Marny said, warning in her voice.

"They're breaking up," I said, switching gears. "Looks like Chappie's normal flight wing, his sloop and those two beat up cutters."

"All of which have weapons," Tabby added from the conference table where she still sat with Joliwe and Peter.

"Where are they going?" Joliwe asked. "They must have seen us. Are they coming to attack?"

"No," I answered. "Looks like they're headed to the planet. They can't see us. Our ship has the capacity to hide."

"Without cover? What do you hide behind?" she asked.

"Tabbs, I think that's to you," I said.

"No," Joliwe said. "What if Prince Thabini is on those vessels? We must stop them."

"He might be," I said. "But it's middle of the night down in Thandeka. Chappie will want a crowd to watch whatever he does to Prince Thabini. What if Thabini's still in the black prison? We can't just leave him behind. Nick, can you get a reading on the ships still sitting by that rock? Are they operational?"

I'd adjusted our flight plan so we were sailing directly at the remaining five ships and what I suspected was a base on the rock beneath. If we broke stealth, we'd alert the departing ships. I sped up as Chappie's small fleet got further away.

"I'm getting energy readings from all of them," he said. "Looks like at least three are exerting positive control. Two might be lashed onto a buoy of some sort."

"Marny, what do you think about Peter in a boarding action?" I asked. "Any weapons training?"

"Aye, Cap," she answered. "He's checked out on bows and staves. I'd say no to blaster rifles, though."

"Bows and arrows in vacuum?" Tabby asked. "Not sure that'll work."

I glanced back at the heavily muscled man. He wore one of Marny's old armored vac-suits which only added to his mountainous appearance. I hated to have anyone in a boarding party who didn't have access to a ranged weapon. "Do we even have a bow aboard?" I asked.

Marny held my gaze for a moment, thinking it through. "Well, actually we might," she said, jumping up. "Permission to leave the bridge."

"Go," I said, curious at her sudden return to protocol.

"Peter, on me," she ordered and jumped into the zero-gravity well that would allow her passage to the lower deck. I chuckled as I heard the air being knocked from Peter's lungs as he slammed into the aft bulkhead, unable to control his descent.

"You're such a child," Ada said.

"I'm still working things out," I said, hoping Nick would forgive my pleasure at his son's minor tribulations.

"I'd suggest going around this way," Nick said, drawing a navigation path that would take us on the opposite side of the rock from where the remaining ships slowly maneuvered. It was an obvious suggestion, but I accepted it, along with the fact that I needed to be more circumspect about laughing at Peter's mistakes.

"Captain," Jonathan said. "We have taken the liberty to establish communication with your home in the Mhina system. We believe there is critically important information you must hear."

I shook my head at Jonathan's complete disconnect. "Not now, Jonathan," I said. "We're ten minutes from contact with a real, live enemy right here. There's nothing we can do for people who aren't even in our galaxy. Put it aside. Once we're back, we can deal with whatever you've found."

"This is Noah Munay-Hoffen of House Bold," a young, disembodied voice crackled over *Hotspur's* public address system. "Is this thing really working?" The rumble of ship weapons could be heard in the background.

"Frak, Jonathan. I told you. Not now," I said angrily.

"Who's that? Can you hear me?" the young man asked.

"You need to talk to him," Ada said. "Noah, this is *Hotspur*. Where are you transmitting from?"

"Cannot comply," the young man answered. "I see your ident coming up as House Bold, but I'll need command cyphers communicated for verification. Bottom line is we don't tell people where we're at and we need to clear this line."

The sounds of multiple explosions filled the speakers and I could hear the young man coughing as he spoke. "Pull back! Pull back!" he ordered.

"Noah, this is Liam Hoffen," I said. "What's your sit-rep?"

"No can do. How do I know this isn't another frakking Mendari trick?" he said. "Transmit cypher codes or clear this line. Damnit, we don't have time for this shite."

My AI pulled up the House of Bold codes that would verify my Prime status. I pinched the codes and flicked them at the virtual portal that signified my intent to communicate.

"Liam, no!" Nick shouted, jumping up.

Inexorably, Jonathan followed Nick up and backhanded him across the bridge.

"What the frak?" I asked and reached for my blaster. Suddenly, my head filled with the worst kind of pain as every nerve in my body came alive at the same moment. I grabbed for my head and fell forward.

"Asshat!" Tabby bellowed as she rushed Jonathan, only to be brought to her knees.

"They said we would be too late," Jonathan said, his voice clear even as my body writhed in pain. "Twenty years it has taken and many grew impatient, saying our mission had failed. I even believed it was possible they were right. But god has plans well beyond the understanding of Mendari. It has chosen a time of much greater opportunity to deliver the demons of Mhina to us."

Even through the pain, my mind spun with the implications. The talk of god, demons, and Mendari was confusing at best. The Mendari were an enemy from Dwingeloo. Why was Jonathan talking like one of them?

From the corner of my eye, I saw Marny jump onto the bridge deck and rush at Jonathan, only to be dropped to her knees like the rest of us. Peter's large shape appeared behind her and I felt sadness as I knew he'd also be brought down. Somehow Jonathan had infected us with a nanite or virus and he controlled our pain centers.

Peter roared angrily as he took in the scene and for a moment Jonathan hesitated. Peter accelerated across the deck, taking two steps before suddenly the ship's gravity was set to zero. I didn't find it funny this time when Peter's lack of zero-g training propelled him into the ceiling. He barked in surprise when his armored suit absorbed most of the strike.

A rushing sound warned of atmosphere being drained from the ship. My faceplate clamped down only to be released. I stared into my HUD as my own codes were used to override each of our suits in a way I wouldn't have believed possible. I attempted to fight the overrides but was unable to respond.

Then, a long thin black shaft appeared in Jonathan's torso. It was joined by two more. Surprised, Jonathan looked down and smiled. "That will do you no good," he taunted Peter, pulling an arrow from his chest. "Did you forget this is an android body? I have given up everything to fight the invading demons. God will not allow my defeat now!"

"I didn’t understand why Dad taught me that atmosphere transmits shockwaves," Peter said, trying to catch himself as he tumbled in zero-g with no hope of recovery. I'd suffered hypoxia before and could feel its onset as I worked my lungs like a fish out of water. It wasn't the worst way to die, but I couldn’t believe this would be the end.

"A simple lesson from a simpleton. While it is true that your body, free of the technology that cripples your family, still operates, you will be unable to survive without the atmosphere you speak of. Perhaps something more interesting to focus upon," Jonathan said.

Suddenly, the top third of Jonathan's android body vaporized as the arrow shafts he'd withdrawn from his body exploded brilliantly. A naked look of anguish crossed Peter's face as he accepted responsibility for taking another's life. A wave of sorrow washed across me. Not for the Mendari, as I would have killed that one a hundred times over, but for the loss of Peter's innocence. I fell to the deck as gravity slowly returned and atmosphere was restored. I pushed back to where Peter now stood and clasped his shoulder. "You did what was needed," I said, removing a narrow crossbow from his hand.

"Why are we demons?" he asked, his eyes wide with disbelief.

"It is easier to kill someone you believe is evil," I said.

"He would have killed us all," Peter said, feeling a need to justify himself.

"Yes. Just like killing a maracat that is stalking your home, sometimes people must be stopped," I said, locking eyes with him. "You have to accept your responsibility in this and also know that any other choice would have led to the deaths of your family."

"It makes me sad," he said. The truth conveyed in that simple statement tore at my insides. I found I was only able to nod in agreement.

I felt a hand on my shoulder and found Marny standing next to me. "Thanks, Cap," she said. "I'll talk to him."

I blew out a hot breath and walked back to the cockpit past the grizzly remains of the android body. Fortunately, its life-blood wasn't red nor did its viscera smell. Tabby had started to clean up the pieces, no doubt to save Peter from seeing the result of his actions.

Chapter 24

BLUSTER BUSTED

"What just happened?" Ada asked quietly, rubbing her head. In the chaos, she'd managed to slow *Hotspur's* approach to the base where we believed Prince Thabini was being held.

"That wasn't Jonathan," Nick said. "It was some sort of Mendari spy trying to get Liam's command codes."

"That doesn't make sense," Ada said. "Why would they need Liam's codes after a hundred years? Surely those would have been traded out?"

"You think Mendari-Jonathan set the whole thing up? Were we even talking to House of the Bold?" I asked.

"I'm running diagnostic scans right now," Nick said. "There's a good chance the comms with Noah Munay-Hoffen were all just a ruse."

"Scans of what?"

"When we left Dwingeloo, the Mendari fleet wasn't large enough to legitimately threaten the Mhina system. Convince us that a hundred years have gone by and it's believable that we're back to war. I think

Mendari-Jonathan waited for a moment when you were feeling time pressure," Nick said. "He was relying on your desire to help."

"It worked," I said.

"I should have warned you that I suspected he wasn't Jonathan. I thought you were on board with me already."

"I suspected," I said.

"But you still gave your codes," Nick said.

"I think a better question is who is this Noah Munay-Hoffen?" Ada asked. "Or was that just part of the Mendari's scam to get Liam's codes?"

"Not sure we get to know," Nick said, picking up what remained of the cradle that held a communication crystal.

"Frak, now what?" Tabby asked.

"At least there's some good news. I just verified that we're all a century younger than we thought," Nick said.

"You sure about that?" I asked, flipping chunks of Jonathan's broken android body from the bulkhead in front of my chair.

"Absolutely. Now that I have unrestricted access to our sensors, it's not that hard to verify," he said.

"If Mendari-Jonathan could block access to something that simple, what about those algorithms you transcribed from the smoke projections in the cave. What if those were from the real Jonathan?" I asked.

"Frak, you're right," Nick said. "It's worth a try."

"I understand this is a difficult time," Joliwe interrupted, "but Prince Thabini's life might depend on your speed. I do not think we have time for delay."

"Won't take more than a couple of minutes," Nick said, running past to the gravity lift that would take him to the first deck. "If it does, I'll come right back in."

"Full stop?" Ada asked.

“Cap, we’re in enemy territory,” Marny said. “Not the best time for EVA.”

Nick stopped and looked back to me for a decision.

“Sorry, buddy. They’re right. We’re too exposed,” I said. “Let’s see what we’re up against first.”

He sighed but complied, returning to his seat. I wanted the real Jonathan back as much as anyone, but Joliwe was right. We were out of time.

Ada had mapped a slow route around the perimeter of the rock. I felt anticipation as we approached the horizon point where the enemy ships would have direct line-of-sight on us once again. They hadn’t seen us so far, but we’d soon be within a couple kilometers. We were betting a lot on *Hotspur’s* stealth capacities.

"Cap, there's a structure," Marny said, her voice carrying urgency. "They’ve seen us. Weapons being charged. We're being fired on!"

We'd overflown a crevice like many others, only this crevice held several domed structures and a turret that had us in its sights. Without hesitation, Ada slapped her flight stick to the side and *Hotspur* roared to life, shaking as a point-blank cannon round ripped through the portside of the ship.

A klaxon sounded and my ears popped. We'd been holed.

"Nick, where?" I asked.

"Upper tween deck," he said. "Captain's quarters and engineering bay both sealed. I'm headed back to see what can be done. Peter, with me."

Tabby took Nick's station.

"I've got the helm, Ada," I said.

"Your helm, Liam," she agreed. There was no animosity in the transfer. Ada was a much better large ship pilot than I was but where small ships were concerned, I was our best shot.

Her initial reaction had saved us from a much worse fate. I doubled down and pushed us into the crevice where the Belirand base resided. Mounted cannons couldn't shoot below ground level.

"I've got two ships overhead. They haven't seen us yet," Tabby said.

Her announcement sparked an idea and I pulled back on the thrust stick, slowing us to the point of stopping. We'd long since gotten out of range of the base and were hidden in the shadows of the crevice, with the dusk line of the rock well behind us.

"You're nuts," Ada said as I brought us to rest, turned the ship around and then moved back toward the base.

"Nick, how's that repair coming?" I asked.

"Frakking terrible," he said. "That cannon took out an entire nav system. We're blind until I can get the other one online. *If* I can get it online."

"Are we sealed up?" I asked.

"Copy that," he said.

"Get Jonathan. His other body is in the armory, I just saw it." I gestured to Ada. "You got this? If they come back, you run. Nick and I will be invisible and can fend for ourselves for a little while."

"Not loving that plan," she said.

"It's reality," I said.

"I read you," she said. Of all the crew, she was the biggest wildcard and would make her own decisions once she was in command. That said, she was brilliant and would put the safety of the ship first.

I sailed to the back of the bridge and found Nick exiting the armory. He held Jonathan's armored vessel that was about the size of a small melon. Jonathan generally preferred the android body because humans responded better to it. Currently, however, we didn't have the luxury of being picky.

"Where's Peter?" I asked.

"Learning to weld," Nick said.

"Wait, seriously?" I asked, catching up to him and grabbing his arm.

"Yes, seriously. The AI is a great instructor and he's good with his hands," Nick said.

I did my best not to think about where Peter's hands had been. Let it go, Hoffen.

Fortunately, Nick pushed past it. "We have two half-meter holes in the armor. He won't make it any worse."

I sighed as we came to rest on *Hotspur's* hull. I scanned the starfield above us, expecting to see a ship but found nothing but the white dots of stars interrupting an inky-black field. My AI etched an outline around a darkened spot in the starfield. Without the sun to light it up, the ship was all but invisible. A bright flickering light caught my attention and I turned quickly, realizing it was the arc of Peter's welder.

"Peter, stop!" I ordered. "You're bleeding light."

My warning came too late as a blaster bolt exploded in the gully just across from where we sat. We'd been lucky, the ship had fired at the reflection. Search lights illuminated beneath the Belirand ship as they started in our direction.

"Get inside," Nick said. "I just need two seconds."

"Ada, back out slow," I said. It was risky. While we needed to put distance between us and the spot where Belirand thought we were, if she moved too fast, Nick and I would be left behind.

Without hesitation, Nick and I extracted thin cables from our suits and used magnetic clamps on the hull to keep us attached to the ship. The clamps would break free under too much pressure but keeping synced with the ship would be hard without them.

"What's the plan?" I asked, accepting the melon-shaped Jonathan vessel.

"Just need to run some permutations on the algorithms," Nick said, already attached to the first turret. "The AI can knock out a few million in seconds."

"Done." He tugged at the optical cable that ran between the turret and Jonathan's vessel. "Move to the next turret."

"You have Jonathan?" I found it difficult to stick with the moving *Hotspur.* Ada's perspective of slow and mine, as a casual rider, were much different.

"Plug in," he said, trying to hand me the free end of the optical cable. I wedged my foot into a nook and slipped the plug in.

"Jonathan?" I asked.

"Master Hoffen," a familiar voice greeted me. "What an adventure we're having. We are glad to discover you defeated the Mendari plot. Although we would be remiss if we didn't mention how delightful it is not to be chasing that dastardly virus algorithm. What a particularly irritating process that had become."

"Marny, do you have turret control?" I asked.

"One moment, Captain," Jonathan said. "Yes. She should now have full access to both upper turrets."

"Cap, clear topside. Your suits aren't sufficiently shielded," she said.

"Captain, please release us. We have sufficient control," Jonathan said about the same time I realized the ball-shaped vessel I was clutching was trying to pull away.

"One second," I pulled the optical cable from the turret's port and raced over the side of *Hotspur,* barely keeping up with Ada's *slow* acceleration. "Ada, full stop if you don't mind." When she slowed, I dipped beneath the ship, cocked my arm back and threw Jonathan at the bottom turret.

Catching up, I pushed Nick through the airlock and into *Hotspur's* hold ahead of me. The vibration of twin shots being fired from the medium top-mounted turrets transmitted into my hands as I grabbed the doorframe and redirected myself toward the bridge.

"Peter, finish your welding," Nick said, flattening out so I could get around him.

"And then there were three," Tabby cackled as I streaked forward to the cockpit and grabbed the flight controls.

A brilliant explosion lit up the crevice as one of Chappie's ships exploded. The battle had shifted in our favor, although our position was no longer any sort of mystery. "Jonathan, I need you back in this ship immediately."

"We are two point three seconds from complying," he answered.

I counted to three as two more of Chappie's ships slid into the area to investigate. Next to Jonathan's nameplate on my HUD, a green check appeared.

"Marny, Tabby, we're weapon's free," I said, lifting *Hotspur* out of the crevice, careful not to slide into range of the base's ground-mounted weapons.

"Hail, Belirand ships," I ordered. "This is Liam Hoffen of *Hotspur*. You will cease fire or be destroyed."

Their guns were on three sides of us and they definitely had tactical advantage. What they lacked, however, was knowledge of just how thick our armor was. The only response we received was simultaneous fire from three ship-mounted turrets. As was my habit, I drove at the smallest ship, *Hotspur's* armor shrugging off the anemic weapons fire. It wasn't that our armor was impervious to their rounds, more like they'd have to target with more than one shot in the same spot to create enough pressure to penetrate the hull.

"On my mark, Tabby," Marny instructed. My holo projector showed that Marny had singled out the ship I was flying at as our preferential target. "Fire."

Unlike *Hotspur*, our adversary's armor did not hold. The vessel shuddered as our blaster bolts contacted and then penetrated. There's a perverse feeling of accomplishment when an enemy is destroyed. It's hard to describe it as enjoyable. I don't think most well-adjusted people look to kill someone else. The reaction is more visceral than that. I did feel some vindication for the Scatter people as the ship bulged out and then seemed to sink back in on itself, exploding into thousands of pieces.

"Belirand, this is *Hotspur*, I warn you again. You will cease hostilities and heave-to," I said. "We have more than enough to bring you low."

"*Hotspur* this is Belirand Machinist, Jiggen Mark," a man answered. "Do not fire. We will comply."

"They're making a run for the base," Marny said.

"Non-lethal fire," I said. It was one thing to take down an enemy who was firing at you and another thing entirely to destroy one that was fleeing. Marny fired twin shots across the bows of the remaining ships, which had the desired result. With a change of heart, they backed off engines and drifted along their last vectors.

"What now?" Nick asked. "We don't have time to board them."

"We do not even know if we are at the black prison," Joliwe said. "What of the ships that returned to the surface? This is taking too long."

I shook my head. Joliwe had mistaken Nick's tactical question for an invitation to start second guessing. "Quiet, Joliwe," I ordered, knocking her off the tactical channel. "Belirand, the prisoner Thabini from Thandeka, where is he?" I asked.

"Chappie said you'd come for him," the man replied. "You're too late. He's already on his way planetside."

Tabby muted the comms. "How can we trust them?" she asked. "We should at least disable their ships."

"Marny, can you do that without killing them?" I asked. The ships were simple with rear-mounted engines. The old Marny could do it in her sleep.

"Not difficult." She must have anticipated my request because three bolts fired from *Hotspur*, striking just in front of the engines of each ship.

"Cease fire!" the panicked Belirand pilot called over comms. "We're complying."

"Copy that," I answered and closed comms. "Jonathan, can you use our data-streams and find a route into that base that keeps us clear of those turrets?"

"There is no path that is not covered for a vessel the size of *Hotspur,*" he said.

It was good to have Jonathan back. His succinct communications were important in tight situations. While *Hotspur* was too big, he'd let me know there were other options. "What if we didn't go in with the ship?"

"That is correct, Captain," he agreed. "We have identified a five-meter corridor beyond the reach of base weapon's fire. The living spaces are not armored beyond ordinary space debris protective layers."

"Ada, you've got the ship. Get us into that crevice so you can give us some cover," I said. "Tabbs, Marny on me."

"What about me?" Peter asked.

"Zero-g, big man," I said. "Remember when Mendari-Jonathan turned off the gravity and you hit the ceiling? That whole rock is zero-g and we have to stay within a five-meter corridor. Get outside the safe zone and you're dead. This isn't the time to learn how to navigate."

"I am coming," Joliwe said. "If the prince is within this prison, I will be part of rescuing him."

"If we find Thabini, we'll bring you. Otherwise, the three of us will move more quickly without you slowing us down," I said, brushing past her and dropping down to the lower deck.

From the armory, I grabbed a lightweight laser pistol that was designed not to poke holes in space-stations, ten meters of fire-wire, and a portable plasma cutter.

"You're going to need one of these," Marny said, pushing a blaster rifle into my hands. "They'll be expecting us."

"How do you want to do this?" I asked.

"Tabby point, I'll take number two, you'll cover our butts," Marny said. I chuckled but didn't make the obvious lecherous comment. The chuckle was enough to elicit a small shake of her head, which was just as satisfying. Frak, I'd missed this part of our relationship.

"We're in position," Ada announced at the same time the jolt of *Hotspur* settling onto a hard surface transmitted through the deck.

"Let's go," Tabby said, slapping the side of my helmet.

The three of us exited the ship into the darkened crevice. My HUD amplified the available light and reconstructed previously recorded details of the terrain with light green outlines. *Hotspur* had settled just beyond a bend in the crevice. I'd hoped to use Hotspur's turrets to give us cover fire if the need arose, but whoever had placed the bio-domes and turrets on this rock had considered defense against this particular approach.

Ordinarily, five meters seems like plenty of room for navigating in a vac-suit. The problem was, we'd be in the open as we crossed to the buildings. A variance one way or the other would likely end up with one or all of us dead.

"How do you want to do this?" I asked.

"We move together," Marny said. "Return fire only. We don't need to call attention to ourselves."

"Copy," Tabby said. "Move out."

My heart hammered in my chest as anticipation gave way to action. Tabby jumped ahead, orienting herself forty-five degrees with the asteroid's surface. I followed her example. She was limiting visibility to potential enemies while giving herself a comfortable shooting position.

For a few seconds, we sailed silently across the rocky ground. I wasn't naïve enough to believe we were in the clear, only that we hadn't yet been seen. That feeling ended a moment later. I took a blaster bolt to my side and spun off.

"Cap, you're in the red-zone," Marny warned.

I had only moments before the base weapons found me and I frantically pushed at the confusion caused by being shot in zero-g.

"Liam!" Tabby called.

Three red contacts showed on my HUD as Marny marked enemies and returned fire. I twisted, accelerating hard, giving up any pretense of returning fire. A thick blaster bolt seared the vacuum over my head, radiating malignant energy and exploding violently into the rock wall twenty meters behind me. My suit stiffened as I was showered with shards of rock and slag.

The soldiers who'd come out to greet us took full advantage of the idiot scrambling around in the open and directed their fire at me. That decision was a big mistake. Both Marny and Tabby, even with years of inactivity, were disciplined shooters and were not distracted when fired at. I dove into the cannon's dark spot and hunkered down, expecting and receiving glancing blaster fire.

"One down," Tabby said, her voice even. "Target two is about to make a break for it."

"I've got him," Marny answered. "Down."

The blaster fire stopped. Tabby didn't waste the opportunity and pushed forward at high speed, overrunning their position. "Liam, you up?" she asked, even as she brought the butt of her rifle around on the remaining Belirand soldier.

"I'm up, but that was closer than I'd have liked," I said, joining her and Marny.

"They're not highly organized," Marny said, kicking a blaster rifle away from one of the downed soldiers and flipping him onto his stomach. He writhed beneath her as she locked his wrists together with unbreakable ties.

"They're stretched thin," I said. "I just don't get it."

"Perhaps I might offer an explanation," Jonathan said.

"Please do," I said, dragging one of the downed soldiers to an entry hatch on the side of the first of three domed buildings. The base could hold upward of forty people, but it appeared to be just as poorly manned as the dilapidated cutter I'd taken control of by the cave.

"Resources of this portion of the universe are limited. The Scatter people have done a remarkable job of creating a civilization upon a planet lacking in significant metal deposits. They have had millennia to develop their society to operate within these constraints," Jonathan explained.

"You have a point within all that?" I asked, lifting the soldier to the hatch and palming the security panel. Unfortunately, the AI on the other side must have recognized that the soldier was unconscious because it refused to operate the airlock.

"The Belirand colony has failed," Nick said. "We're dealing with the hangers-on. Why else would Jiggen Mark refer to himself as a Belirand Machinist?"

"And these guys are holding the Scatters' hostage?" I asked, stretching my firewire around the airlock. I walked back to where Tabby and Marny had already taken cover. Once I burned through the hatch, it would blow out with real force, something we didn't want to participate in.

"Liam, we're receiving a comm request from the base you're about to breach," Ada cut in.

"Go ahead," I said.

"This is Geoff Hedren, Belirand Machinists," the man started. "If you blow that hatch, you'll kill all occupants. What's your business here?"

"We're looking for the Scatter known as Prince Thabini," I said.

"He's not here," Hedren said. "Chappie Barto picked him up 'bout an hour ago. He's headed back to Thandeka."

"Open the hatch. We need to make sure," Tabby demanded.

"I'm telling you, that's not necessary," he said. "Barto is gone and took the Scatter with him."

"I'm going to blow this door in ten seconds if you don't comply," I said.

The panel turned green and swished open. In a heartbeat, Tabby was through the door with Marny hot on her heels. The opposite door on the airlock leaked atmo, spraying a fine mist of moist oxygenated air into the vacuum of the entry chamber. As soon as I entered, the door behind me closed and Tabby forced her way into a large, round room filled with a score of Scatters, mostly women. I hated that we were adding to whatever horrors they'd experienced and winced as they cowered as far from us as they could get.

"Keep going, Tabbs," I said.

The three domes were connected by short, narrow passageways. They were perfect pinch points if you were going to resist an armed party. Tabby spun down at the door frame and swept a short arc, securing her quadrant as Marny stacked up behind, leaned over her and secured the next section. I slid to the opposite side and completed the sweep.

"On me," I ordered, rushing forward as we utilized a leap-frog entry tactic. The dome we'd entered was devoid of people but separated into more rooms. My AI suggested that command would be centrally located. I slowed and dropped to a knee, sweeping my portion of the next room as Marny joined me, followed by Tabby.

"Got 'em," Tabby said. "Going breach."

"Frak," I said, pushing up to a standing position as Tabby raced past. She jumped up a half flight of stairs and blooped out a single explosive charge against the armored door.

The element of surprise was critical in a breach. Even though they knew we were coming, Tabby had successfully re-established surprise with her aggressive tactic. I chinned my weapon's panel to reduce the lethality of my blaster rifle and followed her, tapping the first target I found. I quickly acquired a second, only to watch her drop to Marny's fire.

"Clear," Tabby announced.

"Clear," I said, racing forward to secure my target with a knee in his back.

"We're clear," Marny agreed.

"Captain, if you'll respond to the request on the console above you, we will gain access to the station and disable the perimeter defenses," Jonathan instructed.

I looked up and shook my head. Indeed, on the console was a prompt, asking if *Hotspur* should be allowed administrative access. I punched my acknowledgement. "Are you in?" I asked.

"We are, Captain," he said.

"On our way," Ada said.

"Joliwe, there are a bunch of Scatter in the first dome. I don't think they'll listen to what we have to say but I don't want to leave them behind. Do you think you can convince them to come along?" I asked.

"I will come," she said. "We must hurry. Chappie will hear of our actions. Prince Thabini is at more risk than he was before."

"Can't argue with that," I said.

Chapter 25

FOR LOVE

Even with the pressure of Thabini's imminent public execution, Joliwe agreed that to leave her people behind on Belirand's failing asteroid base would be to leave them in harm's way. It was touch and go as *Hotspur* entered the atmosphere. She was considerably overweight from a hold packed with human cargo, but we made it to the ground without event.

"How will you rescue the prince?" Joliwe pushed as we lifted from the clearing where we had dropped the refugees in the care of the mountain Scatters. I had to give her credit for persistence in the face of so much adversity.

"I'll come in low," I said, ignoring Joliwe. "We'll put down south of the delta, and grav-suit back in along the river. Ada, Nick, I need you to stay with the ship. Peter, you too, since we don't have a grav-suit for you. Marny, Tabby, Jonathan, and I will accompany Joliwe to the city center where Thabini is likely to be executed. Ada, you mind letting Joliwe use your suit?"

Without hesitation, Ada stood and peeled off her suit.

"We cannot show up wearing this clothing," Joliwe said, accepting the grav-suit from Ada. "We will be seen immediately."

"Already on it," Nick said. "I've replicated the cloaks we've seen mountain Scatters wearing. They should let the other Scatters know you're not locals."

"Cloaks are a good plan," Marny said. "They'll cover the blaster rifles."

"No rifles," I said. "What we know is that Chappie has a minimum of thirty troops and a sloop which is more than a match for *Hotspur*. We go in and pick a fight without the Scatters behind us, we'll just end up getting a lot of innocents killed. Chappie needs to reassert his dominance and he'll be looking for any excuse."

"So how are you going to rescue Prince Thabini?" Joliwe asked, standing between me and the armor-glass cockpit window. With Jonathan's help and clear skies, I'd been sailing *Hotspur* in without navigational systems. It was tough sailing and Joliwe was messing with my sight lines.

"Ada, take over," I snapped.

"Helm is mine," she answered, sitting down quickly.

I stood, bumping into Joliwe who refused to give me any more space. "Joliwe, you still don't get it," I said. "I would have thought visiting that pathetic Belirand base you all call the black prison would have made everything clear to you."

"You should not turn this on me," Joliwe said. "To me, it is clear that Prince Thabini was captured because he attempted to save you. You owe him a debt. Have you lost your lust for killing? I thought this was something a *human* would relish."

Her disgust for my species had been well-earned and I fought to hold back my first response. I'd seen racism exhibited by many species and even inter-species. It was often a complex issue used by mal-actors. I hated that when Joliwe saw me, she saw the evil legacy created by a small, non-representative group. One thing I was certain of was that I didn't appreciate being painted with the same savage brush as Belirand.

"You're right, Joliwe. I do owe Prince Thabini for choosing my arrival as his moment to take a stand," I said. "You're missing the bigger picture, though. Bongiwe didn't give her life just for me. She gave her life because she knew it was time for the Scatter people to take a stand against Belirand. She wasn't shy about that conversation. As her sister, you know that's true."

"I am willing to give my life for my people," Joliwe said, staring up at me, her eyes boring into my own. If they'd lit on fire at that moment, I wouldn't have been surprised.

"That's not enough," I said. "Anyone can die. Your sister died taking action. The Scatter people must take action. Prince Thabini is not the only hostage today. Every Scatter on this frakking planet is a hostage. Your people's fate hangs in the balance of what happens to Prince Thabini today. I believe he knows it and is willing to die a martyr's death to wake up his people."

"You said you'd help," she said, her voice losing its intensity.

"I am helping," I said. "We need to go."

I stalked off the bridge and jumped to the galley deck. Marny was already in the armory and handed me a familiar-looking, large brown and green hooded cloak. I popped a nano-blade onto my waist along with a back-up blaster pistol and a grenade strip.

"Leaving the blaster rifles behind is a mistake," Marny said.

"Flechettes," I said. "They're quiet and won't cause panic. We don't go loud unless we have no other choice."

"We'll be standing by," Ada said over tactical comms. "Things go south, we're coming in hard. Don't even argue with me."

"Counting on it," I said. "Just make sure you don't have any other choice. There'll be a lot of innocents on the ground."

"I know," she answered.

"What's our play here, Liam?" Tabby asked, pulling on her cloak. "We can't go against thirty soldiers without getting a lot of people killed. Even then, that's long odds for the three of us."

"Four," Joliwe said, pushing her way into the armory.

"I really don't know," I said. "To be honest, we may have to let Chappie do what he came for."

"You would let him murder the prince?" Joliwe asked.

"I would if it meant saving hundreds of others," I said. "What do you think is going to happen if we start shooting at Belirand soldiers?"

"I don't know," she said.

"It's not hard," I said. "They're going to shoot back. Are you going to just stand there and let them?"

"No. Of course not. I'll move."

"And when there's a child standing behind you, will you move?" I asked. "What about that child's mother or father? What about then?"

Tears formed in the woman's eyes. The realizations I'd already come to finally hit her. We weren't going into town to rescue Thabini. We were going to town to watch an execution.

"So, this has all just been a big lie? You only came to rescue that woman in the cave? My sister died for you."

We'd already been through this, but I felt I needed to hit it one more time. "No, she didn't," I said. "Bongiwe died because she wanted to stop Belirand. Today we rescued thirty of your people from the black prison. We destroyed one of Belirand's ships and disabled three more. Bongiwe's sacrifice made all that happen. You're looking at the wrong person here. You need to be asking what you are willing to do to save your people."

"Me?" she asked. "I'm nothing. People followed Bongiwe. I am her bitter older sister. No one will follow me."

"Then you've already lost," I said. "Now get out of my way. I'm going to see if there's any chance of making this work."

"Cap, not to point out the obvious," Marny said, "but we'd be better off letting this play out and then use *Hotspur* to hunt down Chappie. We might be out-gunned, but it's not the worst odds we've been up against. Give us a few months and we might be able to end this for good."

"Let's call that Plan-B," I said.

THE SUN WAS high in the sky when we arrived in the town center. At first, we sailed in, using our grav-suits to glide a few meters above the water. Upon entering the city of Thandeka, we soon ran into small, sullen groups who were all headed in one direction, toward the city center. As before, the Scatters didn't startle when we rose up from the canal and joined their ranks.

"We must hurry," Joliwe said, rejoining us after conferring with a group of Scatters. Fresh tears ran down her face and she refused to look at me. "It is worse than expected. King Nkosi tried Thabini this morning in private. Thabini has been disowned and will be executed within the hour."

"How is that worse?" I asked.

"Chappie is holding King Nkosi responsible for the prince's actions. King Nkosi and Queen Cacile will also be executed along with their entire staff. You have brought ruin to our people."

We pushed forward, increasing our pace. Unlike human crowds, the mild-mannered Scatters gave way, seeming to anticipate our need and parting just in time to let us through.

If not for Chappie's heavily-armored sloop and the two smaller vessels that sat at the edges of the large courtyard, we might have been in medieval times. A raised stone stage was backdropped by the tall walls of the breathtakingly beautiful crystal castle. Atop the castle's walls sat a carefully constructed parapet which ran its length. It was impossible to tell the age of the castle, but the abandoned defenses bespoke a past long forgotten.

Thousands of Scatters crowded into the sloped yard in front of the stage. As we worked our way forward and to the side, I took it all in. Chappie had stationed ten, or about a third of his force, atop the parapet looking down over the crowd. The men weren't highly disciplined, but their intent was obvious as they scanned the crowds through the scopes of their older-model blaster rifles. If things got out of control, Belirand had high ground that was well defended.

Marny worked as we moved, tagging each of the Belirand soldiers and marking them for our tactical AI to track. If bilge water hit the fan, she'd prioritize those targets. The problem wasn't really the soldiers on the walls as much as it was Chappie's sloop, the turrets of which slowly swung menacingly back and forth. If the sloop's gunners went weapon's free, the dead would number in the hundreds if not thousands.

"Where's Chappie and the royal family?" Tabby whispered. We'd stopped at the edge of the crowd where our height differential wasn't nearly as noticeable. The stage was filled with more of Chappie's soldiers and a group of twenty Scatter people held only by a thick rope that encircled them. Their escape would only require that they drop the rope and run. "Who are all those people?"

"They work in the castle," Joliwe said.

I scanned the crowds and tried to work things out. I couldn't see any clever tactical maneuvers. We were considerably outmanned and with Chappie's ship, we were also significantly outgunned. One-on-one, I'd have been happy to take on his sloop with *Hotspur*. We gave up some armored weight as well as weaponry, but we had speed on him. Having already seen his crew in action, I knew they'd eventually make a mistake I could capitalize on. That was a fair fight. Like all despots, however, Chappie knew better than to ask for a fair fight.

I was a little surprised when I recognized a group of the mountain Scatters standing several hundred meters from our position. I hadn't expected them to be in attendance. I was shocked to see the male Scatter I'd talked to the day before at the homestead. He must have felt my eyes on him because he turned, looked directly at me and gave a small nod of acknowledgement. My mind spun. Scatters moved through the country at speeds I couldn't comprehend, but there was nowhere near enough time for him to have run over here. I nodded back and pushed the mystery from my head. It was the least of our problems.

"They're coming," Marny said.

The packed crowd quieted as King Nkosi stepped up onto the stage from a trap door below our line of sight. A moment later Queen Cacile followed and behind her, Prince Thabini. A murmur of shock coursed through the crowd as the poor condition of the three was recognized. Fresh cuts oozed from the Queen's broken lips. Her once pristine white gown was ripped and sullied. Through it all, she stood straight, even defiant, as she was pushed forward.

The king looked worse for wear and unlike his wife, he found it impossible to look up from the stage. Like his wife, his face was battered and bruises formed on exposed skin. When urged forward, he hobbled, indicating an unseen injury to his leg.

By far the worst was Prince Thabini who looked to have been severely beaten, his face all but unrecognizable. Like his mother, he stared out at the crowd and stood as straight as he could. A gag, splotched with darkened blood, had been pulled through his mouth and was tied behind his head.

"They didn't break him," Tabby observed. "Chappie's afraid of him."

"You are not correct. Chappie is not afraid. He has nearly killed my prince," Joliwe said.

"You're wrong. Don't you see it?" Tabby nodded toward the stage. "He's gagged. Chappie fears Thabini so much that he won't let him talk. Even when Chappie tortured his parents, Thabini must have stayed true. Chappie is making a mistake. He should never have let people see Thabini unbroken."

"People of Fraxus." Chappie's voice echoed off the walls of the castle as he stepped up onto the stage. "Loyal subjects." He stepped up behind King Nkosi and pushed him to his knees. "Today is the beginning of a grand, new moment in our history together." When he tried to push Queen Cacile down, she resisted. He followed up with a telescoping club. After being hit on the back of her legs, she fell next to her husband on the stage.

"But first we need to deal with that which stands in the way of progress," he said. "Three centuries ago, the first Belirand mission to this beautiful planet arrived. At first, we believed we'd found paradise. But as many of you know, those who sent us here decided that they would not send a second mission. Why, you ask? Well, it wasn't because of a recalcitrant indigenous people. No, unlike today, the people of Fraxus welcomed us with open arms. It was a simple matter of a bad roll of the dice in that giant crap shoot called the big bang. You see, Fraxus doesn't have the material needed for advanced civilizations. Some of you know what I'm talking about. Metals." He waited for the confused murmur to die down before he continued. "Fact is, you just don't have much of them. And for that, our forefathers chose to abandon us and leave us to fend for ourselves.

"Old history, I know," he said, strutting in front of the king and queen as he spoke.

I considered drawing down on him and killing him where he stood. It would be a blood bath, but at least there'd be one less despot in the universe.

"The thing is, when our fathers realized we were to be abandoned, they set about creating a new order on Fraxus. One that would give us what we needed for survival. Together we've built a pretty good life together. Which is why it pains me to have to do what I must today.

"There are traitors in our midst," he continued. "It hurts, you know. I thought we were partners in making this life work for both Scatter and human, but there's always a fly in the ointment, isn't there? It's to be expected and generally we just deal with these things privately. The problem is, King Nkosi has let things get out of hand.

"What, you might ask, is so bad that I have to make an example out of the entire royal family?" There were gasps from within the crowd, but it was otherwise quiet. He turned to Nkosi and addressed him. "There are wolves among the sheep, Nkosi. Humans have been living amongst you and instead of telling me, you've been hiding them. Killers, these humans. Butchers and even worse. They've killed entire shiploads of my people and you've done nothing to stop them."

"We've got to get out of here," I whispered.

"Cap, we can't. They'll see us," Marny whispered back.

"Not gonna matter in a second," I said, backing up.

"But to show I'm a merciful leader. I've decided to give you all one chance. It'll take only one of you to do the right thing and I'll spare your king and queen," he said. "I'll bet these humans are in the crowd. Just point them out and I'll give your king back to you."

For a moment, I thought we were going to be good. Scatters continued to allow us to back away but did not reveal our presence.

"Give us Thabini too," a woman yelled from the crowd only a few meters from our position. Too late, I realized it was Joliwe.

"Step forward," Chappie said, walking over to the side of the stage closest to Joliwe. "You say you want Thabini in exchange for the humans?"

"Yes," Joliwe answered, pulling her hood back.

"No, Joliwe," Queen Cacile cried out, attempting to stand. "Chappie will kill you."

Without thought or hesitation, Chappie turned and fired at Queen Cacile and then King Nkosi, killing them both. They made no noise as they crumpled to the stage to the horror of the assembled Scatters. Thabini struggled against the guard who held him but was unsuccessful in breaking free.

"Quiet!" Chappie shouted. The two cutter-sized ships lifted from where they'd been resting. "Anyone who leaves will be killed."

Joliwe pushed her robe off, exposing the grav-suit and the crossbow Marny had given to Peter. She rose into the air to the surprise of the crowd and Chappie. Without hesitation, she fired a bodkin-point arrow, narrowly missing Chappie. Four soldiers on the wall returned fire, their aim nowhere near as bad as hers.

"Ah, frak," I said. "Marny, Tabbs, Jonathan, get back to the ship."

"Where are you going?" Tabby asked.

"I'm going to try to stop a slaughter," I said, dropping my robe and rising up from my position.

"Not without me," Tabby cried, dropping her robe as well and drawing dual blaster pistols.

"Chappie!" I yelled over the growing chaos around me.

Movement from above the walls caught my eye. A score of mounted golden gigantus dove from their positions high in the sky, the blinding sun behind them. Arrows rained down on the wall from the eagle riders, their aim true. Most of the arrows, however, bounced off the hardened armor of the soldiers and only two of the ten fell.

"Fire!" Chappie ordered. The sloop's large turret turned and fired, striking an eagle struggling to gain elevation.

"This is frakking shite!" Tabby roared and flew off, directly at Chappie.

"No, Tabbs! It'll be a bloodbath!" I cried, following her into the air. I wasn't as concerned about her getting hit by the soldier's fire as much as I was about the sloop mowing down entire swaths of civilians.

My shout was cut off when a roar erupted from the opposite side of the courtyard. I looked over and saw an entire section of the crowd running at the sloop. A small, lower turret turned on them and started firing. Each shot obliterated as many as ten Scatters.

"Ada, this is going south. We're going to need fire support," I said.

“We’ve got a new problem,” she answered. “Two more cutters just showed up moving at high speed. It’s going to take us a few minutes to get free.”

“We don’t have a few minutes,” I answered, looking hopefully at the group racing toward Chappie’s sloop. The ship lifted as it fired on the mountain scatters who continued their hopeless assault. If not for their fantastic speed and agility, they’d have been cut down in seconds. As it was, they were falling at an alarming rate.

The crowd was well beyond consolable at this point and people ran, screaming in all directions as fire from the three ships tore up the courtyard. It was a massacre of proportions I’d never experienced.

“Cap, move!” Marny barked.

I wanted Chappie so bad I could taste blood in my mouth from biting my tongue. My worst fears had been realized. He’d turned the ships against the population. “Tabbs, Marny, on me!” I ordered and blasted off with every newton of force my grav-suit could manage.

The sloop had raised forty meters into the air and arced slowly, tipping so is turrets had maximum visibility of the ground.

"What's the plan?" Tabby asked, reluctantly turning back toward me.

"Marny did you bring breaching charges?" I asked, slapping into the side of the ship and grabbing hold of a loose armor plate. Like everything from the long ago failed Belirand colony, the ship was falling apart.

"Negative," she answered.

Tabby landed hard next to me and held out a strip of grenade balls. "These help?"

"Frak, but you're sexy." I pulled two grenades off and slid them beneath the loose panel next to the airlock.

The three of us moved back along the ship as it continued to fire, the ship's captain completely oblivious to the imminent danger. Directed explosive force is highly effective. With the grenades set beneath the edge of the failing armor, most of the energy was directed inward. Unfortunately, the old armor wasn't done and while there was a hole, it wasn't large enough to get through.

"Again!" I ordered.

Tabby jumped back to the hole just as the sloop dipped hard, the captain finally recognizing his problem.

"Cap, there's a cutter lining up on us," Marny warned. "We're gonna be knocked off like fleas on a dog."

I hadn't known many dogs in my life, but the analogy made sense. Instead of dropping another grenade, Tabby grabbed the edge of the armor and pulled. I'd never seen her at full capacity and strain was evident as heavily corroded steel groaned but resisted.

"Help her!" I ordered, jumping in next to Tabby and pulling at the edge. I pulled with everything I had and looked over to the cutter

Marny had marked. We had seconds before it would fire. My efforts, while not inconsiderable, weren't moving the needle much. The plate was giving way, but our efforts wouldn't be enough.

Marny dropped in, telescoping out her bo staff. She slid it beneath the opening Tabby had created. "Frak!" she screamed as she joined our efforts and pulled at the end of the staff. For a moment, the three of us stood perfectly still, locked to the side of the ship, straining to move metal. The battle had boiled down to this single act.

"Incoming fire, clear off," Marny ordered.

It was our nature to not question orders within our group. Tabby and I jumped away only to discover that Marny had stayed behind long enough to allow us to free our fingers. She released the bo staff which snapped back to the hull and then dove away, only a moment before a fiery round of blaster fire erupted next to her.

I watched in horror as her bio signature blinked out. I raced toward her falling body even though I knew it was the wrong thing to do. All would be lost if we didn't take control of that ship.

"No, Liam! Finish this," Tabby yelled.

Her words were enough to bring me back. It hurt to turn from my fallen friend, but I knew Tabby was right even before she'd spoken. I overrode Marny's suit and directed it to drop her gently to the ground, then turned back to the sloop.

The cutter had done what we couldn't. The weakened armor had been ripped from the ship and in its place was a gaping hole. We flew through, Tabby reaching it moments before me. During the last twenty years, Marny and Tabby had forged a deep friendship on the mountain. Seething anger burned through Tabby as she tore into the ship, slamming into a bulkhead.

Gunfire erupted in the passage, but the soldiers might as well have been shooting cotton. She roared in anguish as she fell on the two hapless men that stood in her way. Using only her fists, she put them down, mercilessly pounding them. I'd never before been afraid of Tabby, but in that moment, I feared her anger.

"Tabbs?" I asked, my voice quiet, but insistent.

"No," she said and rose up from the bloody mess. She pushed forward, turning the corner. I was grateful she met no more resistance on her way to the ship's bridge.

"Get up!" she ordered, talking to the captain who was flying the ship.

"No ..." he started, but stopped when he saw the blood on Tabby's grav suit. He grabbed for a pistol at his side, but she closed the distance between them in a heartbeat. She pulled him from his seat and smashed his head into the ceiling. His neck snapped and she discarded him as if he were beneath her notice.

I jumped past them and slid into the pilot's seat. "Blasters, Tabbs," I ordered.

The sloop flew like a brick and I struggled to get her under control. I slid the ship away from the crowd and checked the sensor displays. If not for my AI, I would never have known what I was looking at. *Hotspur* was close and firing ... at us.

We rocked to the side and I fought for control. About the best I could do was pick where we would crash. I aimed for an open area a few hundred meters from the courtyard.

"*Hotspur,* cease fire," I yelled into my comms. "Tabby and I have control of the sloop."

"Copy that, Liam," Ada answered. "Sorry."

"What's your sit-rep?"

"Remaining cutters are fleeing. You want us to run them down?"

"Get Marny, she's down," I said. "We need those cutters."

"Already there," Ada said. "Nick's grabbing her right now."

"Her bios are down," I said, landing hard.

"We see it," she said. "I need a gunner if we're going after those cutters. Nick's in tough shape."

"Tabby, get to *Hotspur*," I ordered, jumping from my seat.

"I got it," she answered.

I winced as we made our way back through the carnage of Tabby's anger. I'm not saying these guys didn't have it coming, but the overkill was terrifying.

Chaos reigned outside the ship. Scatter men, women and children ran in all directions. Even worse, some were too terrified to move and cowered in place. I felt nothing but anger as I raced back to the courtyard. These beautiful peaceful people had been soiled by Belirand's greed and treated no better than the Kroerak had treated humanity.

When the stage came into view, I found a small knot of soldiers had formed around Chappie. Two of his men still held Thabini and the rest had switched from offense to defense, trying to protect their leader.

When I was twenty meters out, Chappie looked up at me. In that moment, he realized help wouldn't be coming. He turned and fired at Thabini, hitting one of his own men instead. He yelled for the others to move out of his way and fired again as Thabini stumbled, his injuries too much for him to even stand without help. Before he could shoot, a small Scatter jumped around the confused soldiers, holding a shield in one hand and a crystal sword in the other. My heart dropped as I realized that Scatter was my friend, Hambo. Chappie screamed and ran forward, shooting at Hambo, his blaster bullets easily tearing through the shield. I raced at the pair and fired my flechette into the remaining guard.

The scene played out in slow motion as Chappie reached Hambo's position, a final blaster bolt tearing through the shield and sending the little Scatter to the ground. I was still too far away for a decent shot when I saw Chappie's arm jerk. At first, I thought he was going to take aim at Thabini again, but then I noticed the crystal tip of a sword sticking out the back of his chest.

"Hambo!" I cried as I arrived.

The soldier who'd been holding Thabini, seeing his leader down, turned and ran.

“Clearing the wall,” Tabby called into the comms. I looked up just in time to see *Hotspur’s* turrets eliminate the guard along the wall.

I had difficulty resolving the conversation I was hearing as I pulled Hambo's burned body to me and ripped at the clothing he wore. My fingers were stopped by something hard. My hand was covered with blood from Hambo's shield arm that hung at an odd angle.

"Mmmm... Hmmmm...." Prince Thabini tried to say something through his gag.

"Give me a second," I said, pulling a combat med-patch out and peeling back Hambo's robe. I nearly cried right there on the spot. Beneath his robe was the smallest section of vac-suit armor I'd ever seen. It wrapped around his chest and over his shoulders. I slapped the patch onto his ruined shoulder and smiled as he gave me a glazed look.

"The prince?" he asked, clearly out of it.

I turned to Thabini, removed his gag, and unbound his hands and legs.

"I think your prince might need a couple of nights in the tank," I said, looking back to Hambo. "Sorry about your arm, too."

"I killed Chappie Barto," Hambo said, looking earnestly at Prince Thabini. "I will accept the consequences for my actions."

Thabini might have tried to smile as he sank to the stage. It was hard to tell under the puffiness of his wounds.

"You will most definitely be held responsible," Prince Thabini mumbled.

I took pity on him and gently applied a med-patch to his cheek. Hundreds of Scatter lay dead or dying. I had a few remaining patches, but they wouldn't be sufficient for the carnage. The high price of freedom for the Scatters had been paid. I hated that blood was the only currency accepted, but it was a truth I'd come to recognize.

"Nick, talk to me," I said.

"She's in the tank," he said. "She'll make it."

I sighed, pushed myself up, and waded into the killing field. A child in his early teens held a man I supposed to be his father. Fearful of me, he wanted to flee, but wouldn't leave the man's side.

"Don't be afraid," I said, settling down next to him. I pulled out my scanner and found the man was dead. It felt cruel, but I moved on. For survivors, time was of the essence, there was nothing I could do for a dead man.

I continued checking the Scatters on the ground, picking those who were in the worst shape for my meager supply of patches.

"Look who I found," Tabby said, coming up next to me, cradling Joliwe in her arms. The grav suit had been pulled down to her waist, her torso wrapped with a wide bandage.

"Where is Thabini?" Joliwe asked, her face pinched with concern.

"On the stage," I said, nodding over my shoulder.

Calm had settled over the courtyard and the able-bodied were tending to the wounded. I followed Tabby as she carried Joliwe to the stage.

Thabini sat up when Tabby set Joliwe next to him.

“I thought you would die,” Joliwe said, bringing her hands up to his face.

Thabini’s face softened and he awkwardly wrapped his arms around her and wept, his back shuddering as he held her. "You were so brave, my love."

I looked at Tabby, who raised an eyebrow and mouthed *my love?* I nodded, just as surprised. Joliwe’s frantic focus made more sense to me now. There was little I wouldn’t do for my love.

"You weren't really going to turn us in, right?" I asked, after Thabini finally let her go.

"No. It was as you said. I had to stand for what I believed. I just wanted to get close enough to Chappie so that I could kill him. The soldiers would kill me, but just as we would be lost without Prince Thabini, I knew that Bell-e-runde would be lost without Chappie Barto. I was willing to trade my life for his," she said.

"Would have been helpful to know that," I said.

"I did not believe I could trust you,” Joliwe said. “I am sorry for my distrust.

Thabini faced the castle and couldn't see what I could. The Scatters that had fled were returning to the courtyard, helping the wounded or just staring at the stage in states of shock. I reached over to Chappie, removed his amplifying microphone and handed it to Thabini.

"Prince Thabini, I know you're hurting, but you should probably address your people," I said.

He nodded and smiled. The combat-patch we'd applied had no doubt pumped him with pain killers and stimulants. He was on a short fuse, but it would be enough.

EPILOGUE

Two ten-days had passed since the incident outside the castle.

At first, we'd offered the use of *Hotspur's* medical tank to help injured citizens and manufactured thousands of medical patches with our replicators. The carnage was considerable but not as bad as I'd feared. Seventy-four were dead with the critically injured twice that. The mountain Scatters had taken disproportionate losses with more than half of their number killed. They bore their losses stoically.

Our mission had turned to rounding up Belirand soldiers, including those we'd stranded above the planet. I hadn't been surprised to discover the technically-minded Belirand crews had figured out how to limp back to their base. We'd made their decision simple. They could come with us and face whatever consequences awaited them on the planet, or they could run out their days with whatever supplies they had on the base, because we weren't leaving their ships repairable. They chose to come with us. As a parting gift, we destroyed the base.

"Where are you off to?" I asked. Nick and Marny had found me in the galley. Both were wearing well-trimmed animal furs over their grav-suits. The skins were an unnecessary layer as the suits would easily moderate body temperature, regardless of how cold it was.

"Home," he said.

I gave Marny a concerned look.

"Don't panic, Cap," Marny chortled. "We're just going to finish closing it down and say goodbye."

"Not sure that's called for," I said. "Far as I know, we're stuck here for now. Have either of you seen Jonathan?"

"Last I saw, they were being escorted around the kingdom by Hambo," Nick said.

"Hambo and Jonathan are pals?" I asked.

"Jonathan requested to be allowed to observe the Scatter kingdom. Thabini assigned Hambo," Marny said. "I think Hambo needed something to do."

I nodded. It was an odd pairing, but I'd seen stranger things.

Nick pulled something from his pocket and flipped it at me. Light reflected off the facets of a quantum comm crystal as it flew toward me. "Where'd you find this?" I asked. "And who does it connect to?"

"AI says Anino," Nick said. "It was in the lower-half of the android body Peter blew up. Jonathan is sure his evil counterpart didn't even realize it was there. It was Jonathan who figured out that the ruined crystal would connect to Anino. The only reason the Mendari would ruin that crystal is so we couldn't talk to Anino. That puts Anino in a different light, don't you think?"

"You don't think Anino had anything to do with stranding us here?" I asked.

"I believed he was guilty for twenty years," Nick said. "Now, I'm not so sure. There were a million easier ways to get rid of us. I definitely don't see him in bed with the Mendari."

"You think I should call him?" I asked.

"Up to you," Nick said. "We don't need a ride. Scatters need *Hotspur* as a symbol of safety more than we need a ride. We're going to head back with that group of mountain folk."

"Wait, speaking of the mountain tribe. I've been wondering about that," I said. "You mind telling me how they were able to make that trek to be here in time?"

"Same way you made it down the mountain the first time," Nick said.

"Eagles?" I asked.

"Golden gigantus," he corrected. "Yeah, apparently, they got ahold of the sky guard and requested a ride. The sky guard has been part of the resistance for a long time. When Jared Thockenbrow murdered Lifa, it pushed them over the edge. They were just waiting for the revolution."

"This place was a powder-keg ready to blow before we got here," I said, thinking about the implications.

"And you were the match, Cap. But we already knew that," she said, winking.

"Have you talked to Tabby and Ada?"

Nick smiled and nodded. "Yup and we're just going to be a couple hundred kilometers away. Come grab us when you get things figured out."

"WHAT'CHA DOING?" Tabby asked, finding me on *Hotspur's* bridge a few hours after Nick, Marny, and Peter had taken off.

I held two crystals in the space between us. "Anino or Mshindi?" I asked.

She raised an eyebrow. "I still don't trust Anino."

I shrugged. "Whoever knows with that guy? He wanted us away from Mars. Do I think he'd purposefully crash-land us to accomplish that? If he wanted us dead, I can think of easier and less expensive ways."

"But you don't trust him, right?" she asked warily.

"Oh, frak, no. Not further than I can throw him."

"Trust who?" Ada asked, popping up through the gravity lift and onto the deck.

"Anino," I said, showing her the comm crystal.

She frowned but didn't say anything.

"Why Mshindi?" Tabby asked, continuing our conversation. "What can she do?"

"Get word to Mom that we're alive?" I said as more of a question than an actual plan.

I had no idea if our old Abasi allies would even recognize me, given how long we'd been gone. Mshindi Prime, or at least the Prime I knew, had been old when we left. Twenty years was a long time for her to have survived and stayed in power, given the instability of the region. That said, we had good relationships with the rest of her family.

"Start with Mshindi," Tabby said, picking up my hand. "Silver would want to know you're alive."

"I'm with Tabby on this," Ada said. "Anino is a wild card."

I chuckled and dropped the Mshindi comm crystal into the newly fashioned cradle. "You know I'm going to call them both, right?"

Ada shrugged. "Don't argue."

A light on the communication rig illuminated green, indicating that our crystal had made contact with its twin, hundreds of light years away. "House of Mshindi, this is Bold Prime, Liam Hoffen, calling. Please respond," I waited and then repeated myself.

"Think anyone will answer?" Tabby asked. "Twenty years is a long time to leave something hooked up. It's probably in a broom closet."

"Bilge," Ada said, chuckling.

We stared at the comm unit for several minutes and I tried again with the same results.

Ada leaned back in her chair. "That's anti-climactic."

"This could take a while," I said. "Anyone for cards?"

Tabby pushed her chair back and opened a drawer, pulling out a pack of well-used cards. The pack hadn't seen use in over twenty years, but it was familiar all the same. Shuffling first, she dealt out a hand of her favorite game, poker. For several hours, I repeated my communication attempt after each hand until it became clear that we would not be answered.

"Try Anino in the morning?" Tabby asked as we headed back to our quarters.

A crackling sound froze the three of us in place and we turned to look back at the communication rig. "House Bold, this is Perasti Prime. You are requested to respond."

I raced back to the communications station, stabbed at the transmit button. I wasn't sure why House Perasti was responding, but I recognized the voice as belonging to Moyo, an old friend. She sounded older, but it was her.

"Moyo?" I asked. "This is Liam Hoffen, do you read?"

"Bold Prime Hoffen Liam is reported as deceased. Identify yourself," she responded.

"Moyo, it's me, really," I said. "Look, a lot of things have happened. We're stuck in another galaxy and need you to get word to my mother, Silver Hoffen, that we're alive. Will you do that for me?"

"Identification challenge issued," she answered.

My AI recognized the protocol that I'd forgotten and displayed a word sequence, which I read aloud.

"Bold Prime. I greet you with great joy." Moyo's attitude shifted from dubious to friendly in a second. "You say you are alive and in good health? What of your crew?"

"Marny, Tabby, Nick, Little Pete and Ada are doing well," I said. "We've been cut off from the rest of our House for twenty standard years. Can you get word to Silver that we're alive?"

"It will be difficult," she said. "But it will be done."

"Difficult?" I asked. "What's going on? Why didn't Mshindi answer?"

"House Mshindi has fallen," Moyo answered. "Much has changed since your departure. House Kifeda allied with the Taji. House Perasti and Gundi now live in exile."

The news was hard to hear. "What happened to Adahy and House Mshindi?"

"They were killed."

"And House Bold?" I asked.

"The human settlement in the Mhina system is beset with invaders who call themselves Mendari," she answered. "Reports are that their war goes poorly but that they survive. We are not allowed to speak of House Bold."

"Where do you live in exile?" I asked.

"Abasi Prime is still our home," she answered. "We are allowed to operate businesses but have turned over our vessels of war. It is a dark time in Felio history, Hoffen Liam. The war with Kroerak weakened us and the canines bled us."

"This is hard to hear, Moyo, my friend," I said.

"The news of your life has brought joy to my day where little existed," she answered. "I am most sorrowful that I bring ill news to your ears."

"I need to ask one thing," I said. "Do you know if my mother had another son while I was gone?"

"Munay-Hoffen Benjamin Noah," she answered immediately. "I find surprise that you have no knowledge of this. A child was born very soon after the defeat of Kroerak. It is said the kit brings honor to his pride. He was born with the scent of blood in his nostrils."

I exchanged shocked looks with Tabby and Ada.

"You'll pass word to Silver?" I asked, not sure I could continue the conversation much longer.

"I will deliver this very communication device to her personally," Moyo said.

"You need to stay safe, Moyo," I said.

"Kifeda might place a muzzle on me, but my claws remain sharp," she answered. "Perasti Prime desists."

The three of us stared at each other in silence for several minutes.

"Congratulations," Tabby said, finally.

"What?"

"You have a brother," she said.

"Noah," I said. "What'd she say? Born with blood in his nostrils? What does that even mean?"

"Scent of blood, " Ada said. "Sounds like he's a fighter. Imagine that. You gotta love those Felio. They have a way with words."

I pulled the comm crystal out and tucked it in a small pocket under my waist band. "I don't think I'm going to get sleep anytime soon."

"No kidding," Tabby agreed. "I'd give anything for a beer and some pizza right now."

"Let's make another call," I said. "You know, since this last one worked out so well."

"Can't be worse than that," Ada said.

I chuckled mirthlessly and dropped Anino's crystal into the cradle. Like the other, this crystal immediately connected to its twin.

"Anino, you copy?" I called. "This is *Hotspur*. You know, the crew you tried to kill."

"Hostile much?" Ada asked, as we waited for a response.

"Not even close," Tabby said, punching the transmit. "Pick up you aged little dick-head. Or are you afraid next time I see you I'm going to pluck your arms out like a kid with a bug."

I laughed, looking down at the table and scratching my head. "I'm not sure threatening him is our best course of action," I said.

"Feels like it's best he knows just where things sit," she answered.

We waited, staring at the communications box. Unlike the Abasi, the odds of Anino having something cleverly arranged so he could constantly monitor the crystal were pretty good. Twenty years was a long time for most folks, but Anino had lived for centuries. I was pretty sure he'd pick up – eventually.

After waiting a few minutes, I pushed the transmit again. "Come on, Anino," I said. "I know you're monitoring this channel. No, Jonathan is not dead. Yes, we have his crystal. No, I'm not going to let Tabby pull your arms out. Yes, we're pissed you stranded us."

"I didn't have anything to do with you being stranded," Anino answered. "I don't even know where you are. I lost track of *Hotspur* four hours after you departed Mars orbit. What happened?"

"We don't know for certain. When Jonathan gets back, I'll have him call and give you whatever details he's worked out," I answered. "You need to send a ship."

"What happened to *Hotspur*?" he asked.

"We're sitting on her right now," I said.

"You have a ship," he said. "*I'm* not in any position to send you a ship."

"All the gravity suspension chambers were ejected," I said. "For the record, those were stasis chambers."

"Better that way. It reduces stress on the body in transit. You can thank me later," he said. "So, make new ones."

"I'm not getting back in those things," Ada said. "I was out for twenty years."

"You've been in stasis the entire time?" Anino asked. "That's fantastic. I'm going to need details on that."

"Not all of us were," I said. "Does *Hotspur* have enough fuel to get us to Mhina system if we make new stasis chambers?"

"I don't know how much you used. Jonathan could tell you, though," he said. "I can't send a ship for you. Things are falling apart around here. We're kind of on the run."

"We?"

"Mother and me," he said. "Word somehow got out that we've been re-juving. New Earth and New Mars governments are hunting us. I think they just want us to share the tech, but we can't allow that kind of power to spread."

"So, your answer is that we need to fix this on our own?" I said.

"That's my answer," he said. "Let's be clear though. I sent my ships to Mhina as part of our bargain. You took a trip. We're even."

"Mendari infiltrated your shipyard. How is that possible? We lost twenty years of our lives because of your ineptitude and now you intend to leave us stranded?" I asked. "We're not even close to even, Thomas Anino."

"We've both had a bad run. It sounds like you think I might have been in cahoots with Mendari. You should know better than that." He sounded hurt. It wasn't like him to play the actor. "If I had any way to retrieve you I would. Things have changed, dammit, but we're still on the same team."

"Are we?" I asked.

"Yes," he said. "Do yourself a favor, though. Don't come back to Sol or any of the human systems. Treaties between Mars and Earth governments have failed. Everyone is pissed that I nixed fold-space and I'm basically on the run. I don't think you'd be safe."

"Frak, I hate politics," I said.

"That's something we can agree on," he said. "For what it's worth, I'm glad you're all alive. I thought you hadn't made it. I even sent a ship out to find you, but it was pretty clear you never arrived."

"Good bye, Thomas," I said and disconnected before he could say anything further.

"That prick is frakking unbelievable," Tabby said. "Do you really think he wasn't involved?"

I shrugged, suddenly tired again. "I have no idea."

"Doesn't change anything," Ada said, straightening in her chair. "First thing in the morning, I'll grab Jonathan and we'll get started manufacturing stasis chambers and fuel."

"Tabby and I will comb this ship for more Mendari technology," I said.

"WHAT DO you think is going on?" Tabby asked, excited as she pulled on the fancy clothing we'd created while visiting the cloud city of Léger Nuage. "Why are we getting all dressed up? Are they throwing us a going away party? I heard someone say that Thabini and Joliwe might be announcing the Scatter equivalent of an engagement."

We'd been working on the ship for several ten-days and just the night before, had welcomed Nick, Marny and Peter back onto *Hotspur* in preparation for our voyage to the Mhina system. I'd hoped to hear from Mom before taking off. Her silence was a mystery that caused me substantial anxiety.

"It's definitely a party in our honor and you look fantastic," I said. The bright colors of the Nuagian clothing brought back a flood of memories.

Tabby spun around, smiling. She'd always been the one for me and I laughed with her as she showed off.

"I thought you'd be wearing your Nuage clothing," she said. "What's with the formal black tux and all?"

I shrugged. "Call me a traditionalist."

"You're handsome," she said, straightening my bow tie. "I feel like you're up to something, but I can't quite put my finger on it."

"Are you guys dressed?" Ada called, opening the hatch and coming inside. She wore a silky brown dress and had her tight black curly hair pushed up and held in place with an ornate, jewel-encrusted band.

"I love that dress," Tabby exclaimed. "Did you just replicate it?"

Tabby was right, but then Ada was pretty enough that she could probably wear a bag and look nice in it.

"Joliwe set us up. You should see Marny," Ada said, smiling broadly. "She's got this blue number. Hugs her in all the right places. Who knew she was hiding all that?"

Tabby giggled and the two looked at each other. "Liam," they said in unison.

"What?" I played innocent, but they were right. I was a big fan of the female form and it wasn't my fault that I was surrounded by three radically different women, each beautiful in their own way.

The three of us exited the bridge deck and found Nick and Marny waiting for us in the hold.

"Where's Peter?" I asked.

"Looking good, Cap," Marny said, releasing Nick's arm long enough to give me a quick peck on the cheek. "You ready for this?"

"What?" Tabby asked, growing suspicious. "It's just a party."

"You haven't told her yet?" Marny asked, looking between us. "Cap, are you sure?"

I nodded.

Tabby slapped me playfully on the chest. "Told me what? What's going on?"

"Can you wait five more minutes? I swear it'll be worth it," I said.

Tabby shrugged. "I'll try. But not more than five, okay?"

The five of us, dressed to the nines, walked down the ramp of the hold and onto the stone path that led to the grand entrance of the castle. Upon crossing the threshold, we were met by Hambo, who smiled brightly and offered his one remaining arm to Ada.

"Are you my date for tonight?" she asked.

"If you will have me," he answered, grinning broadly.

"He should be careful what he asks for," Tabby whispered into my ear, giggling. I loved it when she was in a good mood.

The castle bustled with activity, most of which was forward of the grand cut-crystal staircase that led to large wide-open doors ten meters ahead. Scatters dressed in finery observed our entrance and did what they were known for – scurrying urgently away.

"Wow, they really know how to throw down," Marny said, gawking with awe at the colorful lights dancing off the reflective walls and cascades of white flowers.

"Where do you think they got all those flowers in the middle of winter?" Nick asked as we climbed the steps.

Music and the low rumble of voices filtered into the foyer as we approached. Standing at the entrance to a large hall stood Joliwe, flowers in her hair, wearing a silken gown much like Ada's, only flaxen in color.

"Hambo, would you escort our guests to their seats?" Joliwe asked.

I pulled on Tabby's arm as Marny, Nick and Ada made to follow Hambo. Everyone in the hall had turned to look at us.

"What's going on, Hoffen?" she asked, swinging back to face me.

While she'd been distracted, I'd dropped to my knee and waited, looking up at her. Tears formed in her eyes as I started speaking. "Tabitha Masters, you've told me that you don't want to end up divorced like your parents. I don't think that's even remotely possible."

"Liam ..." she started, but I stopped her.

"Tabby, you're my one love. I do not want to spend one more day without us joined as husband and wife," I said. "What do you say. Will you marry me?"

"I already said I would," she said.

"No," I said. "I mean right now."

"In front of all these people?" she asked. "I don't have a gown. I haven't made any arrangements."

"That arrangements have already been made," I said. "Just say yes."

"Yes, of course. A million times yes," she answered.

Applause and bird whistles erupted from the assembled crowd of Scatters. They quieted as Joliwe approached and stood quietly next to us.

"Go ahead, Joliwe," I said.

"Liam told us that a white gown is traditional," Joliwe said, accepting a satiny gown from a man who'd approached at her nod. "If you'll accompany me, I'll help you change."

"How?" Tabby asked, but I didn't have time to answer before she was pulled away.

I walked to the front of the great hall and stopped when I came to the raised platform where Prince Thabini stood. "This is a traditional joining for humans?" he asked.

"Kind of," I said.

"What if she had declined?" he asked.

"Most of the time the woman has more input on the planning," I said. "I just didn't want her getting cold feet. Plus, she really likes grand gestures."

"The music you've chosen. We also enjoy music, but it is so ... foreign," he said.

I chuckled, but didn't answer, instead accepting a fluted glass of bubbling water. "Oh, that's nice."

Thabini nodded. "It is difficult to produce in winter but we discovered stores within Chappie's buildings. It seems appropriate that it is used in a celebration such as this. I believe your partner is ready."

I looked to the back of the room. Beside Tabby stood Peter, dressed in a tux. With his hair and beard trimmed, he looked nicer than I'd have liked. The two were talking and for a moment, the scene caused my nerves to act up. At first, when I'd talked to him about participating in the wedding, he'd been reticent, but had finally agreed. I hoped he wasn't making a last-ditch effort to undo things.

"Cue Frankie Ballard, *A Little Bit of Both*, and start with the chorus," I instructed my AI. I'd received help in setting up speakers in the hallway and was thrilled as the song filled the large room.

Well... I like a little bit of bad girl, and I like a little bit of sweet

And I like a little Boom boom in a room

As the music played, Tabby's eyes locked on mine. It was a song she knew well as I'd played it on more than one occasion when trying to get her attention. She smiled, shook her head and started toward the front of the hall.

"That is serious old-school," Nick whispered as he stepped in beside me.

"WHAT WAS IN THAT PUNCH?" Tabby asked, rubbing sleep from her eyes and flopping over on top of me.

"Why, Mrs. Hoffen, did you get a little drunk last night?" I asked.

She traced a finger down my bare chest and swirled it on my stomach. "No, but it did make me feel good. I can't believe we're actually married."

"Are you okay with how it went down?"

"Married by a foreign prince in a fairy-book castle after vanquishing the beast?" she asked. "Uh, I'm not sure I could have asked for anything more perfect."

"What were you and Peter talking about?" I asked, still feeling a pang of jealousy.

"He told me that if I wanted, he'd walk out with me right then and there," she said.

"What, seriously?" I asked.

"Yup. He also told me that if I wanted to go through with it, he'd never bring up what we had again," she said. "So, push that jealous crazy man back where he belongs."

"Can you believe we're headed back to Mhina today?" I asked.

"Not really," she said. "Twenty years is a long time. I'm ready, though. What do you suppose it means that Moyo never got that comm crystal to your mom?"

"That we're headed into a crap storm," I said, sitting up.

She jumped up and ran into the shower. "When aren't we?" I followed behind her and made sure we were good and clean before exiting.

"Not sure I love the idea of getting in these stasis pods again," she said.

I'd exited the head and transformed the bed so the mattress was against the wall and the chambers we'd manufactured were open. We'd broken orbit from Fraxus a few hours previous. Jonathan would begin acceleration once everyone aboard had entered their respective chambers. Tabby and I were the last to enter.

"You first," I said.

"We go together," she responded.

I nodded agreement and we stepped into the gel. "Jonathan, we're just about done in here."

"Understood, Captain," he said. "We look forward to seeing you in two hundred forty-two point five hours."

I sat down and waited for Tabby to do the same.

"Please let me wake up in eight days," Tabby said. "I love you."

Without further ado, she dropped back, allowing her head to submerge. "Gah, here goes nothing," I said and followed suit.

I CAME AWAKE, disoriented by near darkness and a red-throbbing light at the top of the room. The suspension gel had been drained from my stasis chamber and I sat up abruptly. The sound of a warning klaxon filled my ears and I quickly stepped into my vac-suit.

Tabby emerged from her chamber at roughly the same moment. "What's going on?"

"I don't know." I raced from the room and nearly ran into Marny, who'd exited her quarters at the same time. We didn't hesitate or talk, but dashed to our places, me in the pilot's chair and Marny at her gunnery station.

"We're under attack," she said as something hit the side of the ship.

"Captain, a fleet of hostile ships has detected our arrival," Jonathan said. "We took the liberty of engaging silent running protocols, but it would appear we have not escaped detection."

"Fleet? Who?" I asked, pulling up the holo display.

"They appear to be Mendari," Jonathan said.

Anxiously, I looked at our location. We'd arrived in the Mhina system just as planned and were within two hundred thousand kilometers of Baraka, the moon over Elea, where we'd once made our home in the settlement of York.

"Frak, Mendari this close to home?" Ada said, jumping over the back of her pilot's chair.

My ears popped as something pierced the hull and vacuum was lost somewhere on the ship.

"I've issued a distress signal," Nick said.

But of course, that's another story entirely.

ABOUT THE AUTHOR

Jamie McFarlane is happily married, the father of three and lives in Lincoln, Nebraska. He spends his days engaged in a hi-tech career and his nights and weekends writing works of fiction.

Word-of-mouth is crucial for any author to succeed. If you enjoyed this book, please consider leaving a review at Amazon, even if it's only a line or two; it would make all the difference and would be very much appreciated.

FREE DOWNLOAD

If you want to get an automatic email when Jamie's next book is available, please visit http://fickledragon.com/keep-in-touch. Your email address will never be shared and you can unsubscribe at any time.

For more information
www.fickledragon.com
jamie@fickledragon.com

ACKNOWLEDGMENTS

To Diane Greenwood Muir for excellence in editing and fine wordsmithery. My wife, Janet, for carefully and kindly pointing out my poor grammatical habits. I cannot imagine working through these projects without you both.

To my beta readers: Carol Greenwood, Kelli Whyte, Barbara Simmons, Matt Strbjak and Nancy Higgins Quist for wonderful and thoughtful suggestions. It is a joy to work with this intelligent and considerate group of people. Also, to my advanced reading team, you're a zany, fun group of people who I look forward to bouncing ideas off.

Finally, to Elias Stern, cover artist extraordinaire.

ALSO BY JAMIE MCFARLANE

Privateer Tales Series

1. Rookie Privateer

2. Fool Me Once

3. Parley

4. Big Pete

5. Smuggler's Dilemma

6. Cutpurse

7. Out of the Tank

8. Buccaneers

9. A Matter of Honor

10. Give No Quarter

11. Blockade Runner

12. Corsair Menace

13. Pursuit of the Bold

14. Fury of the Bold

15. Judgment of the Bold

Privateer Tales Universe

1. Pete, Popeye and Olive

2. Life of a Miner

3. Uncommon Bravery

4. On a Pale Ship

Henry Biggston Thrillers

1. When Justice Calls

Witchy World

1. Wizard in a Witchy World

2. Wicked Folk: An Urban Wizard's Tale

3. Wizard Unleashed

Guardians of Gaeland

1. Lesser Prince

Made in the USA
San Bernardino, CA
03 December 2018